L A

C H A R

www.

ORBIT

First published in Great Britain in 2018 by Orbit
This paperback edition published in 2019 by Orbit

1 3 5 7 9 10 8 6 4 2

ISBN 978-0-356-51110-8

Printed and bound in Great Britain by
Clays Ltd, Elcograf, S.p.A.

Papers used by Orbit are from well-managed forests
and other responsible sources.

Orbit
An imprint of
Little, Brown Book Group
Carmelite House
50 Victoria Embankment
London EC4Y 0DZ

An Hachette UK Company
www.hachette.co.uk

www.orbitbooks.net

In Memory of David Stross,
6th July, 1924–20th July, 2017

Power tends to corrupt and absolute power corrupts absolutely. Great men are almost always bad men, even when they exercise influence and not authority; still more when you superadd the tendency of the certainty of corruption by authority.

—Lord Acton

1: GOD SAVE THE KING

As I cross the courtyard to the execution shed I pass a tangle of bloody feathers. They appear to be the remains of one of the resident corvids, which surprises me because I thought they were already dead. Ravens are powerful and frighteningly astute birds, but they're no match for the tentacled dragonspawn that the New Management has brought to the Tower of London.

These are strange days and I can't say I'm happy about all the regime's decisions—but one does what one must to survive. And rule number one of life under the new regime is, *don't piss Him off.*

So I do my best to ignore the pavement pizza, and steel myself for what's coming next as I enter the shed, where the client is waiting with the witnesses, a couple of prison officers, and the superintendent.

Executions are formal occasions. I'm here as a participant, acting on behalf of my department. So I'm dressed in my funerals-and-court-appearances suit, special briefcase in hand. As I approach the police checkpoint, a constable makes a point of examining my warrant card. Then she matches me against the list of participants and peeks under my veil before letting me inside. Her partner watches the courtyard, helmet visor down and assault rifle at the ready.

The shed has been redecorated several times since they used to shoot spies in it during the Second World War. It's no longer an indoor shooting range, for one thing. For another, they've installed soundproof partitions and walls, so that the entrance opens onto a reception area before the airlock arrangement leading to a long corridor. They sign me in and I proceed past open doors that reveal spotless cells—the unit is very new, and my client today is the first condemned to be processed—then continue on to the doorway to the execution chamber at the end.

The chamber resembles a small operating theater. The table has straps to hold the client down. There's a one-way window on one wall, behind which I assume the witnesses are already waiting. I pause in the entrance and see, reflected in the mirror, the client staring at the odd whorl of blankness in the doorway.

"Ah, Ms. Murphy." The superintendent nods at me, mildly aggrieved. "You're late." She stands on the far side of the prisoner. She's in her dress uniform: a formal occasion, as already noted.

"Delays on the Circle Line." I shrug. "Sorry to hold you up."

"Yes, well, the prisoner doesn't get to eat breakfast until we're finished here."

I stifle a sigh. "Are we ready to start?" I ask as I place the special briefcase on the side table, then dial in the combination and unlock it.

"Yes." The superintendent turns to one of the prison officers. "Nigel, if you'd be so good as to talk us through the checklist?"

Nigel clears his throat. "Certainly, ma'am. First, a roll-call for the party. Superintendent: present. Security detail of four: present. Executioner: present—"

The condemned, who has been silent since I arrived, rolls his head sideways to glare at me. It's all he can move: he's trussed up like a Christmas turkey. His eyes are brown and liquid, and he has a straggly beard that somehow evades his cheekbones but engulfs his neck, as if he grew it for insulation from the cold. I smile at him as I say, "This won't hurt." Then I remember the veil. I flip it back from my face and he flinches.

"Superintendent, please confirm the identity of the subject."

The superintendent licks her lips. "I hereby confirm that the subject before us today is Mohammed Kadir, as delivered into the custody of this unit on January 12th, 2015."

"Confirmed. Superintendent, please read the execution warrant."

She reaches for a large manila envelope on the counter beside the stainless-steel sink, and opens it. There's a slim document inside, secured with Treasury tags.

"By authority vested in me by order of Her Majesty, Elizabeth II, I hereby uphold and confirm the sentence of death passed on Mohammed Kadir by the High Court on November 25th, 2014, for the crime of High Treason, and upheld on appeal by the Supreme Court on December 5th. Signed and witnessed, Home Secretary . . ."

When the New Management reintroduced the death penalty, they also reintroduced the British tradition of greasing the skids under the condemned—letting people rot on death row being seen as more cruel than the fate we're about to inflict on the unfortunate Mr. Kadir. Who, to be fair, probably shouldn't have babbled fantasies about assassinating the new Prime Minister in front of a directional microphone after Friday prayers during a national state of emergency. Sucks to be him.

"Phlebotomist, please prepare the subject."

Mr. Kadir is strapped down with his right arm outstretched and the sleeve of his prison sweatshirt rolled up. Now one of the prison officers steps between us and bends over him, carefully probing the crook of his elbow for a vein. Mr. Kadir is not, thankfully, a junkie. He winces once, then the phlebotomist tapes the needle in place and steps back. He side-eyes me on his way. Is he looking slightly green?

"Executioner, proceed."

This is my cue. I reach into the foam-padded interior of the briefcase for the first sample tube. They're needle-less syringes, just like the ones your doctor uses for blood tests. I pull ten cubic centimeters of blood into it and cap it. Venous blood isn't really blue. In lipstick terms it's dark plum, not crimson gloss. I place the full tube in its recess and take the next one, then repeat the process eighteen times. It's not demanding work, but it requires a steady hand. In the end it takes me just over ten minutes. During the entire process Mr. Kadir lies still, not fighting the restraints. After the third sample, he closes his eyes and relaxes slightly.

Finally, I'm done. I close and latch the briefcase. The phlebotomist slides out the cannula and holds a ball of cotton wool against the pinprick while he applies a sticking plaster. "There, that didn't hurt at all, did it?" I smile at Mr. Kadir. "Thank you for your cooperation."

Mr. Kadir opens his eyes, gives me a deathly stare, and recites the Shahada at me: "*lā 'ilāha 'illā llāh muḥammadun rasūlu llāh*." That's me told.

I smile wider, giving him a flash of my fangs before I tug my veil forward again. He gives no sign of being reassured by my resuming the veil, possibly because he knows I only wear it in lieu of factor-500 sunblock.

I sign the warrant on Nigel's clipboard. "Executioner, participation concluded," he intones. And that's me, done here.

"You can go now," the superintendent tells me. She looks as if she's aged a decade in the last quarter of an hour, but is also obscurely relieved: the matter is now out of her hands. "We'll get Mr. Kadir settled back in his cell and feed him his breakfast once you've gone." I glance at the mirror, at the blind spot reflected mockingly back at me. "The witnesses have a separate exit," she adds.

"Right." I nod and take a deep breath. "I'll just be off, then." Taking another deep breath, I spin the dials on the briefcase lock and pick it up. "Ta-ta, see you next time."

I'm a little bit jittery as I leave the execution chamber behind, but there's a spring in my step and I have to force myself not to click my heels. It all went a lot more smoothly than I expected. The briefcase feels heavier, even though it's weighed down by less than half an old-school pint. Chateau Kadir, vintage January 2015, shelf life two weeks. I make my way out, head for Tower Bridge Road, and expense an Addison Lee minicab back to headquarters. I can't wait to get there—I'm absolutely starving, for some reason.

Behind me, the witnesses will have already left. Mr. Kadir is being booked into the cell he will occupy for the next two weeks or so, under suicide watch. I expect the superintendent to look after her dead man with compassion and restraint. He'll get final meals and visits with his family, an imam who will pray with him, all the solicitous nursing support and at-home palliative care that can be delivered to his cell door for as long as his body keeps breathing. But that's not my department.

All I know is that in two weeks, give or take, Mr. Kadir, Daesh sympathizer and indiscreet blabbermouth, still walking and talking even though he was executed an hour ago, will be dead of V-syndrome-induced cerebral atrophy. And, as a side effect of the manner of his death, my people, the PHANGs who submitted to the rule of the New Management, will keep on going.

Because the blood is the life.

Hello, diary. I am Mhari Murphy, and if you are reading this I really hope I'm dead.

I used to work for the Laundry, a government agency that has been in the news for all the wrong reasons lately. I wanted to study biology, but ended up with a BSc in library science, for reasons too long and tedious to explain. Then I ended up with a job in Human Resources at the agency in question. I was a laughably bad fit, so it wasn't hard to get them to let me transfer out to the private sector. I acquired management experience and studied for my MBA while working for one of our largest investment banks, and was busily climbing the career ladder there when an unfortunate encounter with a contagious meme turned me into a vampire.

As a result of my new status as one of the PHANGs—Persons of Hemphagia-Assisted Neurodegenerative Geheime Staatspolizei (or something like that, the acronym wanders but the blood-drinking remains the same)—I ended up drafted back into the Human Resources Department of Q-Division, Special Operations Executive, aka the Laundry: the secret agency that protects the UK from alien nightmares and magical horrors. But things were different this time round. I was rapidly reassigned to a policing agency called the Transhuman Police Coordination Force, as director of operations and assistant to the chief executive, Dr. O'Brien. Our beat was dealing with superpowered idiots in masks. (The less said about my time as White Mask—a member of the official Home Office superhero team—the better.) When all's said and done, TPCF was mostly a public relations exercise, but it was a blessing in disguise for me because it broke me out of a career rut. When TPCF was gobbled up by the London Metropolitan Police I was re-acquired by Q-Division, moved onto the management fast-track, and assigned responsibility for the PHANGs. All the surviving ones, that is.

A big chunk of my job is to organize and requisition their blood meals, because the way PHANGs derive sustenance from human blood is extremely ugly. The V-parasites that give us our capabilities rely on us to draw blood from donors. They then chew microscopic holes in the victims' gray matter, so that they die horribly, sooner rather than later. But if we *don't* drink donor blood, eventually our parasites eat *us*. Consequently, it fell to someone to arrange to procure a steady supply of blood from dying terminal patients and distribute it to the PHANGs. That someone being me.

Anyway, that was the status quo ante, with me responsible for keeping all PHANGs on a very short leash and available for operational duties—they tend to be really good sorcerers, as long as they don't go insane from hunger and start murdering people—until the horrifying mess in Yorkshire last year resulted in the outing and subsequent dismemberment of the agency.

PHANGs being high-capability assets, I was pulled into Continuity Operations by the Senior Auditor and assigned to Active Ops, a specialty I've evaded for the past fifteen years because I do not approve of playing James Bond games when there are documents to be processed and meetings to be chaired. To be honest, I joined Continuity Operations mainly in the expectation that it would keep my team of PHANGs fed. I think most of us would choose to walk into the sunlight if the hunger pangs got too bad, but I'm not exactly keen to test their limits. Neither do I want to murder my own people. So it fell to me to keep them alive by any means necessary.

Continuity Operations—working against an enemy organization that had infiltrated and captured the government behind our back—were entirely necessary. And when the dust settled, we had a new government—the New Management, led by the very shiny new Prime Minister, who was unanimously voted into Westminster by the grateful citizens of a constituency whose former MP (a member of the cabinet) was catatonic in a hospital bed at the time. The Home Secretary invoked the Civil Contingencies Act and served as transitional PM in the wake of the emergency at Nether Stowe House, but she stepped down without a struggle[1] right after the new Prime Minister took the oath. Personally I suspect the PM had something to do with her resignation, but I have no proof, and as you have probably realized by now, it is very unwise to ask certain questions about the New Management, lest *they* ask questions about *you*.

We are now six months on from the tumultuous scene at the Palace of Westminster, when the Prime Minister took his seat and the New Management presented its program in the Queen's Speech. Six months into rule by decree under the imprimatur of the Civil Contingencies Act, as Parliament obediently processes a gigantic laundry-list of legislative changes. Six months into an ongoing state of emergency, as the nation finds itself under attack from without and within.

Which brings me to my current job.

Five months ago I was notified that it was Her Majesty's

---

[1] To spend more time with her hatchlings, according to *Private Eye*.

pleasure—or rather, that of her government—to bestow upon me the rank of Dame Commander of the Most Excellent Order of the British Empire. That rank came with the title of Baroness Karnstein (the PM's little joke), a life peerage, and a seat in the House of Lords.

The British government gives good titles, but don't get too excited: it just means the New Management considers PHANGs to be a useful instrument of state, and wanted a tame expert on board. Consequently I chair the Lords Select Committee on Sanguinary Affairs and have the distasteful duty to conduct executions, newly recommenced after fifty years in abeyance. Although I *did* get to be the first vampire—as far as I know—ever to wear an ermine-trimmed robe to the state opening of Parliament, so I suppose there's a silver lining . . .

Anyway, that's my CV. A slow start followed by a dizzying stratospheric ascent into government, you might think. But the New Management doesn't hand out honors and benefices without getting something in return. And I've been waiting for the other Jimmy Choo to drop ever since I was sworn in.

An unwelcome consequence of my new position is that I have come to the attention of very important people. This is a mixed blessing, especially when one of them is the Prime Minister himself, Fabian Everyman, also known as the Mandate—or the People's Mandate, if you're a tabloid journalist.

A couple of days after I officiated at the execution of Mr. Kadir—his soul is now feeding the V-parasites of some seven PHANGs, so he's probably good for another week—I'm alert and not particularly hungry as I perch on the edge of a fussy Victorian sofa in the White Drawing Room at 10 Downing Street.

I'm here because the PM invited me for afternoon tea and cakes along with a handful of colleagues from Mahogany Row, the formerly secretive upper tier of the Laundry. The PM is wearing his usual immaculate three-piece suit, and everyone is on high alert. This session is only informal insofar as it has no agenda. In truth, it's a platform for the PM, who is mercurial at best, to rant at us about his personal hobby horses. (Which are many and alarming, and he tends to switch between them in mid-sentence.) It's as exhausting as dealing with an early-stage dementia sufferer—one with a trillion-pound budget and nuclear-weapons-release authority.

"We need to deal with the Jews, you know," Fabian confides, then pauses dramatically.

This is new and unwelcome, and more than somewhat worrying. (I knew the PM held some rather extreme views, but this level of forthright anti-Semitism is unexpected.) "May I ask why?" I ask hesitantly.

"I'd have thought it was obvious!" He sniffs. "All that *charitable* work. Loaves and fishes, good Samaritans, y'know. Sermon on the Mount stuff. Can't be doing with it—"

Beside me, Chris Womack risks interrupting His flow: "Don't you mean *Christians,* sir?"

"—*And* all those suicide bombers. Blowing people up in the name of their god, but can't choke down a bacon roll. Can't be doing with them: you mark my words, they'll have to be dealt with!"

Across the room, Vikram Choudhury nearly swallows his tongue. Chris persists: "But those are Mus—"

"—*All* Jews!" the Prime Minister snaps. "They're just the same from where I'm standing." His expression is one of tight-lipped disapproval—then I blink, and in the time it takes before my eyelids open again, I forget his face. He sips delicately from his teacup, pinkie crooked, then explains His thinking. "Christians, Muslims, Jews—they *say* they're different religions, but you mark my words, they all worship the same god, and you know what *that* leads to if you let it fester. Monotheism is nothing but trouble—unless the one true god is me, of course." He puts his teacup down and beams at us. "I want a plan on my desk by the beginning of next month to prepare a framework for solving the Jewish problem. Mosques, mikvahs, Christian Science reading rooms: I want them all pinpointed, and a team on the ground drawing up plans to ensure the epidemic spreads no further!"

"A, a *final* solution?" Vikram asks, utterly aghast.

The PM looks primly shocked. "Absolutely not! What do you take me for? This is the very model of an enlightened and forward-looking government! The indiscriminate slaughter of innocents is wasteful and unappealing—although I'm sure there are some reality TV shows that could use a supply of Hunger Games contestants, ha ha! No, I just want the pernicious virus of *the wrong kind of monotheism* contained. Starve it of the oxygen of publicity and it'll suffocate eventually, no need for gas chambers, what?"

"But sir," Chris speaks up again—unwisely, in my opinion— "we have a legal commitment to religious freedom—"

The PM holds up a hand: "Maybe *we* do, but *they* don't, and if *they* get out of control again we'll end up with another Akhenaten. That's where they get it from, you know—once you allow one god to take over a pantheon and suppress the worship of rivals, it never ends well unless you're the first mover. But don't worry about the religious freedom issue! It'll be taken care of in the Great Repeal Bill I've directed the Office of the Parliamentary Counsel to draw up." He shakes his head dismissively as one of the police officers refills his cup from a brilliantly polished silver teapot. "Now, on a happier note, I'd like to hear how plans are coming along for the Tzompantli that will replace the Marble Arch those idiots erected in place of the Tyburn tree . . ."

Say whatever else you will about him, Fabian is full of unpleasant and exciting surprises, and always three steps ahead of the rest of us! He reminds me of a certain ex of mine in that respect. But it's a bad idea to enthusiastically applaud everything the PM comes out with. Sometimes he says outrageous things deliberately to smoke out flatterers and yes-men. The way to survive these sessions is to pay attention to how his inner circle react. So I take my cue from Mrs. Carpenter, his chief of staff, who is nodding along thoughtfully, and match my reactions to hers. And that's how I get through the next half hour while Hector MacArthur—who has apparently landed the job of coordinating the festivities for Her Majesty's ninetieth birthday—describes some sort of bizarre titanium and glass sculpture that he asked Foster + Partners to design for the junction of Park Lane and Oxford Street.

Whatever a Tzompantli is, it keeps the PM happy, and that's never a bad thing. When the PM is unhappy He has a tendency to meddle and break things. Last month it was Prince Charles (no biggie: I gather he should be out of hospital just as soon as he stops weeping uncontrollably); this month it was the US Ambassador (who made the mistake of personally asking for a tax break for his golf course in Ayrshire). From the way He's talking, next month it could be the Church of England; and *then* where will we turn for tea, sympathy, and exorcisms?

Finally the fountain of bizarre winds down. "Well, it's been *lovely* to see everyone," the PM assures us, "but I really mustn't keep you any longer, I'm sure you all have important things to be getting on with!" It's a dismissal, and we all stand. "Not you, Baroness Karnstein," He says as the shell-shocked survivors of Mahogany Row file out of the drawing room, "or you, Iris." The PM smiles, and for a moment I see a flickering vision where His face should be: an onion-skin Matryoshka doll of circular shark-toothed maws, lizard-man faces, and insectile hunger. "A word in my study if you don't mind. Right this way."

Oh dear, I think. I follow Him into the entrance hall, where the others are collecting their coats and filing out into the skin-crisping afternoon overcast, then we walk through a corridor leading deep into the rabbit warren of Number 10. Eventually we come to the PM's study. The curtains are drawn, for which I am grateful. There's a small conference table at one end, but the PM heads straight towards a small cluster of chairs and a sofa that surround a coffee table. He waves me towards a seat but I bow my head. "You first, Majesty."

Behind Him Iris briefly smiles approval. Her boss sinks into the armchair and nods at me. "*Now* will you sit?" He asks, and I hurry to comply. In public and in office He's the Prime Minister, but Iris and I know better. He is a physical incarnation of the Black Pharaoh, N'yar Lat-Hotep, royalty that was ancient long before ancient Britons first covered themselves in woad and worshipped at Stonehenge. The Queen may still open Parliament, but she does so by His grace and indulgence. "I suppose you're wondering why I invited you here," He says, then grins like a skull that's just uttered the world's deadliest joke.

"Yes, Your Majesty." I sit up straight, knees together, my hands folded in my lap. I briefly try to meet His gaze, but even though I am myself a thing that can soulgaze demons, it's like staring at the sun—if the sun had gone supernova and turned into a black hole a billion years ago.

"I have a small problem," He begins, then pauses expectantly.

Okay, here it comes. I tense, digging the points of my expensively capped incisors into my lower lip: "Is it something I can help with?" I ask, because there's not really anything else you *can* say when a living god looks at you like that.

"Ye-es, I believe you might." The gates of hell flash me a twinkle from what passes for His eyes. "Tell me, Baroness"—he already knows the answer to the question, He's just toying with me—"have you ever visited the United States?"

Hello again, dear posthumous diary reader.

I know this is a lot to take in all at once, so for what it's worth you have my apologies. But the CV I started with doesn't give the correct context for my position under the New Management. I may no longer be Mhari Murphy, civil servant, from SOE Q-Division, but Dame Mhari Murphy, BSc (hons), MBA, FIC, DBE, styled Baroness Karnstein, and member of the House of

Lords—but I am also, to use a technical term, utterly and unambiguously boned.

This is not my official work journal: I can afford to be honest here.

It used to be Best Practice in SOE for high-level personnel—line sorcerers and staff managers—to keep an up-to-date logbook so that in event of their incapacitation, retirement, or death in the line of duty their work would remain documented. In my experience, if you keep a written record of your wrongdoings you will only provide ammunition for your enemies, so I generally don't do that. I have an orderly mind and I try to apply procedures humanely but exhaustively and keep within my remit. Work journals are for the experimentally inclined—hackers and the like—and my official work journal is mostly just a transcript of my weekly time sheets and performance appraisals.

Prior to CASE NIGHTMARE RED and the Leeds Incursion this was never an issue for me. I wasn't engaged in active ops, and first I was too junior and then TPCF didn't have the same requirement. (Dr. O'Brien doesn't consider it useful to overdocument the antics of half-trained amateur superheroes.) Then everything went topsy-turvy and upside down while Continuity Operations were in effect, and keeping an up-to-date logbook was the least of my worries.

Since the installation of the New Management I've been stuck in experimental, improvisational mode. Nobody has ever chaired a House of Lords Select Committee on blood magic while working for a Risen God. And life, as they say, comes at you fast. Institutional knowledge retention is the name of the game, and it's especially difficult when the institution is vulnerable to ideological purges. If you write something in an official logbook it may be used in evidence against you. But if you don't leave any written record at all, and you die, then you leave your allies at a disadvantage.

Which is why I'm maintaining this secret diary.

And if you're reading this and I'm not already dead, then may whatever gods you believe in have mercy on my soul, because the Prime Minister won't.

Back when I worked with Mo and Ramona on the Transhuman Police Coordination Force executive, we made a habit of going out for a team-building exercise exactly once a week. Team building in this context meant drinking wine until we fell over. When you manage a rapid-reaction force you can't afford to show any signs of stress in the workplace, because stressed-out management is contagious and degrades mission effectiveness. Hence the girls' nights out in a non-workplace environment, with companions who had the security clearance to hear what I was moaning about. Not to mention enough alcohol to provide next-morning deniability if it all got too embarrassing.

I'm pretty sure those sessions saved Mo's sanity, what with her violin gnawing on the corners of her mind. I don't know what they did for Ramona, but she seemed to enjoy it, too. Me, I just needed the regular reminder that I was still officially human. But Ramona isn't around any more—she got recalled, *nobody* seems to know what her people (BLUE HADES, the abyssal Deep Ones) make of the New Management—and Mo, Dr. O'Brien, is unavailable. Or maybe I'm just too much of a coward to talk to her since she . . . changed. As for family, my parents and kid sister aren't cleared to know anything about my work (anyway, even if they were they'd be utterly useless), and I can't vent at Fuckboy because reasons. Which means there's only one person to turn to—and I know exactly how to bribe her.

"'Seph, darling, do you have anything planned for this evening, or are you free for—yes, absolutely! Listen, I need to pick your brain, so shall we make it my treat? I can sign you into the dining room at work and expense it if you meet me at the Cromwell Green visitor's entrance at six—er, expect security screening? But you won't believe the wine list! And all the latest gossip, of course!"

I hang up, then call the maître d'hôtel to reserve a table in the Peers' Dining Room, because they tend to fill up fast on the evening before a debate. The chamber's been uncommonly busy of late, processing a deluge of new legislation. The PM doesn't really hold with new-fangled ideas like the Rights of Man (or Woman), let alone egalitarianism and democracy, but he works with what he's got, and in this instance that means a House of Lords stuffed with life peers.

Most people think life peerages are handed out as retirement sinecures for front-rank politicians. But it's also a means to recruit experts the government wants on tap to scrutinize bills in progress. Law professors, barristers, journalists, economists, historians: the sort of people who can't be arsed going into politics as a career, but who are nevertheless deemed to have Useful Opinions to contribute to Parliament. That's why there are so many life peers, and why they're drawn from a surprisingly broad spectrum of British public life. The old aristocracy barely get a foot in the door any more. The only reason any of them are left is that the Lords Reform Bill got stitched up in a back-room deal in 2012, derailing the most recent attempt at fully modernizing the upper chamber.

Back when it was called the Invisible College, and "computer" was a job description for a working mathematician, the Laundry was funded out of the House of Lords black budget. It's almost inevitable that these days we have people *inside* the House, supervising the muggles. But I still wake up some mornings wondering how I, a nice middle-class girl from Essex, got here, and how much longer I've got to make use of the perks of office before I'm found out.

On the dot of six o'clock I'm waiting in the lobby to meet Persephone Hazard as she comes through the metal-detector arch and retrieves her handbag from the X-ray screening machine. Yes, Westminster has airport-grade security, but the uniformed men and women on duty are courteous and polite, as if you're graciously doing them a favor by permitting them to check your possessions for dangerous items.

"'Seph!" I call.

'Seph looks more like the popular conception of a baroness than I do. Her makeup is understated, her clothing fits with the eerie precision of couture, and her jewelry is discreet. She moves with the grace of a dancer—or a martial arts instructor, which she is. (Mind you, the popular conception is wrong: most baronesses these days are slightly eccentric middle-aged law professors—that, or retired politicians. Sorry to puncture your illusions.) Not for the first time I wonder what I'm doing in this house instead of her. Certainly if the New Management wants a trustworthy pair of hands to keep the Lords on track with occult affairs, we could do worse.

She beams at me, trots over, and kisses both cheeks, stinging my oversensitized nose with her jasmine scent. "Mhari! It's been too long. How have you been?" She leans back, inspecting me. "Is everything all right?"

"Everything is absolutely splendid!" I assure her, with such gushing irony that she blinks. "No, it's not, but how about we leave that until after dinner?" I take her arm. "Been to any good gallery openings lately?"

The Peers' Dining Room in the House of Lords is one of those peculiar British institutions that somehow combines a snobbish conviction of utter superiority with a pronounced cross-Channel culinary cringe. It's easy to believe that in rooms almost identical to this[2], blue-blooded nobles conspired to ravage the Indian subcontinent, colonize North America, deport their criminal classes to Australia, and build a railway from Cape Town to Cairo. It's all polished wood-paneled walls, paintings of distinguished alumnae (mostly of Prime Ministerial caliber, dating to the eighteenth century or earlier), and small tables dressed in crisp white linen, gleaming silverware, and crystal. The occupants, in suits and dresses, look as if they belong in the board-

---

[2] It was rebuilt after the great fire of 1834, and again after the Blitz, so it's not actually much older than my mum.

rooms of British industry. And the stunningly good wine list is subsidized by the nation. "What do you fancy?" I ask, as Persephone reads the food menu.

A minute frown wrinkles her brow. "Hmm. This is a little . . ."

"Mundane?"

"I was going to say, high-end gastropub?" She puts the menu down and shakes her head. "However, the potted confit of sea trout and crab will be an acceptable starter, and I suppose it will go well enough with the baked salmon with tagliatelle as a main . . ."

The British ruling class was never noted for its expertise in haute cuisine. Rumors that they conquered a quarter of the planet in search of a decent meal cannot be discounted. For decades, the dirty little secret of the Westminster dining experience was that the chefs were mostly trained in Paris. This will change when Westminster closes for extensive reconstruction next year—there are rumors that we are going to acquire our very own sushi conveyor-belt restaurant—but for the time being, dining in the House of Lords is like taking a TARDIS trip back to 1955.

However, if your real motive for eating is to line your stomach before exploring the Crown's wine cellar, while discussing your utterly top-secret assignment from Number 10 with one of the *very* few people who share your security clearance, the Lords' Dining Room offers one valuable perquisite that no public restaurant can match: it's the most exclusive and surveillance-free club bar in London.

Over the next hour Persephone and I tuck into posh pub grub as I listen to her make small talk about fund-raisers for charities and curtain-raisers for operas—the stuff she amuses herself with when she's pretending to be a rich socialite rather than the most powerful independent intelligence witch in the UK—and I gossip about the weird traditions and colorful customs of the office I've landed in, but nothing of any consequence.

Finally the casual chat winds down. A different waiter arrives with the dessert wine list—I opt for a tawny port—and once he retreats 'Seph leans back and watches me. "So. Spill it. What eats you?"

"I had a meeting at Number 10 this morning. One of His blue-sky sessions, except that He held me back for a confidential chat afterwards." I shudder, remembering the way He made me feel, like a quarter-century flashback to being a naughty schoolgirl carpeted for giving lip to Mrs. Barnes in History again. "He gave me extra homework, and I'm afraid I'm going to fail the exam."

"Homework." Persephone Hazard tilts her head a few degrees to the left and gives me a raven-eyed stare. "Hmm." She knows exactly what I am, so the lack of immediate reassurance is dis-tinctly unreassuring. "What kind of assignment?"

I've backed myself into this position deliberately so I'll be forced to share the grisly details. There are no excuses for lead-ing her up to this point and then chickening out; so I tell her, which only takes a minute or so, and then I wait.

Persephone thinks for a bit, then finally shakes her head. "I'm sorry," she says softly, then reaches across the table and touches the back of my wrist: "I'm so sorry, Mhari, but I'm afraid you're right: you really *are* boned, and this time not even Mahogany Row can save you."

Hello again, diary, and welcome to this evening's episode of I Am So Doomed.

The PM, as I said previously, likes to meddle. That's the only explanation for my assignment that I can come up with. (That, and the PM is so much smarter than a merely human sorcerer that He's beyond terrifying. He knows *everything* that's going on—I mean, you can't hold anything back from Him. He keeps track of seemingly unrelated items you wouldn't imagine Him being involved in, and then casually pulls them up in conversa-tion and shows how they are interrelated, and it all makes a hor-rible kind of sense.)

"According to the Identity and Passport Office you have never visited North America," He said with an avuncular smile. "Which means that unless you have an as-yet-undisclosed covert operational identity, your biometrics are not on the US immigration department's database."

I stared at the carpet. "That's true," I admitted. When I worked for the bank as an executive assistant, my boss Oscar used to jet around the globe and attend summit meetings. Meanwhile, I was stuck in the office keeping the wheels on his wagon turning and in contact with the ground. Maybe with another couple of years of seniority I'd have made vice-president and gotten to do some jet-setting of my own, but PHANG syndrome happened instead. That put me back inside the Laundry, where any international holiday travel plans have to be pre-approved six months in advance. Finally we hit CASE NIGHTMARE RED—and I gather British Airways laid off a third of their staff last month.

"You have what your colleagues in the trade call a clean face. That will come in handy." The Prime Minister paused. "Have you been following the news from the United States?"

"The—" *What?* I bite my tongue.

"There are signs and portents." The PM smirked. "The President has not been seen outside the White House for eleven weeks, he's not on the news or attending any meetings, he is never available to take my calls—and I've tried. He's not home to the German Chancellor either," he added. "Or to the Prime Minister of Japan."

Oh dear.

"All our usual sources inside the Beltway are distinctly unforthcoming," continued the Prime Minister. "Congress continues to sit, the Supreme Court deliberates, CNN talking heads debate, the various candidates are preparing the groundwork for next year's election campaigns, but it's as if they've all forgotten the Executive Branch exists."

"*What?*" I couldn't help myself; it just slipped out. You don't just *forget* the American President: it'd be like forgetting about the Queen, or absent-mindedly misplacing the Moon. The President is one of—if not *the*—most potent authority figures in the world. And that's leaving aside his role as the leader of a team of four or five hundred politicians and high-ranking civil servants who run the most powerful executive office on the planet. (Ahem: the most powerful *human* office on the planet.) How do you forget *that*?

"It appears that the Vice-President is missing, too," the Prime Minister continued. "A powerful glamour has engulfed the United States of America. It's not the first time, of course—that nation is a shining temple to amnesia with its foundations built atop the bones of vanished empires—but I find it disturbing that a third of a billion people have simultaneously forgotten the existence of the Executive Branch of their government at *just* this moment, with the walls between the worlds rubbing paper-thin and the chittering of unseen things in the darkness growing ever louder, eh, what? I fear a takeover, Mhari. A *hostile* takeover, possibly something coming through the imperfectly sealed gate in Colorado Springs through which that fellow you dealt with last year obtained access to the Sleeper—" He was referring to the unspeakably vile televangelist Raymond Schiller, whom I drained in a luxury apartment in Docklands, and good riddance—"or at the very least, an internal coup within your former agency's counterparts, the Operational Phenomenology Agency." His grin was skeletal. "It would hardly be unprecedented, don't you think?

"So here's your new assignment: you will establish a new agency, recruit agents, and direct them—I have a little list of those who won't be missed, tum-de-dum, I shall send it to you presently—in order to develop and deliver a HUMINT capability directed against the United States. You are to bring the new organization to operational readiness, then lead them in penetrating the continental land mass, peering behind the blackout curtain that has so abruptly descended, and working out who is currently running the show. Ahem: I meant to say *what* is running the show: they're almost certainly not human any more.

"Your team will consist of agents with clean faces who are politically unreliable but sufficiently competent to have some hope of survival in a very hostile environment. In addition to intelligence gathering, they may be called upon in future to conduct extraction and sabotage operations if the situation calls for it, just like the old wartime SOE, hah hah! And while you're about it, don't forget to retrieve the President? He might come in useful."

I squeaked. "You want me to rescue"—*don't say kidnap*—"the President?"

"Only if he's still human enough to be worth collecting." Darkness smiled at me across the table. "You never know, he might not be! It all depends on what's running the United States in his absence, and whether the President escaped before they got their tentacles wrapped around his brain-stem. I won't hold it against you if you can't manage it because *he's* awakened at last and is behind it, you know: *Ph'nglui mglw'nafh Cthulhu R'lyeh wgah'nagl fhtagn*—in his house at R'lyeh dead Cthulhu waits dreaming. But come now, why the long face? Isn't this the promotion you've been waiting for, Baroness?"

I drink inadvisably with 'Seph but manage to avoid getting weepy or maudlin. Afterwards I pour myself into a taxi, head for the office, and set to work designing a new government agency.

Whatever else you may think of the New Management, when the boss commits, He pulls out *all* the stops. There's something refreshingly Churchillian about it, just as long as you're not standing at ground zero of one of His ire bombs. Previous administrations had to worry about expenses scandals and investigative journalists, so penny-pinching and paperwork were the order of the day, but that all changed after His Darkness had a fireside chat with the Dirty Digger, and Mr. Dacre of the *Daily Mail*. Now the headlines all praise the New Management, and nobody dares look below the surface—especially after what He did to *Private Eye*.[3]

When the PM learned about the decrepit state of the former Laundry's premises, He had us—the revenant core of Mahogany Row/Continuity Operations—requisition a whole row of think-tank and NGO offices along Great College Street, a stone's throw from Parliament. Then He had the Exchequer write Facilities a blank check. It came with strings attached, of course. I swear Vikram nearly fainted when he saw the deadline to turn that rat's nest of listed eighteenth-century buildings into a new HQ for the civil service sorcerers. Then, when we slithered past the guillotine blade a couple of hours ahead of the drop dead date, he burst into tears and shouted, "We're going to live! We're going to live!"

Anyway, as a result of the PM's double-edged largesse, I have a gigantic office with intricate gilt cornice-work and an original Adam fireplace. It's about the same size as my apartment, and it comes with a huge sash window overlooking the Westminster School gardens. It's backed by a sheet of bulletproof glass with some sort of fancy photoreactive coating that totally blocks ultraviolet light, so I'm safe from daylight. I can't get over it: I can enjoy the view during office hours without catching fire! And the paintings from the Government Art Collection are—*don't* get me started. Let's just say I've come up in the world. It's a *nice* office, perfectly suited to a baroness who is the head of a new intelligence agency; I hope they let me keep it.

Mind you, I'm not enjoying it right now. I stand in front of the window in my stockinged feet, glass of brandy in hand, glaring at Westminster Abbey and trying not to lose my shit. 'Seph thinks I'm doomed, and I can't say she's wrong with any cer-

---

[3] Scurrilous weekly investigative scandal sheet and thorn in the side of the British establishment, founded in 1961 and continuously published until its liquidation in late 2014, when they tried to blow the lid on what really happened at Nether Stowe House.

tainty. I've been in bad positions before—unreasonable bosses with unreachable expectations—but senior banking VPs usually can't do anything worse than fire you. As for Laundry management, they're mostly amenable to reason, especially if you have friends in HR. But the New Management is another matter entirely. The mere *idea* of disappointing the PM gives me the cold shudders. Reaping my skull for a Christmas tree ornament is one of the least-bad outcomes if I screw this up.

(Oh, and where's the list of candidates he promised me? If He's serious, their caliber will speak volumes about whether He expects me to succeed.)

Anyway, I can at least try to use my time to come up with a plan. So I sit down at my two-hundred-year-old Admiralty desk, pull out an A3-sized sheet of drafting paper, and start sketching out a tentative org chart.

So, let's see: His Darkness has given me an overall goal with two sub-tasks. No, make that three.

Firstly, I need to set up a management team for a new agency with a remit to support HUMINT assets—spies—working overseas. (Normally that'd be a job for a department inside SIS, but this is different: at least the New Management will give me whatever legal cover I need to make it fly, because we are in an ongoing state of emergency.) It follows that I have to be able to insert agents into the United States of America without coming to the attention of the Nazgûl. That's our nickname for the Operational Phenomenology Agency, the Laundry's bigger and better-funded American counterpart, and should tell you everything you need to know about them.

Secondly, I need to deliver on-the-ground answers to certain key questions: Cthulhu: Has he risen? The President: Is he a lizard-man? And so on.

And thirdly, I need to set this circus up so it can continue to operate on an ongoing basis as a permanent agency, not just a one-off project, iterating in pursuit of future goals defined by Number 10.

This is so far above my previous pay grade that just thinking about it gets me chewing my lower lip and looking longingly at the brandy. So I force myself to take five minutes out to de-stress and repair my sun-proof makeup.

While I'm working on the top coat, I carefully reconsider my assumptions. Assume the worst: nobody outside the UK loves us, and in particular the US intelligence community are totally not our BFFs any more. Rather than just dropping in for a friendly chat, my people will be facing a hostile environment, with border guards looking for intruders. Hence the boss's point about clean faces. Oh, and if the Nazgûl aren't already on the alert for reports of vampires entering the country, I'm a chocolate teapot.

As for why His Darkness picked me for this job, I can think of several explanations, none of them good. Why not Mo, who at least has experience of setting up an agency from scratch? Or 'Seph, ditto, only for undercover penetration ops? Neither of them are clean faces, but it's terrible tactical doctrine to put your controller anywhere the opposition can see them, much less order them to lead from the front. Maybe He simply doesn't trust anyone else. Or maybe He really *does* think He's giving me a big break. Maybe He wants me there as a high-level negotiator— risky, but if He's serious about the President, he might—

Let's shelve that for a moment and move on to the PM's specific questions. Schiller, the televangelist in Colorado Springs, worries me. I remember Bob Howard was involved in some classified project to do with him a few years ago—GOD GAME something? I scribble a note to myself to pull the archival report. Maybe it'd be better to get the story from Bob directly, but for personal reasons I'm reluctant to ask him.

The PM's specific tasking is infuriatingly vague. I draw an arrow leading to a box labelled "RESEARCH" and another arrow from there to "RECON" before allowing myself to get sidetracked for a few minutes.

I have a "dirty"—private, unsecured—Samsung phone. I pull it out and google Colorado Springs and then ask the google monster how far it is from London. Nearly five thousand miles! I draw an arrow and a thought bubble captioned "LOGISTICS" and move swiftly on.

Next there's the action-movie assignment: *rescue the President*. Even assuming he hasn't been eaten by tentacle monsters, or possessed by those nauseating crotch parasites Schiller planted on people, that's a big ask. If he's missing, then *either* he's in a dungeon somewhere (and maximum security prisons are designed to be hard to break people out of), *or* our information is wrong and he's still in office and guarded by the Secret Service— battalions of men in black with automatic weapons. I hang these two options off the diagram as an IF . . . ELSE fork, flow-chart fashion, and make an executive decision. If the President is still human but a prisoner, we'll rescue him. If we can't, well, trying to kidnap an unwilling President seems like a messy form of suicide. *Especially* if he's the American counterpart of the PM.

Rule Number One is *don't die*. Corollary Number One is *don't poke things that will certainly kill you*, like high-tension cables and hostile level-six Existential Anthropic Threats. If it comes to it, I'll take responsibility and lay my head on the block. I mean, the PM *might* not kill me if He's misjudged the threat, right? Firm but fair: strong and stable; the slogans of the New Management.

Somewhere in the middle of my elaborate thought-doodle my glass of brandy has emptied itself and, having been refilled, has half-emptied itself again. It's almost two in the morning. I sigh and contemplate my work. "Pathetic," I mutter. I quickly sketch in an org chart with three tails—two field teams of four and an executive branch, also of four—then knock back my nightcap.

The eleven empty slots on the org chart mock me as I turn out the light and head for the door. But they'll have to wait until I get the PM's little list.

The ship of state is a supertanker with a turning circle so vast that it takes years to change course—but there is constant, frantic activity on the bridge as it begins to steer. For the past six months, we have been under the command of a new master, and the ship is slowly coming about. If you are on the outside, watching, you have probably noticed a few changes. A new cabinet, a new government, new faces, new names in the papers. A stirring declaration by the Prime Minister that there will be no referendum on leaving the EU, because He is determined to take us out of the union anyway[4]—He has a mandate to do so, after all, a mandate for strong and stable government.

There have been other changes that don't make the front pages of the newspapers. Windfall taxes on multinationals, subsidies for certain types of agriculture, discussions about food and petrol rationing with the chief executives of Tesco and Sainsbury's—

—The Mandate is preparing for war.

CASE NIGHTMARE GREEN is the codename the Laundry applied to the most likely human extinction scenario resulting from the wide-scale effects of applied computational demonology. That's the branch of the occult that our agency—the bastard offspring of the wartime Special Operations Executive and Bletchley Park—was responsible for (and ultimately failed at) suppressing. Magic is a branch of applied mathematics. Computers are machines that can be used to solve theorems and perform mathemagical operations exceedingly fast (as are certain neural networks, so long as you can immunize them against the extrad-

---

[4] I asked why we had to leave the EU, in one of those informal breakout sessions at Number 10. "Mm, need to get rid of the ECJ and the ECHR," He mumbled around a crumpet. (The European Court of Justice and the European Convention on Human Rights.)

"Why?" I asked.

"Can't bring back the death penalty without ditching the ECHR," He replied. "Also, we need to get rid of free movement. Stop the blighters emigrating."

I couldn't help myself: "Why the death penalty?" I persisted.

He fixed me with a quelling stare: "There haven't been enough human sacrifices of late, as *you* should know," He said.

imensional feeders that like to chew up the brains of magicians). Brains can under some circumstances perform magic, and there are too many brains these days. There are also too many computers. Would you believe that iPhones are a major threat to national security? A current generation smartphone is more powerful than a 1991 supercomputer.

CASE NIGHTMARE GREEN hung fire for a decade, but it finally arrived with a bang last year. That's when the explosion of microprocessors over the past few decades, and the proliferation of meddling peasants who program them, blew past the agency's ability to sweep everything neatly under the rug. CASE NIGHTMARE GREEN weakens the fabric of spacetime to such a degree that ordinary people begin to acquire power through thaumic resonance. Botnets spread through unpatched copies of Windows 2003 running on medical diagnostic equipment, spamming arcane prayers on behalf of things better left unworshipped. Supposedly wholesome bitcoin mining apps are actually running demon-summoning algorithms in disguise. And *don't* get me started on the prevalence of necromantic malware in the app stores.

Nine months ago we hit critical mass. It started, ironically, with a scenario the agency considered unlikely: an invasion by an army of magic-wielding hominids from a parallel universe, fleeing extermination by ghastly horrors that had been attracted to their realm by their excessive use of magic. The *alfär* host caused death and destruction on a scale not seen in the British Isles since the Second World War, triggering a crisis that the enemies of the agency sought to exploit for their own benefit. Ultimately this left our board with no option but to strike a devil's bargain with an only slightly lesser evil—

—who is now our Prime Minister.

If you are to survive under the New Management you need to understand the Black Pharaoh, insofar as it's humanly possible to do so. The PM is brilliant, incisive, and mercurial, and He is definitely not insane. However, His concerns are so remote from those of regular humanity that most people simply don't understand what they're dealing with. So I find it helpful to employ a metaphor in order to explain our predicament, and it goes like this:

The Denizen of Number 10 is the avatar—the humanoid sock-puppet—of an ancient and undying intelligence who regards mere humanity much as we might regard a hive of bees. Our lives are of no individual concern to Him, but He likes honey. As long as we continue to give Him what He wants—honey—He is content to keep us around, and even to tend to us to the extent that it does not inconvenience Him. But the moment anyone thinks to sting the keeper's hand, it will be out with the fly-swatter—or, if we're unlucky, the insecticide bomb.

So we've got to keep Him happy, *whatever* the cost.

The alternative is simply too dreadful to contemplate.

The next day is a Friday, which is generally debate-free at Westminster—lots of MPs have to commute home to their constituencies—and this has knock-on effects in the upper house. Committees tend to shut down at lunchtime. The afternoon is for filing expense claims and reports, and leaving early.

A red box—a battered briefcase covered in red leather, bearing the royal cypher—is waiting with my receptionist when I arrive. "Lauren." I nod, and she gives me a timid smile: apparently I scare people. "Any news?"

"A courier dropped this off for you an hour ago, your ladyship?" (I don't know why she persists with the whole formal "your ladyship" thing: it's technically the correct form of address, but we've been working together for four months and I've even taken her along to a wine bar a couple of times.) She offers me the box.

"Thanks." I take it. It's light, which is a relief. "Is there anything to sign for?"

"No, your ladyship. I mean, they got me to sign for it, but you're covered."

"Okay, fine. Anything else?" She shakes her head. "I'll be in my office if anyone calls, then."

Once inside, I open the box. It contains a slim document folder, and when I open it a single sheet of paper falls out and drifts to the floor. I pick it up, put it on the desk, and resist the urge to swear—I recognize most of the names on it. *Is He insane?* I ask myself. *No, don't answer.* I flush: sweat prickles up and down my back under my suit jacket and I glance up to check that the window coating is intact and I'm not feeling the first signs of daylight-induced spontaneous combustion. I'm just—surprised, and not in a good way.

I sit down and stare at the sheet of paper for about ten minutes, thinking furiously. Then I unlock the top desk drawer, pull out my battered Parliamentary-issued Dell laptop, plug it into the network socket, and fire up the creakingly slow internal email app that Q-Division makes us use instead of something shiny and modern. Then I start typing:

> To whom it may concern:
>
> You have been seconded to a special assignment with immediate effect by express order of the Cabinet Office.
>
> We recognize that some of you have ongoing tasks. These orders override all prior duties. If you experience pushback, refer your management to me *personally* and I will deal with them.
>
> Your attendance at a mandatory all-hands team briefing is required. Report to Briefing Room C, Cabinet Office, 70 Whitehall, on Monday at 9 a.m.
>
> In addition to your normal identification documents you should bring your current passport and any travel documents or visas you possess.
>
> I apologize in advance for any inconvenience,
>
> Mhari Murphy, Baroness Karnstein.

After I hit "send" I sit for a long while with my chin on my hands, staring pensively at the sheet of paper bearing the list of recipients.

What have I done? I wonder. *Is this a deliberate provocation, or some kind of loyalty test? Or does He simply* not care *what we think*? Probably a bit of both, I suspect: the PM is slippery even by the standards of other immortal nightmares.

I've got a lot of work to get through—reports to read, minutes to write, witnesses to call, that sort of thing—but after sending *that* memo to *those* faces I am feeling the weight of isolation on my shoulders, and it is depressing and upsetting. So I copy some names into slots on the org chart I drew up yesterday, stash my papers and laptop in the office safe, and bunk off work for the weekend. Normally I'd take a bunch of unclassified/low-risk stuff home—I like to feel I'm not idling my life away—but for once I don't have the energy. I am losing my detachment: I am in danger of actually getting angry with the PM—which is a life-threatening error. So I resolve to get totally blitzed and stay that way until I can no longer avoid dealing with His little joke, which in practice means I next need to be sober again no later than 9 a.m. on Monday, when I have to look everybody in the eye and explain how we've been sent on a suicide mission.

Civil service pay scales are traditionally shit, and that's before you clamp five years of austerity policies down on top. When I worked in banking I was doing a lot better, but thanks to one or two regrettable early errors of judgement I kept putting off the usual first step on the property ladder, namely hooking up with a partner and jointly mortgaging our souls in perpetuity for a leasehold on a single-bedroom rabbit hutch. Story of my life. I wasted nearly a decade before I realized that life is not a game and there are no save points or second chances. That's when I extricated myself from the Laundry, bought a suit, got a real job, and turned serious about getting ahead. Okay, so maybe I was overreacting, but I signed up for an MBA and grabbed on to the corporate ladder *hard*. Watch me level grind, making up for lost time! But then I got PHANG syndrome and Oscar got himself killed, so I never made it to VP level after all. And I fell back into the shadows.

When I was drafted back into Q-Division, Human Resources went to some lengths to find me secure accommodation. They classified PHANG as a disability for residential support purposes, bless them, which got me free housing. But it was still a room in a Laundry shared house, as if I were a twenty-two-year-old graduate-track recruit: not quite as humiliating as ending up in kid sis's room at Hotel Mum and Dad, but hardly ideal. When you're in your late thirties, a civil service salary, even a management one, means that the London property market is not for you, sweetie—and you're too well-off to qualify for social housing.

But then I got my promotion break via the Transhuman Police Coordination Force, managed to hang onto my seniority when *that* came to an end, and when the New Management arrived with a bang it was *hello* ermine-trimmed robe and Junior Ministerial portfolio. Normal members of the House of Lords don't get a salary, but they *do* get to claim expenses. As a committee chair, I got both. Nice money, but then the London property bubble ate it all.

Saturday evening finds me holed up with a bottle of wine on an IKEA futon in my elegantly sparse one-bedroom apartment in Ilford. My home's under-furnished because, between my mortgage and the requirement to dress like a front-rank politician, I can barely afford to buy a bean bag to sit on. (Apparently if my shoes aren't genuine Louboutins that cost a week's salary, nobody in government will take me seriously.) So I'm working my way down my third glass of Minervois when the land line rings. There's no caller ID on the cheap handset but I answer it anyway, and get Fuckboy.

"Mhari!" He snorts indignantly, then switches to concern so fast I nearly get whiplash. "Are you all right?"

"No," I say, looking at the empty bottle in my hand. "No, I'm really not."

"I'm coming round," he says, and hangs up.

"Fuck," I say, then rummage around behind the futon for another bottle of plonk. I've got a feeling it's going to come in handy.

About half a medium glass later I hear noises from the narrow concrete balcony outside the French window. My flat's on the third floor, but Fuckboy has gotten it into his head that I don't want him to be seen visiting me—at least, not via the street entrance. I stumble over to the glass door and slide it open. He catches me and carefully carries me back inside.

"You shouldn't do that," I tell him.

"You're drunk," he replies, as if that's important.

I lean against his chest, waiting for the room to decide which way it prefers to spin. "Yes, but I'll be sober in the morning, and you'll still be ugly." I pause. It's a quote, and it sounded funny in my head, but—"I'm sorry, I didn't mean it that way. How's Sally?"

"Sally's fine. I got her a new tracking device and she carries it everywhere. She thinks it's for SnapChat and I think it's so I can monitor her location. We're both happy."

"Sneaky," I say admiringly. (Sally is Fuckboy's teen-aged daughter.)

"How are your parents? How's Jenny?" he asks, shutting the balcony door one-handed.

"Much the same. Jenny's angsting over the wedding, I'm trying to keep her from doing the bridezilla thing . . ." Because nothing relaxes you after a lovely day of workplace stress like two-hour-long phone calls from your sister who wants you to sort out her flower arrangements and attend a sizing for a bridesmaid's gown you can't wear in daylight. "Let's talk about something else?"

"Sure," he says. He leads me over to the sofa and I sit down more or less under my own power. "I got the memo." He lances the boil cleanly. "I see you're upset. Problem at the office?"

"Yes." I hold up the bottle. "Grab a glass. We're going to need this."

Fuckboy ambles over to the kitchenette and goes straight to the correct cupboard. I let my gaze linger on him. He's easy on the eye. He may be closer to fifty than forty, but he keeps himself trim and he has buns that make my fingers clench appreciatively. Clear blue eyes and graying once-black hair, now cropped short. Abs and pecs that betray his fitness thing: weights and judo. He wears jeans and a polo shirt, but also para boots, because he may be off duty but he can never let go of the job entirely. He looks as if he's in uniform even when he isn't. Divorced, clean-cut, a senior police officer, and a gentleman when he needs to be. Oh, and he can fucking *fly*.

My Fuckboy is a detective chief superintendent—and an official Home Office superhero. It'd be really cool if it hadn't stalled his career—and if his powers weren't going to kill him, horribly and slowly, over the next couple of years.

"So, are you going to fill me in?" he asks, dropping down beside me and extending a wine glass, stem delicately held between index finger and thumb.

I fill it. "To us—to something or other—"

"—to that." He clinks his glass against mine, and takes a sip. "Smooth," he observes, and leans against my shoulder, pressing up against my space like a big, self-confident tomcat, even though he knows what I am and that things like me kill people.

I take a sip and stifle a sob. "I'm so sorry," I tell him.

"Sorry about what?"

"It's got to be His idea of a joke."

"Hush." He turns and kisses me behind my ear. "I've got your back, whatever it is. Tell me about it."

So I recount my meeting with His Darkness to Fuckboy. And then I tell him, "He wants me to lead the new agency, and I kind of get why. But it feels like I'm being set up to fail. Leading a team of politically unreliable agents—His term for them, not mine—and the secondary goal, that's a suicide mission, isn't it?"

He sighs heavily. "It's bloody ambitious, at a minimum." He falls silent for a few seconds, processing. "And I don't get why He should want you to go out, on-site. Unless there's some elaborate double-bluff in train whereby he's setting you up to be compromised and leak information all over the oppo . . ." He hugs me, as if He can hold fate at bay. "This is why cops shouldn't play spy games," he adds. "I like working within a chain of command that gets held to account if it plays fast and loose with the rules. At least, in theory." A pause. "Should you be telling me this?"

There's no avoiding what comes next. "Yes, because you're one of the names on the PM's list." I pause. "It's totally not fair—I mean, you've got Sally to look after—and I needed you to know, in case I'm sent . . ." I pull back a little, then turn my face in towards his and lick the side of his neck. "Finger-fuck me?" I ask after a while.

"No: you're too drunk."

"Never stopped you before," I complain.

"That was before . . ."

"Before what?"

"Never mind. I think you should go to bed."

"Spoilsport."

He kisses me and puts me to bed, then leaves via the balcony door, floating up into the amber overcast of the London night. And I don't see him again until after the weekend, because tomcat is as tomcat does, and I guess he has other places to be and other girls to visit. But that's okay, because he may not be mine but he's not the boss of me either, and I don't care, or so I keep telling myself.

2: MORNING IN AMERICA

Gilbert Tancredy flees through the warren of neon-lit tunnels beneath the Library of Congress, expecting to die at any moment—but for the life of him, he can't remember why.

His world has narrowed to a sick sense of dread, the pounding of his heart and the breathless burn of his lungs. *Should have spent more time in the gym,* notes the one corner of his mind not yet submerged by the tidal wave of panic. He clamps the clothbound book tight under his left arm as he comes to a junction between corridors leading around one of the conservation suites. High overhead, the exposed book conveyors—larger versions of a department store pneumatic tube system—rumble like oversized aircon ducts. He pauses, unable to sense the footsteps of his pursuers. *Which way now?*

A distant shout echoes down the passage behind him and Gilbert spooks. The nearest door is only a couple of yards away. The label DIGITIZATION 202 doesn't give much away, but if he has to guess it's unlikely to be full of armed security guards. Panting, he tries the door handle. It turns, and he slips inside the darkened room.

The digitization lab is empty. Gilbert sobs for air, gulping as he recovers from his panicky sprint. A scuffling sound from outside brings him back to himself, and he shifts sideways to lean against the door just as someone tries the handle. "Locked," he hears a man say, inches from his left ear. "You and Tom take the right fork, me and Vic will keep going this way. Check every door in case he's hunkered down."

"Yessir . . ." Two pairs of boots pound away, back up the corridor. Gilbert slumps. *Should've called in sick,* he thinks dismally. *Stayed home and offered to take Mrs. Parker's pug for walkies. Washed the car.* (Gilbert doesn't own a car: he commutes by subway, thanks to the DC traffic.)

After a minute or so, Gil calms enough to take stock. Moving lightly on his feet—he's not a small man, both in height and (in recent years) girth—he fumbles around the side of the doorframe until he feels a row of light switches. Illumination reveals a low-ceilinged, cluttered workroom. There are storage shelves on two walls, white-topped benches with lights on articulated arms, cameras and scanners and PCs at workstations. He spots a bulky laser printer sitting on a rolling table in the corner and rolls it in front of the door. Once adequately barricaded, he puts his stolen book down and opens it to the flyleaf.

The book is fussily typeset, with an engraved border of flags and angels framing the title, after the fashion of an earlier century. The words seem to be in English, but some of them shimmer and warp as he tries to read them, making his eyes hurt. No matter: Gilbert pulls out his smartphone and begins to carefully photograph each two-page spread. He doesn't need to read entire words to focus, and the individual letters in the blurry ones are clear enough until he tries to join them up. Then they start to snake around inside his head.

A modern smartphone camera can capture a page of text at nearly the same resolution as a desktop scanner. Gilbert's book is about two hundred pages long, but creeping dread lends his fingertips wings as he flips pages. He doesn't bother with conservator's gloves, even though the book is a rarity. His pursuers were ignorant of its presence in the stacks until he issued an unwise pull request, thereby revealing his own presence: if they find him with it he doubts he'll enjoy the experience.

This is so *not what I joined the Postal Service for,* Gilbert thinks as he passes the halfway point. Perspiration glues his shirt to the small of his back and his hands are shaking. He pauses momentarily to look at the page before him. It's trying to tell him something about a fellow called John Quincy Adams, a former Secretary of State, whose advocacy for a National Observatory met opposition from, from . . . Gilbert blinks, his eyes watering. *Some other politician, perhaps?* There's that troublesome word again, the one that slips past his gaze like a ripple in a glass of water. "A fnord," he mutters under his breath as he flips pages again, photographing continuously. "It's a fucking *fnord*. Huh." A fnord is a kind of word that kids are trained not to notice in kindergarten and that causes deep unease in anyone who sees it. They're fictional, of course—invented by jokey conspiracy theorists, popularized by Robert Anton Wilson, and *this* word doesn't even begin with an "F"—but they're a handy signifier for a hidden layer of reality, like the messages in a cult John Carpenter movie. Except, just like the wholly imaginary fnord, *this* word—the P-word—stubbornly refuses to come into focus in his mind. *Presi*-something. Something *important*. Something important that has gone missing from the world, and he's supposed to know about it, to know why the security guards are hunting him like he's a spree killer on a rampage, why they shot Marilyn in Conservation as he ran away—

I should know this shit. Gilbert flips pages, snapping constantly, then realizes the last two pages are blank but for spots of brown oxidation—he's reached the end. He squeezes his eyelids shut. "What is *wrong* with me?" he asks, frustrated.

Book. Scans. He has a special memory stick in his inside pocket, although he can't remember—now—why he might be carrying it. Or how he's smuggled it into his workplace. Copyright violation is not something Library of Congress staff generally approve of or participate in. The stick is double-ended, with a micro-USB connector designed to plug into a phone opposite the regular connector. He shoves it hastily into place and copies all the photos across. It's only a gigabyte but a subjective eternity passes as he waits, sweating, as the progress bar slowly creeps across the screen.

Finally, it finishes. Gilbert shoves the stick inside a small internal mailer, and dispatches it to the post room via the pneumatic system. Then he carries the book over to a shelf of manuscripts awaiting return to the stacks. As he slides it into the middle of the row, the design embossed on its cover seems to stare at him accusingly: an eye of Horus inside a pyramid framed within a pentagon, sacred geometry flanked by the compass and plumb bob of an architect. *Great Presi-blur-s of the United States of America,* laurel wreaths surmounted by a bald eagle. *Copyright MDCCCLXXXVI.* Gilt lettering inlaid on faded green cloth. Not a very *impressive* book, except that by the itching in his fingertips and the urgent burning heat of the ward he wears on a chain around his neck it *means* something, something important that has been *forgotten . . .*

He shakes his head and turns his back on the deadly book. Hands clean, he switches off the lights, shoves the printer aside, and steps into the hallway. Even before the door closes, he's forgotten again. But it's just as well. To carry any book with the P-word on its cover down here would attract the wrong kind of attention. Without it, Gilbert Tancredy, former USPS Postal Inspector (Occult Texts Division), working undercover as an administrator in the Library of Congress, is just another pasty-faced, middle-aged bureaucrat adrift in a sea of amnesia. If—god willing—the security guards don't recognize him, he'll go home this evening with little recollection of what he's just done, and by tomorrow morning he'll have forgotten about it completely, memories suppressed by the extra-heavy glamour focussed on the Capitol.

Sleep can't come fast enough.

It's late on a Thursday evening in Crested Butte, Colorado, and Gaby Carson is sitting in Studio 2 at WOCZ-FM, reading down her playlist one last time while across the glass-walled booth Glenn (producer on playlist, admin, and mixing desk) and Danni (intern on phones, and occasional on-air conversational snark) bicker amiably over how to run tonight's show. It's a triple-A format—adult album alternative music—with a phone-in element hosted by Gaby, mainly local night owls and the odd trucker trying to keep awake on the long haul up through the mountains. WOCZ's license requires the station to act as a relay for the national Emergency Alert System. The station also still pushes out two hours of live programming every day, as a condition of an old endowment the current owners can't break without losing money. For Gaby it's a step up from her weekly podcast in the direction of actual public talk radio, which is where she's convinced her future lies.

So of course she scowls furiously when Glenn gives her the lead-in and she cues up track one on tonight's playlist, "Video Killed the Radio Star."

"Good evening. This is Gaby Carson, coming to you on WOCZ with tonight's episode of *The Whatever Show*, here in Crested Butte, Ground Zero of high weirdness in America. And we're going to be talking about whatever scares you awake in the middle of the night, but particularly the supernatural—zombies, vampires, and brain slugs. With me tonight are Danni—"

"Hi!"

"—and Glenn, and also Glenn's brain slug, which insisted I play "Video Killed the Radio Star" by The Buggles just now. Say hello, Glenn's brain slug."

"All glory to the Hypnotoad."

"I'll take that as brain-slug for *hi*. Calls are open now, and I'm waiting to hear from you if you've ever seen a zombie, vampire, or a trademarked *Futurama* character here in Crested Butte!"

And it's into track number two, "Scary Monsters."

Gaby sits back. On the other side of the console Danni is listening on her headset while Glenn fiddles with the ASCAP playlist sheet. "Got one for you," Danni tells her: "Billy from Baxter's Gulch."

"And our first caller of the evening is Billy from Baxter's Gulch," Gaby fades down the music. "So, Billy, zombies or vampires?"

"Ain't got nuthin' like zombies or vampires round these parts."

Billy has a three-packs-a-day rasp and sounds defensive, which is a bad start, so Gaby gives him a gentle shove: "So what *do* you have, Billy?"

"Nothin', 'cept a couple of hours ago jes' before sunset I was out chopping firewood an' I looked up and saw me a *dragon*." Suddenly her constipated caller unblocks in a rush: "It came over the north ridge 'bout a hunnerd feet up an' it had bat wings outta *here* an' a long tail with a stinger at the end an' it was moving fast, like a hunnert, hunnert and fifty miles an hour. I only got a glimpse of it, it was an' over the treeline faster than a greased hog's—"

"—Whizzings," Gaby interrupts hurriedly—Glenn has them on a ten-second delay loop but he gets itchy if she counts on him to bleep the show too often—"Listen, Billy, that's really cool but, are you sure it was a dragon? Could it have been maybe a drone or a light plane instead? Or, I dunno, a buzzard? I don't wanna rain on your parade but—"

"—I know me a buzzard an' I know what a light plane looks like an' this was no plane, missy! It had wings like a bat an' scales on its body, an' a mass o' tentacles for a face, an' it hissed like a snake! I know what I's seen and I's seen a dragon!"

"That's really interesting, Billy." Gaby mutes him: "Listeners, have *you* seen a dragon flying down Baxter's Gulch at dusk? If so, I'd like to hear from you!" On the screen in front of her Glenn has rapidly shuffled the playlist around and she nods at him as she brings up "Radioactive" by Imagine Dragons. Two thumbs up. As it plays, the phone lines light up until both Danni and Glenn are busy screening calls.

"Lot of dragons tonight," Glenn tells her. He looks perturbed.

"Yeah, well, give 'em to me. Caller number two, you're on air!"

"Hi, this is Erika, up near Lake Grant"—country-club territory, and Erika's breathless party-girl delivery gives way to a squeal—"I saw the dragon, I saw it, too! It's really big but not like the ones on *Game of Thrones,* I mean it has no legs and a big bundle of squirmy worms for a head and oh my gosh, it's out here *now*! Circling over the club! It's so exciting! Oh look, Biff—" (*inaudible*)—"smartphone, film it now! It's coming back, do you think it's friendly—"

Gaby stares at Glenn for a horrible dead-air second as Glenn shrugs helplessly. "Well, it looks like Erika hung up on us, folks," she extemporizes. "Sorry 'bout that. Next caller, you are . . . ?"

"I'm Adam from Gunnison an' I don' believe in no dragons." A glutinous swallowing sound, and Gaby winces. "The good book says our Lord sent an angel, and he laid hold on the dragon, that old serpent, and bound him a thousand years in hell because he's Satan, so if ya'll seeing a dragon tonight it means our Lord has returned and so's Old Nick—"

Adam is off-air as Glenn mashes the panic button and goes straight into "Fire of Unknown Origin," which should buy them a couple of minutes while Gaby leads into the first ad break and Glenn and Danni play "hunt the sane caller" for her. Gaby looks at her mike in disbelief. "*What* is in the air tonight?" she demands.

"Dragons," Danni giggles.

"Dragons." Gaby makes a curse of the word. "What have you got for me?" she asks Glenn.

"Next caller is Sheila from up near Italian Mountain. You're on-air in two seconds, Sheila. Go."

Sheila is stressed out and her voice wobbles: "You've got to send help, the phones are down and all I got is cell service! There's a fire on the hillside just above Skyland and it's like to go wild if we don't get the Fire Department out!"

Across the desk from Gaby, Glenn sits up straight and looks alarmed. Gaby collects herself before she speaks. "Sheila, I hear you and"—her eyes flicker at Danni, who is dialing the emergency dispatcher—"we're calling them now." (*This had better not be a hoax or your ass is* so *going to get kicked,* she thinks silently.) "What can you tell us about the wildfire?"

"It's not, not a wildfire! This flying thing came over, it was swooping along above Slate River and it sprayed napalm or something all over the Lodge! There's cars on fire and half the hillside's ablaze! It flew off and Jack Silver tried to drive over to see if he could help but then it came back and oh my God his station wagon, it went up like a tiki torch—"

Sheila is still rattling along on the gibbering edge of panic but then Glenn cuts in, earning a glare from Gaby until she hears him say, "Folks, this is *The Whatever Show* on WOCZ with an urgent announcement for everyone in the Lake Grant area. We have a major incident and a possible forest fire. The Fire Department and Sheriff's Department are responding. Please stay off the roads for now, we need to keep them clear for emergency vehicles, but you should pack your bags and be ready to drive out when, and *only* when, the Fire Marshall says you should evacuate. I repeat: sit tight, but be prepared to get out if an evacuation is called."

Danni, across the desk from Gaby, is pale but focussed, listening to someone on the phone. Gaby plugs in and hears the tail-end of Deputy Landau's call—"not a hoax, we have a no-shit fire-breathing *thing* up here and it's attacking the Skyland Lodge—"

The line goes dead. Glenn stares at Gaby, wide-eyed. Gaby shakes herself and cues up "Light My Fire," the Shirley Bassey remix version. "Emergency plan," Glenn mouths at her, and she nods. It's going to be a very long night.

Hours later, Sam Penrose shuffles into the lobby of the Walmart closest to the safe house in the suburbs of DC where his team is standing watch.

Sam is in his early thirties, trim and clean-cut, with the kind of fireplug build that comes with habits learned during a tour of duty in the military. Not to put too fine a point on it, he looks like a plainclothes cop in casual dress, which is more or less what he is, if the cop in question had just been subjected to a week or two of systematic sleep-deprivation torture. There are baggy pouches under his eyes, his stubble has raced past six o'clock at least twice, there is an exhausted slump to his shoulders, and his gaze is bloodshot. His chinos may have been pressed once, and his polo shirt is still passably clean, but a sour odor of desperation rises off him. Whenever he stops moving he sways back and forth very slowly, like a dead poplar just waiting for the right moment to topple over in the forest.

This being a Walmart, Sam's state of exhaustion is not entirely out of place. A number of the other shoppers are wearing their pajamas and shuffling like extras in a zombie flick. He drags a shopping cart free of the gridlock by the entrance and pushes it into the giant fluorescent-lit cavern, leaning tiredly on the handlebar as he peers at his phone, which is displaying a shopping list.

Twelve days, Sam thinks, trying not to mutter aloud. *Two days to go.* He's looking for the bulky stuff first—paper goods—and as he trawls up and down the endless aisles he twitches, for every so often he senses someone stalking him. But whenever he looks round, or blinks, or pinches himself, there's no one there. And blinking is hazardous. If he blinks it feels so good that his eyelids try to stay closed and his consciousness goes sideways and tries to escape out his ears. Sam has spent twelve consecutive days on Modafinil, generic Provigil—a wonder drug for students who need to cram all night before an examination, or fighter pilots who need a "go-pill" to help them fly an eighteen-hour strike mission. But drugs will only get you so far before REM deprivation kicks in, and Sam is clinging to the end of his rope by his fingernails. He's been hallucinating for the past week, hearing the voices of ghosts and seeing things that aren't there. He'd go to sleep right in the middle of the store aisle, if only he could be sure of waking up again.

Shopping list: toilet paper, a 36-pack of rolls, kitchen towels, a 4-pack. Bread, 6 loaves. Milk, 2 gallons. And 12 frozen pizzas,

24 ready meals, 2 pounds of butter, 12 of the live yoghurt drinks that *she* likes, 16 pounds of hamburger patties, a smoked ham, 2 dozen eggs, a few different cheeses. Then a pack of light bulbs, bathroom cleaner, and on to the clothing aisles and a bunch of basics they need. Sam is shopping for a dozen people holed up in a safe house with eight bedrooms and the curtains shut and two standing watch at all hours, sleepless because they're terrified that if any of them go to sleep, something bad will happen.

If only he could remember what.

As he lurches down the household-goods aisle towards the fenced-off cantonment where they keep the firearms and ammunition, the icy claws of dread scrabble at Sam for attention. He hasn't been home in months, Jenna will have forgotten he even exists—*why do I know* that? he asks himself—paychecks aren't being deposited in his account but—*Continuity of Government*—he's still on duty. *I should phone my parents,* the dull voice of filial duty nags in one of his ears, and for a moment he's half certain he's hallucinating his own conscience telling him to do that. *Dad will know what I should do, what I'm doing here. Dad will help.* Except Dad, Lieutenant Brad Penrose (USN, Retired, would be seventy-two at his next birthday), died of lung cancer three years ago.

This mission stinks, he thinks wearily, as he produces ID—forged by the very best, *nobody* forges identity paperwork like the US Treasury Secret Service's counterforgery unit, they know all the best tricks—and signs for five hundred rounds of 357. (If they're going to be in the field much longer, their certification is going to expire. At least with practice ammo Matt can maybe send his people to a private range in the neighborhood, and subsequently confirm that they've been keeping up their training. One less reprimand to face once this clusterfuck blows over.)

Sam is street-savvy, and trained to recognize threats—but he is less effective when his brain is baked to a crisp and lulled into a false sense of familiarity by the dull ambiance of a big box store. Shopping is the true religion of Middle America, and this Walmart is the most eclectic of mega-churches, perpetually understaffed and a bit unkempt, with stock flowing off the shelves and piles of stripped packaging forming cardboard snowdrifts in corners. The shuffling crowds pushing their carts and corralling their bored and fractious children are so familiar that they seem to phase in and out of invisibility beneath his tired gaze. So he is almost at the check-out line before he notices the odd, silvery mannequins.

He's walked past at least half a dozen of them dotted around the store in the past quarter hour: human-sized and human-shaped dummies wearing metallic silver body stockings. But it's only when he pauses to stand in line that he focuses on the mannequin standing by the door and realizes that the dummy's lycra stretches over a very small paunch, and its rib cage is moving.

In a perspective flip that would be dizzying enough even if he wasn't exhausted and hallucinating, Sam realizes that they are not dummies but *people*. People wearing skin-tight silver from head to foot, standing still as statues. He remembers a news article or a what-will-they-think-of-next briefing paper or something about zentai—full-body spandex suits for sports mascots and superheroes and people with a skin-tight shiny fetish. These dummies can't possibly be superheroes—not standing watch in a Walmart, anyway. *Is this some kind of promotion?* he puzzles. It wouldn't be the first: last month you couldn't fight your way past the front door without running a gauntlet of goofy Left Shark impersonators.

But now that he's noticed the faceless, silver-suited man behind the row of checkouts, he slowly realizes that there are more than one. And although it's hard to tell—their eyes and mouths are completely hidden by masks of stretchy silver fabric and they're standing very still—they seem to be watching everyone entering and leaving the store.

A cold shudder runs up Sam's spine and he realizes the leather pouch he wears on a thong under his polo shirt has grown uncomfortably warm. The silver suit nearest to his queue is male.

About five yards down the store, there's a female figure, gracefully posed as any store dummy—but a shop dummy would be modeling sale items, wouldn't it? As he watches, she shifts her weight from her left hip to her right. Five yards past her there's another silver suit, and then another . . .

They're looking for Arthur, he realizes. A trickle of sweat runs down his ribs. The cashier is finishing up with the tightly curled older lady in front of him. *What to do?* He's not carrying his P229, concealed or open. His phone is a burner, never connected to a public carrier. If it looks like someone's going to follow him back to the safe house it's his duty to fall asleep before they can take him alive. But the team really needs these supplies. The last time anyone broke cover to stock up on provisions was four days ago. Mal didn't mention any zentai-suited weirdos staking out Costco—they never use the same store twice—but if this is a new angle, Senior Officer Mattingley needs to know. *You could phone home,* Dad whispers in his ear as one of the silver suits sweeps its face slowly across the row of checkouts, its occult gaze drifting past. *Let a real grown-up handle it.* Sam is thirty-four, a Special Officer in the US Secret Service, married to Jenna (if she still remembers him), father of Brad Jr. and Kyle, and hasn't slept for twelve days. It doesn't get much more grown-up than—*You're too tired for this,* a pernicious ghost whispers in his ear, and Sam yawns convulsively, his jaw cracking.

"Next!" squawks the cashier, staring at him blearily, and he pulls himself together. He unloads his cart onto the belt and she scans everything briskly, almost too fast for him to keep up. He shovels everything back into the cart as she rings up the bill and he manages to drop the prepaid credit card. Bending down, he yawns again but collects it and hands it over. "Tired, huh?" the cashier asks unsympathetically.

"Yeah. Been a long day." The longest. *You should really get some sleep,* his grandfather's shade whispers behind his left shoulder. *Not helpful,* he thinks reproachfully. The ward around his neck is buzzing. It feels painfully hot where it lies against his sternum. The Secret Service doesn't have many left, now that the special office inside the Postal Inspectorate has gone dark. He pays and trudges towards the vestibule beneath the masked haze of the zentai guardians, each step feeling like a mile-long forced march.

Transferring the spoils to the cargo bed of the elderly F-150 is bad enough. Driving home is a special kind of torture, forcing Sam to maintain situational awareness and check for tails. A couple of times, he finds himself drifting out of his lane and opens his eyes to the blaring horns of alarmed drivers. He's not sleeping, merely drowning in fatigue toxins. His eyes burn and he feels as ancient as the mountain peaks beyond the horizon.

The hallucinations seem to come more frequently as he drives. Once, he glimpses a faceless mannequin at the wheel of a supermarket chain's truck. Later he catches a flash of bland-faced silver inside a parked highway patrol car, staring out across the highway. The doors of perception are hanging ajar without need for drugs, and shadows cast by a light other than the sun seem to twitch and jitter just outside his field of vision. He turns on the radio to try and stay awake but its station-seeking is faulty, and it repeatedly cycles between newscasters warning of a forest fire and a preacher wailing about the end of the world. Eventually he gives up and hits the CD autochanger, but it's loaded with Senior Officer Mattingley's college rock collection and he's *heard of a van that is loaded with weapons, packed up and ready to go* . . . Sam shudders convulsively and kills the music right before the next stanza, but his brain serenades him with it regardless: *heard of some grave sites, out by the highway, a place where nobody knows.*

Sam doesn't crash or drive off the highway, or miss his turnoff. He stays within spitting distance of the speed limit until he turns onto a side road, and finally brakes as he enters the driveway to the safe house. Fifty yards up the drive he pulls up and watches his rear-view for a full five minutes, timing it with his watch. There is a pistol in the map compartment under the dash, and much repetition has its location drilled into his muscle memory. But there's no sign of pursuit. Eventually he yawns, then starts the engine again and drives on up the track to the weathered, shingle-fronted house with the drawn curtains and the discreet cameras hanging under the eaves. Reaching the front yard he turns the truck until it's facing back down the drive, parks, and steps out of the cab to present himself to the front door.

"Officer Penrose, returning with supplies," he announces.

"Come forward. That's close enough." Sylvia's voice is harsh, her usual cordiality eroded to its rocky foundations by circumstance. "Okay, Sam. Who is the President?"

"Arthur," Sam answers wearily, then yawns again. He's so tired he barely registers the footsteps of the front-of-the-house crew as they emerge. He hears Senior Officer Mattingley's gravelly voice as if from a considerable distance: "Your ward's taken a hit." As casual an observation as if the ballistic vest he isn't wearing had soaked up a bullet.

"Yeah, there were gimps at Walmart. I mean, silver gimp suits. Dun-don't know what they were but they were guarding the exit, like security. They didn't pull me in but I felt it heat up."

"Silver gimp suits."

"He checks out clean, sir," Sylvia confirms. "No trackers or soul-suckers attached."

"Okay, let's get the truck unloaded."

"Yessir," he slurs, swaying.

Mattingley notices because he steps alongside Sam as he unlocks the tailgate. "I'm bringing your down-time forward," Matt tells him. "Looks like you need it bad."

"Yes sir." Sam hefts four bags full of chilled items. "You're not wrong."

Mattingley nods sharply. "Let's get this lot stored," he says. "Then you can tell us all about the gimp suits."

There's a row house in downtown DC, just outside the museums and government buildings that cluster around the Mall and the

Capitol, that is one of several owned by an obscure but wealthy think tank. Sometimes its donors borrow its conferencing facilities for meetings, and this morning a ground-floor room is filling with private-sector executives. They're here for a face-to-face meeting and a very exclusive in-person backgrounder about a very special government project.

This is not a gathering of actual CEOs, captains of industry who run fractional-trillion-dollar enterprises. Those men (and a few women) have so many demands on their time that a group appearance by them has to be scheduled months in advance. The guests today are merely vice-presidents or above. They are, however, all executives in corporations with a market cap of at least ten billion dollars, and have sufficient authority to spend money and initiate projects. Their employers all have a federal services division or some sort of process for bidding on government contracts, and they're here today because a previously obscure member of the intelligence community has hinted that something really big is in the offing and their attendance would be profitable.

(Also, they've been having very odd dreams.)

The meeting is due to kick off with a presentation about the agency, and then a description of what the agency wants from its suppliers. None of them are familiar with it as yet. But the invitation came via the right channels, and the Global Business Forum offices are often used for para-governmental events like this dog-and-pony show, and all the right faces are here, so . . .

"Hi, Rick! Surprise!" Ira Oates spots a familiar face across the lobby and picks up his coffee mug. Rick Martini from AMD does a double-take across the room as he spots Ira weaving towards him.

"Ira! Hey, what brings you here?"

They shake cautiously, in concession to each other's handicaps—Rick has one wrist in a splint, Ira bears an over-full coffee cup—then Ira shrugs carefully. "Same as you, perhaps? A tender from the Operational Phenomenology Agency?"

"Yeah." Rick's poker face is in play. "Although why they want us here . . ." He shrugs back. Rick is at AMD these days, working on fab line configuration, and Ira is part of Apple's we-could-tell-you-but-then-we'd-have-to-kill-you internal chip design team. Before that, they were both at Intel—but that was long ago. "Maybe they want a better baseband backdoor?"

Ira snorts. "Not going to happen, my friend—" Then he does another double-take. "Celeste? Celeste Travers? What the hell?"

Celeste, who has just arrived, is wearing the power-suit uniform of an older industry. She's the kind of sales manager who only needs to close two deals a year to contribute nine digits of turnover to her employer, United Launch Alliance, a consortium of Lockheed and Boeing that builds satellite launchers. She's smiling, or maybe baring her teeth, at a fireplug South African entrepreneur with slit-like eyes who has been making waves on the internet when his experimental boosters haven't been exploding: a rock star type who's a couple of levels above anyone else in the room. "What's *he* doing here?" Rick mutters under his breath.

"Probably didn't want to feel left out." But Ira's eyes are wide. "This is not what I expected."

"No, really?" Rick nods his head at the far corner of the room. "I see Google, I see Microsoft, I see HP, and they're not even sneering at each other. I see aerospace, emphasis on space. And who's *that* guy?"

"Exxon."

"This makes *no* sense," Ira complains as a bright-eyed host announces that the conference room is now ready and would they please proceed inside.

They file into a compact, well-padded lecture theater with full audiovisual support and power and network sockets at every seat. At the front of the room sets a podium and an A/V desk. The lectern is positioned in the middle of a powder-blue carpet featuring an ornate circular design picked out in silver. Ira finds himself sitting next to Rick and another middle-aged emeritus engineer from a second-tier aerospace corporation. "Ira, from Apple." He offers his hand. "Do you know what this is about?"

"Hi, I'm Frank, Astradyne Corp. And I've got no idea either, except it's something to do with satellites and communications networking." Frank shrugs self-deprecatingly. "So Apple's going into the launch business now?"

"I could tell you but then I'd have to kill you." Ira says with a straight face, then leans back in his chair: "Hey—"

A person steps onto the podium, then walks behind the lectern and opens a laptop that's already plugged in on top of it. They're miked up, wireless, and—

Ira squints. *He? She? They?* Ira can't tell. Can't tell the color of his—or her—suit, can't even look at their face: his eyes slide sideways whenever he tries to look at them.

"Good morning, everyone!" says the person on the podium. It stands in the middle of a glowing silver pentacle in a circle, surrounded by some *really fancy* rippling laser-projected script, almost like the inscription on the One Ring in the Peter Jackson movies. Two figures in skin-tight silver body stockings flank him, standing motionless at either side of the podium. They're covered from head to toe: superheroes anonymous, like life-size Academy Award trophies.

"I'm very glad to see you all here today! We at the OPA recognize that you're all terrifically busy people, so we're going to keep this introduction as short as possible, but we hope to do business with you in the very near future—yes, *all* of you— because we've been tasked with setting up and running a federal government project as big as the Manhattan Project and the Apollo Moon landings rolled into one."

Ira sits up. *Everybody* sits up. Both those programs soaked up a visible percentage of the federal government's entire budget for years on end, and a single project as big as both of them combined is unprecedented. There's as much money at stake here as the Gulf War, all in one mouth-watering, delicious project. He can feel tension rise in the room as the speaker continues, in an odd, rolling cadence that emphasizes alternate words.

"Here in *America* we have lost our *sense* of *purpose,* come adrift from our *destiny.* People feel an *emptiness* in their *souls.*" On the wall behind the podium, a montage appears: crying children, car wrecks, a column of tanks in a war zone. "*We* in the Operational Phenomenology Agency *feel* this deeply—"

Ira pinches himself awake. The cadence of the presentation feels intimately, creepily familiar. It's playing the same chords on his subconscious as the big Apple keynote presentations, back when Steve Jobs was showrunner. The master salesman was a mesmerizing speaker who used every trick in the crowd psychology playbook, mixing neurolinguistic programming, sensory saturation by background imagery and music, and a little something *extra* to captivate his audience. Ira was too low down the totem pole to ever go on stage at one of those events, but he knows how they work. He's even been trained to do it himself in supplier meetings. But this is bigger. The little pinch of magical pixie dust, the *something else* that made it work so well, has been replaced by the entire goddamn Gobi Desert. The speech feels suffocating and heavy, freighted with a willed compulsion to submit and obey, as it batters against his mind. Ira fights it, but his shoulders sag with the strain.

"We have *lost sight* of our national leadership, and it is *vital* that we recover the visionary leadership that we *deserve,* the strong father who *will* make America great *again,* whose mind we can emulate and channel using the magic of computation that has brought us *so many* benefits—

"Which is where *you* can make a contribution, my friends. We have a *vision of a new world,* a world where American ingenuity will leverage our leadership in space and computing to bring about a bright new golden dawn. *We have the technology.* We have software that can *directly* affect physical nature, tools that earlier, less enlightened ages called magic. But it takes enormous computing power to make use of this—not millions or even billions of processors, but trillions and quadrillions, working in parallel to open a wormhole in space that will *reach out* to the *greater power* we serve and *awaken* it to *lead us*. We need *factories* that don't exist yet, high-vacuum beam lines in orbit building billions of advanced microprocessors using rare earth elements extracted from the lunar regolith using mining technologies that don't exist yet.

"And we need it *now,* in the next three years. Undead alien nightmares are awakening from aeons-long hibernation. Their ambassadors are already at work, spreading darkness around the world. Our old allies are turning their faces against us, lost in the gathering storm. Our new allies are weak and unreliable and mean us ill. We need a new kind of arsenal if we are to defend democracy and freedom, and the first step in rebuilding our defenses is to build a hypercomputing cloud in solar orbit, one powerful enough to summon the Lord of Sleep to lead us . . ."

Ira shakes his head. Hot prickling sweat dots his spine, but he can't summon the willpower to stand. He means to block out the soporific droning narrative of the speaker and walk out of the overheated briefing, but somehow he can't quite work out how to move his arms and legs any more. And he is still in his seat when the speaker pauses for breath—their first pause in nearly five minutes—and taps a key on the laptop to start the Power-Point presentation.

Then Ira is out of time for good, as the Black Chamber's geas works its way into his soul and binds him to serve the Common Cause.

A mirror-walled office building in Maryland, formerly the exclusive home of the National Security Agency, plays host to a very different agency these days. Three upper floors of the NSA's headquarters building in Fort Meade, Maryland, have been donated to another agency, the OPA, during its ongoing rapid expansion.

The Operational Phenomenology Agency, known to its friends as the Black Chamber and to its detractors and rivals as the Nazgûl, sprang from the same roots as the original NSA: wartime codebreakers and builders of computers and listening posts. But the OPA serves other objectives. It's not a passive intelligence-gathering agency. Rather, it was established to bring the spectral weight of America's occult intent to bear on all threats, both internal and external. Here are the hex-casters, the shadow wreakers and night haunts. Here dwell the senders of nightmares and the breakers of rebel souls. Their mathemagical scryers and experts in algorithmic arcana have privileged access to the NSA's server farms, which were designed from the outset with dual use in mind. The chained monsters they summon are all bound by the OPA, forced to serve the agency. And the agency is itself subject to the iron bonds of a geas encoded in a steel sigil buried beneath the Supreme Court.

On the same morning that the OPA's speaker weaves a spell of obedience over an assembly of executives, a very small committee meets in a windowless room next door to the Deputy Director's temporary office. There are permanent isolation grids inscribed on the floor, ceiling, and walls—all currently energized—but no black candles drip wax on skulls adorning the Chair's ebon throne, nor do silver zentai-clad blood guards stand motionless in the corners of the room, guarding the witch-queen and her generals. It's almost ostentatiously plain, furnished with General Services Administration tables and chairs. The occupants show no outward signs of the huge occult power under their control.

"Today's updates, General Miller?"

General Miller—a lean, fiftyish fellow—leans forward and bows his head over his blotter. "Oligarch is giving me cause for concern," he says thoughtfully. "There's the ongoing lack of progress with Threshold, but that's nothing new, and the longer it continues, the less scope there is for disruption. Everything else is ticking along. But Oligarch—"

The Deputy Director clears her throat. "Remind me which one Oligarch is? Is it Japan? Or—"

"Great Britain, ma'am."

"Ah, yes." A frown of disapproval mars her office-blonde visage. "Quite a *royal* mess."

Miller nods. "The traitors in the Comstock Office did a number on us, I'm afraid, and the New Management over there isn't inclined to let things slide. We've been trying to reestablish traction but everything we set up gets shut down fast. The Brits are professionals. Also, they've got their hands in our pockets about as deep as we've got ours into theirs. It's as bad as going up against the Israelis."

"Spare me the tedious metaphors. *What* is happening *now*?"

"An uptick in chatter, ma'am." General Miller glances across the table. "Dr. Garrett has the details." Dr. Garrett, a civilian advisor, frowns and looks attentive, but Miller passes over him and ploughs on lugubriously. "It looks like the New Management is reviving their Special Operations Executive. Not the postwar OCCINT side of the organization, but the original wartime agency, the British equivalent of the OSS"—ancestor to the CIA, an active sabotage agency that raised hell during the Second World War—"and it's under the personal control of the PM. They're putting Q-Division personnel in all the key positions. In conjunction with the changes to their military threat stance, it looks as if they're rapidly elevating their nonconventional war-fighting capability, and they've got those Middle Earth geeks to draw on as cadre. I can't speak to their goals, but it looks very bad from here."

"Jesus H. Christ," someone is heard to mutter in the sudden silence.

"How effective are the overtures we've tried since X-day? Technical exploits? Capitative replacement? Lester?"

Lester—Colonel Lester Burns, another department lead—shakes his head. "We've given up trying to engineer an in-office replacement, ma'am. It's proven impossible to obtain contractors of the required caliber."

"By contractors you mean freelance assassins, yes?"

"Your term for them, ma'am. Given that the PM is not in fact human, I'd hesitate to use the term—"

"Theicides, then." The Deputy Director smiles briefly. It's a fey lightning flicker of an expression, as if the tissues of her face have briefly become transparent, to reveal a glimpse of the chromed steel armature they normally conceal. Her smile fades, returning to flesh: "What is the nature of the retention problem?"

Burns gives up all attempt at circumlocution. "The last two ended up dead, ma'am. It's as bad as Castro in the '60s: once word gets out, we end up only able to recruit the desperate or the incompetent. Our first candidate attempted a close-in kill— the Brits keep laughably light overwatch on their high-value assets—so she succeeded in penetrating his personal protection detail. But when she tried to make her move he, uh, he *skeletonized* her. Our second candidate circumvented security at the Palace of Westminster and assembled a sniper station on the Elizabeth Tower. Or at least, he *reported* he'd circumvented security. They replaced his ammunition with inert cartridges and arrested him when he tried to take the shot. They're holding treason trials *in camera* these days and handing down a lot of death sentences— they've got vampires to feed, like us—so if we're lucky they won't notice how flimsy his back story is . . ."

"I see."

"Both times it looks like they had advance warning, ma'am. Or their PM has short-duration precognition. Anyway, I upped the prize money another thousand bitcoin—as high as I could go on my own signing cognizance—but got no takers who passed our first-stage screening. I guess if you want a job done properly you've got to do it yourself."

"Let's not go there just yet, Colonel." The Deputy Director frowns mildly. "We're not at war with them—not officially, anyway—and we don't assassinate foreign heads of government we're not actually at war with. Usually." She flips a page in her agenda. "So we've been kicking his shins and he's pulling on the boots to kick back, is that where you're telling me we stand with Oligarch?"

"Pretty much that, ma'am. We're in tit-for-tat territory, iterated game-theory strategies."

"So what comes next"—the Deputy gazes into the middle distance—"is they'll make a move on us. A warning nudge. The PM's vanity will compel him to send us a message. Won't it?" She stares at General Miller and slowly smiles. It is not a friendly expression.

"That seems likely, ma'am."

"Good." A small nod. "Get your tiger team to generate a list of likely secondary targets and we'll burn down them at tomorrow's meeting, but for now I want you to focus on Threshold. The former resident of 1600 Pennsylvania Avenue is their obvious target—that, and maybe disrupting the next Great Awakening. Anyway, let's aim to mousetrap the British agents when they arrive, shall we? Turnabout is fair play. Meanwhile, I need to give my opposite number a call. Make nice, convince them we're de-escalating."

I'm not much of one for foreign travel, and I've never been to the US before. I don't like flying, and my first impressions on arrival are not very good at all.

We're here under cover as tourists, although I'm damned if I can see why. Air fares are still sky-high despite the resumption of international scheduled flights. We probably stand out like sore thumbs *and* our cover requires sitting in economy seats for more than seven hours, which has not put me in my happy place. Also, Heathrow? Meh. (The one silver lining is that it was possible to arrange for me to stay at least three layers of glass away from daylight at all times until we were aboard, and then to sit in a center-row seat, well away from the windows. Opaque clothes and heavy sunblock will only get you so far, but a VIP pass does the trick.)

I refresh my makeup before we touch down at JFK, and once we reach the terminal we run the gauntlet of a single window-lined corridor before diving into the subterranean guts of the airport and fetching up in a vast, echoing cattle market dominated by a giant flag. On the up side, there is absolutely no death-star radiance to scorch my skin, which would be a bit of a tell. On the downside? It's another giant airport. Yay.

Fuckboy doesn't quite get it. I mean, he can tell I'm scratchy and irritable and he knows in the abstract that I'm outside my comfort zone in daylight, but he doesn't have the gut-deep visceral terror of spontaneous human combustion that I live with. If anything goes wrong, if we have to evacuate the plane using the emergency slides, he'll be the one carrying my blackened rib cage off the runway. But he doesn't seem terribly concerned. It's almost a relief to find myself queuing at passport control in an unfriendly country, under the guns of border patrol agents looking for illegals: at least I know where I stand with them.

It takes us a quarter of an hour to shuffle through the enormous queue to the crappy photo-booth machines, where we present our passports and answer a bunch of tedious questions before being fingerprinted and photographed and given a printout of our details. Then there's a shorter queue in front of a bored man in uniform who collects our papers, checks them, and stamps our passports—I have no idea why they automated only half the process—but he waves us through as a couple, and then we find ourselves in baggage claim. "When do we hit customs?" I ask.

Fuckboy shrugs. "Isn't that next?" he asks. "Hey, did you notice the flag?"

I sniff. "No, I didn't notice the flag." I need a shower. I *deserve* a shower. "Why is the flag important?"

"There's another one over there, past the far baggage belt." He pitches his voice low. "The stars are wrong."

"How do you even—" I squint at the flag.

"They've got the wrong number of points. Seven each, instead of five."

"Huh." Suddenly I have to fight the urge to count them, which is simultaneously the most important thing in the world and an incredibly annoying itch: arithmomania, compulsive counting, is one of the side effects PHANGs like me learn to live with. I force myself to look away, and also to ignore the mirrored observation windows running the length of the hall just below the ceiling. He's right about the flag, and it's so disturbing that I almost miss my Louis Vuitton suitcase tumbling down onto the conveyor belt. I grab it, remembering to make a performance—it weighs twenty kilos, which used to be a lot back when my muscles were merely human—then wait patiently for Jim's bag, which takes considerably longer to emerge. All the while I have an itchy feeling that somebody is watching us, or at least keeping an eye on the travelers in the baggage claim hall. Finally, I take Jim's arm and he escorts me to the customs desk. Just another sightseeing couple visiting the Big Apple, nothing to pay attention to here.

At five in the afternoon—ten at night, back home—I find myself skulking under an awning while Fuckboy haggles with the driver of a black limousine with tinted rear windows. *Not bursting into flames on the drive into Manhattan* will totally fly as an expense account item, I figure—at least, it will if I sign off on it myself—and once again I curse His Ghastliness for helpfully ordering me to lead from the front.

I'm traveling under my real name, as is Fuckboy (aka Detective Chief Superintendent Jim Grey) because we've got visible public profiles and we have to assume that we're on a watch list. The safest cover story is to creatively deploy the truth: we're lovebirds (somewhat true) on vacation together (somewhat false). To add depth and texture I'm wearing an antique Tiffany emerald-and-diamond engagement ring that'll be returned to the jewelers after the mission. Meanwhile, I'm carrying a burner smartphone faked up by CESG that has a totally plausible address book and an app payload that won't hemorrhage state secrets if it's seized. So, the roles we're playing are a medium-high ranking cop and a medium-high ranking civil servant who are celebrating their engagement with a romantic trip to New York because they are in lurve. *Blech*.

For obvious reasons I had to leave all my work back home. A day of forced inactivity in an economy-class death trap, then running the gauntlet of the US equivalent of Border Force, has put me in a bad mood. Not even the prospect of getting to share a posh hotel suite (and a bed) with Fuckboy quite takes the edge off it, because I'm going to be too tired to get up to much. And then we've got a job to do. Also, the traffic on the JFK Expressway is terrifying—and I can take the M25 at rush hour in my stride.

I'm cowering back in my seat and hiding from the windows (even though it's dusk) when Jim suddenly gasps "Wow!" and sits bolt upright.

"What is it, dear?"

"I saw—" I track his gaze out the tinted window, but there's just a blur of traffic and concrete and overhead cables. "Damn, missed them."

"What?"

"I thought I saw a cape," he says, subsiding. "They flew overhead at about a hundred meters, following the road. Silver bodysuit, no wings or anything."

I snort. "Probably a traffic cop." Quietly: "Poor bastard." There are more *soi-disant* superheroes in New York City than anywhere else in the world—it's ahead of LA, Tokyo, and London combined—but they're all doomed. Sooner or later Krantzberg syndrome will kill them. The thaumic feeders they're unconsciously invoking may temporarily give them extraordinary powers, but feeders like to chow down on the neural tissue of their summoners, and if they're not adequately protected, K syndrome—a really nasty early-onset dementia—will get them. I'm immune, thanks to my V-parasites, but V syndrome has its own problems. And now my mood drops like a stone because I can see the yearning on

Fuckboy's face, and it isn't fair. Because my Fuckboy is a super-hero, and if this engagement ring was for real, I could expect to be a widow by the time I'm forty.

"Poor bastard," Jim echoes quietly. A pensive expression crosses his face. "If only there was another cure."

I reach over and take his hand. "A better one," I agree. There *is* a cure for K syndrome, for ritual magic practitioners and "superheroes" alike. It's just that the cure is to go PHANG, and to my way of thinking it's worse than the disease.

You're probably wondering what happened between me getting drunk over the weekend, and me flying into JFK with Jim. So let me start with that meeting four weeks ago, in Cabinet Office Briefing Room C:

I looked around the big boardroom-style table that filled the windowless high-security briefing room a stone's throw from Whitehall. Misery loves company, especially on a Monday morning, and judging by the faces around the table I was definitely part of the "in" crowd.

"Good morning, everyone," I said, forcing myself to smile over my Caffè Nero latte—it's never good for morale when the boss is down in the dumps. "I suppose you're wondering why I asked you here today." *Enough with the clichés.* "This came right from the top with all our names on it." I picked up my folder. "Close the door, please—thank you." Deep breath. "The Prime Minister has instructed me to establish a task force and seconded all of you to it *by name,* as key personnel."

I cleared my throat. "The PM is using an obscure statutory instrument called Henry VIII Powers to reactivate the former Special Operations Executive. Not just Q-Division, but the original sabotage and black-ops organization, founded by Churchill in 1940 to set occupied Europe ablaze. SOE was absorbed by SIS in late 1945. Now it's being reactivated, given new goals, a budget, and a new reporting chain—direct to Number 10—and a whole raft of existing oversight arrangements have just gone out of the window." I waited a few seconds while the uneasy shuffling and throat clearing died down. "My understanding of what Number 10 expects from us is unclear"—it would have been more accurate to say *the Prime Minister is winging it,* but that might scare people—"so for the time being, I'm assuming that His long-term vision for us looks something like"—*the lights on the front of an onrushing train*—"this."

I tapped the space bar on my laptop to bring up the first slide: no PowerPoint here, just a boring PDF of some bullet points generated by software with absolutely *no* power to infiltrate brains. Then I explained the jobs we'd been given. It didn't take long: about ten minutes, start to finish. And then there was stunned silence.

"Does anybody have any questions?" I asked, and waited expectantly, because that's what one does.

Colonel Lockhart was the first to surface, a wrinkled tortoise sticking his head out of his shell and peering around myopically for threats. "That's—" He cleared his throat diplomatically. "Problematic. To say the least."

"Can he do that?" asked Janice, defensive and prickly in this unfamiliar setting.

Lockhart gave her a frosty side-eye: "He most certainly *can.*" He tapped his pen on the notepad in front of him. "Civil Contingencies Act *and* a majority in the House." He swallowed, Adam's apple bobbing above the over-tight knot of his regimental tie. "Our questions should center on how, not why." Another glare. Janice, like me, was a Scrum survivor—our sysadmin/devops deployment expert. She turned PHANG at the same time as the rest of us, survived the murderous attentions of Basil the vampire elder, and of course ended up working for the Laundry. The big difference between us is that she's not even remotely a people person. I have *no* idea why He picked her for this job, unless He thought we needed someone to secure our servers. In any event, Lockhart's disapproval was, to her, like water off a duck's back. Janice didn't even notice it.

"Come *on*, people," I coaxed. "Derek, how about you? You're on scenario development, this has got to be right up your alley, yes?" I flashed him a smile full of pearly gnashers.

Derek actually had the decency to look frightened. "Who, me?" I nodded encouragement. "Well, um, we're supposed to—" He took a deep breath, then another, chest rising and falling so fast I began to worry that he was starting to hyperventilate. "America. Right. I've never *been* to America."

"Not to worry, you won't be going there without a minder," I said, to his visible relief. "You can hunker down in your basement just like a good DM. All I expect from you for now is scenario design and build, timeline management, and the usual contingency planning on top. Oh, and you've got VIP access to Forecasting Ops." I smiled reassuringly. "It'll be just like running one of your weekend LARPs, only in a different time zone, and if you get it wrong the oppo will dial in a drone strike." *On* you, *never mind your minions,* I didn't add; there was nothing to be gained by hounding our chief planner into a breakdown.

"Well, that's all right, then." Derek said, relieved. He pulled out a cloth and began to polish his horn-rimmed glasses. "Where do I start?"

"You start by planning how to get us home in a hurry if it all goes to shit—that is, the away team *and* the high-value target—or, failing that, how best to keep everything out of the adversary's hands. Work backwards from there." I watched as Derek scribbled hasty notes in pencil. "Got it?"

A throat-clearing sound caught my attention and I glanced round the table. It wasn't Fuckboy: too high-pitched, and anyway Jim was leaning back in his chair, looking pensive. Beside him, the wiry schoolteacher-y guy from our SRR ancillary team was scribbling notes as if his exam results depended on it. Then—*oh, her. The kid.* "What is it, Jonquil?" I managed to smile affably.

"Do you really figure this is, like, *for real?*" she singsonged at me. "It's, like, not a loyalty test or something?"

Dear Jesus, fuck you very much. I managed to freeze my face just in time, but not everyone else in the meeting was as quick on the uptake, and Janice just about bit her head off: "*Of course* it's a fucking loyalty test!" she exploded. "Test to destruction. Do this, do that, *oh dear,* well at least you died trying to be useful, don't you *get* it?"

Silence descended, leaving Janice beetle-browed, casting her glare around the table for support. Meanwhile pretty blonde Jonquil, the office intern from hell, simpered and scribbled something in eldritch shorthand on her jotter. "What do you *mean*?" Jonquil poked the bruise. "Why do you think He'd give us a—"

I stood up. I hate uptalk, that upward inflection at the end of every sentence that turns a statement into a leading question. I hate it even more when it comes from the mouths of babes and informers. "Shut. The *fuck*. Up."

Jonquil saw something in my expression that made her bite her tongue. She stopped dead in mid-flow, her upturned face pale.

"Stop. Harassing. The B-Team," I warned her.

"I'll have you—"

"You'll have *nothing*. People," I looked around the table, "just to make things *totally* clear to those of you who aren't political, Jonquil here reports to her mother"—bemused expressions from those for whom the penny hadn't dropped yet—"Mrs. Carpenter, the High Priestess of Number 10." *That* was a bitchy put-down, but not untrue. "Jonquil has *no* official rank within SOE, but she's a SPAD from Party Central Office and you should treat her with the respect she deserves." A Special Political Advisor to the Prime Minister himself, in other words, imposed on the team to monitor ideological compliance with the New Management. Impossible to keep out of the office, and as deserving of respect as a spitting cobra with rabies. If snakes could get rabies. "She's not *in* our reporting chain so much as she *is* our reporting chain." I point a finger at her: "But that doesn't give you license to fuck with my personnel, *especially* when the officer in question is here because the PM expressly requested her participation. If you start a witch hunt, you'll fatally undermine our efficacy before we even get started, and I'm pretty sure He'll take a dim view of that. He wants *results,* or none of us would be here. Am I understood?"

To my surprise, Jonquil backed down. "I'm sorry, Baroness?" she said with downcast gaze, folding her hands in her lap. "Please accept my apologies?"

I made a mental note to check my bedroom for concealed UV flashbulbs and poisonous spiders, then nodded and moved on. "Here—" I opened my red box and pulled out a clipboard and a pile of sealed envelopes—"are your initial individual orders. Paper only, no electronic copies permitted, sign and fingerprint on the attendance list—we'll break for coffee and reading time, then reconvene in half an hour to discuss execution and matters arising." The clipboard circulated, the pile of envelopes diminishing as my team picked them up. "Oh, and Derek? A word with you— I've got a little errand to run tomorrow and I want you to come along."

3: WE'RE ONLY MAKING PLANS FOR JAR-JAR

I'm tired, itchy, and bad-tempered by the time our taxi pulls up on a street in midtown Manhattan, a few blocks from Times Square. Twilight has fallen and the frontage of our hotel is entirely concealed by scaffolding, so I leave Jim to get a receipt from the cabbie while I haul our suitcases into the lobby. We're staying in a boutique hotel which most certainly does *not* fit within our normal travel allowance policy, but which is perfect for our cover story. The door is green-tarnished brass scrollwork and crystal-polished glass panels. And the lobby is all chilly Italian marble and black velvet, with pretty young things in sharp suits staffing the check-in desk.

Sally from Guest Services is handing me my room card and explaining about the complementary wine tasting every evening when her gaze slides sideways and focuses on something behind me: Fuckboy, I realize, as Jim rests a hand on my shoulder. She manages to tear her eyes away from him without prompting, so I keep my smile businesslike: "I'll let you know if we need anything else—" To Jim—"Help me with the baggage, dear?" He trails after me without so much as a backward glance. "Well, *that* was life-affirming," I remark as I lean against the mirrored back wall of the elevator.

"What?" He looks baffled.

"Nothing." The elevator dings and the doors open on a surprisingly narrow corridor. I gather hotels in Manhattan, even upscale luxury boutique hotels suitable for an upwardly mobile couple on their naughty prenup honeymoon, are just as cramped as those in London. (Mo's husband insists that all hotel corridors join up eventually via those doors labelled EMPLOYEES ONLY in a hyperdimensional manifold he calls Hotelspace, but he's always been a few screws short of a full set, and I've long since given up trying to figure him out—not my problem anymore.) We find our suite without too much trouble and it turns out it's actually smaller than my living room, which is remarkable, although there's a bathroom with whirlpool bath, and no less than three TV screens.

"Huh," says Jim, lining up our suitcases and carry-on bags against one wall as if they're on parade. "Where are the, uh . . ."

"I'll sort them out." I pick up the room telephone. "Housekeeping? This is room 1214, I believe there should be some mail waiting for us—parcels? I mean, packages? Can you have someone bring them up, please? Thanks everso." I hang up, then sit down on the end of the aircraft-carrier-sized bed and bounce up and down experimentally. It's a good thing I call Jim *Fuckboy,* is all I can say.

"Packages." Jim grins boyishly, his face losing thirty years in a second.

"Packages. Hur hur." I stifle a yawn. "It's too early for bed and I'm getting hungry. How about we freshen up, and once they deliver the engagement presents we find something to eat?"

"Sounds like a plan," he agrees, and retreats to the bathroom before I can stake my claim, the bastard.

About the "engagement presents."

This is the post-9/11 era, and we spooks have to run the gauntlet of airport security whenever we travel. Which puts a little bit of a crimp on our activities, as you can imagine. When you enter the USA or the UK, before you are granted admission by the passport officer, you exist in an uneasy legal limbo. You are technically outside the rule of domestic law, and your civil rights don't quite exist. Smartphones, laptops, and personal electronics are all subject to search and seizure at the border. Bags can and will be searched. Body cavities can be searched. So if you are an illegal, carrying any equipment on the job will cause you to run an unacceptable risk of exposure. Hence our faked-up phones with the fabricated social media bread-crumb trail and sanitized address books, and my irritation at being unable to work en route.

Which brings me to supply-chain logistics, and our saviors Amazon, AliExpress, and eBay.

As a power couple on an engagement celebration, nobody really blinks at us receiving gift-wrapped packages delivered *poste restante* to our hotel. There are greeting cards, of course, mailed the usual way. A few pieces of discreetly packaged clothing for me, to help with my sunburn vulnerability. Some Mall Ninja toys like pocket knives and LED flashlights for Jim. And some other stuff.

The postal service inspectors scan everything, and UPS and FedEx check the contents of parcels for explosives. But it's astonishing what you can get your hands on if you buy on the big e-commerce sites and know how to use drop-shipping services. Some of the drop-shippers Derek uses will forward anything inside the continental United States. I suspect their main customer base are small-scale drug dealers.

For starters, our *real* phones arrive in tamper-proof packaging from the factory, as do a couple of SIMs from a local phone company. Then magic happens, once both of us type in some really long and annoying passwords we memorized and download the flashable firmware upgrades waiting for us on a website, check some even more annoying long numbers to ensure the firmware hasn't been tampered with, and boot them up. That gives us an encrypted messaging system, OFCUT software—a standardized suite of magic-sensing apps—and dual rear-facing cameras for that extra special sauce. (It's only a matter of time before the powers that be ban the manufacture of dual-camera systems and then brick all existing ones in the name of security;

but in the meantime, it's convenient as fuck for us that they haven't.) The phones we traveled with go in the trash. They were set up in anticipation of being searched or infected with malware by the opposition as we entered the country, and even though we didn't get searched, they were probably logged on our way through the airport and can be used to ID us as recent arrivals.

Now we get to the dangerous stuff.

Derek, in his capacity as mission planner, fucking *loves* Amazon. Amazon doesn't sell firearms, but it *does* sell tasers, handcuffs, batons, and pepper spray. There's also a suit of black Kevlar and ceramic body armor for Jim, more Darth Vader than Mall Ninja. As it happens, neither Jim nor I are certificated for firearms—but we're not the only act in this circus. For example, one of our earlier plans involved members of the SRR (the successor to the SAS) armed with locally sourced Glocks and AR-15s—with aftermarket bump stocks to convert them to full auto, of course. God bless the NRA. But that's not going to be necessary now, thanks to another of Derek's suggestions and an idea of mine.

If we arrived as a single team, carrying all these toys in our luggage from Heathrow, we would be as conspicuous as we'd be if we came with a marching band and passports in the name of James Bond. But because we flew in via different routes in small teams, and our kit came piecemeal on various slow boats from China, piling up in different hotel mail rooms over a period of a week, no single pair of eyebrows are going to be raised. It worked for Mossad in Dubai and it can bloody well work for SOE at three target sites in America. At least that's the theory.

The plan is intricate, and because it involves multiple teams converging on the target from different directions, perhaps some further background is needed.

So, two weeks earlier, in the south of England . . .

"It's preposterous. We're not, not head-bangers! If he insists on us doing it this way, it's going to get people killed." Derek shakes his cupped right hand when he gets agitated, as if he's rolling a set of dice. "Anyway, it's ridiculous! What does he think he's playing at?"

"Fantasy spy games," I say absent-mindedly. "Oh look, we're landing."

"What?" He cups his hands around one side of the bulky green headset: "I can barely hear you!"

That's not surprising: the army helicopter we're hitching a ride in is so loud that even with noise-cancelling headphones I can feel the vibrations in my bones. It's early evening, there are no convenient reading lights back here, and I've been unable to read or write during the flight, so I've had altogether too much time to stare past the flight crew's helmets at the dark front window, imagining what could go wrong. Now we're descending towards Camp Tolkien on Dartmoor, which means that in about an hour I'm going to be interviewing the final candidate for the team. *No, we are going to be interviewing the final recruit,* I remind myself. And *seeing whether Derek's idea for how to use her will work.*

There is a helipad outside the front gate to the compound, some distance from the stack of Portakabins and unpaved car park around the entrance in the razor-wire-topped concrete wall. Our helicopter wallows briefly, then settles with a bump on the pad. "You can unfasten your seatbelts and climb out when you're ready. Captain Perceval is waiting for you at the guardhouse," says the pilot. He sounds relieved to be rid of us.

I scramble out of the back of the flimsy scout chopper and help Derek down—he's middle-aged, with creaky knees and poor eyesight—and then walk, shoulders instinctively hunched, towards the guardhouse. "Mhari Murphy and Derek Blacker to see Captain Perceval," I say, holding up my warrant card in front of the camera. "We're expected."

An apologetic throat-clearing comes from the grille of an entryphone. "Can't let you in without authorization, ma'am."

For an instant I see red. "I'm on your list," I say. "Can't you just—"

Another voice interrupts. "I'll take it from here, Private. Ms. Murphy, please come inside the guardroom." The door opens and I step inside. The room is cramped, mostly a bench beneath a wide armored window, with a side door opening into a back room. A squaddie stands in the far corner of the room, watching me warily from behind a big black gun. Cameras whirr and point at me.

I hold up my warrant card to the unblinking gaze. "Satisfied, Captain?"

"Yes." The soldier lowers his gun to point at the floor as the back door opens and an officer, presumably Captain Perceval, enters. (But he doesn't look away from me, or blink, not even once.) "I'll escort you inside the perimeter, Ms. Murphy. And your colleague, Mr.—"

"Blacker. Is Yarisol'mün ready for us?"

"Jar-Jar? Yes, she's waiting."

I wince at his casual disrespect as I follow Captain Perceval into the rear. We wait for a minute while Derek goes through the same airlock rigmarole with the armed guard and the dual cameras that double as remote-controlled Basilisk guns, then follow him along a windowless corridor. The ceiling is dotted with strange-looking unlit lights. "Ultraviolet LED strobes," Captain Perceval comments, not looking my way, "in case of mages like yourself." I don't bother to correct him. "They're safed for now, but make sure you've got clearance before you enter."

Ah. "Get many break-out attempts, do you?"

"Oddly, no." We come to the end of the tunnel and then another guardroom. "The magi are actually quite tractable, now that they're part of an established hierarchy of bindings again. More so than the regular Host knights, anyway."

"I thought they'd shipped out?"

"Most of them have." He side-eyes me. "What can you tell me?" he asks, his tone cautious.

"Don't trust the PM's sense of humor." Camp Tolkien is two-thirds empty right now, most of the invading *alfär* expeditionary force having been forcibly bound to the Will of the Black Pharaoh and sent to Aleppo, where they are bloodily crushing the Caliphate. What's left are not so much the dregs of the Host of Air and Darkness as an unstable explosive precipitate. "Tell me about Yarisol? In your own words? Why the nickname?"

Perceval looks unhappy. "You know the scene where Jar-Jar Binks steps in the shit? There was a stupid accident in the early days. She was on a detail mucking out the stables. The name stuck because unicorn droppings stink like nothing on earth and bored squaddies think that kind of thing is funny. Also, she *is* a bit clumsy." I feel a chill of foreboding. "That's why she didn't make the cut for Syria. What do you want with her?"

"Oh, just a chat." Behind me, Derek is making frantic hand-gestures signifying deep unease. "You don't think it's odd that she's female?"

He shakes his head as we wait for a guard to unlock the next set of gates and admit us to a central hub with corridors radiating off in six directions. "No, why?"

Because she's a female alfär mage, I don't say. *The* only *female* alfär *PHANG. Half the* alfär *regular soldiers are female, but all but one of their bloodsuckers are male. Formerly male.* "Just curious." The gate unlocks with a whine of motorized bolts and Captain Perceval waves Derek and myself through.

Eventually we arrive at an interview room. There are doors on two opposite walls, a transparent window bisecting it, tables and chairs on either side. The far side of the room contains some elaborate security devices: defensive wards on all surfaces, nozzles designed to spray salt and rice grains everywhere, ultraviolet flash bulbs and paired camera turrets. I've seen the like in the custody suite under Belgravia nick where they hold paranormal arrestees, the so-called supervillains. These are the sort of precautions you'd want for debriefing battle-hardened vampire sorcerers, which makes me wonder what the hell we're letting ourselves in for here.

"I'll be a minute," says Captain Perceval. "Phone if you need anything."

He points at a wired telephone handset on the table, then turns and leaves. The door locks behind us and I look at Derek. "Thoughts?"

Derek looks apprehensive. "You're sure about this?"

I shrug. "We'll see." I'm not sure at all, but the PM's little list of people to bring on board was worryingly specific. And I did a little background reading—just enough to tell me that something smells wrong here.

The alfär, our bloodthirsty hominid relatives from the universe next door, inflict PHANG syndrome on their combat mages to enhance their lethality. To make them a little more tractable, and keep them out of the lines of hereditary succession, they also castrate them—the male ones, that is. The *female* ones are another matter. Or rather, the female *one*. I don't know if the Host that invaded us last year was atypical, but all their magi, with one exception, were male eunuchs. And the PM has sent me here to recruit the shy, weak, klutzy, pathetic excuse for a soldier who is the exception. "Do you suppose—" I begin, just as the door on the other side of the room opens and Jar-Yarisol'mün shuffles inside, accompanied by the captain.

H. alfarensis is our species' closest surviving relative. So close that, like Neanderthals (if any were still alive), they're probably inter-fertile with us and could just about pass for normal on the high street, if you did something about the distinct points on their ears and the psychopathic attitude. They're slim and graceful and look as if they wouldn't be much use in a fight, but appearances are deceptive. Among the first things genome sequencing established was that they've got a variant FOXP2 gene—vital for language acquisition, and implicated in ritual magic performance—and a frameshift mutation in their MYH7 gene that actually makes their skeletal muscles a lot stronger per unit mass. The combination is utterly deadly. When a desperate force of a couple of thousand soldiers, exiled survivors of a devastating necromantic world war, trashed Yorkshire and went head to head with the British Army and the RAF on their home turf, they only lost because of systematic intelligence failures on their part (and their leadership being as mad as a box of frogs).

But the woman on the other side of the glass window isn't the graceful and deadly exemplar of the elven master race I've been expecting.

Yarisol'mün—that's her bare-naked identity, although I mustn't use it to her face unless I'm willing to kill her: *alfär* sorcerers take a really dim view of people misusing their true names—shuffles through the door, eyes downcast and left shoulder hunched defensively. Stripped of all glamour she's a skinny wee thing, of indeterminate age, with pallid skin and lanky blonde hair. It trails to her shoulders and looks like she hasn't washed it for a month. *Alfär* look different enough from us that I can't guess her age, but her file says she's thirty-two and has been a mage since she could crawl, which means she's consumed the lives of maybe three or four hundred helots. (I flash for a moment on Mr. Kadir's expression as I filled the sample tubes with his blood. Who am I to judge?) She wears a grubby orange boiler suit and wrist and ankle cuffs. There are no obvious chains in sight, for her fetters are abstract, and vastly stronger than steel. Her feet are bare and slightly grubby.

She stops moving just as the door closes behind her. She turns as if she wants to leave, then stops.

"Jar-Jar," says Captain Perceval, "sit down, Jar-Jar. Sit." He speaks loudly and slowly, as if addressing a particularly ill-trained spaniel. For a moment I hate him. I force back the impulse to bite out his throat and drink him dry. It's not just the contemptible nickname the asshole camp guards pinned on a vulnerable woman: he seems oblivious to the incandescent beauty on the other side of the window, beaten down and broken by—

What?

I hastily self-assess. No, my ward isn't kicking off, so I'm not under the influence of any external glamour or geas. Yarisol is passive, depressed (I can feel her black dog at the back of my head), *grief-stricken*. She's part of my brood, in need of—

What the fuck? *Okay, so maybe His Eldritch Majesty knows something that I don't.*

"What do you want me to call you?" I ask.

She stares at the floor.

"Jar-Jar," says Captain Perceval, "she answers to Jar-Jar."

Well fuck. "Jar-Jar, look at me," I tell her.

For a couple of seconds she doesn't react, but shuffles towards the chair and fumbles her way into it.

"Look at me," I repeat, then push my will in her direction. "*Look.*"

She finally gives up her attempted shoegaze and peers at me sidelong from under her fringe. Something about her expression, the way it slides away from my face, rings bells. "Jar-Jar," Captain Perceval brays, "this is Ms. Murphy from London, she's a very important visitor—"

"Shut *up*," I snarl quietly. "Captain, has anyone done a psych assessment on her?"

"*What?* Why would we do that?"

She sits upright in the chair and faces us attentively but she's not making eye contact. And—I focus—she's tapping the fingers of her left hand on her thigh in a complex, syncopated rhythm that makes me itch to start counting. She's not much to look at, but in my mind's eye she's *beautiful*, a swirling vision of carmine complexity woven from the strands of a myriad of invocations, her head surrounded by a halo of crimson V-feeders so dense that she *glows*—

"*Service to the All-Highest, Yarisol,*" I say haltingly in the de-fanged dialect of Old Enochian that the People use for everyday speech. "*I am Mhari.*" Abbreviated names are just about acceptable from leader to subordinate, but I'm damned if I'm going to call her Jar-Jar. My Old Enochian is about as good as my school-girl French—coming from the Admin side of things I didn't see the need for it or get any tuition until about a year ago—but it gets her attention. The elven waifu with fangs looks at me properly for the first time: her eyes widen in surprise, and she gasps slightly.

"*Mistress, I meant no disrespect!*"

"*Peace,*" I tell her, then realize Captain Perceval and Derek are both looking at me, baffled and perplexed respectively.

"*All-Highest commands me on a quest. He says you will come. Will you do this?*"

"What?" asks the captain. I look at him and twitch and he shuts his mouth hastily.

"*I obey, mistress,*" she says in a monotone, but something about her aura feels happy, as if a missing piece has just slotted into the middle of her jigsaw puzzle of life. Purposeful.

"*Do you know the—*" I think furiously for a minute. "*The rite of face-stealing?*" Is it even possible for an *alfär* mage to steal the memories and appearance of another person without cross-infecting them with V-parasites? I don't know, but Yarisol is clearly unsuited for this mission without acquiring an additional veneer of humanity that no amount of classroom study will give her, and it would kill two birds with one stone if she can do it.

"*I know of it, yes.*" She nods, a gesture she must have learned from her captors, and I adjust my assessment of her accordingly. Autism manifests differently between human men and women. I've got no previous experience of what it looks like in non-human hominids, so I'll just have to play it by ear.

"*Have you ever performed it?*" I persist.

"*Why would I?*" She's clearly puzzled.

"*All-Highest requires that if, if possible, you take the face and memories of another. Do you need assistance? Agent First of Spies and Liars can help.*" *Alfär* eyes look wide to begin with, and when I mention Cassie by rank Yarisol's nearly tumble out of her head. She glances from side to side frantically.

"*Peace!*" I say. (It translates as "not-pain.") "*Are you true to your nature? Has anyone made you someone else already?*" She shakes her head violently. *"I will not require this of you."* (There is no word for "force"; it is implied by every statement in the *alfär* Low Tongue: a brutally direct language.) *"However, this quest requires you to pass for an* urük.*"* Human. *"Is it your will to join me?"* I ask, as gently as her language permits.

"I obey," says Yarisol, and she looks away again, overcome by emotional overload.

"You can go now," I tell her, and she stands and does her shoe-gaze shuffle over to the door. I tell Captain Perceval: "We're done for now. I'll raise the paperwork to sign her out of here later."

He stares at me. "What was all that about?" He hasn't understood a word of our conversation.

"Above your pay grade." I smirk, giving him a hint of fangs, and he recoils. "Let's just say she's been assigned to me for a special task, and leave it at that."

I shove back my chair and rise. Derek, bless him for being not *entirely* bereft of social skills, is only a moment behind me.

"Mhari—" he begins.

"Later," I warn him and he falls silent. "We'll talk back at the office."

I watch for a moment as the guards take the *alfär* mage away, presumably back to her room in the segregation block, and mentally slot several pieces into place in the six-dimensional jigsaw that the Prime Minister has created for me. Then I smile, because it looks like our plan for Yarisol'mün is going to work.

Meanwhile, the same day that Jim and I arrive in New York, another team is driving across Minnesota.

One does not simply walk into Mordor these days; one drives a rented Cadillac Escalade the size of a county, shiny black and chrome, with a fake walnut dash, and enough black leather to clothe a battalion of Hell's Angels. Pete the Vicar sits bolt upright behind the steering wheel, peering across the bonnet—no, the *hood*—of the gigantic all-American land barge as it rumbles along

I-90. They're approximately two hundred miles from Minneapolis, where they arrived the previous afternoon and spent a jet-lagged night in an airport hotel before collecting their rental.

"Are we nearly there, yet?" Brains singsongs from the front passenger seat, where he is babying a lap-tray full of electronic components.

Pete checks the satnav, and sighs. "Just over seven hundred and fifty miles to go . . ."

Without looking up, Brains says, "I spy, with my little eye, something beginning with M."

Without taking his eye off the ruler-straight expanse of cracked concrete stretching in front of him, Pete replies, "Minnesota."

Now Brains sighs.

Minnesota—at least this part of it—is as flat as if God's own road-roller had spent a million years rumbling back and forth across the landscape, grinding it into grass and ten thousand lakes, oppressed by the gigantic emptiness spanning the horizon. In the far blue distance Pete thinks he can glimpse the peaks of mountains, but they could be hundreds of miles away. He knew in the abstract that the United States was huge, but the landscape they're crawling across right now is agoraphobia inducing: you could lose the whole of England in it.

Neither Pete nor Brains are used to driving on the wrong side of the road, that is to say, on the right. Luckily a ruler-straight interstate in the middle of nowhere is a relatively safe place to train one's subconscious to do a mirror-twist on reality. There's little traffic aside from trucks, although the highway picks up locals whenever they approach the vicinity of a town, losing them again as they leave. Pete scans his instruments once more, notices that they've used almost half the tank of gas, and resolves to stop at the next filling station they pass.

Pete is driving with some trepidation, for his wheels at home are a Yamaha bike and he's finding the Escalade a learning experience. As for Brains, the rubric "don't ask, don't tell" could well apply to his preferred choice of ground transport: his hovercraft isn't road-legal and he's still sore at Environmental Security for impounding his Kettenkrad until it can be thaumaturgically decontaminated.

"Active service," Brains says, disgustedly. "I knew there was a reason I didn't let myself get roped into that stuff."

"It's a bit like cricket," Pete agrees. "Weeks of endless boredom interspersed with the occasional moment of existential terror." Then he flinches as he notices that his right front tire is rolling along the solid white line at the edge of the road. There's no rumble strip to provide a wake-up vibration. "Oh dear."

"How's it coming along?" he asks Brains, to break the boredom.

"Slowly." Brains bites his upper lip. "Need to stop this evening so I can use the soldering iron."

"It needs soldering?" Pete is surprised.

"It's not exactly the kind of thing you can order pre-assembled off the shelf from Radio Shack. I can only do so much while we're bouncing all over the road."

His lap-tray bears a bunch of components: an Arduino board, a couple of shields, a wire-wrap breadboard, some ICs, and a USB power bank. Pete is not, in fact, bouncing them all over the road—his driving hand is steady—but the road surface itself is rough, with occasional potholes that threaten to throw Brains's collection of components to the wind.

"Maybe you should put it away for now and look up a motel we can stop at overnight?" Pete suggests.

Brains frowns. "The sooner we get there, the sooner we can fuck off home again," he complains. "Don't you want to get back to your wife and kid?" He doesn't notice Pete's fingers whiten slightly where they grip the rim of the wheel, or relax a second later.

"Give my regards to Pinky, when you see him." Brains's husband.

"Touché," Brains backs down. "I'm sorry. This landscape—it's getting on my tits."

"Mine, too," Pete admits. "Seriously, though, I can't do more than another six or eight hours of this. And if you take over, firstly you'll be driving through the night—" on the wrong side of the road, at that—"and secondly, we won't be at our best when we arrive."

"Whatever happened to straight in, see what's happening there, straight out and report home?"

"Two thousand miles of interstate happened." Pete drums on the steering wheel.

Pete and Brains have drawn the long straw on this mission. Theirs is the easy if extraordinarily dull task: fly into Minneapolis, hire a set of wheels, drive a thousand miles to Colorado Springs—taking instrument readings for the last five hundred miles using the thaumometer that Brains is assembling in his lap—have a quick look around a few churches just to make sure they haven't erupted in tentacles, and drive back to Minneapolis to catch a flight home. The plan is subject to updated orders from HQ, of course, but it's a simple in-and-out. Which is about all they can be entrusted with, because they're not really field officers: this kind of amateurism is what you get when the capricious über-boss tells His sorting hat to pick names at random out of the House of Those Who Won't Be Missed.

The one real drawback is all the driving the plan calls for. Flying straight into Denver would save a couple thousand miles, but Schiller's people might be keeping an eye on international arrivals. Hence the decision to enter via the state next door, to muddy the reporting chain.

Pete, for all that he looks like a skinny, middle-aged biker, is actually an ordained vicar in the Church of England, and thus ideologically suspect per the New Management. He was sucked into the Laundry when the Eater of Souls made a regrettable but necessary judgement call a few years ago (he needed an expert on pre-Nicene heresies in a real hurry), then Pete accidentally made himself useful during the desperate struggle to defend Yorkshire. When the target of a mission is notorious for its collection of mega-churches—almost unknown in the UK—and has previously been implicated in the Nazgûl's attempt at subverting the New Management, sending a churchman along seems prudent. As for Brains (who resembles a famous mythbusting television personality), he's been in Technical Services for a decade and a half.

Between them, they've got exactly the skill set that seems appropriate on the fact-finding side of this mission.

Jim is through with the bathroom surprisingly fast, and steps back into the dayroom of the suite just as I'm tipping the bellhop who delivered our "engagement presents." By the time I've showered, dried my hair, and reapplied my anti-combustion makeup, he's got our new phones plugged in to charge and is downloading their new firmware. I yawn. "Dinner, or I'm going to fall over," I tell him, which is a little bit of an exaggeration—of necessity I'm a bit of a night owl these days—but it's already past midnight back home.

"Let's take a walk." He pauses.

"I'd better get dressed then, shouldn't I?" I unlock my suitcase, then grin at him over my shoulder because I never get tired of him looking at me like that: bend over, waggle butt, watch Fuckboy's face. Then I tense. There's a note inside the case: THIS BAG HAS BEEN OPENED BY THE TRANSPORTATION SAFETY ADMINISTRATION. *Well, fuck.* I systematically unpack and check that nothing's gone missing, or been added, before I unwind a millimeter and assemble an outfit. I let the chilly sweat in the small of my back evaporate before I put it on. A fully clothed Mhari emerges, entirely sober and professional, as

I silently process all the ways I nearly fucked up just now. "Have you checked your bag?" I say aloud.

"No, should I?"

"Yes, yes you should. But—*not yet*." He freezes over the combination lock. "Wait until your phone's ready and then scan it with OFCUT first."

"Why?"

"Stop thinking like a cop and remember we're illegals, maybe?"

"But—" He bites his tongue, and I can see the gears turning in his head as I hold up the TSA notice. "Oh." He takes a careful step back from his case.

"I screwed up; I don't need you to screw up also. Nobody planted a bomb in my bag so they probably didn't make us, but even so. I got a distinct *being watched* feeling back in arrivals." I shrug. Jim's face is a picture. "C'mon, sexytimes are just our cover story." I tug him in the direction of the vestibule. "Try not to lose situational awareness."

"Thank you for balancing that invigorating bucket of ice water on the door edge, Madame Director." Jim takes a couple of shuddering breaths as I scrawl an amateurish ward on the inside of the door. "Dammit," he adds under his breath, then offers me his arm.

"It was a wake-up call for me, too," I say, sotto voce. "This kind of thing really isn't my cup of cocoa."

"We're amateurs. Babes in the fucking wood."

"Yes. So let's shape up, shall we?"

I know the criteria for Active Service training. Back in the old days—between about 1991 and 2001—there used to be a battery of psych tests, then between two and four years of supervised experience before they'd consider putting an agent into the field. But then everything accelerated out from our control, and we had to cut back training to six months, like an army on the losing side of a war throwing green recruits into the meat grinder.

And now this: people with relevant skill sets being expected to improvise, playing by 1939 rules. Sometimes it works, and the survivors get to write the training manuals for the next generation, but the personal consequences of failure are drastic, and you can't learn from a fatal mistake.

I yawn (and snap my mouth shut just in time as the lift stops and the doors slide open): I'm that tired. Not even Jim squiring me out into the neon-lit twilight of a semi-legendary city I've always meant to visit can stop the yawns coming.

There's this myth that New York is the city that never sleeps, but that seems to only be half-true. A lot of the smaller shops on the side-streets are shuttered and dark, although a few blocks away I can see the illuminations from Times Square. But people dine late in this town, and there are plenty of bars and restaurants still open. Unfortunately, our phones are still downloading stuff, and I didn't think to bring a paper guidebook, so we're stuck with wandering aimlessly until we see something we like the look of.

We end up in a family-style Lebanese diner a few blocks from the hotel in the opposite direction from the bright lights. I'm hopelessly lost and relying on Jim to navigate, because all these ruler-straight roads and high-rise buildings look the same to me. The food's probably good, but I barely taste it on the way down. "No wine for you," Jim says repressively, and I roll my eyes before conceding the point. Maybe tomorrow.

Afterwards, with my stomach pleasantly stunned, I stand on the sidewalk outside and look up at the stars. They're spectacular with PHANG-enhanced vision. "If we go straight back I'll fall asleep," I tell him. "Walk for a bit?"

He nods, glancing around. "Let's get a feel for things." Jim has police eyes: he spent years training and more years working the beat. His gaze is never still, always flickering around when we're in public, assessing and evaluating. Although I've done an accelerated police training course I'll never have his situational awareness. We pass a couple of side-streets where even to my eye transactions appear to be taking place, either bottle-washers sharing a cigarette break or locals engaging in a little bit of extralegal trade. Jim twitches, then determinedly turns away and walks on, which makes me smile.

"Not our circus, not our monkeys," I murmur, and he nods.

We walk for a couple of kilometers outside the tourist areas, I think. Shops seem to cluster by trade. One block is nothing but buttons, trimming, and wholesale beads, another is all fabric importers. But the streets are all deep cement-lined canyons, and whenever I look up I nearly fall over with a combination of fatigue and dizziness. At one point I see a familiar silhouette looming above me: the Empire State Building, comically foreshortened. But there's no giant ape clinging to the airship mooring mast at the top, and at street level it's surrounded by scaffolding. Home—London—is the same, I suppose. All big cities have a lived-in feel and smell of fast food and truck exhausts, in a way that no movie can ever convey.

Finally we turn and head back towards our hotel. "You're sure this is the right way?" I ask, lost as I am.

"Yeah." He nods. "Follow Broadway to Times Square, then go four blocks north and two east." He says it patiently, as if it should mean something to me. "It's not far." Although *not far* in Jim-speak could mean anything. "I could fly it in about a minute, if . . ." He stares upward, wistfully.

"No flying," I tell him, tightening my grip on his arm. Even though it would be fun, doing the Superman and Lois Lane thing. "Nothing that might raise your parasite load. Operational use and emergencies only."

He nods, jaw muscles tensing. We're in potentially hostile territory, and it'd be a really bad idea for Jim to attract the attention of the local vigilantes, half of whom are neo-Nazi thugs.

By the time we get to Times Square it's past ten o'clock local time, three in the morning back home, and even Jim is beginning to flag. There are lots of people about but the shops have either closed or are closing—giant flagship branches of famous trade-marked brands, Skittles and Disney, and cosmetics chains like Sephora. There's a police station in the middle of the square and two black-and-white cars parked nearby, but what gets my attention—and Jim's—is the quartet of silver-suited figures posed motionless on the roof. If they weren't silver they might resemble Autons, the murderous shop mannequins from *Doctor Who* back when I was a kid. No capes, no boots, just silver body-stockings that cover every inch from crown to toe. They face outwards, looking across the sea of late-night idlers like a promise of blood on the wind. Something about them feels terribly familiar. Then I hear them in the back of my head, a distant hungry buzz and chatter. I think back to the "engagement presents" waiting in the hotel room and realize what the mannequins are. I nudge Jim: "They're PHANGs—but not ours. Don't make eye contact," I hiss. They're scanning the crowd, looking for a certain type of trouble. "Let's get out of here. Don't run, and *don't,* whatever you do, power up."

Bless him, he obeys without asking questions until we turn the corner and pass a wall of souvenir-shop windows full of over-priced electronics and tacky made-in-China memorabilia. "What?" he asks.

"They're alert." I shiver, remembering their hungry chatter. (I was fed well—don't ask—before we left: mine is not an active appetite right now.) I would know if their V-parasites were of the same lineage as mine. The infestation riding the people in the silver suits feels subtly wrong, weirdly synchronized, as if they're a single organism in four separate bodies. I can still hear them distantly, the same way I sense members of my own tribe. "Local PHANGs, out in public, standing around on an NYPD shop roof. What does that tell you?"

He stares at me. "Is there a local TPCF?" (Transhuman Police Coordination Force, our very own official team of supercops.) "I mean, New York State or City?"

"Not that I know of—I thought it was all vigilante assholes and the military over here."

It's a puzzler. But then, American police arrangements are utterly weird to British eyes, with every municipality and state and transport authority potentially having its own sheriff's department or police force or state troopers or thief takers or whatever. And that's before you even think about the federal agencies like the FBI and DEA.

"They could be federal. Or city." He squints over his shoulder. "Or you know who."

"Don't say it." We're near the entrance to our hotel. I can recognize that much. "Do you suppose *He* knows?"

"Why else do you think He sent us here, darling?" He slows and turns to embrace me.

"Yes, let's work on our cover story." I lean in close and kiss him lightly as he slides his arms around me. Presently I pull back and lean my cheek against the side of his neck. "Mmm, that's good. Yes, He fucking knew. Or guessed. Jim, something is *very* wrong here."

PHANGs are, of necessity, a scarce resource. We're limited by population density. Each of us needs to consume a minimum of one other human being's life every six months—more if we're actively practicing ritual magic. I'm barely a beginner. Some of my people are well on their way to becoming formidable practitioners (like Alex, but best not to tell the little oik that). However, beyond a certain level, sorcerers with V syndrome need to feed more and more lives to their parasites to keep them in check. An *alfär* battle-mage is the necromantic equivalent of an artillery company, but to function offensively they need to consume a human sacrifice every hour, minimum.[5] PHANGs in New York, working with the NYPD, imply a growing pile of corpses somewhere, tacitly condoned by the NYPD at a policy level, which

---

[5] That's why His Eldritch Majesty packed them off to fight a colonial war in Syria, where the other side are so vile that nobody back home will object.

goes *way* beyond even the usual trigger-happiness we Brits attribute to American cops. PHANGs—hunting supervillains aside—are not an appropriate tool for law enforcement, any more than you'd fire cruise missiles at shoplifters.

"I agree," Jim murmurs. "But I'm exhausted, you're tired, and they'll still be here tomorrow. Let's go to bed." I nod and, leaning on him, we head back to our hotel room.

Two weeks earlier, a couple of days after Derek and my visit to Camp Tolkien . . .

A couple of days after the session at Camp Tolkien, I am required to make another field trip to inspect an agency asset who Derek and Colonel Lockhart insist will come in handy during the terminal stages of Operation YELLOW OLYMPIC. As the asset is nominally owned by the Royal Air Force, we're to be given a proper Ministry of Defense dog-and-pony show—which means suits and briefcases all round. Five of us are in attendance: me, the colonel, Brains (in his capacity as speaker-to-techies), Jim (who I already know is going to be along for the ride), and Jonquil, who thinks she's here to report back to Mumsie, but is actually here so I can keep an eye on her.

It's two and a half hours by train from Paddington to Bristol Temple Meads, but the installation we're visiting is housed in a hangar by the Airbus plant at Filton Airport, some distance out of town. So we set off bright and early from London City Airport aboard an elderly BAe 146 airliner from 32 Squadron RAF, the Queen's Flight. Less than half an hour later we're on the ground again, and I can release my death-grip on the armrests and breathe a sigh of relief as we taxi straight to the hangar where they keep the white elephants.

It's an unpleasantly sunny day. Jim has thoughtfully brought a gigantic black parasol, which he holds over my head as I slither down the air stairs and scuttle towards the human-sized door in the hangar. Jonquil seems to think it's all a bit of a lark and strolls nonchalantly along, whistling tunelessly. Brains is gawping in all directions, head spinning like a radar scanner. I dodge around Jonquil with a glare—which she misses completely, probably because I'm wearing a veil again—and Lockhart, breathing heavily, makes it to the door and stops in front of me just before I slam right through it. "Wait," he grates, fixing me with a glare.

"If I wait I'll burn," I warn him, glaring right back. I can *feel* the sun through my parasol, clothing, and sunblock. I swear the hair on the back of my neck is beginning to smoke.

"No, *really*," he says, and waves his warrant card at the door. "It's warded and there are armed guards." He raises his voice: "Gerald Lockhart, SOE ops, here to see Squadron Leader Bradshaw, VIP party of five. We're expected."

The door opens onto blessed twilight. "Go inside, have your ID ready," Gerry murmurs. Once inside I flip back my veil and then pull out my own warrant card, blinking as my eyes adjust to the huge, unlit indoor space. I can hear feeders chittering, somewhere nearby.

"Identify yourself," grates a metallic voice. It sounds like a Dalek with laryngitis. I startle as someone looms over me, the source of both the challenge and the feeders: brainless crawling manifestations of extradimensional hunger. If bound to flesh they can animate it for a while and use it to infect living people by touch. (Not PHANGs like me, though—we're immune.) In this case, the animated corpse is so thoroughly dead that it's almost entirely skeletonized. It stands upright, bones screwed into a trellis of metal struts, motors, and pistons that whine faintly whenever it shifts its balance. It smells of dry rot and burning insulation. Green luminous worm-shapes are writhing in its eye sockets: "Identify yourself!" a tinny recorded loop screeches from a concealed speaker. "Identify yourself!"

A blackout curtain hanging from the ceiling about four meters inside the doorway blocks my view of the hangar. To either side I see other silver-gray exoskeletons turn and lurch into motion, converging on us, their bony cargo bobbing and grinning inside them like so many gibbeted cyborgs. Some of them carry guns. I will admit to being a little bit creeped out by them. I bare my fangs as I hold up my warrant card: "Baroness Karnstein, from Whitehall," I say as calmly as possible. "I'm expected."

"Baron-ess . . ." The skeleton freezes in position for a second, then takes two jerky steps backward and, improbably, comes to attention. "All glory to the All-Highest!" it screeches.

"All glory," I echo, with a sidelong glance at the other two constructs as they lurch hastily into position alongside the first, and salute.

Then Brains steps over the threshold. His eyes widen. "Ooh!" he says excitedly. "I've read about these!"

"Intruder! Identify! Identify!" screeches the necrotic chorus line, guns swinging to bear.

"Stand down, Harry!" shouts a baritone voice from behind the far side of the curtain. "I say, stand down! Sorry about the reception party, ma'am, we weren't expecting your flight to arrive for another half hour or so and Harry gets excited about intruders . . ."

"So I see. Is it safe for the rest of my party to enter?"

"Nearly! Harry one through four, code whisky tango foxtrot, return to maintenance station immediately." The animated skeletons turn and, with a squeal of under-lubricated joints, march jerkily towards the far side of the curtained-off space. "I'm sorry, ma'am," says the voice from behind the curtain, "but if you can just give them a minute to shut down, I'll get you signed in so that we can proceed."

The curtain directly in front of me billows slightly, and a tall, well-built fellow with sandy hair and an improbably strong jaw steps out. He may not be expecting us just yet, but he's taken pains over his dress uniform this morning, clearly anticipating an inspection. "You must be Squadron Leader Bradshaw?"

"Yes, ma'am. If I can see your ID? Excellent. The rest of your team can enter now. I'll need to check them off individually. Here, I have security tags for you. Please remember to wear these at all times, otherwise Harry will get *quite* irate . . ."

The badge on the lanyard he hands me is heavily warded: my fingertips prickle on contact.

"Colonel Lockhart, sir!" Bradshaw draws himself up. Lockhart nods minutely. "Welcome back to Triple-six Squadron."

"It's a pleasure to visit again," Gerry Lockhart drawls. "Ready for the show?"

"Absolutely!" Bradshaw checks Jonquil and Brains in, then holds the heavy curtain open for us. "Welcome to the squadron."

I follow Gerry past the blackout drape and finally get a glimpse of the hidden magic, a secret deadly enough that they feel the need to deploy Harryhausen bots to guard it. I forget to breathe for a few seconds as I stare up at the underside of a pointy white nose cone eight meters above my head. After a few moments I notice it's flanked by two companions, each lined up on the centerline of the hangar doors like Godzilla's own throwing knives. They're parked amidst a clutter of maintenance carts, air stairs, ground tugs, and other support equipment. People in coveralls are working on two of them, and a fourth aircraft without wings or nose is parked against the far wall of the hangar. The lights are on in the cockpit of the plane looming over me, the heads of a maintenance crewmember just visible in the flight deck side window.

I feel like I just walked into the central atrium of a museum and, instead of a skeleton on a stand, have found a live tyrannosaur staring at me as it sizes me up for a snack.

"Triple-six is traditionally a reconnaissance squadron," Bradshaw explains. "The number used to be assigned to the Royal Canadian Air Force. It was also allocated to a British Army scout helicopter squadron in the seventies, before being publicly deactivated. That's when we took it over." He smiles faintly. "We used to fly recon missions for you people—the kind everything else is too low, slow, or small for."

"But. But." I stare up at the impossible aircraft above me. The first thought that pops into my mind pops out of my mouth: "This has *got* to be a gigantic hole in someone else's budget . . ."

"Not *that* big, but plenty big enough," Bradshaw says ruefully. "The mid-eighties block two refit—that gave us—" he descends into an acronym soup of FADEC and in-flight refueling—"was responsible for the AEW cost overruns that broke GEC-Marconi. More recently, we got into a whole heap of trouble after 2010 because we siphoned so much money from the Nimrod MRA4 modernization program that it got cancelled out from under us. And of course Concorde going out of civilian service didn't help, either. But it's only the third most expensive black project in postwar British history that I know of."

I shut my mouth. *Third* most expensive? I don't want to know. Off to one side, Gerry Lockhart is watching me with crossed arms and a stupendously smug expression.

"Let's continue this in the site management office, where I can give you a full briefing on what our white elephants can do . . ."

The next morning finds Janice, armed with a multitool and a bundle of cable ties, weaving a web of spell servers in the living room of a safe house in the suburbs of DC that Derek found on Airbnb.

Janice and Derek are the tech support half of Team Three, the DC crew. They flew into Dullas International the evening before under separate covers. Janice is not terribly happy about this. Like other PHANGs, she's intensely itchy about going out in daylight. As a Myers-Briggs INTP personality type, she gets anxious about situations she can't control and predict minutely. She's just about got a handle on the portly middle-aged bloke with the pebble glasses and M&S cardigans who she's been assigned to shadow, but trying to cope with Derek (who is even more

Aspie than she is) *and* foreign accents and road signs and everything else simultaneously is taking her close to overload. The lights on her personal control panel would be amber and flashing into red, well out of her comfort zone, if not for the fact that the house is . . . well, it's huge and comfortably furnished, there are blackout curtains on *all* the windows, and there is a stack of boxes waiting for her in the garage (which she can get into through a side entrance without going outdoors).

"Janice?" Derek calls from the open archway that leads to the dining area.

Janice ignores him as she continues to lay out the edges of a very strange graph—the five-dimensional structure of which the Elder Sign is merely a flattened projection into two dimensions—in ethernet cables. A box of Raspberry Pi computing boards and a twenty-four-socket USB power supply sit close at hand, ready to bring the compute nodes of her project to life.

"Janice, I need to go—"

"Derek!" Janice finally snaps. She places the cable she's holding precisely where it belongs, then straightens up and glares at him. "What?"

Derek wilts slightly in the face of her hostility. "There's no need for *that*."

"I was"—she looks back at the cable maze—"concentrating."

"Sorry." His posture screams *not sorry*. "I need to go out. The Library of Congress is open to researchers and it looks like if I get there before 4 p.m. today I can apply for a reader identification card—"

"Library of Congress. Right." Janice regards him through half-closed eyes, then relaxes slightly. "You know I can't come with you."

"I know." Derek gathers his shredded dignitas around him like a slightly baggy sports jacket. "But Forecasting Ops suggested it, and I'm here *now*—"

"So what are you waiting for?" Janice blinks, blindsided. "It's not like you're going to be much help with this." Her shoulder roll encompasses the boxes scattered all over the floor. "Go on, shoo. On second thoughts, buy me a crate of Diet Coke? I'm going to be up all night getting this grid up." She tosses him the keys to the rental SUV parked outside the garage.

Derek looks momentarily shame-faced. "But I can't drive."

Janice glares at him. "What do you expect me to do about that? It's daylight! Expense an Uber."

"An—" His eyes cross.

She walks across the room and leans over him—or seems to: Derek, despite shrinking, is a good fifteen centimeters taller than Janice. "You've got your phone, yes? Is it charged? Yes? Good. Let me show you how we get a ride in the twenty-first century."

Working with Derek is frequently infuriating.

He's terrifyingly bright in some ways but through no fault of his own he spent forty years in a Laundry-run internment camp for cultists, where paper was rationed and any technology more sophisticated than a manual typewriter was forbidden. Personal computers and the internet passed him by completely until he was released a couple of years ago, and he's still reluctant to use the smartphone Facilities issued him, which is why they paired him with Janice. Meanwhile, she can't go out in daylight without burning, so they gave her Derek to carry her fire extinguisher. They work together like they're running a three-legged race—while drunk.

Having bookmarked the safe-house address in Derek's Uber app, Janice is about to return to her network layout when Derek asks, "By the way, what *is* that you're working on?"

"Software-configurable RAID grid." She pauses, a cable in each hand. "Go on, your ride will be waiting."

"RAID grid being . . . ?"

"Redundant Array of Interconnected Demons." She bares her teeth at him.

"Demons!" he squeaks, and clutches his magic dice.

"The *alfär* coughed up this topology. It's an anchor for Phase Three that can be reconfigured as a storage ward or a summoning grid. Now go on, piss off to your library. Take your time. I'll be fine here." As he vanishes round the corner in the direction of the front door she raises her voice: "Don't forget the Diet Coke!"

One of the first things I did when the PM gave me my current job was to establish a Working Group on Best Practices for conducting overseas operations. One of the rules we settled on was that PHANGs should always be partnered with a Renfield—a human co-worker, able to go out in daylight and take care of the little chores that don't come easily to us bloodsucking fiends. This is why I'm travelling with Jim, and why Janice is paired with Derek, and Yarisol is with . . . I'll get round to her later. It's a generalization of the rule of thumb that you never send one agent to do a critical job on their own—the risk of them being run over by a cycle courier while crossing the street may be low, but you don't want to bet your operation on it. So you always send at least two bodies, which is why Pete and Brains are driving across the Great Plains together.

A second rule is to keep chains of command from crossing international borders whenever possible. It's vastly easier for a hostile signals intelligence group to detect long-range communications than a local network, especially if the locals coordinate face-to-face wherever possible rather than helpfully emailing each other their secret plans. Which is the primary reason Derek is in DC—he's handling physical logistics for our mobile teams, a glorified Amazon shopping spree. He's got another task as well, of course, but that's a one-off, while the logistics are ongoing. Meanwhile Janice is there to take care of more recondite support activities, like provisioning the DC safe house with secure wards and a veritable zoo of summonings, in case things go wrong and we need to cover an emergency evacuation.

As for the evacuation, we have a plan for that.

Our operational null hypothesis is that the PM is wrong about everything. There is nothing sinister happening in America. No fountainhead of near-mystical executive power embodying the hopes and fears of a third of a billion Americans has gone missing, nothing to see here, move along now. Everybody forgetting the Executive Branch is just a laughable misunderstanding, a glitch in the news cycle, or something. If this is the case we can close up shop, everybody breathes a sigh of relief and checks in for their flight home, and that's the end of it.

Chances of this happening? Oh, *come on* . . .

Now consider the worst possible case: that Cthulhu Himself has awakened, the Nazgûl are liquidating the presidency—the office, not just the man—as some kind of sacrifice, and we have to get out of Dodge *fast*. If we don't get across the border and out of shooting range, or otherwise fuck their plans up, the Black Chamber come after us with the US Air Force, the Army, the National Guard, Border Patrol, every local police force this side of Canada, and several thousand demons.

Chances of this happening? Oh, *come on* (again).

Most likely the truth lies somewhere in between. Or maybe the PM has palmed a couple of cards and doesn't trust me with the full picture just yet, but is actually maneuvering everything into a favorable position before he lays a smackdown on his rivals.

Either way, though, the business with everybody forgetting the President? And the PM telling me to work out how to rescue him? That's a *hard* problem. So it's a good thing I have the PM's signature on an unlimited black budget—and permission to use some *very* exotic tools.

A final flashback (I promise!): one week before the present:

Yarisol'mün is uneasy.

She sits in the back seat of a snarling metal and plastic box that sways and rattles as it hurls itself along a wide *urük* trail, screaming past other grubby metal boxes with a warble of sirens and a hypnotic flare of blue and red lights from a casing atop its roof. She's swathed in the daylight veil and robes of a mage, but not bound. Two *urük* males in dark blue uniforms with silver badges sit up front, one of them working the lever and wheel that direct the slave-cart's chained burning energy. She can feel their heartbeats pulsing, warm and sticky and full of life—but All-Highest has decreed that she may not feed at will. Consequently she aches with the life-hunger, for the *urük* are miserly with the blood of their slave-farms. Outside her box on wheels other minds flash past, carried by their own *urük*-carts. Along the edge of the track she sees buildings, the squat baked-mud huts of the round-eared ape-men who captured and defeated the Host without granting them the honorable release of a victory sacrifice.

She knows she is supposed to feel shame at her debasement, but she is still alive. And if life were less dismayingly confusing, she could actually be happy.

The pale-haired catspaw of the conqueror's All-Highest (the All-Highest who is now perforce her own lord) is the source of much of Yarisol's confusion. That the *urük* routinely employ female mages is bizarre. That this one is high in the confidence of the All-Highest, and apparently a high leader of their Guild of Spies and Liars, is even stranger. But what the *urük* mage told Yarisol to do is strangest of all, and admits of no understanding. Perhaps one who was not face blind (like Yarisol) would know if this was all an awful joke, but Yarisol—who is used to being the butt of japes and pranks among her own kindred—can see no reason why the *urük* would wish to make sport of her so. To exsanguinate her unto death, certainly: she is their slave-of-war and her life belongs to them, to do with as they wish according to law and tradition among her kind. To torment her for their amusement, or to express their indignation at her existence, mayhap. But this . . . ? She raises her chin in brief denial. *Maybe I will understand afterwards,* she thinks, then falls back into the comfortable repetition of counting mayfly souls as they snap through her mind and are lost to the road unrolling beneath the wheels of the speeding police car.

The car carries her away from the prison on the plain and joins a gigantic path full of cars and other, larger, vehicles, all flowing in one direction. They pass homes and labor camps—so many *urük*!—and gradually the greenery to either side of the road is replaced by more and more buildings, endless buildings, a sea of round-eared *mana*-less *urük,* more than she had imagined the entire world could hold. She loses count somewhere past eighteen thousand nine hundred and three souls when a huge, segmented vehicle running on cold iron rails whizzes past the side of the car-track, carrying hundreds of passengers so fast that her own speeding carriage might as well be stationary. Frustrated, Yarisol bows her head over her lap and tries to shut out their bewildering, ever-changing world.

When next she dares look up, the car has slowed and is wending its way through the narrow streets of a hive-city so vast it hammers her soul with the roar of a million minds. Terrified, Yarisol tries to make sense of the faceless torrent of life around her. The All-Highest who sought to conquer this chaos was clearly mad, she apprehends. This one city alone must contain as many lives as the Morningstar Empire, uncountable millions of *urük* swarming and breeding like insects! And the chosen of the new All-Highest wants her to, to—

They stop, and her keepers ruthlessly open the car door beside her. Eyes screwed tightly shut, head down and shoulders rocking, Yarisol does not resist as the constables take her arms and pull her out of their metallic oyster shell. They march her across an open courtyard, then in through a door that leads to a confusing, busy lobby area where a number of *urük* are engaged in tasks that make no sense. Many of them are uniformed, and their minds are all inedibly warded.

A succession of rooms, waits, and faces ensues. The *urük* babble at each other barbarously. Unlike most of the Host, she hasn't bothered to pick up any of their speech. Words are hard and knobbly and don't get on with her tongue at the best of times, except when she's telling her servitors what she wants them to do—and none of them speak *urük,* or even the Low *alfär* Tongue, so why bother to learn?

Finally she's brought into another room with chairs and a table. It's a lot like the interrogation suite back at the camp, except her chair is more comfortable and there are fussy decorations everywhere. No windows, which is good. The door opens and two *urük* come in: the *urük* mage who was nice to her, and another. She doesn't like the other *urük.* It's a female with straw-colored hair like the mage, but there is no smell of clean blood magic about her. Instead there is an air of meanness, a miasma of malice, and a taste of ancient sorcery that boils and smolders around her head like a halo of death. She bares her teeth at the mage. Words are spoken that mean nothing to Yarisol. "Is this the one you wanted me to see?"

The *urük* mage pulls out a chair. "Sit down, Jonquil, please." There is some meaningless chatter, then both the *urük* females are seated across the table from her. The one who reeks of ancient death and sorcery bares her teeth at Yarisol, who cringes. *Is she going to bite me?*

"Don't smile at her, she doesn't understand," the mage says. Then, in words Yarisol knows: "*Nobody is going to hurt you.*" Her lips curl but there are no bared fangs. To the other *urük*: "Do you know how unusual she is?"

"I thought all the *alfär* PHANGs were male?"

"They are—except for this one. Who turns out to have some very interesting psychological test scores. Serious executive function deficit, face blindness—not just the PHANG variety—and linguistic processing anomalies: if she were human we'd say she had autism spectrum disorder. Almost all *alfär* have deficient empathy—they default to sociopath, by human standards—but Yarisol is different. What does this tell you about her?"

The straw-haired female makes faces that, if Yarisol could

parse them, she might interpret as disgust. "I have no idea?! Except she's got PHANG? I thought the *alfär* sacrificed all their defectives?"

"They do." The human mage smiles. "So it follows that she's not defective—or that she has considerable utility to them. But either way, her existence is an anomaly. Bears further investigation, wouldn't you say? Introspection, even?"

"Yes, but while I'm sure this is all very interesting it's not my department—"

"Oh, but it is, Jonquil!" To Yarisol, she adds: "*This is the one I want you to take.*"

Yarisol doesn't nod, or smile, or hesitate. She simply reaches across the table and touches Jonquil's wrist, as the *urük* mage grabs the woman by the neck and yanks a leather cord up and over her head. They are both magi and they move as one, with lightning-fast reflexes. The merely *urük* woman stands no chance. Her face contorts and her mouth opens as she tries to stand, but Yarisol has not been idle in the days since the *urük* mage came to visit her. She has consulted her colleagues, risking their disdain and contempt, double-checked her invocation, and prepared the Ritual of the Spies and Liars with precision. At the *urük* mage's orders she has been permitted to feed, and to feed more deeply than the others. She has plenty of *mana* for this task.

And so she drinks again, but differently, opening herself to Jonquil's memories and face and identity and name—the *urük* do not guard their true names wisely—and loses herself in the other's mind.

After a fractured, chaotic period, Jar—*Jonquil*—opens her eyes.

Mhari anxiously peers at her over the slumped body of the other woman. "Did it work?" she asks in English.

Jonquil raises her arm and stares at the back of her hand.

"Fuck me," she says, her voice heavy with astonishment and disbelief.

"I'll take that as a *yes, it worked,* not as an invitation, shall I?" the *urük* mage says drily.

So that *was a joke?* Jonquil blinks. Her donor is still out, lying facedown across the desk. Her thoughts race: everything is weirdly clear in places that were fogged before, distant and inchoate where once there was comfort and routine. She doesn't like this newfound sensitivity to nuance much: it itches. "You've got to kill her now," she thinks aloud, "otherwise she'll tell—"

Mhari smiles. Yarisol wouldn't have recognized the expression in a million years before she stole Jonquil's memories and face, but Jonquil knows enough to recoil from Mhari's venomous grin. "Think I'm going to let her off that easily?" Mhari asks easily.

"No! But—"

"Relax. This is all going to plan. Look at me." Mhari peers at the *alfär* mage's face. "Yes, that's good enough to pass. You got it right first time." Her gaze tracks over the stunned, unconscious victim. "Spin up a glamour and give her your old face. We're sending her back in your stead."

"But they'll spot the substitution right away?!" Jonquil-as-is finds swerving in mid-thought far easier than Yarisol-as-was ever could. "You want me to make her look like me? But she's not a—"

"That's stage three. First, you give her your old face. Second, I'm going to put her under a geas to keep her fat gob shut. And third"—Mhari extracts a tablet from her handbag—"she may not have PHANG syndrome yet, but I've got an app for that."

4: AWAKENINGS

There must be a law that civil service offices be as drab and unpleasant as it is humanly possible to achieve on budget, however
much money is available, Gil thinks. The improvised summoning lab he and his co-workers have assembled in the basement
of the GSA office building certainly supports the theory. It's not
that it's cheaply and drably furnished: it's *expensively* and *unpleasantly* furnished, conveying "we're the government, we're
required to be miserable at work." The widespread belief among
some politicians that government can't do anything right—that
the private sector is always better—becomes a corrosive, self-
fulfilling prophecy. Government isn't allowed to be bright and
cheerful, helpful and efficient. Thus, he and his teammates work
in a windowless basement room with vomit-colored carpet tiles
and a drop ceiling stained by plumbing leaks. To free up floor
space they've pushed the original contents to one side, forming a
pile of beige office chairs and battered green desks that rises halfway to the ceiling.

"Are you with us? Gil?" K.J., his boss, is getting twitchy.

He yawns. "Yeah, I'm ready." He shuffles to his place at one
corner of the red pentacle Big Al from Facilities splatter-sprayed
on the carpet with an airbrush. "How about you?"

K.J. sniffs. "Let's keep this on track. Brian? Mindy?" she calls.
Middle-aged, dumpy, and as tightly locked down as a teacher
from a tough inner-city school, she takes a roll call of those present.
Half a dozen assorted government workers from the former Comstock Office of the US Postal Service Inspectorate, now scattered

to the four winds but working for other departments—vehicle licensing, FAA, or, like K.J. herself, bedded in at the GSA under deep cover—they continue the mission. They're the lucky ones who transferred out before the shit hit the fan. Gil has spotted a few of his former colleagues across crowded subway platforms or civil service canteens. They didn't notice him, for which he is very grateful. The prickling of his ward and the faint green glow behind their eyelids tells him all he needs to know.

"Okay, let's see what we've got here. Mindy? The printout, if you please?"

Mindy huffs as she steps over one of the spray-painted lines and carefully lowers a stack of laser-printed pages facedown on the floor, positioning it carefully in the middle of the grid. It's the contents of a memory stick containing a series of photographs that dropped into K.J.'s inbox a couple of weeks ago, the day after Gil's exciting and unpleasant trip to the library. Viewing such scans is not recommended. Opening the files on a computer with an internet connection isn't recommended either. But sometimes there are advantages to working for the government, like having a wide selection of laughably obsolete office equipment to play with, and Big Al has set the team up with an ancient PowerPC Macintosh with a USB interface so sluggish that it took two hours to slurp a gigabyte of scans onto the machine's whirring hard disk, and a processor so obsolete and weird that any modern malware that lands on it dies instantly, unable to even run. One brainless, non-networked laser printer later, they have a printout. The most difficult part of the process was stealing the paper without anybody noticing.

"Places, people. Let's start." Mindy steps smartly out of the pentacle—the summoning space—and goes to stand at her corner of the grid. K.J. peers at the screen of her bulky, trailing-edge laptop. "Interface has gone into safe mode." She scowls furiously.

"Let me see . . ."

Gil bends down and peers at the bulky armored flight case of electronics that is connected to each corner of the pentacle by a trailing cable. "Here's your culprit," he says. One of the serial plugs isn't seated correctly. "Let me power cycle it, and try again?"

Brian snorts quietly. Short, balding, and fussy looking, he's the only one of them who still works for the Post Office—but not as an inspector. "Ten to one it's just another variant Bible, with extra Apocrypha," he opines, peering at the stack of papers on the floor. "Fifty to one it's a history of the Rosy Cross, eighty to one it's another joke *Necronomicon*—"

"That's enough," K.J. says sharply. "Let's not get distracted, people." She's a stickler, which is actually a good thing in her line of work. "Gil?"

Gil flicks the power switch. "Back on. Showtime, folks."

"Going live."

The red pentacle begins to fluoresce, almost imperceptibly in the light cast by the buzzing fly-specked tubes overhead. "I'm getting—" K.J. pauses. "—what was *that*?"

Gil feels a ripple pass through the walls of the world. His ward stings him sharply, and heats up. "I'm getting anomalous thaum flux," he says, reading off the LED display on the front of the repurposed spectrum analyzer that the Occult Texts Division used as a magical bomb detector. "How the heck does a copy of a copy get so hot that—"

"It's external!" Mindy flaps excitedly. "Look, there's nothing inside the grid! The paper is fine, the flux is coming from—" she trails off.

Something nags at Gil's memory, a word on the tip of his tongue that will change everything if he can just give voice to it. "It was disguised as a history book," he says, thinking aloud, "but a history of our country, nothing really ancient. Talking about—" The word slides into place behind his lips, muscle memory clearing a path for it. "*Presidents.*"

"Pre—" K.J. screws her face up. "*What?*"

"Presidents are, are—" He lurches. "I forget?" A dizzying moment of sensory recalibration. "No, something is *making* me forget. The *presidency*. It's, it's really important?"

Brian looks up. Green rectangles of light from the overhead lights reflect off his spectacles. "You're talking about a geas," he says.

"You." K.J. points a dagger-straight finger at Gil. "You said a word. I did not *hear* that word." She looks outraged. "And my ward"—her fingers rise to touch the plain-looking cross she wears on a silver chain—"it's live! Ow!"

"We're being blocked." Gil twitches. "Better power down before—" There's a loud click from the back of the spectrum analyzer and its digital display blanks. Simultaneously, the containment grid loses its fluorescent glow. "Shit."

K.J. looks around. "We're done here, let's pack up and go, people. Go *now*. If the other side are standing watch on DC we just sent up a signal flare. Tear down and get out."

Mindy grabs the manuscript, K.J. takes the laptop, Big Al unplugs the burned-out analyzer and carries it away. Within two minutes there is no sign that anything untoward took place in the storeroom, aside from spray-painted graffiti in the middle of the carpet. And tomorrow morning a crew of contractors is due to rip up and replace the floor tiles.

Gil leaves, turning over the word in his mind. Who or what is a *President*? he wonders—and, equally important, who or what doesn't want him to find out? It's a mystery, but one he and his team intend to get to the bottom of.

It's the Thursday after the fire of unknown origin visited Crested Butte, Colorado, and Gaby Carson is eating a microwave meal in the WOCZ break room—she eats her lunch late on program evenings, then a serving of mac and cheese to settle her stomach right before she goes on-air—when the doorbell rings.

"I'll get it," she volunteers, before Glenn can scowl at her. (Glenn has sore knees and gets grumpy if he has to stand too soon after he's just sat down: right now he's clutching a full mug of coffee in one hand and a hard copy of the playlist in the other.) She pauses at the office door and eyeballs the security camera screen, then hits the button on the entryphone. "Yes?" she demands.

"Who's there?" Glenn echoes at her. She ignores him. Looking at the screen, her first reaction is that a pair of Blues Brothers cosplayers are visiting. Two men in black suits and shades stand on the front stoop. One is tall and skinny, the other short and plump: only they've got no hats and no guitars. One of them looks at the camera directly and for an instant she wonders, frightened, if there are eyes behind the Ray-Bans.

The short, fat one holds up a wallet and a badge. "Federal agents. Open up."

They're leading with a badge, not a battering ram, so Gaby buzzes them in. "Feds," she tells Glenn as the door opens.

"Don't give them anything!" he says frantically. *"Fucking FCC . . ."*

The Blues Brothers reach the front desk (which is unattended outside office hours), and walk past it. There's something oddly disjointed about them, as if they're aliens wearing human skin-suits. The tall, thin one addresses Gaby and Glenn: "I am Agent Smith. This is Agent Jones. We are here to observe."

Observe? What? Gaby blinks. She hears a toilet flushing: *Must be Danni.*

"Who are you again?" she asks. "Why are you here?"

"We are from the Department of Homeland Security," says Agent Jones. His voice is flat, affectless, almost robotic. Definitely *Men in Black,* not *Blues Brothers.* "We are here to help you."

"If this is some kind of joke—" Glenn levers himself heavily to his feet, frowning. Gaby takes a step back, worried. Is that bulge in Agent Jones's waistband a roll of fat or a gun?

"We have a warrant." Agent Smith extends a sealed envelope, then contorts his face into an expression that is probably a new kind of smile that was approved after being beta-tested on Martians. "We are here to observe the programming."

"You don't need to be here to do that!" Gaby flusters as Smith advances on Glenn, shoving the envelope in his face. "Why don't you just tune in like everyone else?"

Agent Jones's face points his empty Ray-Bans at her. "We crave authenticity."

Weird, Gaby thinks with a shudder.

"We're not set up for spectators," Glenn warns him. He opens the envelope and reads quickly, swears under his breath, meets Gaby's raised eyebrows with a brief nod. "This looks . . . *fuck.*" He nods at Gaby again. "This is an investigative warrant from the FCC's OIG for the, the Operational Phenomenology Agency? Whatever that is?" To Agent Smith: "I need to fax this to our counsel and my boss immediately. Until I hear back from them you can wait in there." He waves at the break room. "Keep it quiet while we're on-air, they cheaped on the soundproofing in the studio."

"We need to listen—"

"There's a speaker." Gaby points at it. "You get to hear the raw, unlooped feed, no bleeps or anything, before it gets edited and goes to the transmitter. Is that what you want?"

Agents Smith and Jones nod in unison, like a pair of marionettes controlled by the same unseen hand.

Glenn gets on the fax scanner, but they're out of time before there's a reply, so they take their places in the studio. And they're on-air again before she can snap her fingers. "Hello, this is your host Gaby Carson coming to you on WOCZ with tonight's episode of *The Whatever Show* in Crested Butte, Colorado, capitol of high weirdness in America. And we're going to be talking with you about government conspiracies and cover-ups, Men in Black and crashed UFOs in the hills, and who killed Kennedy. With me tonight are Danni and Glenn, and also two Men in Black of our very own, who just served us with a warrant and say they're from the government and they're here to help us. Calls are open, and I'm waiting to hear from you if you've ever seen a UFO, a Man in Black, or a little gray alien here in Crested Butte!"

As Gaby cues up "Meninblack" by The Stranglers, she glances

through the double-glazed window into the break room. Agents Smith and Jones are standing at parade rest, listening expressionlessly to the speaker. She's not sure they're even breathing. Creepy.

"First caller's on line one," Danni says in her headset. "Jim, out near Peanut Lake."

"Caller number one, Jim, you're on air!"

"Howdy, Gaby."

"Jim, isn't it—near Peanut Lake? Have you seen any UFOs or aliens lately? What are your thoughts?"

"Howdy, hi, well it kinda *depends*. They're not the little gray ones and they ain't got no UFOs, but on the ridgeline up by Magic Meadows there's a place where the trees are all flattened outwards in a circle and there's a scorched symbol in the dirt, kinda like a five-pointed star with an *eye* in the middle, like the Brotherhood—"

Glenn is making a throat-cutting gesture so Gaby cuts Jim off. "That's very interesting Jim, moving on, caller number two, hi! Seen any UFOs tonight?"

Behind Glenn's shoulder Gaby notices Agent Smith frowning as he makes notes the old-fashioned way, with a pen on a notepad.

"Hi! It's Billie Jean again!" She's a regular caller, and Gaby relaxes slightly. Billie Jean is reliably kooky but catches on gracefully when her time is up, and she's got a bright, febrile patter that fills the dead air and holds the audience's attention, even if her stories always turn out to be bullshit. Gaby figures she calls because she gets bored. She should really get her own show. "It's funny you mention Men in Black, Gaby, because there's this one guy who always goes everywhere with a bodyguard of Men in Black from the government, only I haven't seen hide nor hair of him on TV or the internet lately? And I was just wondering if he's been abducted by UFOs?"

"That's interesting." *No it isn't.* "Who *is* this mysterious man, Billie Jean?"

"He's the—" Billie Jean falters, her silver tongue momentarily leaden. "He's the Pres-Presi- oh *damn,*" she wails. "I'm sorry! It was on the tip of my tongue! He's really famous and all and he's at the top of the government and everybody has just forgotten him!"

Agent Smith looks at Agent Jones behind the window, and gives him a slight nod, just a dip of the chin. Agent Jones scribbles on his pad attentively.

"So, mysterious government man guarded by Men in Black, kidnapped by UFOs. Men in Black just like the two we've got right here in the office, huh?" Gaby keeps it light to cover Billie Jean's breakdown, but she's fuming: BJ is a reliable two-minute filler before the ads and she just *doesn't* fumble like this.

"Y . . . Yeah, that's right," Billie Jean agrees. Agent Jones leaves the break room, heading for the parking-lot exit.

"But you can't remember what he does. Escort of Men in Black, huh. Are they hunky? Maybe he's the mayor of Pittsburgh," Gaby free-associates. "I once saw him go past in a motorcade out east, with about thirty motorcycle cop outriders and five cruisers, all with their lights lit up. I thought Christmas had come early. But, huh, no sign of the actual UFOs, right? Remember, people, today we're on UFOs, Men in Black, and aliens. Lines are open." She cues up "UFO" by Sneaky Sound System and breathes a shaky sigh of relief.

They get through the next two ad breaks and half a dozen calls without any untoward on-air corpsing by the call-ins, and only one god-botherer, who is good for amusement value for about two minutes—he's quoting scripture, something about Ezekiel and flaming wheels in the sky being the true origins of UFOs. Some time after Billie Jean's call, Agent Jones comes back in, but the two G-Men in the break room mind their own business. Then there's a call to make the blood freeze.

"Hi Gaby, this is Brother Drake." The voice is warm, male, and has a southern twang. Nevertheless something about it sets

Gaby's teeth on edge. "Brother Drake from the Circle of Friends of the Lord of Sleep, with a message about Billie Jean, who called earlier. There is a reason we don't talk about the Man, why we forget we ever heard of the Man, and a message for anyone who thinks talking about the Man is a good idea: get some sleep and you'll find a whole new perspective. No, really, you should take a nap, and if you don't, then at any rate you should keep your lips zipped unless you want to sleep with the fishes like Billie Jean up by Peanut Lake. Don't bleep this out or you'll be next."

The line goes dead.

Gaby gapes slack-jawed at Glenn for a couple of seconds as Glenn frantically loops backwards to dub over the threatening call with the channel signature jingle. "What the effing eff?" Danni swears on the studio circuit. (Self-censorship in the presence of hot mikes is a reflex in this business.)

"We just had a, a . . ." Glenn's face is pale. "Can you handle this on out, Gaby? I need to call the Sheriff's Department. No callers, just playlist and sponsors." He reads her expression. "Don't get creative." He cues up "Dr. Mabuse" by Propaganda, which is obscure and off-format but buys them a good ten minutes.

"I don't like this," Danni bursts out. Her shoulders are shaking. "I, I quit!" A residual sense of professionalism prompts her to add, "After this program, I mean, not right now."

Glenn is dialing the PD. In the break room, Agents Smith and Jones are putting their heads together, conversing in low, urgent tones. This time it's Smith's turn to leave, striding robotically out the door. Gaby, hands shaking, reorders her playlist and pulls in some backup material. Glenn's right: she doesn't trust herself to go live just now, not after receiving a clear death threat with the promise of a body out by the lake. *Who the hell are the Circle of Friends of Sleep?* she frets. *Is this some kind of bad joke?* The remaining Man in Black in the break room stands motionless, like a cockroach in a cheap suit. She surreptitiously pulls out her phone and photographs him, mentally picturing the doge macro she'll post on the show's Facebook page later, when this all blows over—*very sinister, much Kafka, wow*. Assuming it doesn't end up as evidence in a criminal trial.

Fifteen more minutes squirm by before Gaby can cue up the closing sequence. Glenn cuts back over to WOCZ's syndicated programming for the rest of the night, and they're off-air. Gaby pushes back her chair and stands, forcing stiffening limbs into motion. "Well, *that* was different," she says, stretching. "And I don't mean that in a good way. Glenn . . . ?"

"Sheriff's sent a car." He hunches over, looking rough. "I can't believe that . . ."

"I quit! I said I quit, didn't I? I quit!"

Glenn rubs his forehead tiredly. "Nobody's stopping you, Danni, but do you think maybe you can send Mae an email tomorrow morning?" Mae handles HR for the studio. Danni may be an intern but there are still forms to be observed.

A throat-clearing from the doorway catches Gaby's attention. It's Agent Jones, his suit beetle-black, plump as a false widow's abdomen, dark glasses glinting curiously as he looks around the studio.

"You are resigning, yes?" he addresses Danni directly. "Clarify?" His words are halting, as if they must be internally translated from a language other than human before they can be uttered.

"*I* don't *work* here any more!" Danni singsongs as she picks up her daypack and casts the G-Man a poisonous glance. "I'm going home and you can't stop me!"

"Oh, but I *can*." Color creeps into Agent Jones's voice: the heavy indigo velvet of gloating satisfaction. "You were employed by this station during this program." His blindsight gaze sweeps around the room, beaming out a signal of purest malice. "I witnessed you speaking with callers, and recorded you on-air broadcasting un-American propaganda. You are all under arrest."

Back at the safe house in DC, Officer Penrose is nearly dead on his feet, but before he can unload the spoils of his Walmart shopping spree from the pickup, Mattingley waves him into the front room and shuts the door. "Tell me about the gimp suits," Matt says, tight-lipped and standing uncomfortably close.

"I'm—" Sam yawns, his jaw cracking. "Sorry, sir. Gimp suits. Right . . ." He knuckles his eyes, then unloads the contents of his cop-brain, the ever-vigilant observer who rides shotgun behind his senses even when he's too fogged by fatigue to pay conscious attention. Mattingley listens, his long face getting longer the entire time. Finally Sam runs out of recollections of the silver-suited watchers, and Mattingley shakes his head.

"Okay, you've got three hours to sack out right now. Set an alarm for four. Be prepared to move out by four thirty: we've been here too long."

Sam shakes his head. "Sir, if you think I was followed, don't you think we should evac early—"

Mattingley cuts him off. "If you were followed we'd already be dead. So we've got time. Nevertheless, I want us out of here by nightfall." He hesitates. "You're on PPD during the move. If you think you can handle that?"

Sam blinks. His eyelids don't want to reopen. "Sir. I'll need to load up on Provigil again." He fights off another yawn. "Otherwise, I'm good."

"Good man." Mattingley nods approvingly. "Go get some sleep."

Sam doesn't bother to go upstairs to the bunk room. He simply sets the alarm on his phone and lies down on the sofa and closes his eyes. A moment later the alarm goes off and he opens his eyes. It takes his shaking hand several attempts to unlock the phone, stilling the alarm. Three hours have passed. He sits up, punch-drunk, and stumbles to his feet, leaning heavily on the furniture. The front room's door is open and there's a pile of kit bags stacked just outside it. Agents in polo shirts and chinos bustle about, carrying equipment downstairs and out to the SUVs in the front yard. Sam climbs the stairs to the bathroom, uses the toilet, washes up, and splashes water on his face to wake himself. It's a futile gesture. The face looking back at him from the mirror is a decade older than his years. *Pills,* he thinks fuzzily. Someone's left an opened bottle of Provigil on the sink-side, and he raids it ruthlessly, dry-swallowing the tablets. Then he heads for the bunk room to get ready for his shift on personal protection duty.

PPD requires a ballistic vest, a sidearm, a windbreaker or similar jacket to conceal the equipment, and more consciousness than Sam can currently muster, even after three hours' sleep—the most he's had in a week. He checks his Sig Sauer carefully before he holsters it, wondering who Officer Mattingley wants him to guard.

The house is buzzing as the seven men and four women of the Secret Service team move their gear out to two F-150 crew-cab trucks and two armored Escalades. Mal is up on the roof with a Barrett, standing watch. Sam shoulders a couple of kit bags (keeping his right arm free) and hauls them over the second Escalade's tailgate, then turns to go back. There's a stranger standing just inside the front door, looking out at the activity with an odd expression. Crow's feet at the edges of his eyelids, salt-and-pepper hair tending towards white, once neatly cropped but now growing slightly wild. He seems to be a well-preserved sixty, tall and lean. Something about the way he holds himself signals that he's used to being the center of attention. Sam is instantly on guard. "Hello." He nods.

The stranger gives him an avuncular smile. "Hello, Sam. Forgotten me again?"

Sam blinks. *Something* about this man is screamingly familiar, as if he's known him half his adult life . . . "Arthur?" he guesses.

"Very good." Arthur nods approvingly, like a paramedic checking a car-crash victim for signs of concussion. "Matt says you and Sylvia are my shadows this afternoon. Can you remember anything about me? Anything at all? From last time, maybe?"

Anything about . . . Arthur. *Arthur.* "You're OSCAR," Sam dredges up from somewhere. OSCAR is Arthur's Secret Service codename. The SS assigns these names to the people they provide bodyguard details for, the really high-ranking senior politicians like the, the—Sam frowns. The word is at the tip of his tongue. "I'm sorry, sir, it's the, uh, hostiles messing with me again."

Arthur nods. "You'll remember more as you get woke," he reassures Sam. "The geas sinks its fangs into you while you sleep, but you'll be okay." He glances at the Escalade. "You think we're about loaded up?"

"I'll go check, sir. If you'd step away from the front." Without quite knowing why, Sam finds that he's standing between OS-CAR and the open doorway, scanning the drive, his right hand hovering just inside his open jacket.

Senior Officer Mattingley clears his throat. "Let's move out, people. The next safe house is waiting for us, we can be there in forty minutes if we leave now."

Sam and Officer Sylvia Haas lead Arthur out to the second Escalade and sit to either side of him, as Officers Murphy and Cho clamber up in front. Sam feels extremely rough, but at least he's no longer hallucinating. Also, he has a feeling that being PPD for OS-CAR is *really* important, not just a senator or congressman—he's something else. The word stubbornly refuses to come to his tongue. Something powerful and symbolic, like the Stars and Stripes or the Pledge of Allegiance. This is an important job, that—

"Any word from the First Lady?" asks Arthur.

"Nothing to pass on," says Sylvia, "but her team's status canary is still green. We'd know within a couple of hours if anything happened to them."

Arthur sighs unhappily. Another jigsaw puzzle piece slots into place as Sam realizes with a twinge that the First Lady is important to him, and that Arthur hasn't seen her any more recently than Sam has seen Jenna, Brad Jr., and Kyle—*the First Lady is his* wife, *the wife of the*—

Sam shakes his head as Murphy starts the engine, then settles back to keep watch.

"All good, eh?" asks Arthur.

"You can depend on us, Mr. President," says Cho, as the convoy moves out, making haste to move on to a new safe house. "We'll keep you safe."

[Transcript of PowerPoint presentation delivered to private-sector stakeholders.]

CLASSIFIED: SECRET NOFORN OPA GODWAKER

[Slide 1]

- Welcome to the Operational Phenomenology Agency
- Defending the USA against alien threats since 1929
- Now integrating proactively with NSA, NRO, Homeland Security to deliver a Safer Republic

[Slide 2]

The Threat

- Iterated computation has direct and indirect side effects on the structure of reality
- Too much thinking → attracts alien intelligences/ computational feeders
- Historic origins of "spells" and "demons"

[Slide 3]

Examples of Weaponized Magic

- Curses, geases, bindings, summonings, containment grids, sacrifices
- Ritual magicians are susceptible to K syndrome
- (Computers are not)

[Slide 4]

We Are Not Alone

- Zombies: origin, invocation, containment, and binding

- Vampires: origin, containment, binding, and feeding
- Non-human species co-resident in Earth's lithosphere and abyssal regions
- Alien hominids from elsewhere in the metaverse

[Slide 5]
The Singularity
- Moore's Law: computing ⟺ thinking
- Exponential up-slope, no end in sight
- Big Data: "The Cloud" is Hell (literally)

[Slide 6]
Necromantic Cosmology and Existential Anthropic Threats
- Alien Gods are Existential Anthropic Threats
- Summon the *wrong* one and humanity ceases to exist
- But we are here (so no alien forerunners in our universe have made that mistake, so far)
- Summon the *right* one and we can keep the wrong ones out

[Slide 7]
The Elder Gods—part 1
- Emergent climax ecosystems of an ancient alien singularity, or Satanic Creation?

Either way, they're bad for humanity (and un-Christian)
- Historically, worshipped as a pantheon
- Mystery cults persist into the present day
- Establishing toeholds on Earth as the Computational Singularity looms

[Slide 8]

The Elder Gods—part 2

- Our enemies:
  - ❑ **N'yar Lat-Hotep** ("The Black Pharaoh")
    Has taken over the UK, is active in Australia,
    Middle East, North Korea
  - ❑ **Czernobog**
    Slavic/Russian mystery cults, extensive
    infiltration of KGB, possible Kremlin links
  - ❑ **H'astur**
    Not obviously active (yet)
  - ❑ **The Sleeper**
    - ▪ Worshipped as Jesus by the Church of the
      Golden Promise
    - ▪ Partially awakened but failed to fully revive in
      2014
    - ▪ Threat level: high

[Slide 9]

The Elder Gods—part 3

- Our allies:
  - ❑ **Dread Cthulhu**
    - ▪ Currently sleeping
    - ▪ Pledged to the service of the OPA by His
      priesthood
    - ▪ **Full immanentization requirements are
      costly:**
    - ▪ In excess of 10^9 directed human sacrifices
      (simple genocide is insufficient)
    or
    - ▪ Successful deployment and activation
      of PROJECT GODWAKER orbital
      hypercomputer

[Slide 10]

PROJECT GODWAKER

- Variable-inclination orbital swarm of > 4,294,967,296 invocation nodes
- Invocation node: solar-powered neurocomputing node manufactured in orbit from Lunar regolith
- High-bandwidth quantum-encrypted prayer links for peer-to-peer summoning coordination
- Hyperdimensional Dho-Na curve geometry supported by breakthrough in deep neural-network systems

[Slide 11]

Launching PROJECT GODWALKER: Requirements

- HLV Capability: Falcon Heavy *or* NASA SLS required for > 370 tons into Lunar orbit (20 launch minimum)
- Deployment of Lunar Space Elevator (PROJECT MOONSTALK) from L1 to Lunar south pole
- Deployment of > 1GW of photovoltaic panels in L1 to power and provision GODWALKER Surface Installation (est. weight: 1000 tons)
- Deployment of Phase 1 Von Neumann robot factory to Shackleton Crater (est. 2000 tons)
- Shackleton to L1 lift of GODWALKER nodes into orbit via ascender

[Slide 12]

PROJECT GODWAKER Time Frame

- Development of Heavy Lunar Surface Engineering capability
  - 2–3 years
- Development of Phase 1 Von Neumann factory
  - Ongoing

- Design of GODWAKER node block 1 spacecraft
  - 15–30 months
- Fabrication of L1 solar power station
  - 9–30 months

[Slide 13]
PROJECT GODWAKER Budget
- Maximum wartime priority—see Manhattan Project, Apollo Program
- Initial $120Bn allocation for FY2015 (approved unanimously by Congress and Senate)
- FY2016 allocation to be decided (will be approved unanimously)
- CBO Assent: unconditionally granted
- Enabling Act to permit conscription of any necessary resources (approved unanimously by Congress)

[Slide 14]
Ph'nglui mglw'nafh Cthulhu R'lyeh wgah'nagl fhtagn
All Hail the New Flesh!

Meanwhile, in London:

In the middle of the table sits a rotary-dial telephone. It's almost a century old, made of wood and brass and bearing the royal crest of King George V's Post Office. A separate speaking horn hangs from a hook on its side, connected to its polished case by a very modern wire-wrapped cable (clearly a recent repair). The telephone is not connected to a wall jack. It sits on the conference table in the middle of a complex double ward, two concentric Möbius loops that glow silvery blue and eat the perspective of everything within, so that the phone's boxy construction seems like a three-dimensional shadow cast by an object in a higher-dimensional realm.

This is the hot line. Formerly stored in a secure vault under the New Annex, it is now installed in the White Drawing Room at Number 10 Downing Street. The Prime Minister's staff meeting room is the demesne of Iris Carpenter: former Active Ops Manager in the Laundry, then prison inmate, and most recently, the Prime Minister's High Priestess and Chief of Staff.

Iris sits by the telephone, flanked on her left by the man who consigned her to prison for six years (no grudges are held: their relationship was and is *complex*), and on the right by a former subordinate, still *technically* a subordinate, possessed of terrifying power (and, thankfully, a degree of maturity he lacked back in the day). "Well, this is a pretty pass," she mutters to herself, and wipes her palms on her trousers. "What do you think, Michael? James?"

"It's Bob, not James," the body on her right grunts resentfully. "I know what you're thinking, and you're wrong. I'm infinitely more human than those fuckers."

"Language, Mr. Howard," chides the Senior Auditor.

"Okay already!" Bob's voice rises. "I *don't like* them," he adds apologetically. "They give me the willies." He crosses his arms tightly, almost hugging his shoulders. "Brrr." Most of the people in this building wear business suits; Bob wears a hoodie and combat pants, but nobody dares give him any flak. *They give* you *the creeps?* Iris thinks rhetorically: *Have you looked in a mirror?*

The Senior Auditor snorts. "I'm sure they don't like your face either, Bob, but that's the whole reason you're here, isn't it?"

Bob grunts. "It's *so* nice to be wanted for my sparkling personality and scintillating conversation. Although, isn't this room—" he gestures at the doors leading to the Terracotta Room— "adequately warded?"

"It's more than warded. The PM saw to the protections on Downing Street in person as soon as He moved in," Iris reassures him. The SA gives her a sidelong look. "It's not as secure as the new eyrie will be when it's converted, but needs must." The legacy architecture of Downing Street can't be protected from occult attack as effectively as a steel-framed skyscraper, which is why the New Management will be moving into the penthouse of the Shard once it has been converted. But converting the tallest skyscraper in Europe into an occult fortress takes a lot of work, and (figurative) sacrifices must be made in the meantime. Which is why Iris can't even have a quiet phone chat with her opposite number in North America without bringing the Eater of Souls along as metaphysical muscle.

Not that she's happy with Bob. Iris still hasn't forgiven him for unintentionally massacring most of her congregation, cocking up a *very important* summoning which might have shaved four years off the critical path to the New Management, and always being late with his timesheets. But they're on the same team now, working to a common shared goal, and a big part of good management is knowing how to work with what you've got. So she indulges his little snits for now. There'll be time to make adjustments later, once His Majesty's rule is secure.

She considers the Senior Auditor in turn. The SA is potentially even more dangerous than the Eater of Souls, and he has played the Svengali to her Trilby for many years. He, too, is supposedly on the same team—indeed, he was instrumental in striking the devil's bargain that made the team possible in the first place. But he hides his deadly light behind the guise of an amiable old don, collegiate and tweedy. It's never easy to be sure what he's thinking. "Dr. Armstrong?" she asks.

"Ready to proceed when you are, Mrs. Carpenter," he says gravely.

Iris takes a deep breath, picks up the speaking horn, and enters a three-digit number on the antique rotary dial.

"This is Downing Street. We're ready to talk to the Directors. They're expecting this call."

For long seconds there is nothing on the line but faint white noise. Then Iris hears a voice—or rather, the absence of static, speech modulating the sound of silence to convey information. *"This is the Director's office. You can hang up now."* The crypt-voice disappears: after a few seconds of mundane line noise she hangs up.

The summoning grid connected to the phone's base energizes. The far wall of the formal drawing room fades into a misty void stippled with pinpricks of un-light. A conference table limned in smoke takes shape, with three suited figures arrayed along the far side. Their faces are indistinct, but not in the same manner as the Prime Minister's visage, which memory refuses to grasp: in their case, smudges of darkness outline the presence of features too indistinct to see in the first place.

"Good, ah, afternoon," says the figure in the middle, a languid roll of one bony wrist suggesting a glance at a watch. Her voice—the pitch is feminine—is mellifluous and warm. "I am the new Deputy Director. With me are Operations Director Black and Senior Agent Green. To whom do I have the pleasure of speaking?"

Iris keeps her face expressionless, even though she is aware that the hotline of the damned renders her and her companions' features as bland and unmemorable as those of their counterparts. "Good morning, Deputy Director. I am the Prime Minister's Chief of Staff. With me today are two representatives of your counterpart agency: the Senior Auditor, and a Special Assistant to the Director of Operations." She uses no names, even though the Deputy Director certainly knows who they are. The bound entities that provide this hotline service can find uses for an imprudently uttered name. "You wanted to talk?"

The Deputy Director is disconcerted. "I was expecting my opposite number. An agency-level officer, not executive branch."

Iris resists the impulse to smile. The hotline is metaphysical, not electronic, and immune to interception by normal means—also, it resists recording. But it has certain drawbacks. It interprets intent, rather than transmitting speech directly, and it has a bad tendency to distort emotional color or facial expressions. They are either ignored completely, or morphed into something terrifying and abhuman, like a shadow show projected on the wall of Plato's cave by a projectionist with strangely articulated claws instead of hands.

"There have been some changes to the line of command," Iris says blandly. "Melting stovepipes are quite the 'in' thing this year. In particular, the Prime Minister has *personally* assumed control over the agency. Unlike your presidency, which—"

She stops. The projected image of the Deputy Director's head has split open vertically from top to bottom, revealing a raw and bloody skull with unusual dentition, almost as if her flesh is a shriveling seed pod for her skeleton. Clearly some emotional nuance has been mistranslated. After a moment the edges of the bloody wound begin to ravel themselves together, from the bottom up. "Please do not mention that title again, or I will be forced to terminate this call," the Deputy Director says primly, once her lips and palate have reassembled themselves and her canines have retracted. While her voice has the flatness and lack of affect characteristic of the link, her words quiver with rage.

Interesting. Iris allows herself a faint smile, knowing that the Deputy Director can't see it. Bob stares at their adversaries with the intensity of a hawk. On her other side, Dr. Armstrong frowns, but keeps his insights private. "*You* asked to speak to us," Iris says. "What exactly do you want?"

"Dialog." The Deputy Director shrugs, an exaggerated gesture, almost burlesque, immune to malign mistranslation. "There has been a marked decline in communication and collaboration between our organizations over the past year, and this hasn't been good for anybody."

That's putting it mildly. Occult operations were not included in the UK-USA intelligence sharing treaty of 1945, and over the decades an unhealthy rivalry developed between the Black Chamber and its various European OCCINT counterparts. After the turn of the millennium, relations deteriorated to the point of open hostility. In the view of the Laundry's executive oversight tier and expert practitioners—Mahogany Row—the Americans' Operational Phenomenology Agency has been taken over by the eldritch horrors it is supposed to hold in check, in the most disastrous case of regulatory capture ever. But from the perspective of the Nazgûl, the Laundry is the lapdog of a hostile alien god.

"Let us set aside recriminations and the apportionment of blame for a joint subcommittee to chew over, shall we? I believe a case can be built that mistakes were made on both sides. What is important is that we keep lines of communication open. The Ancient Ones are rising from their sleep of ages. We have a common interest in the survival of the human species, and it's detrimental to that survival if we work at cross-purposes."

Operations Director Black straightens upright and declaims: "We are aware of your recent problems with Pastor Schiller and his inner temple. Schiller went rogue: your problems could have been avoided, if you had come to us—"

If looks could kill, Bob's death-glare would cause Operations Director Black to spontaneously combust. The Senior Auditor, usually imperturbable, gives Black a chilly stare. Beneath the table, Iris's hands clench into fists. She forces herself to take a deep breath before she responds. "Perhaps if you refrain from insulting our competence it would be easier to find common ground," she observes. Not adding: *We know Schiller was working for you.* "Again: What is this really about, Deputy Director?"

"Intelligence sharing. Forces outside our control are at work on all fronts. Our response . . . to the coming crisis may regrettably be too little, too late. Factionalism and internal disputes weaken our ability to respond effectively. The . . . executive entity . . . you referred to earlier is currently outside our control, and we fear that a rival faction may acquire it and use it as a focus for a hostile zero-day offensive."

Is he talking about the US President? Iris thinks frustratedly. "What kind of zero-day offensive?" she asks.

"A focus for the will-to-believe of a third of a billion humans is no small thing," intones Senior Agent Green. "If the chief . . . executive . . . falls into the wrong hands, they will become a sacrificial dagger held to the throat of a nation." Her speech sounds almost pained when she utters the word *executive*.

Bob bristles for a moment, then finally explodes. "You don't know where he is? You've fucking *lost* him?"

Agent Green recoils. "I would not put it so strongly—"

The Deputy Director raises a spectral limb. "That is not as much of an overstatement as one may wish."

Dr. Armstrong nods. "Rest assured that if we locate your missing *President,* we shall be sure to let you know."

It warms the cockles of Iris's heart to see the way the Nazgûl twitch when the SA utters the title, and brings joy to her soul to note his carefully ambiguous phrasing. She beams at them, deliberately courting a malicious misrepresentation of her expression. "Yes, indeed," she affirms. "And if it leads to a resumption of cordial relations between our two powers, so much the better for everyone, yes? In fact, there's a lot to be gained by everyone from cooperation. Perhaps we could share our lists of what we stand to gain, by way of motivation?" The Deputy Director's shade is nodding. "You could call off these, ah, *unhelpful* attempts at imposing a capitative change on our government, and we could, in return, shelve any plans for a robust response, which would in any case be a tiresomely expensive diversion from our real mission."

The Deputy Director's shade is no longer nodding. "I think that we would, ah, find such a proposal very welcome indeed, and I will convey it to the steering committee at once, if that is indeed a formal proposition on your part." Iris nods. "Perhaps we should move forward by scheduling one of these chats on a regular basis—perhaps weekly? I think it helps enormously to clear the air, don't you? We could even prepare an agenda for our next call."

"Yes," Iris agrees. "That sounds like an idea I can get right behind." A pause. "As for your comment about internal factionalism, I am aware that your government has many agencies with conflicting agendas. We can make allowances. But we do have a pressing concern, which is, whose agenda overrides all others in your agency? The OPA disagreeing with the NSA and the State Department is all very well, but do your various internal departments all answer to the same oath-holder?"

"Oh yes." The Deputy Director nods emphatically. "We do. I am quite sure of it." She reaches across the spectral table towards an invisible telephone. "I look forward to our next conversation, Mrs. Carpenter." And the hotline session ends.

"*Bitch,*" Bob hisses, nailing Iris's mood, if not her preferred phrasing. He glances at her. "She cut us off deliberately, didn't she?"

"I'd say so." The Senior Auditor pulls out a white cotton handkerchief and dabs at his forehead. It comes away stippled with red.

"I suppose, coming from our friends in the Black Chamber, that sort of parting shot is not unexpected," Iris hisses between gritted teeth. She yanks up the cuffs of her jacket and tugs off the knotted bracelets of human skin tied around her wrists. They sputter and smoke as she drops them in her empty teacup. "Damn them."

Bob squints at the smoking ward-fetishes. "Cute," he says. Then to the Senior Auditor: "Bluff, or double-bluff?"

"Time will tell." Dr. Armstrong stares pensively at some inner vista.

"People," Iris says crisply, ignoring the first-degree burns on her wrists. "What did we learn? What did we disclose?"

"They want us to think they're in charge," Bob says, almost automatically. "That they've got a unitary command authority. But"—his gaze sharpens—"the Deputy Director is new. And she was surprised to get you."

The Senior Auditor nods. "And you know what that means. There's been an internal power transfer and they haven't got—

or they want us to think they haven't got—their feet fully under the table yet. So we're still in time . . ."

Dear diary: Rewind a week.

Recall that this is a posthumous confession. If you are reading it, I should be beyond embarrassment. Even the New Management can't do worse than Restoration-era judicial practices, like digging up Cromwell's head and sticking it on a pike years after his death. Symbolism counts for a lot among the living, but if you're already dead you're beyond caring. (Don't argue, I'd like to keep my illusions.)

I, Mhari Murphy, am loyal to the government of the United Kingdom. However, I'm not a blinkered fanatic or an idiot. A government is a vast, intricate machine whose components are people and which is controlled by code—legal code. Most employees spend a fair amount of their time pursuing their own personal agendas, and although "do the job, collect the paycheck" is usually high on their list, it's seldom the only item. There is endless scope for backbiting, rivalry, and internecine feuding and plotting. Perhaps it's my HR background speaking, but sometimes it seems to me that that's *all* that ever happens. My job was just to repair or replace the damaged components of the human machine when the gears started to grind. Now, at a slightly higher level, it's my job to help debug the programs—the legal code—that keep my chunk of the machinery running smoothly. Which would be a fuck of a lot easier without rivals trying to break things, wouldn't it?

Now, any government with a unitary executive—such as the New Management—is susceptible to courtiers who use their privilege of access to the royal ear to settle scores with rivals. The PM is of course fully aware of this *at all times*. But it may serve His purposes to let others—those who haven't quite realized how far beyond the merely human He is—believe that He isn't, and to permit them to think they can manipulate Him for personal advantage. Sociopaths battling for territory are more highly motivated to excellence if they are terrified of being taken down by their rivals, just as ordinary people are motivated by hope of a reward if their work exceeds the requirements of duty.

In short, although we all serve the same Dread Majesty, we don't automatically march in lockstep. Which is partly why I'm recording this: by way of insurance, and to ensure that I don't go to hell without an honor guard.

Last Wednesday evening, I entertained Dr. Armstrong with dinner in the Lords' Dining Room, and afterwards we had a little chat inside the big containment ward in Persephone's attic.

"Obviously I can't tell you anything that will compromise you," he said, with one of those amiable smiles of his that admit to no discomfort at being trapped in a pocket universe four meters in diameter with a hungry vampire, "but you should be aware that it's fractal contingency plans all the way down."

"That's nice to know." I smiled back at him.

"The trouble is, the oppo also have contingency plans. And informers." His smile faded. "We have met the enemy, and they is us."

I shook my head. "Which opposition are we talking about here? The Nazgûl, or the Cult?" We both understood this to be the Cult of the Black Pharaoh, the Prime Minister's brownshirts: fanatical loyalists from back before his rise to power. Some of them have made good in the New Management—Iris was a High Priestess of the Cult and went to prison for it, prior to her rehabilitation and promotion to Chief of Staff—but others remain problematic. They've taken the ascendency of the Mandate as their own imprimatur to steal anything that isn't nailed down and cut the throat of anyone who gets in the way—on an energized sacrificial grid, of course, so the necromantic mojo flows up to Himself. (They think this will buy His indulgence. They might even be right.)

"Both, but the American OPA comes first. Make no mistake, the Nazgûl are our biggest threat right now. They've had years to turn the continental internet backhaul into conductors for a gigantic geas, and they've used it to impose amnesia on their own population's symbolic occult focus. The presidency was originally modeled on the eighteenth-century British king-emperor's powers, which can in turn be traced back to the Roman imperial cult—the *genius* of the emperor, in the original meaning of the word 'genius,' referred to his power as a begetter and supervisory spirit, a godlike being. So we're talking about someone who is revered as an emperor by over three hundred million people . . ." He trailed off, lost in thought.

"It's not news to me that the President of the United States is important." I nudged him. "But why make everybody forget him?"

"Because it creates a god-sized occult power vacuum. They're building a machine to awaken—to call—his replacement, and it's a lot easier to install a new deity if the old one has gone missing."

"This is that Sleeper business again, isn't it? Schiller's patron?"

Dr. Armstrong sighed, so deeply that it almost came out as a groan. "I wish it were! There are many sleeping gods. The one the Nazgûl are trying to immanentize is . . . well, it's another class-six entity, like the PM. Or rather, like the puppeteer pulling the strings behind the PM's face—the one who hasn't fully arrived yet, but is busy building His nest and incubating His eggs. *It's*. Whatever—gender is meaningless in this case. We probably can't stop the Nazgûl from carrying out Project Godwaker, but we can make it a lot harder for them to do it if we break this geas, and it'll be vastly easier to crack the geas if we have the willing cooperation of the actual President."

"This Project Godwaker," I said carefully. "Am I permitted to ask how we know about it?"

"Ah-hmm, yes, a good point. Yes, you can ask." Which I took to mean that I shouldn't.

"All right, then let me see if I've got this straight. The mission to Colorado Springs is some kind of diversion or a side-quest, because we already know, by means I have no need to know of, that the Nazgûl don't yet have their very own elder god. And therefore the PM's little joke about kidnapping the President of the United States, is, is . . ."

"Not a joke at all." His fey smile slipped out.

"But that's—isn't kidnapping a foreign head of state an act of war?"

"Correct! Which is why you're not going to kidnap the President. You're going to convince him that it is in the best interests of his nation to cooperate with you to lift the geas, and offer him all necessary assistance, including political asylum if he wants it. But if anything goes wrong—"

"The PM's hands are clean," I said, slotting it all into place. "Huh. But. Hmm. What about the Vice-President? I know they have a continuity of government arrangement in case the President is compromised or resigns—"

"Or if he dies, yes. But they can't remove a living President from office without impeachment by Congress, or proceeding in accordance with the Twenty-fifth Amendment, which requires their cabinet and VP to take action, at which point they revert to the existing rules of succession. None of which can happen unless they drop the amnesia field."

"Neat," I said, admiring. This is a problem I know. It's like that embarrassing situation where you find a VP in Finance with their fingers in the candy jar up to the elbow, to the tune of a couple billion in unwise leveraged options, but you can't prosecute them or fire them without admitting that your assets are down to pocket lint and pencil shavings, thereby triggering a run on your bank. Perversely, the worst kind of misconduct is the hardest for an organization to admit to.

"So . . ." I say, "if the POTUS is willing to cooperate, we can use him to crack the geas and drastically weaken the OPA, thereby advancing our own interests, plus the US government owes us one—insofar as they ever admit to owing anybody anything, at any rate. And if he won't cooperate, well, nothing ventured, nothing gained. If the OPA find out we're paddling in their pool our excuse is to point at Colorado and shriek. Right?"

"Right." Dr. Armstrong nodded.

"But." I frowned. "This whole plan relies on them not having the President on lockdown. What about the Vice-President?"

"They've got her already," Dr. Armstrong said grimly. "It looks very much as if they only missed the top dog by accident."

"Ah." I've suddenly got a sinking feeling. "And if they find him working with us—"

"—If the President dies, the constitutional succession rules take over, and the Nazgûl are back in control of the situation." The SA pinned me with a flat stare, like a bug on a display tray. "Which is why, once you make contact with the President, you need to extract him by the fastest possible means. If you don't they'll kill him—and blame you."

5: ON DEATH GROUND

The landscape around Colorado Springs looks alien and other-worldly to British eyes. Mountains soar preposterously high into the blue yonder, wearing a shawl of snow most of the year round. The altitude of the gentle, sloping plateau that defines a local ground level is higher than the highest peak in the British Isles. Suburbs exist in name only. Back home they'd qualify as rough countryside, with houses spaced so far apart that you can't see one from its neighbor, towns that are barely a short run of "historic" shops and buildings, and "Founded in 1906" written on sign boards without apparent conscious irony.

Pete and Brains approach their destination close to lunchtime on the second day, having broken the journey overnight in a motel in North Platte. That morning they drove a little over a hundred miles along US 85. Five miles short of the US Air Force Academy, they reach the turn-off leading to the compound of Golden Promise Ministries, near Palmer Lake.

Pete is driving again as Brains fidgets with his thaumospectral analyzer. The road is steep, winding, and alarmingly narrow. "Wish I'd brought my bike," Pete observes, as he brakes hard to keep the Escalade from lurching drunkenly as it corners.

"You and me both." Brains frowns. "There's no contamination here, all my readings are showing is thaumic background." He taps the project box that holds the guts of his instrument. "Nobody's summoned anything here in, well, ages."

Pete drives on slowly. After a few miles they come to an abandoned gatehouse. Driving past the raised barrier they eventually come to a compound like the residential quarters of an army base. Rows of houses, barracks, chapel, warehouses, a building cryptically identified on their map as "spinal injuries/forced maternity ward." The windows are dark, and there are no parked vehicles. Drifts of last year's dirty snow obstruct the side-streets. "This place is abandoned," says Brains.

"And that's a very good thing." Pete pulls up outside the building that is flagged as a chapel. "Coming?"

"Aw, must I?" Brains releases his seat belt and clambers down from the SUV, analyzer in hand.

Ten minutes of walking around in the cold convinces both of them that the compound is abandoned. The analyzer stubbornly insists there's no active thaum flux present, just a higher-than-background level of decay events: magical fallout from previous years. Up close, there are signs of neglect: peeling paint, broken window panes, seedling trees pushing through cracks in the sidewalk. "Abandoned in place," Pete affirms. "One last thing."

Pete walks over to the medical building and tries the front door. The handles are chained together and held by a padlock, now rusting. He bends his head and stands in silence for a minute, then walks back over to the Escalade. Once in the driver's seat he sits motionless, lost in thought.

"What?" Brains asks eventually.

"'Seph told me about that place. Asked me to take a look. I'd say it's abandoned. Wouldn't you?"

"Yes. What is it?"

Pete shakes his head. "Don't ask." He starts the engine and begins to turn the big SUV around. As they head towards the exit checkpoint he relents. "I like to think that there's lots of good stuff in the Bible. Advice and ideas that can help us lead a better life. But it's a mixed bag. Parts of it don't fit, other parts seem to be borrowed from other religions, or written in the third century. Then there's the bad stuff. Cults who add their own apocrypha and outright fakes to scripture. You've got to exercise careful judgement, lest you follow a road signposted for heaven and wind up in hell." He shakes his head. "Schiller's people took that turn: they enthusiastically embraced evil in the name of love. But you know what they say about the wages of sin."

And that's all he'll say until they're in Colorado Springs.

"Next stop, the Universal Life Church," Brains reads from his phone's memo pad. "Where's that?"

"Put it in the satnav," Pete says tiredly. "Let's get this over with."

They drive along ruler-straight highways that crawl across a sloping plain, passing vast shed-like buildings spaced infinitely far apart, past fences and ornamental walls and the occasional strip mall. Eventually they come to a wall punctuated by driveways that lead to a demolition site. A chain-link fence bars access, and a forbidding sign looms above it: CONSTRUCTION SITE. Brains checks his instrument. "Too hot to mess around with, but it's all decay products. Nothing active here," he announces. "Let's go."

A guard in a rent-a-cop uniform is slouching towards them as Pete backs and turns the Escalade. He buzzes his window down: "Wrong turn!" he shouts. The guard shrugs and waves them off towards the main street.

They're taking a lunch break in a diner beneath the oppressive sky, when Brains's phone emits an urgent turkey-gobbling sound, pauses for dramatic effect, and repeats the squawk. "That's odd," he says, frowning.

"What is it?"

"Message from the DC office."

"What—"

"Give me a minute to decrypt." Brains's temper is short and Pete's usual good humor is strained, so they sit in moody silence while Brains unpicks the meaning of the message. "Right," he says to himself, then a moment later, "Right" again.

Pete bites his lip.

"We're to pick up a passenger," Brains finally says. "Late addition, another team member. They flew into Albuquerque this morning, and they're currently on a Greyhound bus. We're to stand by for further instructions about a local job. After which we're to go to DC."

"What?" Pete's patience finally boils over: "But that's nearly two thousand miles!"

"If there are three of us and we take turns driving we should be able to do it in a couple of days," Brains says doubtfully. "Allow four hours a day for meals, showers, and toilet breaks? We could do it in two days, if we average fifty miles per hour."

"If they could fly into Albuquerque, why the devil can't we fly out that way?" Pete stares at the wreckage of a burger and tater tots on the plate before him. "And what's this about a local job? I give up. Anyway, aren't you kind of assuming that they expect us to drive?"

"Well, yes . . . ?" Then Brains sits up, a dangerous glint in his eye. "What else could they have in mind?"

"Don't ask." Pete shudders. "If there's one thing the past year's taught me, it's that things can always get worse."

The female *alfär* mage is having *fun*.

At least, Yarisol *thinks* she's having fun. It's difficult to be certain of such things—she doesn't have much experience to draw on. She *should* be having fun, if she were like everyone else, or at least she should be experiencing the absence of not-fun, because she's not trapped in the camp any more. The camp was comfortably predictable, from the bad weather and the locked cell doors to the petty cruelty. (Cruelty from the warrior caste towards anyone whose face didn't work properly, placid contempt from the other magi, sneers from the *urük* soldiers guarding the camp.) But she didn't know differently before. Now she's sharing her head with the distilled extract of Jonquil the party girl, and it's all *terribly* confusing.

Jonquil is the daughter of the High Priestess of the God-emperor who has lately usurped power over this *urük* kingdom. She aspires to high rank herself, riding the coat-tails of privilege. But her thought processes and memories feel oddly *wrong* to Yarisol.

Jonquil obsesses over facial expressions and appearances, and recognizes nuances of emotional color in speech that completely elude Yarisol. Jonquil finds it easy to read minds and intent. It's like the *urük* woman glides across a social ice rink where Yarisol finds only broken ground that crumbles beneath her feet.

But Jonquil is also deeply, maddeningly stupid. She can no more grasp the essence of *mana*, formulate macros, or compose spell-sonnets than a brightly painted parrot could. At best all she's good for is repeating cantrips, and pretending to understand the true knowledge that comes as easily as breathing to Yarisol.

Jonquil likes clothes and men and is at home in *urük* society, but she's essentially a people person. All she's good at is manipulating victims. Yarisol, in contrast, finds humans—*alfär* and *urük* alike—enigmatic and baffling obstacles, although she can warp reality and melt flesh with a gesture. If she can turn Jonquil's preposterous hypersocialization to her own ends, she'll be unstoppable.

But first she has to get past Jonquil's mother, the High Priestess.

Iris, Jonquil's mother, has summoned her to a breakfast meeting in *Downing Street*. She is due to fly out of *Heathrow* only three hours later. These are places of some differing significance to Jonquil, and the clash of requirements throws Yarisol's executive dysfunction into high relief: Wear formal robes for her presentation before the throne of the All-Highest, or dress for comfort on a long-haul flight? In the end she lets Jonquil bubble to the surface for long enough to settle on a trouser suit and comfortable flats, plus heavy sunscreen. She hands her carry-on luggage to the bemused police officers at the door. "I am on my way to the airport after this meeting?" she explains, forcing herself to meet the hulking *urük* guard's gaze directly and phrase every statement as a question. "You can guard this for me?" She gives him a little push with her will, then enters the lair of the lich-king.

The High Priestess is chatting in the break room with a handful of skinny, intense-looking youngsters whose minds feel juicy and weak. Jonquil is tempted to snack, but forces herself to wait. The *urük* mage's people have provided her with a vial of fresh blood which she carries in her pocket. She intends to consume it at the last possible moment before she passes through airport security. After all, she has no idea when she'll be able to get a meal in the Western Empire.

Iris looks up. "Morning, dear!" She stands, and Yarisol takes a moment to dredge up the appropriate reaction from Jonquil's memories. She air-smooches, millimeters away from Iris's face. "You're looking rather smart this morning."

Yarisol pulls up the right self-deprecating expression from her shadow's muscle memory. Her face aches with the effort of half-smiling while concealing her teeth: a glamour will only get you so far. "Got to keep up appearances, Mumsy?! Flight to catch, special priority lane and all that?"

"Yes. About that . . ." Iris searches her face for some insight, then abruptly turns and presents Jonquil with a china cup of coffee, made exactly the way her daughter likes it. (Yarisol, who *hates* coffee, forces herself to take an appreciative sip.) "Makeup?"

Yarisol wails in a corner of her head, but Jonquil thinks on her feet: "Got to hit a TV studio on the way to the airport, Mhari positively *insisted*, it's a stupid last-minute scheme of hers to fake some digital point-to-point traffic to confuse the . . . listeners?"

It's a terrifyingly thin excuse, but it seems to satisfy her not-mother, who nods. "Good. And you're quite clear on our objectives?"

"You can rely on me?!" Jonquil drops the bright and bubbly tone slightly, allowing the obsidian edge of her commitment to show. Her mother's eyes harden approvingly. "The sacrifice will be retrieved? The traitors will reap their reward?!"

"Excellent." Iris smiles at the face-stealing mage who wears the features of her daughter, evidently not suspecting that the real Jonquil lies mute and stunned in Yarisol's cell, in the prison camp on Dartmoor. She stands. "Before you go, His Majesty asked after you." She flicks an imaginary piece of lint from her daughter's lapel. "It's a great honor and I don't want you to disgrace me. Come along now!"

Her five minutes alone with the denizen of Number 10 threatens to make her late, but rank has privileges: Jonquil is whisked off to Heathrow in the back of a blue-light-flaring police car. Consequently she arrives early, breezes through the pre-clear queue with hand luggage only, and flies into the west aboard a British Airways airliner. It is her first trip aboard an *urük* sky-cart, and it is both delightfully strange and disturbingly half-familiar to her. She drinks the free whisky in business class, becomes giggly and then sleepy, finally recalls that she has not consumed her meal, and makes her way to the toilet to let crimson life bleed across her tongue. Then she dozes the rest of the way to Albuquerque.

Derek's trip to the Library of Congress is not a self-indulgent act of tourism. But there is such a thing as Need to Know, and Janice, as a back-office operator, doesn't have as much of it as she thinks she does, so he doesn't explain. Derek, meanwhile, knows far too much—which is why this is his sole piece of tradecraft on the mission, and very much a training-wheels outing.

You will meet a tall, dark stranger . . .

When Derek asked Forecasting Ops for input on ways to maximize the chances of success for the mission, they recommended a trip to the library and an approach to a particular member of staff. Forecasting Ops are notoriously Delphic, not to mention prone to disappearing in a maze of temporal paradoxes when the shit hits the fan. (They actually vanished completely for three or four months around the installation of the New

Management, written out of history so thoroughly that Boris in Mission Support proposed establishing an experimental oracular subdivision.) But something has frightened them back into existence—something even more terrifying than being the subjects of a government led by the Honorable Member of Parliament for Thebes North. They are now being grudgingly cooperative, at least insofar as anyone can make sense of their predictions. And actually telling Derek to go to *this* place and talk to *that* man? It's unprecedented transparency, by their standards.

Derek directs an Uber to take him to the nearest metro station, then rides the subway into the center of DC. Being a tourist is a great excuse for head-swiveling curiosity, and although it's a cold winter day by local standards, it'd be a warm spring morning back in London.

Derek hasn't been abroad since he was twelve years old—a school trip to Italy was the limit of his travels—so he has only a vague idea of what constitutes normality here, but something, he feels, isn't quite right. Maybe it's the silver, life-sized human statues spaced on plinths, or the purple balloons trailing tentacular antennae and clusters of cameras overhead, like so many cyborg Portuguese men-of-war. Or the way the uniformed police march robotically back and forth, wearing badges with a seven-pointed swirling star that sucks the gaze in if it lingers for too long. His ward pulses just slightly faster than his heartbeat, feeling warm and oddly moist. This is not a place to loiter, Derek feels, lest one attract the gaze of hidden watchers.

Derek is unworldly but not naive. He knows from experience that he has zero aptitude for skullduggery and spycraft, and isn't terribly good at people things in the first place. But he checked back with Forecasting and asked them to confirm that he had to run this errand himself, and Magic 8-Ball said *yes*. So here he is, wandering around the pillars and porticoes of a *beaux arts* building across the road from Congress. There is a leaflet with a map of the public areas of the library available at the front desk. Derek puzzles over it, shuffling along nearsightedly behind a Korean tourist group.

There is, in spycraft, a type of professional known as a Gray Man, so-called because they're almost impossible to spot. They're so unremarkably average and nondescript that a living watcher's eyes slide straight past them. Machine vision systems capable of doing better in real time are seldom found outside of the lab yet. Derek is not a Gray Man: he is Gray Man's seldom-spotted sibling, the Man of No Consequence. He is portly, middle-aged, and peers out at the world through thick-lensed glasses perched on a bulbous nose beneath a precarious comb-over. He's easily spotted, but once spotted he's almost automatically dismissible. Derek has difficulty getting served in bars, or paying in shops, unless he resorts to waving his arms, telegraphing his distress in semaphore. So despite the fact that he wandered in off the street and attached himself to a wildly dissimilar party, nobody spares him a second glance. If they ever do, they assume that he's harmlessly lost and leave it to someone else to redirect him to where he should be.

Nearly forty years in captivity, spent DM'ing a very peculiar role-playing game, has left Derek with an eerie ability to glance at a building's floor plan and infer the likely layout and functions of the blank parts of the map, the implied spaces where secret rooms and hidden treasures lie. The tourist map is a very abbreviated schematic, showing only the general layout of the parts of the library that are open to visitors, but ... *yes,* Derek thinks, there's a door labelled "staff only" right about *there,* fronting that large blank area, and it's secured by a badge-reading lock.

Derek ambles over to the door and pulls his warrant card from the breast pocket of his shirt. (He wears it on a lanyard out of long habit.) He taps it on the lock reader, a prickle of cold sweat springing out on the back of his neck. At home, the warrant card opens doors, no questions asked. In this place, who knows? Worst case, alarms may be ringing in a security office.

But after barely a second the lock clicks open. Derek pushes through the door and lets it swing shut behind him, then returns the card to his pocket. He hurries onward, following the urgent nudges of a wristband he wears. It's destiny-entangled with a twin, which is worn by the remote viewer in Forecasting Ops back home who is leading him to his rendezvous.

Derek makes his way past workrooms identified by number, through fire doors, down a staircase, and along a high-ceilinged subterranean passage roofed with pipes and tubes. He read about the railway that ran down here, once, an early underground line that connected the Library to the Capitol buildings so that senators and congressmen could consult its archives (or, more likely, sneak in and out for a liquid lunch without running the gauntlet of the public at the main entrance). There are many secrets in underground Washington DC, and Derek has an itch to peek behind some of those closed doors. But he has a job to do, and besides, the wristband is urging him towards a door bearing the promising label, "mail room."

Derek opens the mail-room door. A middle-aged man in a short-sleeved shirt and tie is working on a computer at a desk alongside a wall covered in shelving and sorting baskets. He glances up. "Can I help you?" he asks.

Derek lets the door close. "Are you Gilbert from the Comstock Office?" he asks.

"Who sent you?" The mailman jumps to his feet, clearly agitated. "What do you want?"

Derek backs up against the door and smiles nervously. "I'm looking for the President," he says. "I'm told you can put me in touch with him?"

Morning rolls round soon enough and because part of me is still running on UK time I awaken several hours earlier than I'm happy about—until I roll over and see Fuckboy watching me from the other side of the gigantic bed, wearing a smug grin and a sheet tented over his nether regions. The grin is a challenge, so I snarl and pounce on him. Another hour passes before we tire each other out enough to get up. It's a very pleasant hour, which is good because today is going to be tiring and annoying—and that's if everything goes right.

Over the hotel breakfast—which is weird as fuck: Why do they call the scones "biscuits" and smother them in white sauce and call it "gravy"?—I observe Jim across the table. He's unshaven, his hair spiked with sweat, and he's wearing yesterday's travel clothes because he showers after breakfast. He's an unselfconscious mess and so gorgeous I can't take my eyes off him. So I don't even bother to pretend not to stare, because it's consistent with our cover story, and I'm suddenly desperate to commit this moment to memory. I am, I gradually realize, *happy*. And with this happiness comes a terrible apprehension that it's all going to be ripped away from us. It's going to come to a painful end sooner rather than later, because we're doomed.

"Penny for your thoughts?" he asks over the rim of his coffee mug.

"DC today," I say, sticking strictly to work instead of the conversation we really need to have, the one about us. Or the other one, about the traitors and the informers and the deep game the mad gods are playing with screaming chess pieces who bleed. "We should check the train timetables, I guess, but I think they run hourly or more often from Penn Station." Wherever that is: there's a map app for that. "I'll wear a hoodie and pretend to sleep."

"Isn't that a bit risky?" he asks.

I shrug, uncomfortable. "It's daytime, everything is risky." We could hire a van and I could hide from the sunlight in the back, but roads are riskier than rail or air travel. Or I could crouch in a suitcase and Jim could carry me as luggage—he's monstrously strong, when he needs to be—but four hours in a suitcase would be hellish, and carries other risks besides. "I'll do the sunblock thing and stick to shadows, and we can time it so we arrive after 6 p.m. Does that work for you?"

I chug my glass of orange juice. Hunger is a mild buzzing behind my eyeballs: I fed to the point of discomfort the day before yesterday, fed like a leech until I felt like I was ballooning dizzily towards a splattering explosion. Trying all the while not to think about what—who—I was feeding *on*. I overfed because I didn't know when I'd be able to feed again, fed because I was going on a mission overseas and other people's lives depended on me. Not because the hot red life trickling down my throat tickles like the onset of the most ecstatic orgasm ever, not because the sense of warmth and happy tranquility when my V-parasites are well-fed is like an opiate afterglow. (Even though it is.) I fed strictly for duty—I blink. Jim is watching me intently. "What?"

"Nothing," he says, in a tone that means the opposite.

So here's what happens:

We finish breakfast, go upstairs, and agree that he's going to hit the shower while I check in with head office—we have prearranged codes—but I look up while Fuckboy's stripping off and I can't help myself. We jump in the shower together and hump frantically until the water threatens to run cold (this is a big hotel: the water *never* runs cold) and we have to get out. Jim gets dressed, but pauses in the doorway on his way out while I'm online confirming our arrival and verifying that everyone else is in position. I pretend not to notice the frank, lingering look he gives me, but I'd be offended if he didn't stare at me sitting naked and cross-legged on a towel.

After he leaves I dry and get dressed. My own outfit mostly consists of the one-piece bodysuit. With the hood rolled down around my neck and the gloves stashed up the sleeves it looks like I'm wearing tights and a layered turtleneck, just right for late February. I pull a black dress on over it, then a winter coat and hat for outdoors. I glance at the slatted blinds that keep the thin winter sun-glare off my skin. *I'll be fine,* I fret, *as long as nothing goes wrong.* So then I retreat into the bathroom and set up my smartphone's front camera to serve as a mirror while I apply lip gloss and war paint that make it look as if I'm wearing too much makeup rather than factor-100 sunblock.

It's after eleven and I'm beginning to get worried when Jim finally slips back through the door. "Mission accomplished," he says. "Two first-class tickets on the Acela from Penn Station to Union Station, departing at 3 p.m., arriving just before six. Paid for with cash." He flourishes two tickets like airline boarding passes. "You're looking very smart," he remarks appreciatively.

"Dress for the fugitive head of state you want to impress," I shoot back, although he's not wrong: with the right accessories and a pair of heels I could be on my way to a posh reception somewhere. "How about you?"

He shrugs. Under his top coat he's wearing a dark suit and an open-collared white shirt. I feel another flash of lust, even though there's not enough time to get up to anything. "We've got a couple of hours to kill. I was thinking we could do lunch and act like tourists? Then a last-minute dash for the station."

I nod. "Let's do it."

We've paid for the room for a week, money up front. Our luggage is a decoy in case anyone is watching us—it's intended to suggest we'll return for it. News flash—we're not coming back here. Passport, warrant, and credit cards go in a travel pouch under my dress. We're wearing or carrying everything we expect to need. Anything else we can buy along the way.

Jim shoves his own necessities into a briefcase, then puts on a smart tie. We take the elevator to the lobby and I put on my hat and sunglasses as we walk into the sun glare, looking like just another pair of lawyers or bankers stepping out for lunch. Then reality bites and the skin on the back of my left hand stings. *Damn.* I pull my gloves on with inelegant haste and the stinging subsides to a dull burn.

"You okay?" he asks as I hurry to catch up.

"Forgot my gloves," I say, tight-lipped. Between the broad-brimmed hat and my sunblock the rest of me is fine.

"I'm sorry—"

"Not your fault. Where are we going?"

Jim leads me downtown and east towards Fifth Avenue. I decide I like the canyonlike cross-streets. They're shady at ground level. The north-south avenues of Manhattan are another matter: they're a killing ground for unprepared PHANGs. I let Jim take point as we head due south, skulking in his broad-shouldered shadow.

Eventually he stops. "I thought this looked like it'd be a good place for lunch," he says, waving me towards a menu stand just inside one of those canvas awnings they hang over the doors to keep the wind out. (It's above freezing today, but the breeze has a raw edge.)

I glance at it. "Seems okay," I agree. French bistro grub. It's nothing I can't get back home and the prices are outrageous, but that's not the point.

"After you."

We get a table as far away from the window as possible, with good lines of sight. Jim keeps an eye on the front door while I watch the stairs leading down to the kitchen and bathroom—our bug-out route. It's lunchtime but the restaurant is only half-full. The diners are mostly up-market office workers. The real finance action is all the way down south, but they come uptown to spend their loot, so we blend in. I smile at him as he rereads the menu, and he meets my gaze with a grin of his own. I'm pretty sure he's imagining me sitting on that hotel towel: in fact I'll be most disappointed if he isn't, and I don't give a shit whether this is unprofessional behavior. "They do an oyster platter," he remarks, and I just barely manage not to snicker.

"Let's not get carried away?" Fuckboy spots the waiter approaching. I manage to keep a straight face as we place an order. No oysters, just the lunch special and a small glass of wine for each of us. I feel obscurely disappointed, so I pinch myself and remember, *this is just a cover story*. We're friends with benefits, that's all. The engagement bling and lovey-dovey shit isn't real and there's no happy-ever-after waiting for us. Let's get real: he's a middle-aged divorcee with a teenaged daughter and a red sports car, and he's going to die of early onset dementia in a couple of years. Meanwhile, I'm a state executioner living under my own suspended sentence of death, a carrier of the most vile blood-borne disease imaginable. The nation we serve is ruled by a sadistic clown-god who is building a glass-and-chrome skull-rack on Marble Arch and uses human sacrifice as an instrument of state policy. And we're playing spy games in a city on a continent where *something even worse* is tapping hungrily at the window, waiting to come in. Doomed lovers in late Weimar Germany had it easy in comparison.

But when he looks at me like that I can still kid myself that I'm happy.

We make inconsequential chitchat until the food arrives, then eat in appreciative silence. It really is quite good. The restaurant continues to fill up, but we have a couple of hours to kill before we make our way to Penn Station. I'm most of the way through the main course (I decided to pig out and go for the duck cassoulet) when Jim tenses infinitesimally, lowers his cutlery, and begins to track something behind me.

I give him my best, falsest, New York smile and ask, "What is it, dear?"

"Get your camera out," he says conversationally.

"Camera—" *oh fuck*. Then I hear the mindless static chittering of approaching V-parasites. Don't know how they found us here, but that's for later.

"Did you ever watch *La Femme Nikita*?" he asks. "The Luc Besson movie version, not the shitty remake?"

"You're thinking of the restaurant fight scene, right?" He nods.

By this time I have my phone in hand and unlocked. I raise it and use the front camera to peek over my shoulder. My skin crawls as I spot them. Two mannequins, their head-to-toe suits silvery-blue in the dimness of the restaurant vestibule, scanning for—well, if *I* can feel *them* at this range, *they* can sure as fuck feel *me*—

OFCUT firmware: loaded. A targeting box frames Jim's head; I angle my phone away from him. "Going to get messy in three, two—"

"Go *now*—"

I turn as Jim picks up his steak knife and draws his arm back. Time seems to slow. The light fades to red, the air around me feels hot and viscous as syrup, and the voice of my V-parasites rises from a quiet purring to a harsh screech of hatred and rage. As I bring the basilisk gun round I feel a huge surge of energy beside me, then Officer Friendly hurls his knife. It's an invisible blur even to PHANG-accelerated vision, but I hear the thud of impact as I hit the firing button on my basilisk gun and light up the nearest hostile.

The moving mannequin sparkles for a fraction of a second, then flames spurt from it in all directions. (*It*. I'm distancing myself, aren't I? It makes the flashbacks easier to handle.) Great gouts and streamers of sparks like a phone battery exploding flare across the white linen table cloths and well-dressed office workers to all sides, lighting up the ceiling, the slamming thud driving needles into my ears as the front window blows out. *Splash one*.

The second mannequin gathers himself and leaps over his comrade's flame-gouting skeleton, which is still falling apart—all of this takes a fractional second—and he twists and kicks off the ceiling ten feet overhead, bearing down on me. Or he would be, if he hadn't punched his leg right through the overhead paneling and set himself spinning. His parasites' scream of rage and hunger deafens me as I bring my phone up and aim it at him—then realize the screen of my Samsung is impaled on the second joint of my right thumb. When I fired the basilisk app I punched right through the screen, the circuit board, and the stainless steel back. Which ruined my nail polish, and now it's getting really hot.

Shit. I throw my chair at him, then do a rolling forward somersault down the stairs. I rip the burning-hot phone off my thumb, tearing my glove up some more. Smoke and sparks boil out of it. The first screams of fear and pain begin to arrive from the other diners as I tumble across the landing. *Where's Jim? Don't panic.* When Officer Friendly cuts loose, he's close enough to Superman for government business: he can look after himself. *As long as nobody bites him. Don't think about that.*

Then I hear another, most unwelcome, sound. Looks like the Seventh Cavalry is piling in upstairs—and they're not ours.

I slam into the floor at the bottom of the staircase and kick off. A flash of silver at the top of the stairs, then muffled thuds striking the floor around me. *Are they shooting at me? Fuck that shit.* I throw my phone at them, gushing smoke and bursts of blue-white flame—lithium batteries are quite impressive when they cut loose—and the shooting stops as I hurl myself along the corridor to the kitchen. Heat, stainless steel, the sluggish shouts of human chefs. *Where's the knife block?* I grab a big Sabatier-K in each hand and as a silver figure dives through the door I hurl one overhand. I duck below the center island. The chefs stand as if frozen, implements in hand, mouths opening as my knife embeds in the wall. I grab a heavy skillet as a metallic blur whips round and bears on me and I bring it up just in time to catch a double-tap of slugs that were meant for my chest.

There is a *click* from my assailant's gun and he reaches for his reload. But he's unaccountably slowed almost to human speed. Maybe he hasn't fed recently? I leap and scream wordlessly and bash him over the head with the pan. Then I'm past him. A squat extractor duct disappears through a panel in the wall, a covered-over window. I slam a steel Crock-Pot into it so hard that the pot crumples. Brick dust sprays everywhere. I dig my fingers into the extractor ductwork, tear it away, and scramble out, sharp edges tearing a rip in my coat. I've lost my hat somewhere along the way, and I'm in a cellar with a skylight, so I yank my fake turtleneck up and over my face before I jump and haul myself up into the alleyway behind the restaurant.

I'm halfway to the end of the alley when there's a thud behind me. I whirl and get my hands up just as a very dusty Fuckboy— tie askew, coat dripping something horrible, and I can't help noticing he's bleeding from a graze on the back of one hand—lands in a crouch. A small avalanche of bricks and drywall fragments bounces harmlessly off his head and shoulders. "Mhari?"

"Go! Go!" I blur towards the side-street, Jim right behind me. Abruptly I feel a great lassitude as a knot of hunger twists in my gut. I've been running on PHANG mojo for almost thirty seconds. It's incredibly draining. I force myself to straighten up my posture and slow down. "Anyone following?" I gasp.

"Think I lost them." He stops abruptly. "A dragnet, I think. We must have pinged their radar last night. *Fuck* that was close." Suddenly his arms are around me and I'm burrowing my face into his chest. I wrap my arms around his waist, inside his coat, before either of us quite realize what's happening.

"I thought I'd lost you." I take a deep, sobbing breath as I try to get my shit together and make sense of the past minute. "How did you get out?"

He strokes the back of my neck as if soothing a frightened animal. "When in doubt, go through the walls. Their backup tried to swarm me but I punched two out, then went up three floors, through the sidewall into the next building over, then back down the outside." I feel rather than see him cringe in remembered guilt: "I don't even want to think about the property damage. Architecture is fragile. How about you?"

I haul in another lungful of sweet, blessed air. "Live-action *Nikita* re-enactor here, with added vampire mojo. I broke my phone, but other than that, it was nothing." Like hell it was, but I'm not *ever* telling Officer Friendly that. I sniff at him. "Your coat's wrecked and you've got plaster in your hair. Did you get mixed up and try to role-play *Leon* instead?"

"You smell of smoke and *your* coat's wrecked, too." He lets go of me and we step back, then he grins. "But we've got two hours before we have to catch our train. I think this calls for evasion and a change of appearance?"

I take hold of his proffered arm and conjure up the fakiest ever fake Barbie squeal of ironic delight: "*Let's go shopping!*" Because I've got a government-backed credit card and I know how to submit an expense claim.

Rewind a week—again.

"What about our other adversaries?" I asked the Senior Auditor.

"Which ones?" Dr. Armstrong looked mildly amused.

"The internal—" I began, then thought better of it.

"Ah yes, that." His amusement faded.

I took a deep breath and looked around the interior of the black dome. Actually, there was nothing to see: just the two of us, our chairs, and the circle of floor beneath us, inscribed with the circuitry of Persephone's security grid. It was more than airtight: I could barely hear the chittering of my parasite load. Stay here too long and I'd starve into dormancy, but not before the SA and I ran out of oxygen to breathe. This wasn't a timestop grid, like the one the *alfär* used to store their alien weapon-beasts, or Basil used to stash his victims between blood meals. It was a spacestop grid: time continued at the same rate as on the outside, but shielded by an event horizon.

"We're quite alone in here, I assure you."

"Yes, I—"

Dr. Armstrong made a steeple of his fingers. "Conan, what is best in life?" he quoted.

"What? Now you're being annoying! I don't understand." *What has some macho Xena knock-off got to do with—*

"I apologize." He sighed. "It was a quote, but I meant to illustrate a point I haven't made yet. What *is* best in life? Go on, Mhari, that's a serious question."

What is best in life? Well, how about being able to go about in daylight without being forced to cover up and wear vampish clownface? How about not feeling this bitter thirst all the fucking time, a reminder that my life is built on death? How about not being expected to carry out executions? How about us not being collectively enslaved by an ancient evil as the alternative to human extinction?

I was about to open my mouth and say some of this, but I choked on my tongue just in time as I realized that these were *not* the best things in life: they were among the worst.

"What *is* best in life, Michael?" I asked, staring at my nails by way of studied ironic emphasis. "How about *you* tell *me* instead of tap-dancing around a shitty metaphor?"

He gave me a long stare. "Our first priority is the same as it ever was," he said: "survival. Not all of us, or any of us in particular, or forever, but survival is the principal goal. It's the function of all life forms to persist for as long as possible. If nobody and nothing survives, nothing matters. And I don't know about you, but I'm deeply uncomfortable with that."

Eh. I nodded cautiously.

"We're human, and mere survival isn't enough," he continued after a moment. "We have executive function and theory of mind and language. *We make plans.* It's what makes our species so spectacularly successful. But we need to have some hope for the future, we need to be able to think we see light at the end of the tunnel, or we despair and we give up and then we die. If you like, our biggest adversary is our own fear. So, Mhari—before we discuss threats—what do you hope for? I want to know what kind of future you would *like* to see."

"I—"

"Be honest, now," he said with an impish grin, then without pausing for breath added, "Onyx, Hadean, Cantabrian, Luciferous: Execute Sitrep One."

"Subjective integrity is maintained. Subjective continuity of experience is maintained. Subject observes no tampering." It was my own voice speaking through my own lips, but I wasn't moving them.

"Now execute Sitrep Two, Mhari."

I heard myself say, as from a great distance: "V-parasites at zero point eight, stable. Interference at zero point one five, rising. Subjective compliance at zero point nine five, stable."

"Good." His voice was tense, over-controlled. "Now I'm about to go off script before terminating this session, Mhari. I want to apologize in advance for any distress this may cause you . . . what future do you hope for?"

All the sensible inhibitions which would normally stop me vomiting my innermost feelings in a co-worker's lap had shut down. Distantly, I knew I should be furious. I should be throat-rippingly enraged, locked in a seeing-red, fang-extending haze of murderous blood hunger. But I wasn't. I felt calm, almost placid, as I said: "I lost hope two years ago." *Put* that *in your pipe and smoke it, Dr. Armstrong.*

But instead of looking shocked, he frowned thoughtfully and nodded to himself, as if I'd just confirmed an unwelcome line of speculation. "I'd like you to think back to what it was like before you lost hope," he said. "And tell me what you wanted from your life."

I almost threw up. "What most teenaged girls want? Boyfriends who respected me, a rewarding, enjoyable job, enough money not to feel hard up? Later, a romantic wedding to an adoring husband and a house, then a couple of cute babies who'll grow up into adults I can be proud of?" *And a magical pony on top.* "I got the job," I added, just a tad bitterly, "and I can't say I didn't get the boyfriends, at least some of the time." But the rest was a smoking crater.

Dr. Armstrong tried another angle. "When did you give up hope?"

That was easy. "PHANG fucked up everything. And my boyfriend at the time"—well, okay: Oscar was married to someone else, but he'd been threatening to divorce her for ages—"was one of Basil's victims."

"Oh dear." The SA shut up and looked at me. "How did PHANG syndrome fuck things up for you?" he asked.

I was incredulous under the thick blanket of externally imposed apathy, but the oath of office compelled me to give the clearest factual answer to the question that I could formulate, rather than just swearing. "PHANG syndrome is contagious, lethal, and blood-borne. I can infect a victim by drinking their blood. Nobody knows whether other bodily fluids create the feeder link, but I don't want to find out the hard way on someone I like." *Or love.* "So it's strictly condoms or non-penetrative sex, and as for babies"—*too late*—"nope." I swallowed bile. "But that's the easy bit. You know I have to feed, and you know what feeding does to the donors. I'm an obligate cannibal, Mike. If I don't kill people, I will get sick and die horribly. And not just me: the others are in the same boat. I never wanted this! I'm trying to minimize the damage by organizing blood distribution and finding *an approved source of donors*—" I retched.

"Exit supervision," he said hastily. "You can stop now."

Fury descended on me, but I bottled it and sat, head down, choking with rage and shame.

"Was that *entirely* necessary?" I demanded as soon as I could talk again.

"Yes. Look at me." I looked him in the eye and saw the faint green glow reflected there slowly dim. "You seem to be in a bad place, Mhari. And we're trusting you with a lot of lives. That's why somebody had to ask you these things. To make sure you don't simply give up and die halfway through the job, taking everybody else with you."

"I'm not going to give up *now*," I snarled, making an oath of the simple fact. My own life might be a desolate wasteland, but if I gave up it'd all be for nothing, wouldn't it? At least if I kept going *now* someone else might benefit. Not the donors, and especially, please God, not the New Management, but . . .

"Let me tell you what I—and the rest of the inner circle, the team who set up Continuity Operations—are working towards," said the Senior Auditor. "Let me tell you what keeps *me* going through the night. Then you can make up your own mind if it's enough for you."

And he told me, and it's going to change *everything*—but not yet, and first we have to survive the New Management.

6: LEVIATHAN'S REPRESENTATIVE

Gilbert's first reaction to the stranger in the mailroom is flat-out terror. He's deathly afraid that the sudden appearance of the man with the British accent means that his cell has been cracked by the enemy. Second thoughts strike him before he can speak: there is no earthly reason why the Nazgûl would toy with him this way. They'd go straight for the kill.

"Who sent you?" he demands, heart pounding. He looks around for a weapon he can grab, but the Library of Congress basement is lamentably short on such things.

"I'm from the British government," says the stranger, raising his hands warily. "We want to help." *The British?* Gilbert stares, hard, trying to understand what's going on. He doesn't *look* like a British spy, although Bond movies are a dubious guide to reality at best—a portly, middle-aged, short-sighted James Bond? Wearing a gray button-up knitted vest?

"You *are* Gilbert Tancredy, formerly of the Occult Texts Division of the Postal Service Inspectorate?"

Gil stares at him. There's no point denying it, something very strange is happening here. "That's me. Who are *you*?"

"Derek Blacker from, ah, your former agency's opposite numbers—"

"—What, the Royal Mail inspectors?"

"No." He grimaces. "An organization you haven't heard of, we do secret stuff for the government—but we're *not* like the Nazgûl," he adds hastily, then spoils it slightly by adding, "I hope not, anyway." An uncomfortable pause. "Did you know Bill McKracken?"

Gil unwinds very slightly. The name is familiar. "Not sure. Why?"

"He"—Blacker deflates—"he died, actually. In London, enemy action. One of yours. We owe him."

Blacker is so quintessentially, bumblingly amateurish that Gil is at a loss to understand how this could be anything other than what it looks like: an onrushing train wreck. "You mentioned the P-President." The word is hard to pronounce, but gets easier every time. "Why?"

Blacker shrugs, then reaches into a pocket and pulls out a couple of translucent dice. As he bounces them on the palm of his left hand Gilbert sees there's something very odd about them, almost as if they're not cubes but shadows cast by some species of higher-dimensional object. "An oracle told me I'd find you here," he says apologetically. "We need to arrange a meeting between the President and one of our people. It's very important. We know the Nazgûl are looking for him, and Forecast—our oracle—said you were our best bet for finding him first. Before they do."

"A meeting." Gilbert is still disturbed, but at least this is something concrete he can latch onto. "Why?"

"It's not in anyone's interests for the Nazgûl to get their hands on the President. As an allied power, we can help."

That's a non-answer if ever Gilbert has heard one, but at least this encounter now makes some kind of—admittedly surreal— sense. "I can't put you in touch with the President," he says, "but I can forward your request to somebody who can arrange something. *If* the President people think it's a good idea." Derek looks at him oddly, and for a moment Gil wonders if he misspoke. Blacker refers to the President as if it's the title of a person. *A person on the run from the Nazgûl,* he suddenly realizes, and it makes a horrible kind of sense, although he can't quite put his finger on why that might be so. Maybe this President person was somebody high up in the Postal Service Inspectorate? Someone who knows where the bodies are buried?

"I'll need some way to get in touch with you," Gil tells him.

Blacker puts his dice back in his pocket and pulls out a cheap clamshell phone. "Here. Turn it on some time after four and listen to the voice mail: it has instructions for you. Keep it turned off *except* when you're actively using it."

He holds it out. Gil takes it cautiously. "Why?"

"Basic SIGSEC—use it too often, traffic analysis can tell an adversary that it's hostile and they can home in on it." Gil stares at the phone as if it's a poisonous snake while Blacker continues. "I'll call it once, with rendezvous details. You get to use it to call me back—just once—to say go or no go or amend the rendezvous. After that, you get rid of it. Understood?"

Gil nods. "Like a drugs drop."

"Exactly, I think." Then the British agent looks puzzled.

"What is it?" Gil asks.

"Can you point me towards the exit? I'm lost."

Agents Smith and Jones have taken up positions between the broadcasting studio and the lobby, so there'd be no easy way out past them even if Gaby figured it would do any good. They're Feds; they know where she lives, they know where her dog goes to school.[6] Glenn harrumphs indignantly and Danni protests shrilly but it's not making any difference. "Why?" demands Gaby. "We haven't done anything!"

"But one of your callers did," Agent Jones tells her. "You will come with us now. Maybe you can tell us why they called."

"Stand up slowly," says Agent Smith. "Keep your hands where

---

[6] This is not just a figure of speech: Dinah, Gaby's full-sized French Poodle, does indeed go to obedience school.

I can see them." A pistol materializes in his hand like a malignant card trick. "Move!"

Gaby stands, shaking. It feels unreal, more so than the sasquatch and dragon reports that are the meat and drink of her show, the reports of UFO abductions and cultists that cluster in this corner of Colorado. Perhaps they're just the creative outlets of bored locals: it hardly matters to her mind, as long as it keeps her listeners going through the night. But Men in Black holding her at gunpoint in the workplace are emphatically something else.

"Out front! You first!" Smith waves Glenn over to the door. "Kneel!"

"I can't—" Glenn wheezes. He's middle-aged and is always complaining about his joints. Jones grabs him by the arm and pushes him down and forward, twisting the arm behind him to force compliance, but instead of kneeling Glenn gives an agonized wail and falls badly. "My knee! My knee!"

"On your front! Hands behind your head!" shouts Smith, but Glenn is in too much pain to comply. Gaby watches, appalled, as Smith kicks him. "Shut the fuck up, motherfucker! Stop resisting, stop resisting, you are resisting arrest!" Another breathless wail, and Smith kicks him in the side of the head. "Next!" he screams at Gaby, quivering with rage. Jones, standing behind him, shrugs uncomfortably, as if to say, *What can you do*.

"He's got arthritis," Gaby tells them, as if reason will work on fists and boots: "He's due to have his knees replaced next month." *Was due*. Glenn lies horribly motionless and slack.

"Hands behind your backs! On your knees!" Gaby, at least, is flexible enough to kneel while Jones steps round his partner. He's zip-tying her wrists when the alarm siren goes off.

"What the fuck!" Smith casts about wildly, then raises his gun and fires two shots through the open fire-escape door. In the confines of the studio the gunshots feel like fists pounding the sides of her head. Danni has escaped into the nighttime darkness, and the siren wail of the door alarm is deafeningly loud—but not loud enough to stir Glenn. "Come on." Jones grabs Gaby under one arm and hauls her towards the front door. "You search the parking lot," he shouts at Smith, who is already halfway out onto the fire escape. "She won't have gone far."

Jones drags Gaby out into the reception area, then goes back into the studio briefly. He re-emerges shaking his head. "Come on." He shoves Gaby, pushing her off balance, then drags her through the front door.

"Wh-what—Glenn?"

"He's not going anywhere. Come on, we're leaving." There's a gigantic SUV in the car park—a Navigator or a Suburban or something—and Jones pushes Gaby over to it, then pops the rear door. "Get in." Gaby is shaking. She eyes the running board. She's not a tall woman, and after a moment Jones seems to realize that with her wrists bound she can't pull herself up. "Fuck." He grabs under her armpit, and boosts her onto the seat.

"He killed Glenn," she whimpers, struggling upright. "Who *are* you?"

Jones smiles horribly from the open door. "We're from the government, and we're here to *help*."

"Help? You're not helping us!"

"Indeed." He reaches up and pulls off his Ray-Bans, folds them, and stows them in a pocket. A febrile green glow that owes nothing to the street lighting writhes within his eyes. Gaby recoils, whimpering.

A minute later, Agent Smith lurches into view with Danni's body slung over his shoulder. The opposite door opens and Smith and Jones push her onto the bench seat so that her head flops in Gaby's lap. They've zip-tied her, hand and foot, and she's out cold, a bruise already forming on her forehead. A minute later the trunk opens and they roll something heavy inside. "Let us depart, Brother." The two agents wrap seat belts around their passengers, close the doors, and climb in. Jones puts the SUV in gear and drives slowly out of the parking lot, not turning on his lights. As they turn onto Whiterock they pass a police cruiser heading the other way with light bar flashing.

Are they really Feds? she wonders, panicky, as she stares at the back of Agent Jones's head. Glenn seemed to think they were, and he read their papers, but Glenn is—she shies away from the thought—dead. Or at least very deeply unconscious. *Is this an abduction?* Smith and Jones drive in silence. After a minute Danni begins to stir, moaning incoherently. There's a compass display in the rearview, and Gaby realizes they're turning west, heading towards the trail up to Peanut Lake. *Brother. Brother Drake,* she realizes. Friends of Sleep. But the agents arrived at the studio *before* the broadcast. *What the hell?*

"Are—are you with the Friends of Sleep?" she asks hoarsely.

"I told you, we're from the govern—" Agent Jones begins, just as Agent Smith says, "Yes."

Agent Jones clears his throat. "We are the Friends of the Lord of Sleep, and we're from the government, and we're here to *help,*" he explains.

"To help our Lord," Agent Smith clarifies, "not you."

Outside the side windows, the road has run out of houses and street lights. They're driving between trees now, and the street has narrowed and is winding uphill. *I could call 911, if I had my phone,* Gaby thinks helplessly. But her phone is in her bag, back in the studio. "Why are you taking us?" she asks, desperate for anything that could shed light on her abductors' intentions.

"A ward is weakest in the center of its working," Jones says, as if by way of explanation. "And here we are furthest from the coast, the border with our Lord's demesne. Breakthroughs happen. Wild apprehensions of the starry wisdom. Weakenings of the gates of memory that let old loyalties bleed through."

"I don't understand any of this!" Gaby wails, close to spilling tears of frustration.

"It's good that you don't," Smith says, his tone warm and reassuring. "If you understood, you'd either be one of them or one of us—"

"—One of *us,*" Jones echoes. "*Initiates.*"

"Mad, now!" Smith sounds abominably cheerful.

"Instead of which you're one of the flock."

"Please let us go? We haven't done anything to you! We don't know anything!"

Jones hisses quietly, like an amused snake. "Ignorant sacrifices are the best kind."

"Sacri—"

"You were safe until your colleague bleeped out the warning, but he spoiled everything for us. Now we'll have to use you, instead."

"Use—*me*?"

The road steepens and the SUV jolts, rocking from side to side as it descends towards the lakeside. "One of our High Priests— an initiate of the inner temple—wrote, 'The tree of liberty must be refreshed from time to time with the blood of patriots.' What do you think Brother Jefferson meant by that? Are you a patriot, Miss Carson?"

Danni moans quietly, and stiffens, straining at the zip ties around her wrists. She's coming round.

These people are mad, Gaby realizes, *and they mean to kill us.* An icy calm grips her. She doesn't know what she can do to stop them, but the idea of being slaughtered like Thanksgiving turkeys is repugnant.

"Why are you doing this? I mean, what purpose does it serve?" Gaby asks, speaking to cover up the click as she pops her seatbelt latch. The metal buckle is blunt-edged so she can't saw at the zip ties with it, and her wrists are pinioned behind her, but if this is a rental car the door latches may still work—

Smith tries to explain again. "The genius of the republic is maintained by constant sacrifices and the blood-soaked rituals of the initiates. Sacred geometry and dark secrets under DC, this much you and your listeners already know of. But in these trying times, as the stars come right and the walls between the worlds thin, it takes more than ritual and intent to compel a nation to serve the will to power. By the sacred cabling of AT&T and Comcast we bind the routers and ties of a continent together and broadcast the sacred timing codes that underpin the great working, the geas of forgetting. Using them, we, the servants of the Black Chamber—be we Friends of the Lord of Sleep or officiants in the Mysteries of Central Intelligence—act to buttress our nation's magical boundaries against intrusions from outside. But the center cannot hold without reinforcement. Your program is a weakness, febrile leakage from the realm of chaos and the void beyond the world. We were sent to monitor and report, if necessary to close you down—but thanks to your producer's bungling malice, it will take a broadcast anchored in your blood to rewind the damage you have inflicted on our nation's defenses."

The SUV slows as the dirt track between the trees levels out. *Is this slow enough?* Gaby nerves herself as she realizes she's out of time. She twists and scrabbles behind her back for the door latch, then feels it click open. Night and darkness breathe down her neck as she kicks hard against the transmission hump and pushes herself out of the moving vehicle. It's a bad fall, and her momentary fear of going under a wheel is driven out of her mind by the force of impact. Stunned, she rolls over twice and lies prone, gasping for breath as her head spins. The SUV rolls onwards and she collects herself enough to realize that if she stays here she will certainly be killed. She rolls over on her front and pushes herself up—a hot needle of pain stabs through the joint of her left knee—then with a shuddering gasp she rises to her feet and staggers between the trees.

The darkness is near-total, despite the crescent moon riding low overhead. It's a bitterly cold night. Gaby's nostrils flare. She can smell lake water standing, not far away. Dead leaf mass and pine needles underfoot, a whiff of snow hanging in the air. The crunch of tires on dirt ceases. Doors open, shouting ensues.

Gaby stands up, a couple of feet back from the road. And she's still standing, nerving herself to step back into the road and walk away from the lakeshore when—with barely any warning—another car, its lights out, ghosts by dangerously fast with a buffet of wind and a crunch of tires on gravel.

She ducks back further as the new arrival brakes to avoid the SUV pulled up on the shoreline ahead: then she drops and rolls for shelter as shots ring out.

The Greyhound station in Colorado Springs is a single-story brick-and-concrete structure the size of a gas station. During the day, floor-to-ceiling slit windows admit pale winter light that spills across the ranks of plastic bucket seats bolted to the floor. The amenities consist of toilets, a row of coin-operated luggage lockers, and a vending machine. It's as bleak as the visitor room at Camp Tolkien, Yarisol realizes, although there is a comforting sameness to its bland walls and floor tiles, and as it's past sunset she is happy enough to sit and wait for her ride. The handful of other passengers she shares the waiting room with ignore her.

Yarisol flew in to Albuquerque around lunchtime, wearing Jonquil's face and holding a passport in her name. After a brief misunderstanding, one of the limos from the taxi rank proved willing to drive her to Colorado Springs. It was a journey of some six hours, broken only by gas and toilet stops and the quiet weeping of the driver. Yarisol is not needlessly cruel, but she has little understanding of *urük* ways, and once she's settled on a course of action she sticks to it, and the last bus of the day for Colorado Springs had left half an hour before she reached the airport concourse.

She spent the flight over assimilating her memories of Jonquil. She is an alien to Yarisol, who doesn't quite grasp how other *alfär* souls work, let alone the lumpen round-eared kind. Jonquil is dazzling and sharp enough to draw blood with the cut direct, a social animal who takes what she will and serves the All-Highest as a god. So along with the disguise, Yarisol chooses to use Jonquil's awareness as a kind of prosthetic theory of mind, to help her understand the complexities of social interaction. She is determined to make full use of it, and to hold tight as many of Jonquil's memories as she can once the imprinting begins to fade (as it inevitably will, after a few days). So she practices by engaging in cunning wordplay and jest with her driver, and when he balks she motivates him with the razor-sharp edges of nightmare, stopping just short of inflicting so much distress that he loses control on the highway.

Reaching the Greyhound station at eight o'clock, she dismissed the driver from her attention and went inside to sit down. The annoying *urük* followed her, gesticulating and yammering something about payment until she handed him the black plastic card she had been given for expenses. That silenced him effectively. Then she settled down to wait.

It is now five to nine, and night has fallen. The station is about to close, and Yarisol is becoming uneasy. She counts the floor tiles once again, just to be sure they haven't been breeding between eyeblinks, then checks the clock. *Urük* count time in base-sixty units, which leads to some interesting if bizarre symmetries . . . but where are her colleagues? If the station closes, will she have to remain inside all night, or will she be required to leave? (Jonquil's memories imply the latter, but she was not the sort to hang around bus stations after dark. The lack of a conclusive answer to this question, once it occurs to her to ask it, is a maddening itch.)

An older *urük* in a drab uniform shuffles out of a windowless back room, turns to lock the door behind them, then says, very firmly, "We're closed now."

At just that moment, a somewhat younger *urük* enters through the front door. He wears a black leather jacket and jeans, but has too little hair for the biker look, according to Jonquil's fashion-critical eye. Laugh lines crinkle around his eyes as he looks around. He spots her and approaches, raising a hand.

"You can't come in here—" begins the bus station attendant.

"Jonquil?" the new arrival asks hesitantly. "I'm Pete, Mhari told me you needed a ride."

Yarisol stands up, surprised to discover how she has stiffened during her hour of sitting on a throne of polymerized coal oil. "It's no trouble," she says.

"You can't come—"

"Be silent," she says, glancing at the old *urük*. His eyes bulge and he mouths something at her, then turns and staggers towards the back office, clutching his throat.

"This way," says the one named Pete, his laugh lines vanishing. "Will that wear off?" he asks.

"Probably." Yarisol reconsiders. "I see no reason why not," she hedges.

"Do you have any luggage?"

"No." This is not strictly true: a suitcase and carry-on accompanied her on the flight. But they were inconvenient to carry and she didn't see the point, so she left them at the airport.

"Then"—they reach the doorway—"you take the back seat." Pete points at a big cart, mud spattered across the shiny black paint around its wheel arches. "Don't do that again," he advises, "at least not for trivial offenses."

"It is not acceptable?" Yarisol asks him, forcing a hang-dog expression. (She is proud that she now understands this facial contortion: Jonquil's peculiar sensitivity to human physiognomy might be rubbing off on her.)

"No." Pete opens the back door of the car and she climbs in. "Brains? Meet, uh . . . who are you *really*?"

"Mhari told me I'm Jonquil now?" she says, trying to be helpful. "I borrowed Jonquil's face, but some bits are fading? So you, like, see through her? Back in camp they called me Jar-Jar?"

The balding man in the driver's seat makes a choking noise.

"Whoever gave you that name was not being nice," Pete tells her. "Belt up, we've got a long way to go. What do you want us to call you?"

Yarisol thinks for a bit. She cannot give them her full, true name, and apparently the name the *urük* soldiers gave her is bad, but she finds the idea of inventing her own alias pleasing. "Call me Jon," she says, after a minute.

"You're *alfär*," says the driver, his tone abnormally even.

"Yarisol is *alfär;* Jonquil is, like, human?" Jon giggles at her humorous insight.

"Brains—" Pete says.

"I'm . . . okay. I think." He grips the steering wheel with tension-whitened fingertips.

"Brains's husband was injured during the Host's invasion," Pete explains. "You weren't involved were you, Jon?"

"Invasion." Jon hunches forward and wraps her arms around her torso, a very Yarisol gesture. With an effort of Jonquil-esque will she straightens up, relaxes, and flashes an insincere grin at the driver's mirror. "Can we be friends?" A moment too late she remembers that she's not supposed to show her teeth, and realizes this goes double to *urük* scholar-soldiers warded against glamour. The big *urük*-cart swerves, but stays on the road and doesn't hit anything. "Oops," she says, and remembers to clap a hand over her mouth only a couple of seconds too late.

Brains sighs. "*Fuck.*"

"Would you rather work with the real Jonquil?" Pete asks him. Jon tries to puzzle the meaning out of this question for the next couple of miles as they drive in silence, but it sounds like no question at all—*a rhetorical question,* the irate ghost of Jonquil's memory calls it.

"Maybe," Brains says tersely.

Pete changes the subject. "Why are you here, Jon?"

"I am an accident," the part of her that is Yarisol recites placidly. "Papa get—got—loose in slave pens before other magi chop his balls off. Mama died in childbirth."

"*Wha—*"

"—Too much inform—"

"—Female magi are troublesome, said the All-Highest—old All-Highest, All-Highest-before-last eighty-five times over—so in normal times there are only male magi in the Morningstar Empire." Her voice flattens as she lapses from English into the Low Tongue. "*This one is accident.*" She bows her head and rocks.

"Forget I asked," Pete tells her. "Jon? Jon? Can you hear me?"

She keeps on rocking, too disturbed to reply. Jonquil memories tell her that this is *not neurotypical behavior* and the realization brings a flood of disorienting insights. The *urük* have lots of words for this sort of not-normal. The *urük* don't kill their not-normals as soon as they show their differences; they keep them around, even when they're old and useless. The new All-Highest's officer, the baroness, the one who found her—with a shocking stab of insight, Jon realizes that Mhari, too, is a blood-mage, one with high status and power, even though she's not like Yarisol.

"Jon? Why did Mhari send you to us?"

Jon relaxes slightly and pulls the tattered shreds of her Jon-quil persona tight around her as she allows the All-Highest's words to escape. "This is the heartland in the middle of the for-getting empire. This is where the border is furthest and the geas is weakest. We are ordered"—by word of the All-Highest him-self, who is meddling in Baroness Karnstein's scheme—"to steal a sacrifice from the enemy, then with their assistance open a door that will let the Forgotten Emperor address his subjects. I am a mage: you are not, but all our skills are necessary."

"The . . . Emperor?"

"How the fuck should *I* know what the Prime Minister was talking about?" Jonquil asks irritably. "That's *your* job!"

She harrumphs as she crosses her arms and looks out of the window, falling fully into Jonquil's character, so she doesn't see Pete blanch in the mirror.

"Where is this sacrifice?" Brains asks skeptically. "What door?"

Jon blinks slowly. It's nearly time. All-Highest's instructions, delivered in His office at Downing Street, were most anoma-lously specific. Oracles are usually vague, but as All-Highest par-takes of the nature of a god, perhaps this makes some sense . . .

"Turn on the radio?" she says. "Tune to WOCZ-FM? That's

where we will learn the name of the sacrifice we are to retrieve, on *The Whatever Show* at ten of the clock."

OSCAR and his team have settled into the next safe house and Sam is busy moving the groceries from the back of the pickup to the kitchen when Mattingley finds him. "Sam, I've got an errand for you."

Sam straightens up. "One moment, sir." He turns and puts the pair of gallon jugs of milk he's carrying on the table. "What do you need me to do?"

Matt nods acknowledgment. "You can finish unpacking first. But I need you to run over to the Metro station in New Carrollton and pick someone up."

"Pick—" Officer Penrose comes to full alert. "Sir?"

The polite monosyllable is code for *have you taken leave of your senses*? But Mattingley pretends not to notice. "He's a former federal agent, and OSCAR needs to hear what he has to say. Your job is to meet him, confirm he's not a ringer, and get him here without picking up a tail. If he's clean, then afterwards you're to get him back to a Metro station."

"A *former*—"

"—Not everyone has forgotten who or what they swore to protect, Sam. We're isolated and undercover but we're never alone, remember that."

Sam blinks. His eye is watering and he's only half-certain it's because he's been awake way too long.

Officer Haas gives Sam a quick briefing. He finishes unloading, then types the rendezvous into his phone's turn-by-turn navigation app. This should be a straightforward job, but something about it sets his teeth on edge. The President's security is too important to risk, especially under current circumstances. The way everyone forgets about him, forgets the entire goddamn Executive Branch, every time they go to sleep—so that even his own personal protection detail have to be reminded who and what he is whenever they wake up—scares the crap out of him. Scenarios for a single point of failure breed like fever dreams in the corners of his imagination. All it would take is a canister of fentanyl in the HVAC and then, even if the knock-out gas didn't kill them, the presidency would be *over*. They'd be sitting around with their thumbs up their asses while the black hats stormed the premises. Sam isn't paid to have an imagination or anticipate unconventional threats, but even he can see how precarious their situation is. What this must be like for Senior Officer Mattingley—he shakes his head as he puts the truck in gear and moves off.

Driving through the outer suburbs of DC and across the state line into Maryland, Sam forces his mind onto the job. His phone is maddeningly insistent about taking the direct route, but at least it recalculates the route rapidly when he deliberately detours onto side roads, doubles back on his path, and checks for signs of pursuit. Not that there are any. It's mid-afternoon of a late winter/ early spring day in the south. The air outside is a chilly sixty degrees, but at least there's no risk of sleet or snow—Maryland roads turn into apocalyptic chaos at the first hint of icing conditions. By the time he's made the RDV and got his man, it'll be getting dark. Sam pushes back tiredness, scans the traffic immediately in front of and behind him again, and drives on.

It's early rush hour when he gets to the station, and the big park-and-ride is starting to empty out. It's not hard to get in, but finding a parking space involves lots of frustrating queuing as he waits for tired commuters to get their wheels on and leave.

Parking, Sam pulls on a baseball cap, the brim low over his forehead, then heads for the station lobby. A train has pulled in and people spill across the platform, for this is the last stop on the line. He walks over to the kiosk and buys a Pepsi, then positions himself alongside the doorway to wait. *Don't mind me*, he thinks, *just another ride-share pickup here*. It's method acting, of a kind. Occasionally he glances at his watch, or pretends to check the baseball score on his phone. His side-eye scan relies on positioning and reflections in windows rather than direct gaze, and he's at pains not to present his face to the CCTV cameras.

The stars and stripes hang on the wall above the steps down to the platform, but something about the flag makes Sam itch: it's *wrong*. Eventually he works out what it is: there are too many stars, and they don't have the right number of points. If he looks at them too long they begin to swirl like pearlescent whirlpools, sucking his gaze into their black-hole hearts. He shudders. At least there are no silver mannequins standing watch in the shadows here.

Trying not to let his eyes close is a torment, but eventually an office worker emerges from the platform in the wake of the crowd from the third train. Middle-aged, once muscular but running to fat, something about him screams *civil servant* to Sam. Also, he's looking around. Too damn conspicuously, in Sam's opinion, so Sam moves to head him off. "Gil Tancredy?" he asks.

Tancredy jumps. "That's me!"

"This way." Sam waits until they're on the wheelchair ramp outside. "Do you have some ID?"

"You're supposed to take me to the President, aren't you?"

Sam's voice hardens. "ID, please."

Tancredy seems extremely nervous—as well he might. "I'm going to reach into my coat pocket," he says, before slowly pulling out a wallet. Sam nods and keeps his hand well away from his waistband. So far, so good. Tancredy pulls out a badge: "Postal Inspector. Yeah, I know it's cancelled. I'm with—was with—the Comstocks."

This is the correct answer. Sam quickly scans their surroundings. "Follow me," he says, then heads for the truck.

His contact doesn't balk until they get to the black crew-cab pickup. "I haven't seen *your* ID," he challenges, wary of getting into a truck with a total stranger.

Sam doesn't have the heart to tell Tancredy he could have shot him just about any time after he entered the station. "You want to see the President, that's Arthur Savage, previously Governor of California and chair of the Screen Actors Guild?" He raises an eyebrow. "Head of the Executive Branch, in case you've forgotten it, like everybody else?" He squeezes his eyes shut briefly, resisting the gathering headache. It's making him slightly short-tempered.

Tancredy's expression is that of a priest who, fearing himself forsaken by his faith, witnesses a true miracle: "Yes! That's him!" He clears his throat, visibly holding back his excitement. "He's still free! And you are?"

"Secret Service Officer Penrose. Come with me." He may be lacking the dark suit, earbud, and shades but he's still the real deal. He flips Tancredy a glimpse of his badge, discreetly searches him for weapons, relieves him of his phone, then climbs in and drives them away from the station.

By the time Sam has driven in circles for half an hour, with Tancredy head down with his coat over his head for most of it, it's full dark. Sam isn't an expert evasion driver but he's done the standard course and kept in practice, and he's pretty certain nobody's following him. So he voice-commands his phone to dial Senior Officer Mattingley when he's about five minutes out.

"Matt here. Report."

"Penrose, I have a Gilbert Tancredy, Comstock group."

"What's your ETA?"

"Three minutes."

"We'll be waiting. Mattingley out."

"When I pull up," Sam says calmly, "I'm going to wind down the windows and I want you to keep your hands in full view on the dash. Treat it like a traffic stop. We're all a little twitchy and sleep-deprived right now."

The current safe house is much like the last: a bland McMansion with a discreet fence out front, set well back from the road behind a thick hedge for privacy. Sam drives up to the garage, winds the windows down, and puts his hands on the wheel with the cab light on while the gates whine shut behind him. Officers with drawn weapons close and check the truck out before Mattingley gives the all-clear. There's a faint whimper from Tancredy: Sam looks round and sees his passenger staring.

"You're clear to step out, Mr. Tancredy," he assures the postal inspector.

"I—I'm not used to this," Tancredy admits, dabbing at his forehead. "Second time this week, goddamn it."

"Second time?"

"Guns." Tancredy shudders, then steps out of the cab.

Sam leads him into the front hall, then the dayroom where— as usual—the curtains are drawn. Rather more unusually, the President is waiting for them. He rises from the sofa to offer Tancredy his hand. "Sir," Tancredy croaks, visibly overcome. "It's—I was having a hard time believing—"

"It's all right," Arthur says to Sam: "I'll take it from here."

"Yes, sir." Sam notices Officers Haas and Cho are present, doing their best wallpaper impersonations while remaining ready to body-check Tancredy if he acts up. OSCAR is in safe hands. Sam steps back into the doorway and takes up his own position.

"I'm pleased to meet you at last, Mr. Tancredy," says the President. "I've been told what your unit used to do for our nation." A brief expression of pain flickers across his face. "You've got my undivided attention. What can I do for you?"

"Sir." Tancredy draws himself up, almost standing to attention. "When the OPA initiated their takeover of the Postal Service in the run-up to the . . . broader . . . takeover, my team was ordered to disperse and go underground inside other agencies. We were hit by the same amnesia whammy as everyone else, but we continued to coordinate and work on the problem, and regained partial awareness a week ago."

His grimace speaks volumes, and Sam stifles a sympathetic yawn. It's bad enough being part of a team working shifts in the same base, able to reorient each other at every awakening. The thought of trying to maintain situational awareness if he were living at home, sleeping and waking in isolation each day, doesn't bear thinking about.

"Yesterday we were contacted by an agent of the British government." Sudden tension grips the room. "He said they're concerned and don't want you to fall into the hands of the, the Nazgûl—that's what he called them—and they want to help. He says a high-ranking representative of the British government is in town and would like to meet you. I was given a burner phone—" He cringes at Mattingley's expression. "I didn't bring it here, I'm not that stupid!—but if you think it's appropriate we can set up a meeting."

"That's very—" the President pauses. "Matt, you have something to say?"

Mattingley focuses on the Comstock guy. "Did the Brit say how he found you?" he asks.

"Uh, yes, sir? He said something about an Oracle. The Oracle told them where to find me and indicated I was their best channel for getting a message through to you." Tancredy looks as hopeful as a puppy that's just learned to pee on command.

Mattingley nods. "Sam, would you mind taking Mr. Tancredy through into the, the kitchen"—he means somewhere out of earshot—"for a few minutes?"

"I—" The President pauses, then smiles blindingly at Mattingley. "Okay, fine, *you* tell me what's going on?" He's waiting expectantly, arms crossed, as Sam leads the Comstock agent out of the front room and closes the door behind them.

"Come on," Sam tells Tancredy. "I don't know about you, but I could do with a cup of coffee." And something a little stronger.

"Copy that. What do you think is going to happen?" Tancredy asks, still slightly awestruck.

Sam forces himself to smile benevolently. "I wouldn't like to guess. Go on, it's through there." As he steps behind the Comstock agent he crosses his fingers. Tancredy seems like a straight-up guy: he really hopes that, when OSCAR and the head of his protection detail finish tearing strips off each other over the unwisdom of bringing an untrusted person inside the secure zone,

Mattingley won't order him to take Tancredy out back and shoot him.

The Operational Phenomenology Agency maintains satellite offices in a number of cities, and a plethora of sites in and around Washington DC. In the wake of its takeover of other government agencies last fall, the OPA has expanded and taken on additional personnel, for whom new office space had to be obtained. As most of its new client organizations are part of the federal government, most of these personnel need to be based in and around the capitol.

Only one currently existing building is large enough to accommodate what the Black Chamber will become when the starry gates open and their Lord finally returns to resume his rule. So the Army Corps of Engineers is overseeing the construction of a huge new strip of office buildings along I-395—demolishing anything in their way—to hold the office workers who will presently be displaced when the Black Chamber takes over the Pentagon building.

Ninety feet directly beneath the center courtyard café in the middle of the Pentagon—previously known as the Ground Zero Cafe, because when the bomb dropped that was where it would most likely detonate—there is a deep subbasement office with ferroconcrete walls and a filtered air supply, accessible by discreet elevators and staircases from all five wings of the main building. It was designed as a deep command bunker back when the worst threats were raids by long-range Luftwaffe bombers bearing conventional explosives. Obsolescent since the morning of July 16, 1945—it won't withstand a direct ground burst from an atom bomb, much less more modern munitions—it still possesses certain uses. Being deep underground and equidistant from all the other wings, it was well suited as a switch for SCAN, the Army's automatic switched communications system, and later for AUTOVON. AUTOVON led to ARPANET, the predecessor of the internet, and the secure exchange in the basement played host to one of the first IMPs—Interface Message Processors—outside of academia. By the early 1980s a lack of rackspace led the DoD to relocate their hardened exchanges to a site closer to the 1950s-sized mainframe halls. And it was then that the empty bunker was taken over by a shadowy affiliate of the National Security Agency, tasked with waging occult warfare against the enemies of the nation.

The past six months have brought some changes.

There is a pentagonal main room inside the bunker, and within it there is a ceremonial maze, inscribed in blood and silver that glows with a soft fluorescence, converging on a dais at the heart of the design. The labyrinth takes the shape of a pentacle aligned with the building overhead: at each corner stands a motionless sentinel clad head to toe in occlusive silver fabric. Robed in black and crimson silk and shod in slippers of disturbingly pale leather, the Deputy Director paces her way through the maze. In her left hand she bears a jewel-capped scepter carved from the femur of a dead pope, and in her right hand she bears a gold-plated chalice made from a skull that once served Josef Stalin as an ashtray. As she walks she recites a prayer of allegiance and propitiation, its cadences and grammar those of a variant dialect of Old Enochian.

It's a large room—the blast-redirecting partitions have long since been removed—but it feels tight, almost claustrophobic, all sight lines converging on the throne that surmounts the dais at the precise center of the Pentagon. Below this room there is a subbasement crammed with backup generators and air and water filters, and above it is a floor packed with switches, network hubs, and a quantum computing mechanism that refuses to confirm or deny its own sentience—but this level is given over to the labyrinth which forms a powerful containment grid, and the grid encloses the dais, and the dais supports the wards and the cradle, and the cradle bears the backless throne.

Dry-swallowing, the Deputy Director approaches her ruler's mouthpiece.

The backless throne is a rococo nightmare, Louis Quinze by way of H. R. Giger. Everything about it is subtly wrong. Its seat is set at the wrong height for human knees and its legs (all seven of them) have four joints (two of which bend the wrong way) and end in barbed ebon claws. But the throne is by no means the worst part. Silver chains thick enough to anchor a truck rise from the corners of the dais and converge on the throne's occupant, who is manacled at throat and thorax by solid metal bands, as if they might murder any supplicants if left unrestrained.

The occupant tracks the Deputy Director as she walks the path, and for a moment she sees through the living corpse to the animating intelligence beyond. It regards her from all seven compound eyes, frond-like emerald antennae waving lazily as they taste the breeze from the air conditioning. Then she blinks, and her vision fades back to the formerly human body of her liege's Mouthpiece.

"*Master and mistress of time, ruler of space, let your miserable slave abase herself before you and bask in the ecstasy and terror of your regard,*" she recites in Old Enochian, as she completes the final loop of the maze. "*Glory,*" chorus the five silver guardians of the corners as she approaches each vertex; "*Glory to the Lord of Sleep.*" They speak in unison, a single voice emerging from many mouths.

The Deputy Director reaches the end of the glowing labyrinth and goes to her knees before the dais. Then she bows her head and lowers the tip of the scepter to dip into the skull chalice. The stark shadows of the room pool within it and ripple like a dark fluid, as if it is full of blood rather than the absence of light. After a few seconds the shadows overflow the brim and drip across her lap.

"*Rise and approach our vessel.*" The occupant speaks with a voice like wind sifting through the debris of long-forgotten tombs.

The Deputy Director stands, not without effort (for she is in early middle age), and steps onto the dais. In front of the throne stand plinths with supports for the scepter and chalice: she places them in their niches and bows three times, then steps between them and bows to the occupant.

"*Brief me,*" says the Mouthpiece of the Lord of Sleep.

The Deputy Director stands to attention, and begins to list the significant developments of the past day, translating fluently into the language of the ancient ones, the tongue that controls reality itself. For the most part there's not a lot to report: 95 percent of the time the government runs on cruise control, a huge juggernaut of bureaucracy rumbling predictably along its tracks. Even the presidency, an office freighted with a mystical level of respect by the citizenry, has so little room for maneuver that officeholders with diametrically opposite ideologies can often appear identical from outside the Beltway.

As she delivers her briefing, she examines the throne's occupant for signs of deterioration. The Mouthpieces of her Lord are small endoparasitic projections of His multidimensional self, constrained by the physical reality in which humanity dwells. Small autonomous organisms in their own right, at this stage in their life cycle they are linked to the will of their Lord and control a human vessel from within, using it to communicate with their servants. When the true resurrection is finally engineered, her God will manifest fully in this reality, no longer filtered through these biological sock puppets, tiny parodies of His true self.

This particular Mouthpiece speaks through the body of a man in his late twenties, Middle Eastern, with matted beard and straggly hair. The CIA delivered him from some undisclosed interrogation operation, listed as surplus to requirements and available to the OPA to be used to destruction. His crimes, while alive, are no longer of any importance. His unseeing eyeballs glow softly green, tendrils writhing in their luminous depths; his orange jumpsuit is soiled and caked with filth, and he is emaciated. Three of his fingers that still have nails are in need of a trim; his other fingertips are blood-crusted ruins tipped in naked bone. His body writhes slowly atop the throne, as if impaled and trying to ease a gut-deep agony. Even though the mind of the occupant is long since gone, erased to make space for the senses of a great one who cannot (yet) fit within the walls of this universe, the peripheral nerves still deliver signals, and deep spinal reflexes twitch muscles in an attempt to minimize the pain.

The Deputy Director recounts her conversation with the minions of the Black Pharaoh, provides a situation update on THRESHOLD, GODWAKER, and other esoteric codeword programs, and winds up with a swift rundown of various ongoing tasks, including the pursuit of the President. By the end of it, nearly an hour later, her mouth is dry, her throat is sore, and her knees are stiffening. The occupant, for his part, is still fully attentive, although tears of blood trickle down his cheeks when she mentions the latter affair.

"*Do you have any commands, Lord?*" she asks.

"*This mouthpiece is failing,*" says the body on the throne. "*We require a replacement.*"

"Yes, Lord." Procuring a new host body to serve as the mouth and ears of her Lord will not be hard, nor is this the first time she's had to replace one: the feeders sent by her Lord consume their victims almost as rapidly as V-parasites. She waits attentively for further instructions.

"*There is a disturbance in the heartland,*" says the mouth of her Lord. "*Tools of the Black Pharaoh, guided by His Oracles, are at work in Our lands. They seek to free the god-emperor from the sea of dreams. This cannot be permitted.*"

"No, Lord." The Deputy Director bows her head, hiding her frustration. Her Lord is trying to be helpful, but she already knows that the British are stirring up trouble. The trouble with the Lord's help is that the Lord has difficulty focussing on minutiae such as street addresses and safe houses.

"*They come in . . . teams.*" The Lord lapses into English for the final word, and the Deputy Director shivers: the current mouthpiece clearly needs replacing very soon, ideally as soon as this audience is over. "*One group in* Colorado Springs *traces the footsteps of the former High Priest of the Sleeper in the Pyramid, cursed be his name. Another group in this temple fastness*"—the Enochian word shares the meanings of royal palace and capital city—"*seeks to raise the god-emperor.*" They mean the President. "*You must stop them.*"

Tell me something I don't know, the Deputy Director thinks frustratedly, then tells him, "*I hear and obey, Lord.*" After a pause, "*Do you have further instructions for me?*"

"Go," the Mouthpiece says dismissively. "*Seek for us a new garment of flesh, that our eggs may be clothed in life when they conduct the orchestra of our awakening. Continue to build out the thinking machines that sing hymns to our vastness, that they may power our thoughts. Continue to prepare the chariots of our ascent to the heavenly spheres, that the weakening of the false vacuum shall proceed apace. And defend Our lands against the unbelievers. That is all that is required of you now. You will be summoned if further words are required.*"

The Deputy Director bows deeply, and begins to retrace her path, retrieving the scepter and chalice along the way. She does not look back at the Mouthpiece of the Lord of Sleep, the sock puppet of Dread Cthulhu impaled atop their throne. Behind her, unseen and unwatched, the decaying once-human body stares into the shadows and begins to eat another finger.

Three and a half hours later Jim and I are sitting in first class on an implausibly slow express train—I've seen faster tortoises—and I have begun to hope that we've gotten clean away from New York. At least, we gave it our best shot.

After our interrupted lunch, I had dragged Jim into Macy's, made a beeline to the restrooms to tidy up, then rushed us both through all eighty-six floors of clothing. It was strictly utilitarian shopping: one change of hipster-casual outfits, one of business attire, and a shoulder bag for each of us. After we'd paid and changed, we dived down to the subway for half an hour of switchbacks we hoped would shake off anybody who was following us and hopefully confuse the enemy about our intended destination.

Along the way Jim tried to buy me a replacement phone, but it turned out that anything you can buy in a drugstore is too underpowered or insecure to run our firmware, and anything you can buy in a mobile phone shop requires you to give your date of birth, bank details, bra size, blood group, and your great-grandmother's email address. Even if I'd been willing to give them all that, the setup process would have eaten at least an hour of our evasion time. So we noped out of the T-Mobile store, and for about the first time in eighteen years I was totally phoneless. It felt like going commando in a miniskirt on a Saturday night in town, even after Jim sent an email to ensure that there'd be a shiny new Samsung waiting for me in DC. Not knowing I could check my team's timesheets on my phone at 3 a.m. felt profoundly *wrong*.

But my lack of a phone isn't what gives me the ugly, sick feeling as I sit in the train, beanie pulled down, periodically moving my scarf away from my mouth so I can take another sip of coffee while I wait for the other shoe to drop.

"It may not happen," Jim reassures me quietly. He reaches across the table—we're in opposite seats—and takes my hand. "It was a busy restaurant and there was a lot of running and shrieking happening."

I tighten my grip on his fingers. "Yes, and the condom was *just* a little bit torn, and I was just a *tiny* bit over the drink-driving limit, and there were only a *few* drops of blood, sweetie, and *you* are whistling past the graveyard." I keep my voice low. There's nobody in the seat behind Jim, and nobody across the aisle from us, but I'm still acutely self-conscious.

"Most of the blood was theirs. Ill-gotten or otherwise."

I try to think of a way to change the subject without being

obvious because I don't want to alarm him, but I'm getting the hunger again, and the nauseating dread isn't helping. I've got a feeling that this is what Mr. Kadir must have felt like, waiting for me to arrive. It's like a horrible cloud hanging over my head, waiting to drop and choke me to death. Except it's not me, is it?

"If they could sample you—"

"—I'm immune to them—"

"—Track and trace, love." My stomach twists again. I wish he wouldn't use that word. "Law of sympathy and contagion, isn't that what the double-domes call it? They can set sniffers on it, those eyeless multidimensional dog-things—"

"—Hounds," I say, helplessly pedantic. They're not the worst. You can shield yourself against hounds by taking shelter in a non-Euclidean space, or you can even banish them with the right kind of demonological pepper spray. But I don't want to tell him the worst I can imagine, because to speak your fears is to give them shape, and the well of terror is bottomless.

"—Or automated face recognition on CCTV, remember we're coming into Washington DC."

I steal a quick glance at him. He's wearing his cop face right now, doing his best move-along-now-nothing-to-see-here public-reassurance shtick. It's heartbreaking: Officer Friendly is trying to comfort *me*. He thinks *I'm* scared. But *he's* the one who should be bricking it.

"Jim." I smile, squeeze his fingers again, and put just enough extra force behind it—a little mental shove—to remind him that I'm not as easy to break as I look. "We are on this train, and they are not"—*I hope*—"and when we get off we will have support—"

His phone rings, the peculiar trilling tone of the end-to-end encrypted voice service we use internally.

I watch Jim take the voice call. He cradles the phone delicately in his right hand, rock-steady despite the seasick wobble of the train (I had *no idea* any developed nation was worse at track maintenance than Network Rail back home). There's no sign of tremor, although I should have bought him a nail file when we were shopping—he chipped a couple. He listens intently. I focus on his eyelashes, which are long and almost feminine, in stark contrast to his square jawline and buzz cut. *I want this man in my life,* I think, *but I only have him on loan. This cover story was a big mistake.* I can't maintain an appropriate professional detachment.

"Yes . . . huh . . . okay, do that, I'll tell her, thanks. . . . Yes, you, too. Bye." He ends the call and looks at me pensively.

"What?" I ask.

"That was J. She's got a phone waiting for you, and D. has made contact, or so he says. I think there's some difference of opinion as to what constitutes contact." His lips thin. "When we get in, let's catch the underground a couple of stops before we get a cab, shall we?"

"Yes—" I begin, just as he says something like "*Fuuuh,*" and slumps sideways against the window.

Time crystalizes around me. I reach out instinctively and grab his phone before it falls. The light through the window, barely tolerable, is brightening ferociously as the chittering in my head gets louder. I can hear them: not mine, *theirs,* the same ones I heard in Times Square and in the restaurant. They've found him and they're excited, it's a new lunch buffet and I can feel tiny invisible mandibles digging in across the table from me—

My ward is buzzing and growing hot but I'm not the one of us who's in immediate danger.

I take Jim's hand and press his index finger against the sensor on the back of his phone, turn the screen towards me, and desperately search for the OFCUT suite. He's put it in his quick launch bar, clever lad. I tap it and lean across the table towards him, forehead to forehead in desperation, feeling him twitch. It's the onset of the seizure I've been expecting for the past three hours.

So cold.

The main screen comes up and I finger-crawl through it by muscle memory, thanking whatever guardian angels keep an eye out for lovelorn vampires that we both use the same countermeasures app. And here it is, the icon for the firewall: not an internet firewall but a cognitive blockade, an electronic version of the protective wards we use.[7] I set it running, then wrap Jim's fingers around his phone. A furtive glance tells me nobody has noticed Jim's slump or my blur of motion—only seconds have passed. I can still hear the chittering, rustling noises around him, a sound like bacon in a deep fat fryer and a smell like stale blood. What else can I do?

I reach into the mock-turtleneck collar of my bodysuit and tug on my ward, which is still vibrating and warm. I pull the cord up and over my head. It snags on my wooly cap for a few seconds and I smell burning skin as I stuff it over his neck, then hunker down in my seat and tug my turtleneck up. The back of my neck stings horribly and *still* nobody's noticed anything wrong. I stare across the table and check Jim's fingers on the phone, the ward around his neck—he's got one of his own, the more the better—as I wrestle my hat and scarf back into position onehanded. I can't help Jim if my head is on fire. I grab his other arm, the one that's slipped down behind the table, and pull it up until I can hold his hand, wishing, *willing* him to stay alive, to fight back, gorge rising in my throat.

His eyelids flicker. A few seconds later he half-grunts/half-coughs. His hand squeezes convulsively, and if I was the old Mhari Murphy I'd scream because his grip is bone-crushingly tight, the super-strength cutting in. "Muh-whuh—"

I nearly faint with relief before the truth comes crashing home. It isn't over. In fact, it's barely begun. "Jim. Jim? Can you hear me?"

His eyes open. I lean towards him urgently. "Smile for me?

---

[7] It sucks battery like crazy. Brains told me that it's based on a thing you use to generate bitcoins, although I think he was messing with me—as if money-grubbing mathematics preferentially attracts soul-sucking parasites.

Can you raise your right arm? Now your left? Say something, Jim—"

FAST: Face, Arms, Speech, Time. Catastrophic K syndrome often starts with a transient ischemic attack, a mini-stroke. V-parasite infestation—transmitted by having your blood supped on by PHANG-symbionts—looks much the same at first.

"What," he says, dazed.

"Smile and raise your arms," I tell him.

"What?"

"Just do it—"

"—My phone—"

"—Don't let go!" My urgency gets through to him, or he's becoming more aware, more focused by the second, because he frowns and then meets my eyes, alert. Superpowered recovery is part of the Officer Friendly package, but it's not going to last.

"What happened?" he demands.

"You—" I realize I'm short on air: I take a couple of deep, gasping breaths—"had a seizure, I dropped my ward and the OFCUT on your phone on you, it passed. About twenty, thirty seconds." Gasp some more. "V or K, can't tell which, but we've got to get you inside a containment grid or—"

My vision is blurring. After a moment I realize the gasping is turning to sobs. For a few seconds I was sure he was dying, and it wasn't like the scene at the restaurant. I've never been so frightened for somebody in my life: I felt totally powerless. You can't punch extradimensional parasites out of your boyfriend's brain. He was pulling on his mojo like crazy back there, fighting the silver mannequin people. It'd be just our luck if he's fended off K syndrome for a couple of years, only for his feeders to get bored and start nibbling on his cerebellum right now, although the K syndrome will stop progressing if he just never uses his power ever again. But what really worries me is that he left bloodstains back at the restaurant. If one of the adversary's PHANGs sampled his leavings, the V-parasites—

—Oh god, I sensed V-parasites while he was seizing.

It is *them.*

And as he looks at me I realize that he understands, because he just gives me a little nod, a jerk of the chin, and says, "How long do you think I've got?"

We humans—or ex-humans, in the case of some of us—are used to thinking of ourselves as being the top of the food chain. But we are not at the top of the food chain—not even remotely. Plenty of things eat us in various ways. Let's start at the bottom, with the microscopic. Viruses, bacteria, protozoa: these are familiar, everyday threats. In our line of work, those of us who formerly worked for the Laundry run into others. Feeders in the night are a classic—mindless feeders that take over a human nervous system and control its body, spreading by touch, as deadly as a high-tension cable and about as intelligent. So are K syndrome parasites, which are drawn to people who carry out thaumaturgic invocations in their own heads and like BSE chew their victims' brains into soggy, bleeding lace. The closely related class of C-parasites thankfully prefer the taste of our silicon chips.

V-symbionts are a little different. They provide certain benefits to occult practitioners as long as their host feeds them blood samples from other people, on whom they feed via some kind of link—the law of sympathetic magic is apparently some kind of macroscopic quantum entanglement—but they ultimately cause much the same damage as K syndrome.

There are macroscopic threats, too. Sharks. Big cats. Basilisks. Firewyrms (I refuse to dignify those things by calling them *dragons;* real dragons should be elegant reptilian predators, not sea slugs with wings that vomit acid). Hounds. Unicorns. (Don't get me started on unicorns.)

But threats on this level mostly only eat your body and soul, one or both at a time.

About bodies: I am one, and I contain multitudes. It's true: I consist of an ensemble of approximately thirty trillion cells, working in concert to sustain life, with roughly the same number of bacterial and fungal passengers along for the ride. The Republic of Mhari contains five thousand times more cells than there are humans on Earth, but is somehow both more *and* less than the sum of her parts. If all those cells die, then I am, by definition, dead. But the relationship between cell-citizens and the Republic of Me is less obvious than you might think.

At any point in time some of my cells are dying and being replaced, and the me that exists today consists almost entirely of different cells from the me of a couple of years ago—although I'm still *me*. But if you were to separate all my cells and then keep them alive in a mad scientist's test-tube collection, *I'd* be dead, though all my bits live on. The Republic of Self can be dissolved, or taken over in a coup, or drastically reformed. I harbor this illusion of unitary identity—but in reality I'm what biologists call a superorganism, a swarm, an ensemble entity. *I* am not *me*: I am Hobbes's Leviathan, or Leviathan's Representative.

Oh, and that's not all. Cells are complex things, full of intracellular machinery, much of it descended from free-living bacteria in the primordial whatever the hell we evolved from that swallowed one another and became symbionts. (Don't ask me how: I'm not a microbiologist.) Each cell is, in fact, a micro-Republic of Cell, which makes my body a gigantic bickering United Nations; and as for the feeders in the night? That's what happens when the alien mothership from *Independence Day* turns up and zaps the White House. V-parasites? Tiny evil Blood Nazis, occupying and regimenting and restructuring the body politic, making some of the trains run on time but imposing a state of permanent war—practicing genocide on other people.

Which brings me to Fuckboy's little accident.

Our pursuers found a drop of his blood and fed it to one of their PHANGs. Maybe they took blood samples from everyone in the restaurant (they seem blasé about collateral damage). They probably got me, too, but as I already carry my own strain of V-parasites, I'm resistant to being hacked. Whatever the case, though, one of their PHANGs has now got a lock on him. And like good little Blood Nazis, they're munching away on his gray matter, and they will continue to eat until he disintegrates, or more likely until a blood vessel gives way and he bleeds out inside his own skull.

Like a state—like these United States—his body is being taken over in a cellular coup d'état so far below the level of his awareness that he's powerless to do anything about it. The coup is in progress and insurgents are marching neurons into the sports arena and gunning them down. The gates of the capital are open and the tanks are rolling. He's probably got a week left, two weeks, tops. Long enough to complete the mission. That's all.

Meanwhile, at Filton Airport:

As evening falls, the blackout curtains inside a hangar at the private airfield are pulled aside and the hangar main doors open. A small convoy of maintenance vehicles roll out, but most of the pre-flight work has been done indoors, out of view of spy satellites.

Ground crew in RAF uniforms swarm around the doors, then withdraw. Half an hour passes. Finally, a tug noses into view, its towing arms clasped around a wheel, overshadowed by the big white bird's droop nose. It casts a long shadow on the apron as it inches out of the hangar, turns onto the taxiway, and comes to a stop. The Concorde is closer to a spacecraft or a strategic bomber than a regular airliner. It takes days of painstaking maintenance to send one into the sky for a few brief hours, bellowing hoarsely on four afterburning engines that leave a faint smog trail.

Back during the 1980s and 1990s, the RAF Concordes were painted in British Airways livery, with tail numbers that matched civilian aircraft. Their flight plans from the British Aerospace maintenance depot here at Filton were listed as test flights or civilian charter joyrides. While the RAF Concordes flew, the BA craft whose markings were duplicated remained tucked out of sight, providing an alibi. But the supersonic airliners retired from civilian service over a decade ago. Since then they've flown infrequently, and only at night, and there's no point maintaining the pretense. So when Concorde 302 flies, it's in plain white thermal paint, with a pale pink and blue fin flash, and an RAF serial number high and proud on its tail fin.

Another ten minutes pass as the ground crew hook up a generator. Eventually a puff of smoke emerges from one of the inboard engines, and then the other engines spool up in sequence. Technicians scramble to detach the generator cart. Then the tug uncouples, and everyone clears the area as the pilots run through the last pre-takeoff checklists and the engines stabilize.

For this flight, 302 is taking off with a full fuel load—over 98 tonnes—and only a relief crew for passengers. The two flying Concordes have limited passenger seating, most of their cabin being reserved for specialized cargo. There are no sorcerers on this flight, and the summoning grids spaced along the fuselage are de-energized. The flight plan on file with the destination airfield in Canada hilariously mis-describes the Concorde as a Russian heavy bomber paying a goodwill visit, but that's okay. They'll be arriving after nightfall, under tight security, and even so, the prospect of a Tupolev 160 dropping round for poutine is less preposterous than the truth.

Canadian Forces Base Goose Bay, in the north of Labrador, doubles as Goose Bay Airport. It's a port of entry, with border-services agents able to handle private flights carrying no more than fifteen passengers. It has a runway long enough and solid enough to take heavy military aircraft, and, more importantly, it has hosted the RAF in the past. There's no permanent detachment there, but a hangar and barracks have been prepared and ground crew capable of turning around a Concorde flew in a week ago.

"302 Heavy, you are cleared for takeoff."

Despite the resumption of funding for the program under the

New Management, it has been nearly a year since a military Concorde last turned onto the runway at Filton, wound up its engines to full power, applied reheat, and launched itself into the Atlantic sunset. But 302 Heavy thunders down the runway and soars away as if it is all perfectly routine, leaving a medley of car alarms beeping in its wake. And the penultimate piece of the Prime Minister's chess set finally moves into its position on the board, ready for the endgame.

7: CRITICAL-PATH DEPENDENCIES

Pete has learned many things in his four years of working with the Laundry. He's seen a lot, including some things that he would never have voluntarily signed up for, the sort of horrors that make ex-soldiers sit bolt upright from their sleep, weeping inconsolably. But his former day job—he is still a vicar, and his bishop is remarkably reluctant to raise a fuss about his apparent conscription by a secret government agency devoted to issues which can best be described as ungodly (or worse, *wrong* godly)—taught him a lot about helping people. And he's had a lot of practice helping families suffering from experiences that are simultaneously mundane and far more horrifying than anything in a movie: deaths from cancer and dementia, the loss of babies and young children, that sort of thing.

All things considered, he's coped pretty well. But the cracks are beginning to show in his self-assurance, for he is close to certain that they are all damned. Pete is no biblical literalist, but he can't ignore the metaphorical stench of brimstone that dogs the Prime Minister's footsteps. *God is gone and Heaven has fallen: Who do you pitch in with, Beelzebub or Satan?* He has struggled with this question privately, but can find no better answer than the Senior Auditor's: *We fight on so that something that remembers being human might survive.* But now he finds himself riding shotgun while Brains drives through a land overshadowed by amnesia, trying to find common ground with an *alfär* vampire with autism-spectrum disorder who is hosting a magically induced secondary personality. And the first word that springs to mind for his condition is *godforsaken*.

"This sacrifice we're supposed to retrieve," he says, thinking hard before he continues. "Are they a person? And are we rescuing them from being a sacrifice?" *Don't ask about the Door or the Forgotten Emperor,* he thinks uneasily, *just take it one step at a time.* It's pretty clear from her intermittent repetitive actions and gaze avoidance that Jon is stressed out. Whoever thought it was a good idea to stick her on a commercial flight to a foreign country on her own was—well, he'll write them a stiffly worded memo when he gets home, with copious references to the Disability Discrimination Act. Maybe set HR on them about enforcing policy. With the shreds of the Jonquil persona peeling away from the irrefrangible bedrock of Yarisol, the emergent Jon chimera is worryingly fragile. Maybe he's overly pessimistic and Jon will cohere, but right now the most likely outcome he can see is the PHANG in the back seat going into a noisy meltdown. And the prospect is making the skin on the back of his neck crawl.

"Sacrifice," echoes Jon, tapping her fingers on the center armrest. "Radio."

"It's all right," Pete says, as calmly as he can with a stressed-out vampire fifty centimeters behind his throat. "Brains, I'm going to try to figure out how the radio works. Jon, there are going to be some loud noises for a minute or so, but I'll make everything all right."

Back home, Pete rides a Yamaha. His wife has an ancient VW camper. His exposure to modern in-car electronics has been roughly doubled by this trip. Nor is Brains any help. So Pete grapples for a few minutes with something called "Sirius XM" which, to British sensibilities, appears to originate from another star system. Eventually he works out how to turn it on and finds a channel broadcasting from the planet of the overexcited pizza salesmen. A few tentative button-presses later, he's channel-hopping between the payday loan shark frequency and the Realtor™ network, who between them appear to own 60 percent of the channels on the satellite service. "Ah, I think I'm getting the hang of this," he says, poking the "scan" button optimistically.

"... coming to you on WOCZ with tonight's episode of *The Whatever Show* in Crested Butte, Colorado, capitol of high weirdness in America. And we're going to be talking with you about government conspiracies and coverups, Men in Black, and crashed UFOs ..."

"That's it!" Pete exclaims, just as Jon says, "Sacrifice!"

Brains swerves but manages to regain control without hitting anything. "What?" he complains.

"Pull over," says Pete, "I can't google while you're driving—autocorrect."

Brains grumbles under his breath but ferrets out a dirt driveway and gets the land yacht turned around. (The nearest actual parking spot is more than a mile behind them.) The eerie synth-backed warble of The Stranglers comes on-air. "How long is this going to take?" he asks.

"Should be an hour-long slot," Pete mumbles. He's staring at a program listing on his phone. "It's not loading. Can you get us somewhere with more signal? I'm trying to find the studio's address."

"It'll be a canned session," Brains insists as he drives back towards town.

"Not according to the home page. It's a live radio call-in show, so ... huh."

"What?"

"Satnav." Pete resorts to monosyllables when he's preoccupied. Right now he's dividing his attention between his smartphone screen and the SUV's navigation system, which is as overblown and supersized as the rest of the vehicle. "It won't let me enter a destination while we're moving."

Brains stands on the brakes, provoking a squeak of distress from Jon. Moments later a horn blares and lights speed past. "*Car park,*" Pete says between gritted teeth. "*Not* the middle of the road." He glances at the rearview mirror apprehensively. Jon is massaging the side of her neck where the seat belt tightened painfully.

Five minutes later they blunder into a lay-by. Brains parks. Pete considers telling him that the right-hand wheels are on the curb, but reconsiders. Brains's temper has been fraying, and the consequences of triggering an outburst with Jon in the back seat are not something Pete cares to contemplate. "Right," he says, and punches in the address of the WOCZ-FM studio. "This should take us to the station's HQ, assuming it's not an admin building or a glorified post office box."

"You think we should go there." Brains crosses his arms across the steering wheel.

"I think—"

"You *must*?" Jon breaks in breathily, a residuum of Jonquil's personality reasserting itself. "Like, it's important?"

"Why?" Brains asks mulishly.

"Because *listen*—"

The music has been replaced by more chatter, a request for phone-in callers, a sponsored message from the Roofing Royalty®, then a couple of minutes' chatter between someone called Gaby and a caller as drivelingly inane as the worst on Capital FM back home. Then there's more music, and a call-in that raises the hair on the back of Pete's neck. ". . . from the Circle of Friends of the Lord of Sleep, with a message about Billie Jean, who called earlier. There is a reason we don't talk about the Man . . . you should keep your lips zipped unless you want to sleep with the fishes like Billie Jean up by Peanut Lake. . . ."

"Fuck, fuck, *fuuuuck*—" says Brains, as Pete simultaneously says, "Drive!" And hits the "go" button on the navigation screen.

"We will be in time?!" Jon interro-exclaims.

"Does this mean what I think it means?" Brains asks, but Pete is fresh out of answers.

Sticking within spitting distance of the speed limit—the last thing they need right now is the attention of local law enforcement—

it takes Brains nearly twenty minutes to drag the SUV halfway across town. Their destination is one of a row of drab, windowless business premises. They could be anything from call centers or car showrooms to supervillain lairs or radio broadcasters—

"Look on the roof?" says Jon. "It has *satellite dishes?!*" She gives the last two words an odd emphasis, as if she's never seen such things before. Perhaps she hasn't, Pete considers.

Brains pulls over before they get to the building. "What now?"

"We wait," Jon says flatly.

"Wait for what?"

Pete's scalp crawls. The radio is still playing but there are no more phone-in callers. It's just ads alternating with canned music, like any other robot playlist channel. "Peanut Lake," he says, drumming his fingers on the dash. He calls up the satnav again. "Brains, please kill the headlights."

Brains doesn't argue. He reaches into the door pocket and pulls out the thaumic analyzer he assembled the day before. "I'm not picking up anything above background here."

Peanut Lake is a few miles out of town, up in the hills. They're towering mountains by British standards. Pete sets up the satnav to guide them there. "Who the hell are the Friends of the Lord of Sleep? Are they a cult—"

Lights come on behind the building. A few seconds later a big SUV, similar in size to the one they're sitting in, peels out of the parking lot and drives past them.

"Follow that car," says Jon.

"How do you know—"

"Just do it," says Pete. "If they're not heading for Peanut Lake we'll find out soon enough." *And I'll eat the hat I'm not wearing right now,* he adds silently.

Brains drives off, keeping his headlights off. "This is really stupid," he points out. "I'd like to remind you that we're unarmed in Middle America. They have *guns* here. You've seen *The Matrix*? Guns, *lots* of guns. Toddlers learn to clean their teeth with them instead of flossing. Oh, and we're about to run out of street-lights so I'm going to have to light up and then they'll see—"

"One, you can hang back," Pete tells him. "Look, they're heading for Peanut Lake. And two, we're not here to shoot anyone. We're here to observe."

"Be observing, not be shooting," Jon agrees. "Better way."

A mile out of town Brains opens the windows. They're going relatively slowly—it's dark, the road is narrow and unlit, and he's trying not to overhaul the car in front—and the chilly breeze bears the scent of unfamiliar foliage. The reflected noise of their passage reverberates from the trees and embankment on either side.

"About half a mile to go," Pete reads off the screen. They're rolling downhill now, and the road curves tightly as it narrows. "Lights out!" he says urgently. "Lights—"

Brains kills the sidelights but keeps coasting forward. "Slow—"

Pete briefly glimpses something out of the corner of his eye, back among the trees. *Someone hiding?* he wonders.

Seconds later, the road widens and the trees vanish as they enter a broad open space at the side of a body of water. A pair of headlights switch on directly in front of them, blindingly bright, flanked by open vehicle doors. Jon squeals again and Brains stands on the brakes, hard. There's a popcorn crack, then another. "Shooting!" Brains gasps, then throws the SUV into reverse gear and starts to back up. "Fuck!"

Pete slumps down in his seat, trying to hide in the legwell. He can't see for headlight dazzle. An emerald speckled glare from the back seat reflects off the satnav screen and the mirror as Jon sings an eerie singsong ditty in a language not meant for a human throat. His ward heats up alarmingly. Brains's thaum analyzer bleeps a syncopated commentary, and then two flares light up the night to either side of the parked SUV, as the shooters sheltering behind its doors ignite and burn like human torches.

Pete looks round, blinking. Jon beams manically at him, her hair standing on end. Perfect dentistry sparkles in the reflected light of the burning cultists. "Fun-fun!" she giggles, her eyes glowing with the wild and inhuman joy of *mana* unleashed.

Brains stops the car and climbs down. "Careful—" Pete begins.

"Checking for survivors," Brains says tersely.

"Back there—" Pete turns to look back the way they came.

"I've got this." Brains approaches the parked SUV, its open doors, and the two blackened bodies burning on the banks of the lake to either side of it. "Two down, body in the back seat, cuffed . . . checking the boot. Another body. Fuck."

Pete stops beside the open rear window of the Escalade. "Did you know this was going to happen?" he asks Jon, keeping his tone as gentle and even as possible, even though he wants to scream.

"Not be shooting!" she says, and giggles. It takes him a moment to realize that it's shock on her part, not satanic amusement. "Wasn't sure I could do that. Look with both eyes, and"—she taps the end of her nose—"see double, see zero, be the basilisk you want to be? Walking death Barbie!" She giggles some more, then starts free-associating random nonsense names for her new-found ability to kill with a hard stare. Tears slowly trickle down her cheeks: whether they're the joy of the damned or the damnation of joy, Pete can't tell.

Pete suppresses a shudder, swallows, and looks back up the road. "I saw someone back there and I'm going to investigate. Come along. But don't do that again unless they attack us first, please."

In normal circumstances, the President of the United States is one of the most heavily guarded individuals on Earth. Although notionally just another elected politician, the POTUS is surrounded by trappings befitting the King-Emperor of a planetary power—a presidential palace, pomp and ceremony, jet planes and escorts and bodyguards. Protecting them is one of the main missions of the US Secret Service. On foreign trips their retinue numbers in the hundreds and the President travels in an armored car only cosmetically distinguishable from a tank.

But current circumstances are anything but normal, which is why Senior Officer Mattingley and his team are tense and constantly fighting exhaustion. There are fewer than a dozen of them, trying to do the job of an entire battalion—and furthermore, Mattingley has to assume that everything he knows about procedures for organizing presidential security is known to the adversary stalking them.

It's been downhill ever since the morning three-plus months ago when America forgot the President.

Sam is part of Matt's team because of happenstance: he was one of the officers on the graveyard shift the day everything went wrong. The White House and the Executive Office Building operate around the clock, but many of the desks are only fully staffed half the time. (Notionally they're only staffed during office hours, but presidential teams attract workaholics.) The big man himself usually sleeps for at least four hours a night. While much of the White House security detail is uniformed branch, two special officers are on hand at all hours, in case the First Lady gets a hankering for Dunkin' Donuts, or the President gets a bad case of insomnia and decides to work out. It's not all about body-slamming crazed assassins to the ground and being able to provide mouth-to-mouth in an emergency: part of it is about knowing which kitchen drawer they keep the corkscrews in.

So Sam just happened to be sitting in the ready room at about five o'clock that morning, wrapping his mouth around a mug of coffee in an attempt to stay awake, when he felt a strange tingling up and down his spine (as if an army of ants were marching across his future grave) and the bracelet-charm-ward-thing he'd been told to wear two months earlier heated up suddenly, causing him to spill his coffee and swear.

The wards were a new development. The armory began handing them out three months earlier, along with dire injunctions to wear them at all times while on duty. Sam didn't believe a word of it at the time. Occult, paranormal crap was not a recognized threat to the President. But odd bits of news had been filtering in. Monster attacks in Japan, a rash of weirdness in Europe, the entire British government going nuts. It was all a bit like email security in 2012; you don't know much about it but you can't ignore it any more because it's leaking like crazy in all directions and, who knows, maybe the Russians have something to do with it? So, when the order to start wearing these bracelets and necklaces came in, his response was, better safe than sorry. Sam didn't get to be a Special Officer assigned to the White House by cutting corners and disregarding security-related orders.

"Did you just feel something?" he asked Officer Cho. "Did your ward heat up just now?"

Dan shook his head. "Not that I noticed." But he rolled back his shirt cuff all the same, to check: "No, feels normal to me." He shuddered violently. "Spiders on the back of my neck—"

"Nope, I don't see no spiders here."

"I'll just go check the suite anyway." Cho rose and headed for the passage leading to the master suite, where the President and First Lady were—hopefully—sound asleep. Sam shook his head and checked the alarm panel and camera feeds once more. Nothing seemed to be wrong, and indeed, he didn't realize anything was truly wrong for another four hours, when it became clear that nobody was turning up to relieve the night shift that morning.

At six o'clock, OSCAR was up and at the gym; six thirty and FLORENCE, the First Lady, was also awake and active. But none of the morning-shift domestic staff had checked in. Sam swore quietly and got a fresh batch of coffee going. At seven, his and Dan's relief officers were overdue. So were the first early-bird staffers. Something was wrong. "Tell me we haven't all missed a public holiday by accident?" he complained.

"Let me call in." Two minutes later Dan was even more baffled. "The office say they've never heard of us!" He hung up hard. "I'm escalating."

"Let's ask Matt," Sam suggested. Mattingley, in the security office on the ground floor, ought to have some idea what was going on.

Over the next hour things got weirder and weirder. Nobody turned up for work—not regular employees, not political staff, not even their Secret Service relief team. All of the night staff were baffled and irritated, but stayed at their posts, waiting. Mattingley sent Cho, Penrose, and two other officers to check the Executive Office Building. That, too, was deserted: lights out, night shift hanging on for their relief, nobody coming in. By eight o'clock Sam and the others were back at the house itself, reporting to Mattingley. "Catch an eyeful of this," Matt told them, pointing at one of the TV screens in the senior officer's room. It was the morning briefing on C-SPAN, a round-up of the news. "What's missing?" he demanded.

Cho swallowed. "Are *we* missing, sir?" he asked after a minute.

"OSCAR clued me in and I've been keeping an eye on this for half an hour," said Mattingley. "You're right. C-SPAN should be all over today's trade talks and the commerce bill in the house. But they're not. It's all crap about committee hearings, even on the news crawl. It's like they've forgotten the White House exists. And," he added, "he says nobody's returning his calls."

"This is crazy!" Sam opined.

"You think so?" Mattingley fixed him with a reptilian stare. "Go to the front door and tell me where all the tourists have gone."

That morning got progressively stranger. Mattingley sent a couple of the domestic staff and one switchboard operator home, with orders to phone him and report what they found. Which was that everything seemed normal, except when they asked children, spouses, and a tourist guide about the President they got nothing but blank stares. After an hour of fruitlessly working the telephone tree, Mattingley went off-site himself with Murph and one other officer. He personally briefed an increasingly irritated and confused OSCAR, swearing him to stay under lockdown, and left Dan and Sam on close protection duty. Under normal circumstances it would have been reckless dereliction of duty—but it was glaringly obvious that these were not normal circumstances.

They called in Marine One to pick up the President, but the Executive Flight Detachment at Anacostia-Bolling weren't taking calls. The White House Military Office wasn't picking up the phone. Neither was State. Nor were anybody else. They'd called for STAGECOACH, but the Secret Service garage where the presidential state car was parked didn't answer. OSCAR even checked the hotline to the nuclear response center. It was disconnected. Matt walked out through the staff entrance and hailed a taxi to the HQ building on H Street, where he discovered a huge reorg in progress.

"We've been reassigned to counterfeiting," he announced when they gathered in the Ready Room at ten thirty for takeout pizza that he and Murph had the foresight to collect on the way back. "Investigating Ruritanian card-skimming gangs."

"Pomeranian," Murph corrected around a mouthful of Hawaiian.

"Whatever." Mattingley shook his head. "Sir, what do you want us to do?"

The President's shrug telegraphed eloquent bafflement. "I have no . . . *idea*," he said slowly, "but can you tell me that this definitely isn't some sort of attack?"

The word hung in the air like a live grenade. "Sir, it's no kind of attack we've ever planned for, that's for sure. If it's deliberate, it'd take some kind of—"

"—Occult power," the President interrupted. "Something powerful enough to make everyone forget we even exist."

Mattingley was already on his feet. "I can't tell you that for definite, sir, but if it's true we need to move you and FLORENCE to safe locations immediately. Our normal channels are all fubar'd because everyone who wasn't wearing a ward or inside the White House overnight has *forgotten*—"

"Then improvise," said the President, with the twinkling smile that had won him his Academy Awards before he went into politics. "See if you can remind people, pull in more officers, get an improvised team rolling. If it's an occult attack, we've got to have some sort of agency for countering that, haven't we? Let's see what communications can find, what they can do for us. Then we can wake the nation and work out where the attack is coming from. If it *is* an attack."

"Let's move, people."

The morning became a blur of activity. Mattingley sent out officers to pick up all the wards they could find in the armory at HQ. To bring in a very confused consultant on thaumaturgic threats who only remembered the President when they dragged her into the Oval Office to meet OSCAR face-to-face. To round up vehicles, to wake up all the regular White House personal protection officers they could find and haul them in, by physical force if necessary. And to prepare a series of anonymous short-term Airbnb rentals on the fringes of DC for fleeting overnight visits. Around noon they confirmed the sleep/attack hypothesis, when Cho took a catnap and, on awakening, became confused. The temporary staff magic expert was set to work calling colleagues, to start up an emergency countermeasures team. Not long thereafter, the first improvised field team moved out. By that point, all the Secret Service officers were just about jumping out of their skin at the least noise. Something was very wrong, and everyone was waiting for another shoe to drop. A normal attack would have been accompanied by saturation media coverage, frenetic activity, and probably a list of demands. This complete absence of chatter was deeply unnerving. How did you respond to a deafening silence, shouting into a void where nobody could even remember why they ought to be listening to you?

Then, at one o'clock, the President's Blackberry rang.

Jim is still weak and a bit shaky when our train pulls into Union Station, but he says he can walk. So I get a cab to drop us a few blocks away from Janice and Derek's safe house, and try not to freak out every time Jim stumbles on a crack in the pavement. Not that I have any idea what to do if he keels over on me. Local medical services won't be able to help. We've got travel insurance for medical expenses—part of our cover—but the thought of abandoning him in a foreign hospital scares the crap out of me. Not to mention that he's a big chunk of one of the critical paths for this operation. Jim is not only our tank: he's my rock.

See, the PM didn't give me much time to set this operation up, so I'm copying someone else's game plan, with suitable modifications. When you copy, always copy the best. So I'm stealing a leaf from Mossad's playbook: specifically, the page that describes how they assassinated Mahmoud al-Mabhouh, co-founder of Hamas's military wing, in a Dubai hotel room five years ago. Clean-face agents can operate with impunity despite intensive CCTV monitoring and security because they're on clean passports. They had the luxury of using forgeries—biometrics are ubiquitous today, but first-time-out agents have no suspicious history. The team entered via multiple ports of entry, working in small cells that converged just in time to do the job, then evacuated before the body was found.

Not that we're planning on assassinating someone. (At least, not this time.)

It's a little after dark when I get to the bland front door and lean on the doorbell. Jim stands behind me, legs braced apart, shoulders slightly slumped. He resembles a cut-price Frankenstein's monster. The door opens: "Trick or treat?" I chirp, doing a little welcome shimmy to keep in character while Janice gets out of the way. (You never know if the neighbor's curtains are twitching.) "Get Derek," I quietly tell her. "We've got a problem."

Janice looks at me with huge, dark pupils—the hall light's off—and scoots back inside. I take Jim's hand and get him inside lest he keel over on the sidewalk.

Derek ambles gormlessly down the staircase, one shirt tail waving free, just as I'm getting my shoulder under Jim's armpit and hauling him towards the living area. "What's the matter—" he begins, then recoils as I snarl at him.

"Jim's been bitten!" I raise my voice: "Janice, did you get that grid up?"

"It's through here. What—"

"Dragnet in New York. Hostile PHANGs. We threw them, but Jim got tagged. Can you configure that thing for containment? I want him inside and isolated ASAP."

"An isolation grid?" Janice is in the living room with what I mistake at first for an old-school hifi stack, before I recognize that the LEDs on the front panels have nothing to do with audio equipment. A rat king of cheap computing modules, each the size of a Gameboy, forms a loose circle on the floor. "Right here, he'll need—"

"Sofa," Jim mutters, and begins to zombie-shuffle towards the nearest soft furnishing. "I feel like crap," he rumbles as he collapses onto it. "World's worst hangover, without the beer to earn it. Doesn't seem fair."

"Sit," I tell him. Derek peers nervously around the front hall archway. "Derek, make yourself useful and get Jim something to drink." Alcohol *won't* hurt right now, may actually reduce his stress level. "The adversary has PHANGs," I continue, pacing a hole in the carpet. "Watch out for people in silver bodysuits—"

"Zentai suits?" Derek offers hopefully.

"Whatever they are—full face and hand covering? Yes? Where did—"

"They're all over the Mall and the federal buildings," he says, confirming another of my fears. "The suits let them go out in daylight."

"Well fuck." Janice pauses. "Why didn't *we* think of that?"

I decide not to draw her attention to my own sartorial choices: "Because we don't want to stick out like a sore thumb." Deep breath. "Jim, you're going to sleep inside a powered-up grid—Janice, you know the geometry Basil used to keep his food fresh? That'll block the V-parasites temporarily—"

Jim draws breath. "Now hang on a moment—"

"—You're going to live in this grid except when you absolutely have to come out, and we're going to get you home in one piece—"

"Wait!" he says, summoning up his police voice. It's not exactly a shout, but it *carries*. He looks around at us in the resulting silence. "What?"

Janice stalks towards him, clutching a wreath of cables. "Jim." She glances at me. "He's been bitten?" she asks. I nod. "Jim. PHANG infection. You know the basics?" He nods. "No, I really don't think you do." It's still too abstract: I don't think he really gets it. So, because she knows I'm too chicken to show him, Janice *smiles*.

Back when we contracted this unfortunate condition—that's as much a euphemism as calling the US Civil War "the late unpleasantness"—Janice was my team's system administrator and go-to devops person. Alex Schwartz, math PhD and utter flange bucket, rediscovered the dark theorem that installs V-symbionts in the wetware of anyone who studies it, so this is entirely on him. Alex's special sauce was a really nifty animated infographic that turned PHANG syndrome, from something only dedicated psychopathic sorcerers get after years of study, into a drive-by strain virulent enough to take root in a dumb HR manager—like me. And he excitedly demo'd his discovery to everyone on the team. I try to keep the more florid symptoms of my disease to myself but Janice has rather fewer social inhibitions and an aversion to cosmetic dentistry, so when she smiles she *really* bares her incisors.

Jim recoils. "Shit!"

"I'm a vampire," she says. "This is me coming out of the closet, no, coffin. It's not just theoretical, Jim: a vampire has fed on your blood, and what happens next is that their parasites chew on your brain until you die. Unless you get in the fucking grid *right now*."

"Do it," I tell him. "We can figure the rest out later." Inasmuch as he has a later. "Grid up or die, Jim." He moves as if to stand and I'm there in a split second, taking his weight on my shoulders. "Jan, chuck a cushion or something on the floor there. Derek, raid the kitchen, grab any snacks and soft drinks you can find, shove them in. Jim, let's get you settled. Oh, Derek? He's going to need a bucket."

Whoever sampled him while we were on the train—over an hour ago, now—must know they got someone, but there were plenty of other people at the restaurant. They'll be working through the blood samples, trying to figure out which one belongs to the enemy. Probably stashing the rest as power-ups for later. If we're lucky, there'll be a layer of oversight so they can't simply drain everyone instantly. But they could decide to end Jim at any time—this minute, an hour hence, maybe tomorrow—and if he's not completely isolated from all thaumaturgic resonance, the first sign will be when he strokes out. If he's shielded, they may figure he's already gone. Or make a note to try later. Whatever: it broadens our options slightly.

Two minutes later Janice pushes a button and Jim, along with the inner ring of cabling, silently vanishes from sight inside a dome of utter blackness. "How much air does that thing hold?" Derek asks. "Assuming time continues to pass inside it?"

"About"—Janice scowls fiercely—"we need to drop the grid and ventilate at least once every three hours, to be on the safe side. Say, for ten minutes at a time. Let's check in an hour and see what he thinks."

"How do you know?"

"I did a SCUBA course once. I'm not an expert, but air consumption is one of the basics."

So once again Janice proves that not only is she a nerd, she's a *useful* nerd who gets to stay on the team. Yay, Janice, have a gold star. I turn my back and breathe a sigh of relief, then go sit down. There *is* a solution to Jim's situation, as it happens, but it's not a pleasant one. I've got a couple of hours to figure out the best lever to use to convince Jim that he wants to open door number two: weepy violin over Sally's impending orphanhood might do it, but it's a bit unsubtle—

Sometimes I hate my better instincts.

It's not the way the man stands in the middle of the road with his hands outstretched that convinces Gaby. It's that the first words out of his mouth are: "Do you need a ride back into town? Are you hurt? Is there anything I can do to help?" Spoken in a painfully polite British accent.

Open arms, no obvious weapons, and he's asking if she needs help. He's not one of the Men in Black, and if he's one of the crazies from the Lord of Sleep, then they've gone international. But he knows, or somehow guesses, that she's here and needs help. Gaby doesn't have a lot of trust right now. Her heart is pounding, and her hands and the small of her back are clammy. "Stay back!" she shouts. "I have a gun!" It's a stupid bluff, she realizes immediately: it'll be obvious as soon as he realizes her wrists are zip-tied behind her.

The man in the road slowly lowers his arms and puts his hands inside his jacket pockets. "No you don't, and neither do I." His voice manages to blend patience with sincerity. If it's a bluff, it's a better one than hers. "The men you escaped from won't be shooting anyone else. Do you need help?"

A second, shorter figure walks towards him from the lakeshore, backlit by headlights. Gaby squints into the glare and realizes it's a woman. Beyond any rational consideration, this is what finally convinces her that the strangers are safe. "Who are you?" she asks, stepping out from behind her tree but staying tense, ready to bolt at the slightest hint of trouble.

"We heard you on the radio," the man begins as the woman steps up beside him, arms akimbo, and interrupts: "Opener of Doors." She, too, has a foreign accent, but on top of that there's something else wrong, some sort of speech impediment. She bows elaborately, flourishing her hands as she does.

"Not now, Jon," the man tells her, in a tone of mild exasperation.

"Opener of Doors!" Jon is quite insistent.

"Sorry." The man faces Gaby. "I'm Pete, this is Jon, she's on the spectrum, please make allowances. Our friend back at the lakeside is Brains."

"Doors!" Jon is practically bouncing up and down with frustration. "Doorsdoorsdoors!"

"I think Jon is saying she'd like to visit your studio. Jon, we need to talk about other things first. Uh, Ms. Carson, do you know what happened to your colleagues?"

"Oh god, oh god, oh god." Gaby cringes as realization cascades down on her in an icy deluge. "The Men in Black arrested us, they killed Glenn and hurt Danni—"

A distant shout from the shoreline. "Hey! Stop arseing about, I need help here!"

Pete shrugs apologetically, then turns and walks back towards the lake. After a moment of indecision, Gaby stumbles after him, unbalanced by her bound arms. Jon stands in the road, shoulders rounded and head bowed, muttering under her breath, then she turns and trots after them.

Gaby stumbles to a stop on the lakeshore. Two big SUVs face each other, the newcomers' and the one she escaped from. The latter is flanked by two fitfully smoking fires, indistinct objects smoldering on the muddy ground behind open doors. A smell of charred pork hangs heavy on the night air and her gorge rises.

Pete, who she now sees has shoulder-length hair in a ponytail, bends over, gasping, and that's the last trigger she needs for her stomach to rebel.

"This one's breathing but the guy in the boot is—" She barely hears the shouter, Brains. She staggers, unbalanced by her bound arms, but someone—Jon?—supports her and shoves her hair out of the way. As she stands doubled-over, subsiding into dry heaves, she feels someone sawing at the zip ties. A moment later her wrists come free and she wipes her eyes, then rubs her wrists.

"Mm, I love the smell of napalm in the morning," Jon intones flatly, then giggles.

Gaby has a shocked impulse to slap the other woman—then recalls Pete's advice. *On the spectrum? Right.* Inappropriate outbursts—are they part of it, or is she just an asshole? Or is something else up with her? Gaby finishes throwing up. "Water," she gasps. Someone thrusts a plastic bottle at her, which she accepts gratefully. It takes her a moment to register it's Jon. She rinses and spits, then hands the bottle back as she straightens up. Determinedly avoiding looking at the charred husks, she staggers in a wide circle around the SUV and back towards the open tailgate, where a bald, middle-aged guy with a beard is shining a flashlight inside. Something drips on the mud below, black in the shadows.

"Fuck," she spits.

"They shot him." Bald guy—Brains—looks at her with hollow eyes. "I'm sorry." He steps aside. "Your friend—"

A groan from the cab sets Gaby scrambling. She barks her knee on the edge of the door. "*Oww.* Danni!"

Danni lies lengthwise along the bench seat. Brains has cut the zip ties and rolled her into the recovery position but she's still unconscious. "I'm really worried, she needs medical attention. Where's the nearest clinic?"

A shudder of relief turns Gaby's knees to jelly. *Is there anything we can do to help?* Pete had asked. "Back through town to the highway, then—" She judders to a halt. "No, can't get an ambulance down here fast enough, be quicker to drive her ourselves—"

Pete materializes behind her. "Tell you what," he says, "how about we drive you and your friend back to WOCZ-FM? You can borrow my phone and call an ambulance to meet you there while we're on the way. We're foreign tourists," he adds apologetically. "You know what number to ring, right?"

"That'd be great!" She takes a deep breath. "But this—"

"We'll have to move her," he says calmly. "Brains, if you can take her legs? Ms. Carson, you can ride beside her, with Jon on the other side, if you can keep her upright and try not to jar her head—I think she's got a bad concussion? We'll take you back to your studio—"

"Thank you, thank you!"

The good Samaritans ease Danni into the back of their vehicle. Jon mumbles under her breath in a foreign language that sounds like a demon swearing, but *they're helping*, Gaby realizes gratefully, and leaves the thinking to her rescuers. She's had a nasty shock, and if they want to help she should be grateful and let them. "Jon was looking forward to seeing your studio," Pete tells her as Brains turns the SUV around. "Would you mind showing her around while we wait for the ambulance?"

"Oh, there's not a lot to see—" Gaby demurs, but Pete hands her his phone, unlocked, and then she's busy phoning in a 911 call and holding Danni steady while Brains drives. And so what if they've got the WOCZ-FM studio loaded in their GPS, and Jon's eyes glow faintly as she chants? These are good people and they want to help her, and the smoking bodies on the beach will still be dead in the morning.

Sam was riding shotgun in the anonymous sedan—not one of the Secret Service's fleet of presidential transports, but a black rental Lincoln from Hertz—when the phone in the President's pocket rang. They were stuck in traffic near Dupont Circle. His shoulder blades tensed.

"Don't answer that—" Mattingley began, a fraction of a second too late.

"This is Arthur." The President, in polo shirt and Ralph Lauren shades, managed to look both relaxed and pissed off simultaneously. "Who is it?"

Senior Officer Mattingley frantically mimed something at him. After a moment the President blinked, then thumbed his Blackberry onto speakerphone. "You'll have to say that again, I didn't quite catch it."

The President, for all that he is charming, charismatic, erudite on the most surprising topics, politically astute, and plays a mean round of golf, can sometimes be a bit naive about security. Sam had seldom been as terrified as he was at that moment, stuck in sluggish traffic feet away from a radio-emitting device identifying the highest of high-value targets in the middle of a decapitation strike. Previous POTUSes weren't allowed mobile phones at all. This one only got his secure, locked-down Blackberry thanks to vehement insistence and the personal connivance of the director of the NSA, whom he had appointed—

"Good afternoon, Mister President." The speaker's voice was female, self-assured. "I am the Deputy Director of the Operational Phenomenology Agency, our nation's primary magical defense force. I'd like to apologize for being so slow to reach out to you. As you can imagine, we've been in crisis mode today, trying to get a handle on the situation."

Something was wrong with this picture, Sam realized. *Very* wrong. Not that he doubted for a moment that the Deputy Director was the real deal, or suspected her of being a hoax caller who had somehow got hold of the President's personal phone number *and* managed to avoid succumbing to the creeping amnesia blanketing the nation. But there was a protocol for heads of agencies to use when reporting to the chief executive, and the caller wasn't following it. Judging by the faces he glimpsed in his peripheral vision during his scan, Sam figured that both Mattingley and the President himself were also alert to this. The President, in particular, wore the same fixed grin that Sam had occasionally seen on the face of a prosecuting attorney closing in for the kill.

"What exactly is the nature of the situation, and why am I hearing this over a direct voice call rather than through regular channels? Why are you, a Deputy Director, calling me, rather than the head of your agency? And after a six-hour window during which all our normal continuity of government operations appear to have fallen by the wayside?"

There was a dry chuckle. "Ah, sir, what an interesting question." The Deputy Director paused. "I am calling on your voice line because your absence from the executive residence has not gone unnoticed. It may make it harder for us to ensure your safety."

Mattingley and the President exchanged glances. "I don't recall seeing your organization listed in the daily briefings. Or reporting any current threat profiles. Again: Who are you, and what's going on?"

Their driver spotted a gap in the traffic and gunned the limo towards it. Horns blared for a few seconds.

"You really should reconsider, sir. If you return to the White House at once we can lock down the perimeter and make sure no threats can reach you."

Sam mouthed an obscenity. Mattingley mimed hanging up, but the President was clearly out for blood.

"I'm not yours to command, ma'am, whoever you really are. I'm your Commander-in-Chief, in case you've forgotten, and if you're truly part of our nation's civil service then you'll know that there's a chain of command and I'm above you on the org chart. What is going on, why is nobody answering my calls, and what the hell *is* this?"

"What this is is an emergency, *sir*." Sam boggled: The Deputy Director thought she could scold the President? "The Operational Phenomenology Agency deals with occult threats. Magic, for want of a better word. It's real, an applied science or sciences in its own right, and the nation is currently facing an existential threat. Hence this action. Now, please will you return to the White House? I cannot vouch for your safety otherwise."

Sirens rose in the distance, distinctly audible through the sealed windows.

"I don't like your attitude," Arthur sniped, his control momentarily slipping. "You aren't answering my questions, you're making demands, and you're verging on insubordination. So let me make this an explicit order: *tell me* what the hell is going on. Why has everybody forgotten the Executive Branch?"

"I don't take orders from you, sir. Let me make this plain: the President does not *rule,* the President *leads,* within the framework defined by the Constitution. There is a difference. The nation is confronting a situation that is not only unprecedented in our experience, but potentially devastating. There was no time to bring you up to speed on the matter, and uninformed meddling would inevitably make matters worse, so in accordance with our operational guidelines we have enacted a binding geas, a magical compulsion if you like, upon the entire nation, to disregard your existence. Without the support of hundreds of thousands of civil servants and millions of soldiers you can't fuck things up, and we can do our job without human politicians jogging our elbow out of ignorance. Now, I need you to return to the White House *immediately.* I'll have further instructions for you once you're there, but for the time being I just need you to sit tight—"

More sirens, rising. Their driver yanked the wheel sharply left, then hauled the Lincoln into a hard turn onto a one-way street, going against the traffic flow. He swerved around an oncoming bus and braked to avoid a delivery van, but his passengers paid no attention.

"What the *fuck* are you talking about?"

"Mr. President, we are your Deep State: we take our orders

from a higher authority. My instructions are to assume direct control of the federal government, so I'm giving you one last chance: you must *immediately* return to the White House, or—"

Arthur wound down his door window and hurled his Blackberry in front of an oncoming dump truck. A moment later their driver pulled a sharp right turn, narrowly avoided sideswiping a pickup, and accelerated again. As the President closed the window he looked Mattingley in the eye. "Think they were tracing us?" he asked.

"With a Stingray, who the hell knows? You did the right thing, sir, for what it's worth."

"I wish." The President closed his eyes, momentarily looking a decade older, then opened them again. "Well, I think that cleared things up nicely, don't you?"

"Yessir. Jesus. A magical coup. Deep State bullshit." Mattingley frowned. "Who do they think they are, the CIA in 1974?"

"I don't know." The President's expression hardened. "But I know this much: if I go back, they win. And I can't let that happen."

Two weeks prior to mission start:

"Tell me, Baroness, have you ever met one of the Nazgûl?" asked the Senior Auditor.

I tried not to pull a face as I sipped at my teacup while I perched primly on the edge of the carnivorous sofa. The SA's office resembles the private den of an endearingly eccentric English public school headmaster from the 1950s, rather than the headquarters of one of the most powerful sorcerers in Europe. In addition to the saggy sofa, it's furnished with a wooden banker's chair, a battered leather-topped desk, cast-off mismatched side-tables and bookcases, and dusty curtain drapes that cover the bay windows. Which I am informed overlook a landscape not of this world, and the office as a whole is too large to fit inside its allocated space on the building floor plans: but that's all par for the course, and at least I'm in no danger of being accidentally fried by a stray sunbeam.

"Can't say I have," I admitted. "Not unless you count Ramona."

"You only met her after she slipped their leash: she doesn't count." Dr. Armstrong gave me a fey smile as I sipped my tea. (There is an International Standards Organization specification for brewing tea—ISO 3103, based on British Standards Institution BS 6008—but the SA violates it egregiously, every time, by using roughly triple the prescribed quantity of loose-leaf Assam, resulting in a bold and somewhat bitter brew.) "It's all for the best that they don't know you any more than you know them. It doesn't do to become predictable in this game."

I resisted the urge to roll my eyes. "Explain. What should I be alert to?"

"Their organizational traditions and outlook," he stated crisply, suddenly so businesslike that I jerked and barely avoided spilling my tea. "Surprised?" He raised an eyebrow at me.

Keeping my face carefully frozen, I put my cup down on the occasional table. "Do tell."

"An organization's internal culture channels the way its agents attempt to discharge their duties, how they perceive their mission," said the SA. "You've spent most of your working life in just three or four large organizations: the police, a multinational investment bank, the Laundry. Oh, and a couple of universities and the House of Lords, but they don't count because they're research roles, very academic." (I personally wouldn't describe the House of Lords as a research posting, but I suppose the committee processes do a lot of analysis work on the effects of draft legislation, so . . .) "But consider. Banking is all about risk management. The Laundry was about a different *kind* of risk management. The police don't work that way, they're about risk *suppression,* and clean-up afterwards, but it's still risk-centric." He grinned. "What is the Black Chamber about?"

"The—what—" And just like that, he had me standing outside the windows of my comfort zone, looking in. "You tell me?"

"Ancient history lecture coming up." Dr. Armstrong leaned back in his antique chair, coil springs squeaking underneath, and gazed at the ceiling. "During the eighteenth and nineteenth centuries, most of the chancelleries of Europe had Black Chambers whose job was to open and read the post of nobles and dignitaries. The United States was unusual in not having one until the twentieth century, when during the First World War the State Department set up a Black Chamber for monitoring international telegraphy. Because of the Zimmerman Telegram and all that," he added. I made a mental note to look it up on Wikipedia later. "Anyway. It got shut down in the late 1920s by a particularly idealistic Secretary of State—'Gentlemen do not read other gentlemen's correspondence,' Mr. Stimson said—but was resurrected during the next war, and it evolved into the National Security Agency. The American equivalent of GCHQ, our codebreakers."

So far so much bureaucratic genealogy: I half-expected him to haul out a family photo album and start cooing over baptismal portraits of baby espionage agencies. Holiday snaps of middle-aged directors in three-piece suits whooping it up at classified seaside resorts. But then he threw in a surprise.

"It turns out the Black Chamber *wasn't* abolished in 1929. Only the Cipher Bureau was disbanded. The real work continued: a bunch of occult research, largely mumbo-jumbo but containing some nuggets of unspeakable truth, that had been going on in DC since the 1780s. Originally it was the Grand Masonic Lodge, influenced by the Illuminati, who maintained an Esoteric Texts Repository in the Library of Congress. But the BC took it over and expanded on it, and during the Second World War they turned it into an *offensive* occult agency. John von Neumann worked for them, and a chunk of Manhattan Project funding was siphoned off in their direction. That's where the budget for Vannevar Bush's Memex machines came from, like the one in Dr. Angleton's office.

By the early 1950s they were focussed on penetrating the wards around the Kremlin and trying to second-guess whether the Reds were in league with Blue Hades."

By this point I was shaking my head. "Please stop. Too much?"

The SA looked chagrined. "Sorry, sorry. I lived through the tail end of the necromantic cold war: it brings back memories. Shoggoth Gap and all that."

"You're telling me—" I picked up my teacup and wet my lips again. "You said they were an *offensive* agency. Surely you don't mean they were a cold war weapon?"

"I'm afraid that's exactly what I mean," said the SA. His eyes glittered.

"But that—" I stopped.

There are generally two types of secret agency: defensive and offensive. Defensive agencies focus on things like counter-espionage—catching spies—and paranormal protection. Offensive agencies focus on sending spies and actively sabotaging their rivals. In the UK, SIS, the Secret Intelligence Service, does the spying stuff; MI5, the Security Service, sticks to counter-espionage and anti-terrorism duty. Of course, in some areas there's a hot mess of overlapping responsibilities. GCHQ used to be a code-breaking, electronic espionage agency with a tiny defensive electronic security department embedded in it. Very unbalanced. The NSA was the same.

If the OPA are anything like the NSA . . .

"For decades, the OPA has been long on offensive capability and binding non-human entities to service," Dr. Armstrong continued. "We try to retain our humanity in the Laundry, or at least remain on speaking terms with it—exceptions like Dr. Angleton and Mr. Howard aside, of course. The OPA have traditionally been less restrained. DAEMINT, they called it, use of daemonic servitors for intelligence."

He must have noticed my reaction at that point, because he gave me a pained little smile as he nodded. "Yes, and like yourself. Now consider Case Nightmare Green, which we are currently experiencing. The cosmological conjunction. Too many thinking networks in too small a volume of spacetime. All thaumic resonances amplified. The Lovecraftian Singularity. Ask yourself how many unaltered human beings are on the list the PM handed you for SOE field ops, then ask yourself how much worse it must be inside the OPA."

"Do they—" I paused and started again. "Are they suffering, in your opinion, from regulatory capture?"

He nodded.

Regulatory capture is a management disease of task-focussed organizations. Suppose your job is to run nuclear reactors. They're risky things, so there needs to be a regulatory oversight authority to keep an eye on the folks running them. But they're so complex that the only people who really understand what's being regulated are the operators. So when it's time to staff the regulatory authority, who ends up running the regulator but the very people they're supposed to be overseeing? Honest risk assessment becomes impossible when the supposedly well-controlled regulators are captured by the operators.

It's not just nuclear reactors, either. It could be food safety, or airliner maintenance, or pharmaceuticals, or covert operations agencies. *In particular,* offensive covert agencies that rely on bound, superhumanly intelligent alien nightmares as force multipliers.

"Oh dear," I said faintly, and drained my cup to minimize the risk of a spill due to my shaking hand.

"More tea, Baroness?"

"I'd rather not." I put my cup down.

"The Nazgûl have been successfully colonized by a parasitoid superorganism—a group mind, if you like. They're cultists, but not the boringly simple religious fanatics we're used to over here. They dedicate their minds to the service of the great dreamer, dread Cthulhu—who, contrary to the more popular imagery, doesn't have bat wings or tentacles, that was just Lovecraft's seafood phobia speaking. Think exoskeleton and ovipositor and parasitoid brain-control maggots—at least, we *think* he's a megascale vespiform, that might be just another juvenile instar—anyway. Bootstrapping their lord to full immanence is a big job, and partly thanks to you, that maniac Schiller blew their best opportunity."

"Thank you!" I don't get the opportunity to bask in the SA's praise very often.

"You're welcome." He continued: "But they're nothing if not persistent, and now they're trying again. This time, they plan to use a computational brute-force attack. They're preparing to build a gigantic swarm of orbital solar-powered processors so huge it'll eventually eclipse the sun: a thing called a Matrioshka brain. Brute forcing the solution is inefficient, so their hypercomputer has to be really big to run **cthulhu.exe**. When I say big, they're planning to dismantle entire asteroids and planets for construction materials. Eventually they may dismantle the Earth, although I suppose BLUE HADES and DEEP SEVEN might express reservations on that account."

"Good grief." Words fail me.

"I hasten to emphasize that all this lies a few years in the future—a decade, perhaps, if we're lucky. I mention it just to demonstrate why it's imperative that we kneecap them *now*, before this insane scheme gets underway. I am reasonably certain that the US government—those bits of it that haven't been co-opted by the Nazgûl—would take a dim view of them dismantling the planet out from under the lot of us. They're as much under alien occupation as we are, but the fight isn't over yet. The long-term goal of your organization is to link up with the domestic opposition and help them."

8: A GAME OF VAMPIRES

Mattingley and OSCAR confer for some time. Sam, temporarily off watch, holes up in the kitchen, where he discovers a high-end bean-to-cup machine. This is good, but thanks to his run out to pick up Tancredy he's the last to get to it, and the first cup of espresso is lip-curlingly foul, rancid with bitter oils. So Sam rummages in the kitchen drawers for the manual, turns to the maintenance section, and begins to systematically field-strip and clean the coffee maker. He has the parts laid out neatly in a row on the kitchen counter and is degreasing and polishing them between yawns when Sylvia Haas looks in on him.

"Sam. Busy?"

"Routine maintenance." He stifles another yawn. "If you want a brew I'm afraid you'll have to wait—"

"It's not that. Matt wants you?" Sam tenses. "They've finished yelling and Arthur basically ordered Matt to send the Postal Service guy home. So I figure you've got another taxi run—"

"Gotcha." Sam is relieved. The President is a decent guy. Senior Officer Mattingley is a decent guy. Sam's a straight-up guy, too, he likes to think. Still, he was nerving himself for the order to shut down Tancredy. The stakes at this table are far too high to let ordinary human decency get in the way of cold-blooded expediency. "Do I have time to finish up in here first?"

"Normally no, but"—Sylvia takes in the disassembled coffee machine—"I'll check." She heads back into the house and Sam begins to reassemble the grinder and feeder assembly. Half-clean is better than nothing, he thinks. Officer Haas used to be as well-groomed as any other officer on White House duty, but the insane shift arrangements are taking their toll. Her hair is getting oily and lank, eyes red-rimmed, no energy to spare for makeup. The guys have it easy, he realizes; they're expected to look a little rough. He yawns again as he clips the bean feeder into place. There's a muffled clank from behind the closed door to the laundry room next door. He ignores it at first, but then, bubbling up from the sluggish depths of his subconscious, comes a realization that nobody has entered the laundry room while he's been in the kitchen, and the machines aren't running either. *Something*— Sam's hand goes to the butt of his service pistol—*is* wrong.

With his left hand, Sam picks up the filter head and drops it into the empty water tank, then rattles the tank to make some noise as he tiptoes towards the laundry-room door, holding his gun muzzle-down and safety off. He puts the tank down at the end of the counter and takes up a position alongside the door.

"Sam—" Haas enters the kitchen. Her voice catches momentarily, then she continues speaking, "Matt wants to know how long until you can get the coffee maker working again? He wants to put in an order: latte with an extra shot for himself, double espresso for Arthur—" Meanwhile, she draws her gun and moves into a shooter's stance to cover the other side of the laundry room. She raises an eyebrow at Sam: *You sure?*

Sam nods. "Let's get started," he says, and, bringing his weapon to bear, swiftly kicks the doorknob.

Someone is standing right behind the door and they grunt as it hits them, but the sound is drowned out by Sylvia's pistol as she fires three times and steps sideways to clear his line of fire. Sam crouches and shoots through the door at chest height.

The reply is an immediate burst of automatic fire, spraying through the doorway and drywall at waist height.

Sam's ears are ringing. Someone is shouting, "*Cease fire!*" The blind spray of bullets missed him somehow. He scrambles backwards towards the nearest cover, sliding on a smear of fresh blood that is sprayed across the kitchen floor. There's a big island in the middle of the kitchen and as he rolls around it he shoulder-checks Sylvia, who gives an agonized grunt—*she's been hit,* he realizes—but there's no time because the next step in this dance is a flash-bang and then they storm the house—if he hadn't been working quietly in the kitchen and one of them hadn't stumbled, it would have worked—

Out of time. There's a rattle of automatic fire from the front, then the deafening crack of the .50 caliber upstairs as the officers on watch light up the infiltrating hostiles. Sam covers his eyes and opens his mouth in a yawn: the kitchen flashes bright as the noonday sun with a concussion that feels like slamming a door on his head.

Ears ringing and mind a blank, Sam rolls round the side of the kitchen island and shoots at the blurry silver figures storming the room. He knows he's going to die now, but he can buy time for the others. Sylvia, lying in an expanding ruby puddle, doesn't move. Sam concentrates on shooting repeatedly, and at least one silver figure goes down in front of him. Then a mule-kick hammers him in the chest. He pulls the trigger again and the slide locks open. Muscle memory prompts him to reach for a spare magazine, but his left arm isn't working and there are more shots behind him, and now the pistol is too heavy to hold and everything is too dark.

The shooting dies down. Sam and Sylvia took the brunt of the main incursion; Mal and Cho, the sniper team on the rooftop, spot and kill six more intruders out front. The shaken survivors move quickly, hustling out to their parked vehicles without grabbing the gear they've just unloaded. OSCAR and Mattingley are the last out the door, almost a minute late: Mattingley delayed by overriding his charge's angry demands to say goodbye to those who remain behind.

Sam lies on the kitchen floor, unseeing, and forgets his President for the last time.

Gilbert Tancredy hunkers down on the jump seat in the load bed of the big SUV, listening as the President turns the air blue. They hurtle out of the suburban driveway, nose to tail with a pickup full of twitchy officers openly pointing automatic weapons in all directions. The POTUS is a scatological artist, Gilbert realizes. It'd be absolutely hilarious if the circumstances weren't so awful.

Two miles and three turns later the President winds down. "How many people did we lose?" he demands.

The anonymous-looking man with the crew-cut hair and distant gaze holds a walkie-talkie to his mouth. "Mattingley. Roll call."

Over the next couple of minutes the other vehicles call in. The atmosphere in the cab is suffocating even though the AC is running full blast. "We lost three, sir," Mattingley finally reports. "Haas, Penrose, and Jensen. Haas and Penrose were in the kitchen when the bad guys came in. They went down fighting. Jensen was in the dining room, took a stray bullet through the drywall. Cho and Berry are both walking wounded, stable but they could use a medevac."

"Do you have any of those knock-out pills left? You can dose them up and leave them at an ER. If they lose consciousness they'll forget about me again and they won't be able to tell the OPA anything."

"I'll consider that as a last resort, sir. But if the OPA can do this thing to our memory, who's to say they can't reverse it at will?"

"Fuck."

Here goes nothing, Gil thinks as he clears his throat.

"What?" demands Mattingley.

"Is there anything my people can do to help, sir?"

"Hold that thought," says the President. "Matt. Where are we going now?"

The senior officer sits up straighter. "Sir, we have a couple of fallback houses as diversions, and the lamplighter team is setting up more of them ahead of us. But we had zero warning of that attack. I think either they picked up Officer Penrose leaving the rendezvous with Mr. Tancredy here, or the lamplighters are compromised. We can't move to our alternates until we know one way or the other. So for now we hit the highway and keep moving. If we have to stop we'll stake out a motel for a few hours."

"Right. So we're going nowhere in particular." The President's tone indicates how much he thinks of this plan, which is very little indeed. "Mr. Tancredy, do you have any insights?"

"Wh-wh-what"—Gil doesn't normally stutter, but his mouth doesn't seem to want to work properly—"Sorry, sir. What about the Brits?"

"What indeed," says the President, then pauses thoughtfully. "Mr. Tancredy, do you have anywhere else you need to be today or tomorrow?"

"Uh, sir? I don't think so. I mean, if you need me—"

"Just checking." Arthur closes his eyes and tilts his head back.

"Sir?" asks Mattingley.

"While they run us from pillar to post we stay too focussed on survival to think strategically. Which is what they want." The President opens his eyes. "Here we are, running around Maryland trying to wake up people one or two at a time, get enough together to form a cell, a spark of awareness within an office here or a department there—woke people who see what's happening and can form a shadow government in exile, a resistance. Except—" He wets his lips. "—that's pretty much exactly what *they* did to *us,* under our nose without us spotting it. They're better at this game than we are. Hell, they're playing with us, keeping us busy and grinding us down. This is, what, the third ambush in six weeks? The first we've taken serious casualties from, but . . . they only need to get lucky once. We need to be lucky every time."

"Sir, we—"

"We need to change the rules on them!" Arthur snaps. "They wouldn't be chasing me if they didn't think I was some kind of a threat to them. Even if it's just providing a figurehead, symbolizing something. Mr. Tancredy. Your group. How many of you are there? What can you do?"

For the next half hour Gilbert gives the President a briefing on the background and current status of the Comstock organization, to the extent that he can—he wasn't senior management, let alone executive level, to begin with, and since the amnesia spell took hold he's lost track of everyone but his local stay-behind cell, embedded under deep cover in other government departments. "We actually forgot about you for about two months, sir," he says ruefully. "In addition to the geas, the bad guys have been trying to erase the presidency from the historic record. We ran across a book they hadn't destroyed or removed from the stacks in the Library of Congress, and while we were trying to figure out what was so important about it we woke up, and since then we've been sleeping in shifts—working to stay on top of the amnesia."

The President nods. It's a story he's heard before. Individual government workers accidentally waking, forming networks with friends and colleagues, staying loyal, keeping the mission alive. No geas is 100 percent effective all the time, according to the double-domes from the Thaumaturgic Research Office at DARPA: if it fails one in a million times, that's a third of a thousand awakenings every morning. But if those who are fully aware are isolated, the next time they sleep they'll forget everything again. And convincing someone that an outrageous ritual has caused them to forget the constitutional bedrock of their society is *hard*. For every hundred who remember one morning, ninety-five will have forgotten on the morrow. Maybe one in a thousand awakenings will infect others, creating a group of loyalists. There may be a hundred groups scattered throughout the federal machinery at any time, but as long as they remain isolated, they can't swim against the tide of forgetfulness.

"Matt, new orders."

"Sir?"

"I want you and Mr. Tancredy to get in touch with this British ag—" His tongue refuses to say the word *agent*—"Person, and

set up a meeting. Figure out how to do it safely—pick them up
and bring them to me, then drop them off afterwards, I mean."

"Are you sure about this, sir?" Mattingley's expression is grim.

"Yeah, I'm sure." The President is silent for a minute. "The
OPA have put me in a box: I need to break out. If the devil himself offered me a treaty right now, the only question I'd ask
would be whether *they* put him up to it. So let's find out what
they want, and hope their help costs less than my soul."

I have a mission to run, and it's mostly still on track except for
that one troublesome element, which is the inside of my head.

I have trust and abandonment issues. Put it down to my shitty
privileged family background. When my parents divorced, Dad
remarried and got religion and moved to Australia. He didn't want
to deal with a teenage daughter. I mean, he didn't exactly wash
his hands of me—he paid child support on time—but he wasn't
interested in dealing with teenage me on my own terms. Either I
agreed to come live with him in the arse end of Queensland and
attend his church and be his idea of an obedient Christian
daughter, or I could go live with Mum. Meanwhile, Mum had
her own ideas of what she wanted to do with her life. I think she
was secretly embarrassed that she'd gotten married at twenty-
two and had her first baby at twenty-three and another at thirty,
and then she wanted a second chance. Jenny, being nine, was
manageable in a way that I, prickly and awkward at seventeen,
wasn't. So while I wasn't exactly homeless or starving, Mum
mostly ignored me. It was made clear that I had to make my own
way, be strong and independent as soon as possible. I spent my
first decade as an adult owning my mistakes, although luckily I
avoided Mum's particular marital mishap—shacking up with an
early-twenties partner did *not* work out for me—but I never got
the kind of support most people seem to expect from their family.

I've known Jim for a couple of years—since we worked together in TPCF management—and we've had this friends-with-

benefits thing going on for about six months. I'm pretty certain that if it wasn't for the shitty state of the world, and the fact that I've got PHANGs and he's a superhero, it'd be rather more than a casual fling. So when the PM put Jim's name on the list for this operation, it seemed like an all-around good idea for us to do joint cover for our part of the job. We both got into the spirit of things, and it was all fun and games until . . . well, you know what happened. Silly me, I knew it was too good to be true, so why am I surprised it exploded in my face?

It's three o'clock in the morning and we're alone in the living room. Janice and Derek are elsewhere in the house. I admit I may have snarled at them until they went away. I'm lying on the sofa about two meters from the edge of Jim's containment grid, staring at the LEDs flickering on the router, and I'm wondering what it will feel like to die.

He's safe for now, locked inside the eye-warping absence of light that is the containment zone for another seven minutes. It's on a timer. While it's up, he's safe. But it's got to shut down for ten minutes to let air circulate so he doesn't suffocate. While it's down, the enemy V-parasites could start up again at any moment, killing him. About five hours ago we got a coded message. Because the mission is still on track we're going to have to pull him out and repurpose the grid for its intended use in the morning—as anchor for one end of a field-expedient ley line. Unless Janice can work some kind of fucking miracle we won't be able to protect him *and* simultaneously do the job we came for.

My Fuckboy is probably going to die today, and the worst thing about it—about me—the thing that I hate about *myself,* is that I'm angry with him for letting me down. It's infantile, I know, but he's *mine.* He's not allowed to die. I'm not here, I'm not in this situation, I'm not about to go through the any-last-wishes interview, the how-did-you-rate-your-employment-experience out-processing with him. It's all so fucking unreal.

I continue to stare at the flickering LEDs, and it takes me a while to realize that the lights themselves are burning steadily, and it's my eyes that are watering and making them flicker. I wipe my eyes. This waiting is bad for me. Why didn't we pare the exposure window to the bone while we were planning this? (Because airliners get delayed or diverted, and cars and trains get held up by traffic and accidents, of course. Contingency time is useless wasted time, right until you need it.) I blink again, and between my eyes closing and reopening the black hemisphere vanishes and I'm looking at Jim lying on an air mattress, gazing in my direction.

"Hey," he says, with a tired smile.

"Hey yourself." I pat the sofa beside me. "Come on over? We've got ten minutes." My heart somersaults, because really we might only have ten seconds . . . or not. But we can't keep the dome up the whole time or he'll suffocate.

"Better idea, why don't you join me? Uh. Toilet break," he adds, standing up. I notice he hasn't used the bucket in the grid. "I'll be back in a minute."

He stretches and strides out of the living room. I sit up and inhale deeply. There's a stale, heavy odor, like a bedroom that hasn't been aired properly. I pick up my tablet and walk over to his nest. Bucket, air mattress, USB-rechargeable camping lantern, extra booster batteries. *Right.* I make myself useful by swapping in fully topped-up cells and plugging the old ones into the charger while I wait to hear a toilet flush. Two minutes gone and he's still alive. I have an eerie, momentary flashback: I'm standing beside Mr. Kadir who is strapped to the execution table, his expression blank and slightly disgusted as I fill sample tubes from the vein in his arm. Only instead of the crap terrorist wannabe it's Jim's face looking up at me. I shudder convulsively and swallow. *How could he do this to me? To us?* I close my eyes and practice mindful introspection. *Not his fault,* I tell myself. *It was enemy action.* But I can't put a face to them, so I'm unconsciously channeling it towards the nearest target, even though it's inappropriate.

I'm still doing the deep-breathing thing when the door opens and Jim pads back in. He's shed his shoes and socks, I realize. "Hey again. How long have I got out of the box?"

I check my phone. "Six minutes, then in you go."

He walks over to the air mattress and drops down into a cross-legged squat. "C'mere."

For a moment I balk, but then I realize it almost certainly doesn't matter if I get trapped inside the grid when it powers up again. I'll be stuck until six, but showtime isn't until some time in mid-morning, for maximum inconvenience to folks like me. I walk over and sit down next to him.

"So," I say, then find I've run out of words.

"So," he agrees, his expression grave. He glances at the USB batteries and the lantern. "Hang on." He picks up the lantern and switches it on. "It gets really dark when the grid powers up," he explains. "I got caught out the first time."

"Yes, well." I lock eyes with him and we're both silent for a precious minute.

"How much—" He shakes his head. "Let me rephrase: What happens next?"

"We—" I swallow and reach for the tablet. "I'm supposed to conduct an exit interview. I kid you not."

"An *exit* interview?"

"You're—" His double-take would be comical at any other time. "Seriously?"

I nod. "If an employee quits for any reason we're meant to record a bunch of details, basic Q&A stuff for statistical analysis of HR trends. Obviously, it doesn't apply to sudden violent deaths: it's more a retirement or outplacing thing. But if someone has a terminal illness, that's covered—in case it's work-related. So, exit interview." I shrug.

"Fuck."

"It's . . . I wasn't expecting it so soon." Or to be the only HR person in position to collect the data. "So, um, *This Is Your Life* . . ." I swallow again. For some reason I'm having trouble holding my shit together. "Fuck it," I say.

"I'm not dead yet: While there's life there's hope, right?"

"Not really." I feel another flicker of irrational anger. "Listen, Jim, there are only a couple of ways out of this. We can try to stash you in a grid for the rest of your life, but that's some real boy-in-the-bubble shit right there. Or we can hunt down and kill the PHANG who's got her teeth into your gray matter, which *might* work—or it might just make their V-parasites finish you off on the spot. Nobody knows, because we've never done that. Maybe the *alfär* know, or the Nazgûl, but *we* don't. Anyway, we have no way of tracking down that vampire—for all I know they're back in New York. There's a third option which we don't talk about and which might not work because—again—we've never tried to do it to someone who's already being parasitized, and finally there's the door labelled FINAL EXIT. But options one and two"—the living room vanishes, replaced by a perfect blackness broken only by the pale glow of the lantern—"options one and two are vanishingly unlikely, you'll hate yourself if you take option three, and option four is maybe hours to single-digit days away."

Jim scoots round and stretches out beside me, crosses his arms behind his head, and smiles at me hopefully. "And then I suppose there's an option number five, which we don't talk about outside a powered-up grid?"

I roll over to face him. "There is no fifth option," I tell him. Jim isn't cleared for the stuff some of us only talk about inside secure grids, with no written notes. The die-before-disclosing stuff. But I'm not lying to him about this. "No secret trapdoor, no last-minute reprieve. You're trapped in here with me and I'm one of the monsters, remember?"

Jim turns on his side so we're lying nose to nose. He reaches over with his free arm and places his hand against the small of my back. I have the sniffles. "Don't cry," he says softly. I've upset him now, and that only makes it harder to stop.

"You don't want option three," I manage.

"Let me be the judge of that." He pulls me close and I bury

my face against his shoulder. "I've . . . I think I've got a handle on the downsides. But just in case I'm wrong, tell me, hypothetically, how would it work?"

There's a Sheriff's Department cruiser with flashing lights parked outside the WOCZ-FM building when Brains pulls into the car park. "Lights, action, story," Pete murmurs as he turns on the cabin light, cracks his window, and puts his hands on the dash. (They've been briefed about how to interact with American law enforcement: staying in the vehicle feels really weird—it's the exact opposite of the routine for a British traffic stop—but if it keeps things friendly, he's all in favor of it.) The building door gapes open. An officer walks towards them, keeping his right hand close to his holster. "You can't stop here—"

There are more flashing lights at the end of the street, coming closer. "Bill?" Gaby calls from the back seat. "Bill Murphy? Is that you?"

The sheriff's deputy tenses. "Gaby." He stares at Pete. "What's going on?"

Pete smiles and crosses his fingers that Jon will keep her shit together. "Uh, hello, Officer? My friends and I are tourists. We took a wrong turn looking for our motel and nearly ran over Ms. Carson here, and her friend, who's in a bad way, so we offered her a lift back here to meet the ambulance—"

And indeed there *is* an ambulance, turning into the car park with lights spinning and a sudden blare of air horns. Driving licenses and passports are presented, paramedics take one look at the unconscious Danni, and Deputy Murphy undergoes a remarkable change of attitude. Crested Butte is a small town, and Gaby and the deputy went to the same high school. Having someone he knows reassure the deputy that they're just good Samaritans passing by is better than any diplomatic credentials.

Jon keeps her head down and manages not to fidget too conspicuously while Murphy and his partner fire questions at Pete,

Brains, and Gaby. For some reason they don't notice her sitting in the middle of the back seat, doing whatever it is she does that sets Pete's ward tingling. Magic of some kind, he assumes, then sets the thought aside as he does his best to look like an over-helpful tourist. The cover story they agreed on is very simple. They're traveling off the interstate because they want to see the country. Having taken a wrong turn they were flagged down by Gaby, who was staying with an unconscious Danni. Her story is the hard part, and took Jon most of the drive back into town to bind to her tongue. It sticks as close to the truth as possible without mentioning gunfire and burning bodies on the lakeshore. Men in Black came to the studio and abducted her and Danni. She doesn't know what happened to Glenn; they argued, and then dumped the two women on a back road. She thinks it was a robbery attempt gone wrong. Pay no attention to the strangely helpful tourists behind the curtain of mind-fog spread by the alien magus. Given that Crested Butte is the kind of place where the sheriff's deputies carry shotguns loaded for Bigfoot in the trunk and the locals believe in dragons, the only unusual thing about the Men in Black is the lack of a prior UFO visit.

Eventually Danni is strapped to a stretcher, loaded into the back of the ambulance, and driven off to Gunnison Valley Hospital, thirty miles away. The officers have already been through the studio. "They didn't take nothing," Deputy Murphy says, shaking his head. "This is your purse isn't it, Gaby?"

Gaby nods. "May I . . . ?"

"Here y'are, ma'am." He hands it over without comment. "Is anything missing?"

Gaby roots through it. "Phone, cards, lipstick. Huh, what do you know?" She holds her keyfob up. "It all looks to be here."

"Well, if that's so . . ." Murphy glances at his car. "Listen, we need to go find Glenn. Will you be all right locking up here?"

Gaby nods. "I've got a couple of calls to make before I go home, but these kind people offered me a ride, and their friend"—a nod at the back seat—"was asking after a look around the studio. I'm sure I'll be fine."

The skin on Pete's neck crawls as his ward lights up, responding to the backwash from the wave of *you gotta believe me* boiling off Jon. Deputy Murphy's gaze defocuses. "Give the dispatcher a call if you figure where Glenn's gotten to, ma'am. If you're sure you'll be okay we'll be on our way now. I'll need to ask you some questions tomorrow, for the follow-up."

He turns and sleepwalks back to the cruiser, and his partner drives off without a backward glance. Gaby stands motionless and slack-jawed in the car park. "Hey, don't overdo it," Pete tells Jon.

"Overdo? What?" Jon peers at him from under her blonde-dyed fringe. "Overdo?"

"We don't turn people into puppets, Jon, it's bad manners." He gestures at Gaby. "We need her to let us in so we can do the job, that's all."

"Oh." Jon climbs down from the Escalade and stretches. "The job. The job. The job."

Brains shares a worried glance with him. *Is she coming apart?* he mouths. Pete shrugs.

"Gaby?" Pete asks. "Can you show us around? Like you promised?"

Gaby shakes herself. "What? Oh, I was asleep on my feet, dreaming. It was *really* strange . . ." She blinks. "Are you coming?"

Brains grabs a small suitcase from the trunk of the SUV and follows Gaby inside. Pete and Jon trail behind. Gaby drifts through the studio offices as if sleepwalking, but is awake enough to gesture at each room and explain its function. It's a surprisingly small office suite, but, as she explains, 90 percent of their content is syndicated from Sinclair or Clear Channel. WOCZ may be one of the rare stations that is still independently owned and operated, but the invisible monkey's paw of the advertising industry has brought them to heel, just like the big chains. There are two remaining broadcast studios, only one of which is in use at any time. Here's the server room and the phone switch. Here's the mixing desk and the no-longer-used rack of canned signature tapes, kept more as historic memorabilia than for any utility. Routers and decoders for the satellite systems. There's a transmitter on the roof, but the main FM broadcast mast is halfway up a mountain a couple miles out of town. And this is the break room.

"You look tired," Pete comments. "Wouldn't you like a nice hot coffee?"

In her hypnotic haze Gaby is highly suggestible. "I'd love one," she says. "Wouldn't you? Here's where we keep the supplies—"

She doesn't see Brains open his suitcase and set up his tools in the machine room, or see him disconnect the SAGE ENDEC unit from the Emergency Alert System rack, slide it out, and unscrew the top of its case. She's busy setting up the drip machine and asking Pete how he and his friends take their coffee, and Pete is only too happy to keep her distracted while Brains replaces the PROM on the main circuit board with one he flashed in the motel room the evening before. It doesn't take long. Gaby is showing Pete the broadcast suite when Brains ambles inside and picks up his mug.

"Back with us?" Pete asks, unable to quite keep the edge out of his voice.

"Sure." Brains nods. "Restroom break," he says in Gaby's direction, although she's so absorbed in a monotone explanation of her program format that it's anyone's guess whether she got the hint.

Pete nods encouragingly at Gaby and sips his coffee, then glances at Jon. "That's enough," he tells her. "We should drink up and go; it's getting late and we've got a long way to travel tomorrow."

"Thank you for coming out here—" Gaby breaks off to yawn,

stretching her arms above her head. "Where was I?" She looks confused.

Pete smiles. "You were just telling us you've had a very long day, and so have we." He puts his mug down. "I think we're done here."

I'm about to break the fourth wall again, dear reader. So sorry (not sorry).

If you've been paying attention to this journal—*really* paying attention, that is—you'll have accumulated some questions by now, both obvious ones and non-obvious.

Let me tackle the non-obvious one first: what you're reading here is *not* a sanctioned workplace journal, but the unexpurgated and politically perilous truth. I'm writing it down for the usual reason—to prevent loss of institutional knowledge if anything happens to me—but doing so outside work, which is a huge security violation. It's for the SA's sub-rosa task force, whereof we do not speak, and if it falls into the wrong hands my skull will probably end up decorating the Prime Minister's Tzompantli.

I *am* keeping an official workplace journal as well, under lock and key in the office, but I'm a whole lot more circumspect in what I put in it because I'm pretty sure Iris's minions are reading over my shoulder. Iris is a fan of Cardinal Richelieu: "Give me six lines written by an honest man, and I will find something in it with which to hang him." This means that when you see me express an opinion in this account, it's what I *think*, but not necessarily what I *say*. And if you compare it to my official journal, you'll see the opinions expressed there are exactly what the New Management would expect of a loyal servant.

Now, you may well have other questions, concerning my methods. Such as, "How does she know what happened in that meeting of aerospace and tech-sector executives? Surely she wasn't there?" Or perhaps, "The labyrinth in the Pentagon basement is home to a necrotic human mouthpiece who speaks with the voice of Dread Cthulhu—*really?*" Or even, "Do you expect us to believe *that?*"

Reader, I work with the intelligence sources I've got access to. These include remote viewing, divination, and the gnomic utterances of Forecasting Ops, as well as more concrete material such as Gilbert Tancredy's debriefing transcripts and the satellite uplink from 302 Heavy. But in some cases I just have to make do with educated guesswork.

History is written by the survivors, a narrative they compose to explain events to themselves. So the historicity of journals like this one—their accuracy and authenticity—is a function of the reliability of the narrator.

I like to think that I'm a hard-headed realist, but I can't be everywhere at once, and I can't swear to the gospel truth of events I didn't witness and have no direct record of. Critical parts of this narrative depend on circumstances that will forever be inaccessible to us: erased from the record, or even edited out of the timeflow of our universe. If the Mouthpiece of the Lord of Sleep orders the Deputy Director of the Nazgûl to send out for a Desi Chinese carryout, then there's probably a restaurant somewhere with a written record saying *General Tso's Chicken* and *Gobi Manchurian*—but if the city in question has been inundated by BLUE HADES or lightly nuked by North Korea we're not going to be able to prove it. Human knowledge has hard limits, and when I reach them, I have to wing it.

I'm not a professional historian—I only studied it to "A" level—and I have, perforce, winged it quite a lot in preparing this account. I know relatively little about the opposition, who they are, and what makes them tick. I don't understand them the way I understand Iris and her murderous little helpers from the Cult of the Black Pharaoh. To say nothing of Jonquil, Iris's backstabbing daughter, or even Yarisol—who, for all that she's a non-neurotypical elven vampire sorceress, is less alien than some of the minions of the Operational Phenomenology Agency.

So here's my take on the OPA.

They're a modern intelligence organization—in other words, a bureaucratic enterprise tasked with providing intelligence to policy makers and executing covert operations in accordance with their orders. All large organizations are either superorganisms whose cells are human bodies, or very slow artificial intelligences that use human beings as gears in the Babbage engines that run their code. Pick a metaphor and stick to it: I prefer the biological one, but it's a matter of taste. Some of the superorganism's cells are formed into organs that carry out various vital functions. Human Resources is the liver and kidneys, dedicated to purifying and excreting unwanted toxins. Quality Assurance and Standards are the immune system, stamping out rogue cells and insidious infections and other parasitic activities. Project Management is the circadian rhythm, and board-level executives form the cerebral cortex, the source of the organism's emergent self-directed behavior. Behold Leviathan, anatomized.

Different countries have different bureaucratic cultures, and different cultures are prone to their own distinctive types of malfunction. In the UK we're unreasonably prone to regulation by accountancy or, failing that, tradition. Whereas in the US intelligence community, Taylorism and rule-by-MBA run rampant. They're prone to random reorgs and overstaffing, so wherever they can they try to outsource ancillary work. And their executives counter this by trying to reduce the number of human bodies they employ.[8]

The preferred ways of reducing the number of employees in the twenty-first century are automation and outsourcing. About 80 percent of the NSA's total body count are actually employees of various consultancy firms, because that way they don't show

---

[8] Human beings are annoyingly unpredictable and susceptible to non-standard behavior, like emailing dick pics around the office, suing the boss for sexual harassment, or stealing terabytes of classified files before scampering off to Moscow.

up on the org chart. Their remaining internal managers can point to the black boxes that do the job and sneer, "Employees? We don't have no steenking employees!" (Tell that to Edward Snowden.)

In the case of the OPA, with its emphasis on alien extradimensional nightmares, they outsourced their tentacle monster fighting capability to the thaumaturgic equivalent of Blackwater and Palantir, organizations staffed by tentacle monsters. Then regulatory capture ensued, and the monsters ended up running the asylum.

Now ask yourself, what are the goals of monsters?

Many of the worst monsters are regrettably human. We know—history has given us the tools to interrogate them—the goals of Adolf Hitler and Heinrich Himmler, of Stalin, Pol Pot, Hernán Cortés, and Andrew Jackson. They're all too bloody human—more human than I—and all of them can claim a much higher body count than any vampire. (A thought I console myself with when I'm feeling weepy and maudlin after downing my monthly blood meal.) *I* haven't even caught up with the Yorkshire Ripper, never mind Harold Shipman: as monsters go, I'm an amateur.

So much for human monsters: now consider the inhuman ones.

We know the goals of the members of the *alfär* host—the Host of Air and Darkness. They're the surviving military force of a non-human hominid species that evolved on another version of our own planet. They're repugnant and in many cases downright nasty, but they're no harder to understand than, say, a particularly bloodthirsty tribe of chimpanzees—if chimps invented Blitzkrieg and were as pretty as Peter Jackson elves: it's all about survive and prevail, primate dominance hierarchies redux.

Other monsters are harder to get a handle on. I have spent time in the presence of the Black Pharaoh's avatar, the Prime Minister. He presents Himself as a human being, with human-scale goals, but He is always at least one jump ahead of us in any conversation. I have the impression that we might not be able to understand His true, esoteric objectives, even if He was willing to share them with us. His humanity is a mask, although it's intended to be a seductive one.

In the case of the OPA's leadership, *we don't know* what their ultimate goals are, and arguably we *can't*, any more than the dodo birds of Mauritius had any clue about the ultimate objectives of the human sailors who hunted them to extinction.

We have established some of the OPA's proximate goals through observation, signals intelligence, technical monitoring, oracular activities, and (occasionally) phoning them up and asking. We know about their plan to dismantle the inner planets of the solar system, turn them into a gigantic orbital Dyson swarm of solar-powered quantum processors running the code necessary to reboot Cthulhu (who isn't dead, merely exiled to an inaccessible computational state), then hand over power to their Dread Lord. This is understood. But their long-term plans—what they expect to *do* once Cthulhu returns—remain opaque. Maybe they're like Iris's people, who think if they willingly throw in their lot as servants they'll be able to surf to survival on the coat-tails of their chosen deity. Or maybe not. There's simply no way to be sure.

So when I present you with a description of a scene involving our friend the Deputy Director—I'm tired of that title: let's call her DeeDee from now on—presenting the Mouthpiece of Cthulhu with a bag of Cheetos and a bottle of Old Buzzard and begging him for guidance, please grant me your conditional suspension of disbelief: this may not be exactly how it happened, but it's close enough to serve as a placeholder for our adversaries' activities, upon which you can base your interpretation of subsequent events.

Back to the story . . .

DeeDee stands before the Mouthpiece once more, scrutinizing the avatar of her dead god for clues.

A week has passed, and the signs of the Mouthpiece's physical deterioration are now unmistakable: the end is annoyingly close at hand. The once-human body is now visibly degrading, entering its penultimate instar, despite the best efforts of the medical support team with their IV drips and parenteral nutrition line. Muscle and soft tissue liquefies. Hair and skin sloughs away in patches to reveal the chitinous exoskeleton of the avatar. The Mouthpiece's face has gone soft and floppy, lips sagging open to reveal mandibles taking shape within. His eyeballs have clouded over beneath their unblinking lids. Soon the remaining human flesh will sag loose. The inner arthropod will pick and chew at it, increasingly voracious, recycling the biomass to fuel its growth as it matures.

To witness the emergence of a perfect miniature copy of the sleeping god from within the flesh of the Mouthpiece is one of the great privileges of DeeDee's post, but sadly, there comes a point at which the emergent vespid endoparasite can no longer enunciate human words. The deep buzzing of her wings and the harsh stridulation of her yellow-armored legs are unsuited to human communication. When it reaches this stage, a new human host must be brought before the Mouthpiece, who will lay her holy eggs in the new flesh. Next, the High Priests (of whom DeeDee is one) will perform the Rite of Reincarnation, whereby they dedicate the outgoing Mouthpiece's mortal husk to the new brood. This all takes time, and more time as the spent remains are sent to an SCP Repository for preservation. Further days pass as the dominant larva from the brood (only one survives) migrates to the host's brain stem and assumes control. Days during which Her guidance will be unavailable.

"*Approach our vessel,*" buzzes the wasp inside the decaying skin.

DeeDee rises from her obeisance and walks forward, stopping at arm's length. "*Glory to the Lord of Sleep. How may I serve you?*"

"*This vessel is failing, and we have come to a decision about its replacement,"* says the Mouthpiece. *"It comes to us that there exists a perfect host body that will serve our immediate need for a mouthpiece, and also compel the submission of the renegades who resist our will."*

The Mouthpiece stridulates again, rubbing its chitinous hindmost legs against its rotting abdomen to produce a grating, buzzing sound. Fatty, blood-streaked tissue oozes around the edges of the open wounds.

"Who is this new host my Lord desires?" DeeDee asks cautiously. She can make a pretty good guess, but it's a bad idea to put words into the mouth of the Lord of Sleep. At best one risks offending them. At worst—

"The body is that of the one named President,*"* buzzes the Mouthpiece. *"It will make a fitting brood sac for my larvae."*

This is not an order that DeeDee is happy to receive. The President thinks he's free, but in reality he's contained—he hasn't travelled more than a hundred miles from the Capitol at any time since the geas descended. Meanwhile, his team is doing a splendid job of finding (and thereby exposing) every ad-hoc cell of Sleepless government workers in the DC area. The President makes an irresistible bellwether, and at the current rate, in another couple of weeks, statistical analysis suggests the Sleepless problem should be entirely suppressed. On the other hand, keeping the Lord of Sleep happy is a higher calling, and it occurs to her that the Lord of Sleep, for all that they are utterly inhuman in their thought processes, might be onto something.

"Let me just be completely clear on this—you want the President *to be your next mouthpiece?"* The Mouthpiece nods, sagging on its throne. *"May I ask what purpose this serves?"*

"The power of President *is all that sustains the remaining Sleepless. Once we subsume his form, the rebels will succumb to us."*

Well, *that* makes sense: everything will run just that bit more smoothly. Reassured, DeeDee bows before the throne. *"It shall be done, Highness."*

The Mouthpiece's lips sag open, revealing a split mandible. *"Make it so: My Lord hungers."*

There is a single, very tarnished silver lining to the utter shit-show of Jim's situation: we don't need to bother with condoms any more. My symbionts will protect me from anything Jim might give me, including pregnancy. So I dry my nose and calm down, we undress each other and cuddle for a while, then abruptly he rolls on top of me and I wrap my arms and legs around him and we rut like it's the end of the world. I shudder and chew his shoulder gently as I come, and feel the unfamiliar dampness as he shudders convulsively. Afterwards we lie in a sticky tangle, stroking each other gently. It's good sex, and it still totally sucks. I should be happy, not sad.

"A penny for your thoughts, love," he whispers to the curve of my ear.

I plaster myself along the length of his body, feeling the heat of his core radiating through me. "I don't want you to die, but I'm afraid you're not going to like the side effects of option three." That is, of self-infection with PHANG.

I run him through the basics at high speed. The extreme ultra-violet photosensitivity. The symmetry-broken auto-prosopagnosia. The *drastically* upgraded immune system. The ability to draw on the V-symbionts for accelerated reflexes and strength. The dental hypertrophy. And lastly, the Thirst. The Thirst has lethal consequences—Jim totally gets that, from the receiving end. But I feel him tense up and withdraw emotionally as I try to explain it from the other side. "The Thirst never completely goes away. It aches like a stomach ulcer." (I had one once: a medication side effect.) "Worse when you haven't fed. When you feed, it subsides—or maybe that's the endorphin rush." (Because, believe me, when your V-symbionts get their fangs in, the reward kick they give you is orgasmic.) "It takes a lot of willpower not to feed promiscuously." (Only about half of the Scrum had what it took. The others are dead.) "You know that old vegan slogan, 'meat is murder'? I'd like you to imagine you're a vegan with a life-threatening incurable illness that means you've got to eat steak tartare with every meal."

"You sound like you hate yourself," Jim says.

"When I stop to think about it, yeah. But I've had a lot of practice in avoiding looking too closely at what I have to do to survive." Compliance with the mile-high stack of social expectations you grow up with as a girl turns out to be mandatory if you want to get ahead in business. Be blonde, be skinny, and don't forget to smile, bitch. Buy the right shampoo, perfume, cosmetics, dress, shoes, and you *might* be acceptable, but really you're just deplorable. I worked for years in a high-visibility corporate role where I had to wear hose, heels, and lipstick to fit in. Confronting just about any manifestation of sexism, however aggressive and unpleasant, was a fast track to career failure. I've been walking a tightrope over a river full of piranhas all my life. You learn not to look down, or you go mad.

"I didn't look like this before I transitioned. V-symbionts modify you to help you hunt better, and they work with whatever you've got." (If you're mouse-blonde and female, they'll turn you into Vampire Barbie whether you like it or not.) "I'm a fake, it's just predator camouflage."

"You're not a fake." He runs his hand down my flank slowly, possessively. I shiver. "What happens to my existing powers if I take the red pill?"

"I don't know," I tell him truthfully. "None of my people started out metahuman. Existing thaumaturgic practitioners don't seem to lose their mojo when they turn, though. If anything, they got stronger—and it cures their K syndrome. But we can't count on you remaining mission-effective afterwards."

"Shit." He pulls back from me, and I feel the chill of sweat evaporating.

I didn't bring my Fuckboy along on this trip just for the sake of the happy fun sexytimes that shore up our cover story: he's got a vital part to play. Jim is the type of metahuman we call a tank (subtype: flying). He finds it totally annoying, because when he acquired his powers he was already a Chief Superintendent, the equivalent of a colonel in the army, fasttracked for promotion within the Met. Two years later he's *still* a Chief Superintendent (or was, before the PM pulled his name out of the hat). Turns out that being called out of meetings to punch bank robbers is a career black mark when you're senior management. But we're not dealing with London Metropolitan Police internal politics any-more, and we *did* have a role for a skytank with anti-terrorism command experience. We had to ditch his armor back in the hotel in New York—the suit that came in our parcel drop, along with my "engagement presents"—but we could probably hack something together from the sporting goods and military surplus in DC—if he wasn't already a mission kill.

"Right now, with your current threat status, you're not mission ready," I tell him. "Worse, you're tying up one of our critical-path capabilities." (The containment grid we're lying in right now.) "And I'm not going to order you to transition, because it's irre-vocable and there's only about a 50 percent survival rate. Next time the grid powers down I'm going to get on the internet and expense you a ticket to Heathrow, seat class no object, on the first available flight." (And cross my fingers that hostile PHANGs don't kill him before the plane lands.) "Then we'll work out some other way to continue the extraction. Are we clear?"

Jim stares at me for a whole minute before he shakes his head. "You've forgotten something."

"What?"

"If you *don't* turn me, I'm going to have to live the rest of my life in a containment grid." His chest heaves and I have to force myself not to reach out towards him. "Forget about me for a bit, and ask yourself, what about Sally?" (*Fuck,* I think. I wasn't ruth-less and manipulative enough to go there myself, but he's gotten to it without me.) "Don't you think she deserves a father?" he adds, a little callously: "It's not as if the New Management doesn't have an involuntary donor program to keep PHANGs alive as long as they're useful. You need me for this job, Mhari. Turning me is the best way to keep it on the rails. We can work out the rest after we get home."

"You don't know what you're asking for."

"Yes I do." Seen by the twilight glow of the camping lantern, the planes and lines of his face are harsh. "The PM gave us a job. He expects us to do it by any means necessary, not chicken out halfway. What do you think He'll do if we disobey him? How do you think He might punish me? Or you?"

"You don't think He'd—" A sick, ugly realization creeps over me.

"Honey, do you really believe all the prisoners being executed to keep you PHANG people alive are guilty? Do you really think an ancient god-emperor who wants to build a fifty-story-high rack to hold His sacrifices' skulls in the center of London will blink an eye at torturing our entire extended families to death just to set an example?" His eyes are hollow pools of fear. "Do you *really* think that helping the Americans out from under the glamour of an ancient nightmare automatically puts us on the side of the angels? You're not that naive—"

"I'm trying to save you, Jim!"

He shakes his head. "You're too late. We're *all* too late. Do you really think disobedience is an option, this late in the game?"

"No."

The next thing I know, his arms are around me, cradling me like I'm someone precious rather than a thing that belongs in an unmarked grave with a wooden stake through its heart. He pulls me close and hugs me, and I let him because I'm weak. "I'm not going to let you throw the mission away in a stupid attempt to save me from PHANG syndrome. Turn me and we'll sort the rest out later." He tucks his chin against my shoulder and whispers four fatal words into my ear: "I love you, Mhari."

"I love you, too," I say with a shiver. And if he wants to imagine it's because I'm happy, I'm content to let him. He doesn't need the burden of knowing that every other man who's ever said those words to me is dead.

In a hangar at Goose Bay airport, the RAF ground crew are prepping 302 Heavy for what might be its last flight.

The RAF's Concordes are somewhat different from the airliners that served Air France and British Airways for three decades—almost as different as the production airliners were from the flight-test prototypes. Built to the Concorde B specification two years after commercial production ended, they have wing leading edge modifications, improved engines, and extensive use of carbon fiber composites to reduce weight. Then the defense establishment got hold of them, and, as is the case with every major long-term procurement program with an unlimited black budget, succumbed to the impulse to tinker. The cost overruns spiraled, but were blamed on other projects—the Nimrod AEW and MRA4 programs didn't exactly collapse under their own weight.

Concorde was the first airliner built with a computerized fly-by-wire control system. During the 1980s, engineers from GEC and Ferranti upgraded the RAF airframes, ripping out the flight engineer's station and replacing it with first-generation digital engine management computers. Then they used up all the weight savings they'd made—and then some—installing an in-flight refueling system. Concorde is a thirsty brute, and the designers opted for the flying boom system, which meant the RAF periodically had to borrow Dutch and Australian tankers until a suitably modified Airbus could be purchased. Concorde in high-speed trim has absolutely terrible out-of-cockpit visibility. Maneuvering close to other aircraft, and other operational requirements, necessitated the addition of high-definition cameras and in-cockpit screens.

And some of the other modifications were even more peculiar: the summoning grid grounded to the airframe in the forward passenger compartment, for example. Or the instrument stations for the six thaumaturgists required to open an extradimensional portal big enough for an airliner to fly through. The TROC and OBC camera systems sourced from Fairchild and ITEK, more usually mounted on the SR-71 spy plane. And so on.

The less said about the Gadget in the fuselage of 304 Heavy—the one we all hope will never fly—the better.

A civilian Concorde takes seventy-two maintenance hours of attention on the ground for every hour it spends airborne. The military version is even worse, closer in its care-and-feeding requirements to a space shuttle than a regular plane. Like most British aircraft of a certain vintage, each aircraft is a unique, hand-finished artifact, and 302 Heavy has its fair share of eccentricities, one of which is the bail-out hatch.

The original prototype Concordes had two hatches: one for the flight crew up front and one in the back, between the engine pods, for the test engineers. A tunnel surrounded by railings dropped straight down to the lower pressure hull of the aircraft. In an emergency, the crew were supposed to grab their 'chutes, drop down a fireman's pole arrangement, and free fall away from the stricken airliner. This was always a fraught procedure, because the speed at which a Concorde falls out of the sky is not much lower than the speed at which the slipstream stops a parachutist exiting a plane—in fact, it was considered so risky that nobody ever tried it to see if it was survivable. Nobody was crazy enough. Until now.

302 Heavy differs from airframes 301 and 303 in that it has only a single hatch in the lower fuselage, near the rear of the passenger cabin. But this hatch is larger than the original ones, is surrounded by high-visibility markings, can be illuminated, and retracts inwards so that it can be re-sealed after use. There's also a cable winch. Because, at a cost of more millions of pounds than

I care to think about, 302 Heavy has been modified to trail a
trapeze and capture net in flight . . .

It's past midnight before Brains pulls back into the parking lot
of the motel. Bone weary, he parks the big SUV nose out, strad-
dling two spaces in front of the doors to the rooms they've
taken. Sitting in the front passenger seat, Pete's face is a mask
of shadows cast by the distant streetlights. "I'll take the sofa
in your room," he says, pre-empting debate. "Jon can have
my bed."

Brains nods, momentarily ashamed of his instinctive assump-
tion that Pete would be more twitchy about sharing with him
than with Jon. "Yeah, that's fine."

Jon, who has been leaning against the headrest, yawns and sits
up. "Are we there yet?" she chirps.

"Yes, we're there," Pete replies. Brains feels a stab of guilty
relief. The former vicar is unconsciously reassuring. He shows
no outward sign of unease as Jon opens her door and hops down.
"Here's my room key," Pete says, handing her a gigantic plastic
key ring. "Are you going to be all right on your own?"

"It's a—" Jon looks momentarily baffled, then her expression
clears. "—a hotel room?"

"A motel," Pete explains. "Like a hotel, except all the suites
have separate doors that open onto this car park. Look, there's
your front door. We'll see you tomorrow, at eight."

Jon nods. "A motel. Like a hotel. I can do this." She strides
over to the room, her steps oddly jerky, but opens the door and
goes inside without any fuss. A moment later the light comes on
and the curtains twitch shut.

Brains climbs down from the driver's seat in time to see Pete
vent a sigh of relief. "Everything okay?" he asks.

Pete nods at the door to Jon's room. "*I'm* fine. And I think
she'll be fine now."

"What's up with her?"

"A patchy memory overlay, I think. Yarisol—the person under the memories—is totally unequipped to deal with everyday life, both because she's *alfär* and her culture is wildly alien to ours. Also, she's non-neurotypical even by *alfär* standards. So she's relying on Jonquil's memories as a guidebook. It works most of the time, but whenever she falls off the edge of Jonquil's map she falls back on *alfär* rules. Whatever they happen to be. Hence the business on the lakeshore." Pete swallows queasily.

"Yeah, that." Brains gestures: "Inside." Pete follows him into the motel room and draws the curtains and shuts the door. Brains continues: "What she did back there. How safe do you think we are?"

Pete drops his bag on the tan corduroy sofa and shrugs off his coat. "She's an *alfär* mage. *Safety* isn't the word that springs to mind . . . but for what it's worth, I don't think she means to do ill by us." He pokes at the coffee machine on the sideboard next to the elderly looking TV. "I'm more worried about her overloading in public and disengaging."

"Disengaging?" Brains raises an eyebrow.

"Come on, you must have met people with a touch of Asperger's before?" Brains blinks, taken aback. Pete is perceptive about that sort of thing, part of the counseling side of his job, Brains thinks. Or maybe it's just that he, himself, isn't. There's something odd about Pete's expression, although he can't quite put his finger on it, so he nods tentatively. "Jon finds people hard to read and unfamiliar situations alarming, but she only took action when somebody tried to shoot us. I think, under the circumstances, we should be grateful, shouldn't we?"

Brains shudders. "She's a gorgon. Or able to emulate gorgonism." Brains has been dealing with basilisk weapons for well over a decade, and he's read the background history. The medusa gaze is a—thankfully rare—symptom of a particularly unpleasant brain tumor. Victims tend to go mad long before the cancer kills them; watching everyone you love explode in red-hot cinders must be ghastly. But normally gorgonism is uncontrollable. "Jon did it *deliberately*."

"She's a blood-mage. Anyway, I got an email while you were driving. The real reason we picked her up is she's our ride out during Phase Three. Tomorrow morning." Pete fiddles with the sofa until he works out how to unfold the top cushions into a slightly lumpy mattress. "Where's the spare bedding—"

Brains retreats to the back of the suite and raids the closet for a spare pillow and a quilt. He finds himself yawning. "I don't get how she did it," he complains as he delivers the supplies to Pete. "I don't like it."

"Just tape a sign to her back saying OTHER END TOWARDS ENEMY," Pete says, a trifle tetchy. He's not had enough sleep either, Brains realizes.

"I'm going to bed."

"You do that." Pete yawns. "I'll set an alarm for seven thirty. Then we should bring everything in from the car and clear the front room so Jon can do her stuff."

9: MHARI'S BIG DAY

Mission start time T minus six days.

I'm twitchy about taking time out this close to D-day, but if there's one unforgivable sin in any organization, it's forgetting to keep your manager informed. The Prime Minister—*damn Him for meddling*—wants to be in direct control of the revamped and rebooted Special Operations Executive. Which means I have to visit Downing Street to brief Him in person on progress towards YELLOW OLYMPIC, invariably during daylight hours. Can I just say "fuck my life" and leave it at that? No? Didn't think so.

Of course there's more to the new SOE than YELLOW OLYMPIC. It's a small but significant stakeholder in the national security infrastructure that the PM is revamping in preparation for the Umbral Defense Review later this year, so I have to sit through an hour and a half of activity reports delivered by a variety of other departments before I can contribute my own three-minute summary of how the organizational rollout is progressing (TLDR version: I have delegated it to Colonel Lockhart, he knows what he's doing). The projects being reported on range from the tedious[9] to the gruesome.[10] But at the end of the regular reports,

[9] Specification and outsourcing procurement of an online food-rationing system: Is the contractor to use SAP, Oracle, or an open-source stack?
[10] The National Transplant Service is having difficulty procuring the materials for a symphony orchestra string section consisting of pale violins, cellos, and

when the meeting is over and everyone rises to leave, the PM tips me the nod. "Baroness, if you'd care to join me, please? You, too," He adds to Iris.

We follow His Majesty through the warren to His private office, where tea and scones are waiting, the Black Pharaoh having lately displayed an unexpected sweet tooth. I perch on the edge of the sofa beside Iris and sip my tea tensely, wondering if they've seen through me. I'm feeling very much out of my depth.

"According to Forecasting Ops, right now you're wondering if I can see right through you," the PM tells me.

I return my cup to its saucer with only a slight betraying rattle. "I suppose if they say so, it must be true," I bluff. "So busted."

The Mandate laughs delightedly. "Capital, Baroness! Your double-bluff was a low-weighted probability," He confides. "I believe you win this round—on points."

"*What* round?" I ask, irritated and slightly frightened. "Are you playing games with me?"

"Yes," He says, with evident amusement.

Iris, however, glances at her watch with thinly veiled impatience. "Treasury report in eighteen minutes, sir," she reminds Him.

"They'll wait." A languid wrist-twirl takes in the shuttered windows, beyond which lie the Downing Street gardens. The windows are bulletproof and the wooden panels conceal armored steel cores, the legacy of an IRA mortar attack in 1991. "This is *much* more important."

Oh crap, *He thinks talking to* me *is more important than talking to the Treasury?* "I find that hard to believe," I manage to say.

His Infernal Majesty leans towards me confidingly. "You have imposter syndrome," He says, "but paradoxically, that's often a sign of competence. Only people who understand their work

---

double basses. No, I don't know why He wants such a thing. In fact, I don't *want* to know.

well enough to be intimidated by it can be terrified by their own ignorance. It's the opposite of Dunning-Kruger syndrome, where the miserably incompetent think they're on top of the job because they don't understand it." He winks—I think—and adds: "It screws with precognition, you know. Almost as much as the DM's dice. Makes you unpredictable."

Huh? What?

I must shake my head or give some other sign of incomprehension because the PM takes it as His cue to monologue, slightly patronizingly. "True clairvoyance is probabilistic, and depends for its effectiveness on the pettifogging determinism of the incompetent. Any idiot can execute a detailed plan—and by sticking to the plan even when things have begun to tilt off true, they make it easier for an adversary's predictive assets to pin them down. But I've pushed you out of your comfort zone by placing full responsibility for this new agency on your shoulders. You will have to make momentous decisions with inadequate preparation, and follow through on them." His smile reveals a flash of something like shark teeth, or perhaps a dental bridge made out of razor wire. (I shudder and abruptly forget the details, losing everything except a disturbing memory of whiteness.) "You will have to make up your own mind and improvise on the fly, in the field." His smile-like expression widens alarmingly. "And that will make it much harder for the adversary to anticipate you."

I lick my lips. They're dry. "What if I just stick to Plan A?" I ask.

"That would be extremely foolish of you, and I don't believe you're that stupid, Baroness. Although I expect the view from atop the Marble Arch Tzompantli would be quite spectacular." His smile gapes like an Aztec trophy skull.

Did He just threaten me with—yes He did. I swallow. "First you give me a set of conflicting goals, now you're telling me to make my own assessment of which ones to prioritize—and if I get it wrong I'm dead?"

"I have complete confidence in you, Baroness. Ah, that is to say, *the government* has complete confidence in your ability to negotiate at the highest level with foreign powers. To identify with Our goals and plot a course towards the optimal outcome of these negotiations. And an essential element of negotiations is not to show your hand too soon. Now here are your real instructions—"

He blathers on for a bit and I zone out, my attention sliding off-kilter to the soothing drone of His voice. It's just verbal wallpaper, adding nothing and signifying naught: in one ear and out the other. His words are as instantly forgettable as His face, and I lose my memory of them as soon as He stops.

"You trust me to negotiate with the President?" I ask. *First you wanted to know if Cthulhu had awakened yet, then you wanted me to bring the President back here, now you want me to negotiate with him? Make up your bloody mind!* I want to shout.

"If I let you recall what I want, then the Nazgûl's seers will know, too." Something about that last bit doesn't quite make sense to me, but before I can ask Him to clarify, Iris taps her watch. The PM nods, then rises. "Alas, I have to go to my Treasury committee meeting, Baroness. No rest for the wicked! I've given you a toy box, and I expect you to pleasantly surprise me. Confusion to the enemy!" He taps two fingers to His forehead as I stand, and He shakes my hand, with a sensation like thousands of tiny stinging insects running over my future grave.

And then we're done.

The besetting vice of high office is the temptation to micromanage, to take direct control of a small, concrete, easily understood subsidiary operation and start issuing orders, to the detriment of the chain of command (and the neglect of the big picture). The reason micromanagement is a vice is that it's a temptation to self-indulgence: it's too easy to get carried away. Taking on a low-level coordinating role while retaining the full executive authority and fiscal responsibilities of senior rank is like playing a game you've mastered on the lowest difficulty level. DeeDee knows it's naughty but the Lord of Sleep himself has ordered her to do this thing so her ass is totally covered, and the prospect of getting her hands dirty is irresistible.

DeeDee is accustomed to running an organization with hundreds of management cells working under her, supervising tens of thousands of bound servitors directly, liaising with budgetary oversight committees at federal agency level. In contrast, managing a handful of surveillance and pursuit teams and a coordination committee liaising with the various DC police and security services is *fun*. She's actually about to work out in the field for the first time in over a decade. Admittedly she's embedded in a headquarters team based in a mobile command center, with a Marine Corps helicopter squadron on call for logistic support and the entire weight of all of DC's police forces behind her— but, *fieldwork*!

"Good morning, everybody!" DeeDee announces brightly from the front of the briefing room. It's a full house today. Besides her core team (PA, communications tech, Assistant Director (Operations), and two silver-suited blood guards), she's facing a mob drawn variously from the Secret Service, the FBI, the United States Capitol Police, the DC Metropolitan Police, the Pentagon Force Protection Agency, the Marine Corps, Homeland Security, and the Parks Police. About the only federal enforcement entity not present today is the Postal Inspection Service, which is in the doghouse as far as DeeDee is concerned. The back of the room is packed wall to wall by nearly twenty more blood guards, standing eerily motionless.

"You're here to minimize interagency communication bottlenecks and reduce the risk of blue-on-blue fire in today's operation. Which, in case you haven't reviewed your briefing"—she flashes them a friendly grin, because she knows that everyone has felt mysteriously compelled to read and memorize the back-grounder her PA sent out the evening before—"is all about taking down a terrorist cell that we've been tracking around the DC area for the past few weeks before they assemble and commit the atrocity they've been planning."

Just about everyone in her audience sits up and leans forward. News of a high-profile terrorist incident is guaranteed to get their undivided attention, like a blood-dipped rag before hounds straining at the leash.

DeeDee makes a peculiar gesture with her left hand, which she conceals from her audience behind her podium. "The group in question are highly trained and motivated political subversives protecting a kingpin they call the *President*." Her hidden fingertips are briefly suffused by an electric glow as she utters the word, and she tenses, but none of her audience show any sign of woken recognition. "They believe that if they can seize control of the national media on their own terms, they will be able to spark a mass public uprising against the federal government. We've been tracking them for some time"—*nearly 227 years*—"and we believe that in the next two to three days they intend to activate multiple cells around the nation and commence a preplanned campaign." She smiles grimly. "We're not going to give them the chance. Instead, we're going to round them up and shut the President's conspiracy down hard, wherever possible taking them in possession of materials sufficient to secure a conviction for treason or sedition."

For the next hour, DeeDee delivers a quick rundown of the order of operations for today. She introduces the various team leads to one another, explains the role of the blood guard in liaising with her command center, and how she wants the so-called Presidential Protection Detail and their secondary terrorist cells to be detained, held incommunicado, and prepared for interrogation. "Zero hour is sixteen hundred," she sums up. "And please remember, it's essential that we apprehend the so-called President *alive*. The other cells are fair game and I expect you to prioritize neutralization over capture, but my boss is *particularly keen* to question the terrorist leader in person. So let's make sure that happens."

There is a rumble of approval from her audience. *They're good people,* she thinks, *the best.* "Let's go to work!"

The grid shuts down twice more in the night. After the second time I mumble my apologies and retreat to the sofa, leaving him on the sleeping bag with a tablet for company. There's some light reading on it: a low-classification orientation backgrounder on PHANG syndrome I wrote for briefing outsiders with clearance. I warn him there'll be an exam later, if he lives long enough. (If he's serious about turning, I can probably walk him through the process using the tablet as a teaching tool: *damn* Alex for inventing such an easy-to-understand visualization. If you could broadcast it over a TV channel . . . my blood runs cold at the thought.)

But Jim's plight is a problem for tomorrow, and right now I need some "me" time to clear my head. So I lie on the sofa, tense and anxious. If I wasn't me I'd totally fire myself right now: I'm not fit to run this project. Fact is, we need the grid and we need Jim's special talent. They're both critical-path dependencies. But thanks to me screwing up and being spotted by the adversary in New York, Jim's life is in immediate danger, and I'm desperately worried it's impairing my managerial objectivity. Remind me again whose great idea it was to have him on this team? I mean, just because His Majesty sent me a list of names with heavy underlining, and some strong hints from Forecasting Ops, I didn't have to plan to use his peculiar talents . . . hah hah, only kidding.

Eventually I find I can no longer lie around, so shortly before six I write up a sitrep and send it via secure email for the boss's afternoon briefing. There are some new reports waiting for me, including one from parts west—Yarisol has arrived, Brains and Pete have done their thing, and they're awaiting extraction, which means, *fuck,* Jim has to be out of the grid by nine at the latest. The big white bird is ready to fly at two hours' notice. All the pieces are converging on their zero-hour locations, which means that it's time for Derek to make a call and roll his lucky dice.

Derek has the second bedroom at the back of the house. I nudge the door ajar and take a quick look. He sleeps with the curtains drawn, bundled up under the quilt like a plump blood-filled burrito. His snores are far cuter than the rest of him, I decide, and he's had plenty of sleep, so I hop onto the end of the bed and remorselessly peel the duvet back from his face. "Rise and shine!" I carol in his ear. He emits a pulse of terror sweat as he spasms awake: it smells heavenly. "It's going to be a bright, sunny day and I need you to make a phone call!" I singsong at his stunned face. Or, if I'm honest about it, his more-than-slightly terrified one: Possibly I should have delegated his wake-up call to someone who doesn't have enhanced dental assets? Too late to worry now. I see he's wearing PJs, so I step down from the bed, taking the duvet with me. "Coffee downstairs in five!" I trill, then go next door to roust Janice.

Janice is already up and dressed, not to mention grumpy. "What was *that* in aid of?" she asks. She's packing her suitcase, clearly thinking ahead.

"Misery loves company." I shrug. "My offer of coffee stands. We need a briefing while Jim's available."

The kitchen is still comfortably dark. I set the coffee machine going, then wait in the living room for the grid to power down. "Keep it off for now," I tell Janice. To Jim, a trifle waspishly, "How do you feel?"

Jim sits up, rubs his forehead, and yawns. He's skinned down to underwear and is in the sleeping bag. "Not bad," he says, then stills, listening. "I can't hear them. That's a good sign, right?"

"Yes. Okay, I need you to clear out of the grid and suit up now." I see the tablet. "Did you do your homework?"

"I found the visualization," he says. "It made my head hurt, like a random-dot stereoisogram, but I couldn't make head nor tail of those, either."

Huh. "Maybe Janice can talk you through it later—"

"—Now wait a minute—" she tries to interrupt.

"—But right now we need the grid clear and reconfigured as a ghost-road endpoint." That's what the *alfär* call the extradimensional paths we know as ley lines. They're stabilized wormholes, I think, but as we're dealing with Jon and she's forgotten more about this stuff than we've ever learned, we'll use her terminology. "We've got people coming through in a couple of hours."

"But I thought you wanted Jim isolated—"

"Yeah, about that," Jim tells her. "It's not going to work: keeping me in a grid for life, I mean. So I vote we just get on with the mission and worry about fixing me later—you never know, I might get an opportunity to find and kill the PHANGs who hooked into me."

Janice peers at him dubiously from under her fringe. "Mission first?"

"This is not a democracy, people," I remind them. "But for what it's worth, Jim's right and the mission comes first." I've had time to think, unfortunately. There's a lot riding on us. I will be really upset if I lose anyone, especially Jim (who am I fucking kidding? I'll *distraught*), but I'll deal with it when I get home. For now, the mission comes first, because if we fail, the PM will blame all of us. "Derek." The man himself is just shuffling downstairs as I speak: he gives me a hangdog look. He looks as crumpled as an empty crisp packet. "Coffee's getting cold."

Derek nods wordlessly and heads for the kitchen. I wince as I hear the crackling of his knee joints. He's the oldest of us by quite a way, and he's in poor shape. Maybe I shouldn't have ridden him so hard, but he reliably manages to annoy me, and—

I snap my fingers. "Phone," I call after him.

"What?"

"I need you to phone the Comstock guy. Leave voicemail. Tell him to set up a meeting with the President at 11 a.m., or on the hour at any subsequent hour, the sooner the better. Party of two, me and Jim. They get to decide when and where and call us back on your burner number."

Derek returns from the kitchenette, holding his near-overflowing coffee mug in a death-grip. "A meeting with the President. Right."

"Oh, and I want you on standby to roll your dice some time today, at zero notice." I grin at him and he twitches, slopping coffee on the cream carpet.

"What? I can't just—"

"Oh yes you can," I tell him. "It's a straight-up, two-way choice between Plan A and Plan B, but I don't want you to make the roll until I call the shot."

"Oh, *now* I get it. Is that the real reason I'm here?"

"Yes, Derek," I tell him, "we hauled you four thousand miles out of your comfort zone just so you could make a saving throw vs. Cthulhu. Happy now?"

The thing about Derek is that his dice are almost as strange as he is. And he is pretty strange to begin with. Take a bunch of teenage D&D players, rounded up during the Satanic D&D Panic of the early '80s. Drop them into Camp Sunshine, the Laundry's detention center for occult offenders. Now release all of them except the Dungeon Master (who would be diagnosed with Asperger's if it happened in the 1990s, but consequently strikes the ignorant interrogation crew as just possibly being fucked-up enough to be a type of cultist they've not previously encountered). By the time they realize he is, in fact, harmless, he's been institutionalized. That's Derek.

Derek spent a third of a century moderating a very weird role-playing game as rehab therapy for a constantly changing audience of captured cultists. Quite how weird his game had become was something we didn't actually establish until his dice became a problem that could no longer be ignored.

If you roll a normal d6—a cubic dice—repeatedly, the mean of the random number sequence it outputs is 3.5 $((1+2+3+4+5+6)/6)$. Derek's d6 dice, which he made himself out of god-knows-what raw materials he found in Camp Sunshine, and which glow with Cerenkov radiation, aren't weighted . . . but when you roll them they average 3.1415926535 and so on, grinding endlessly to converge on an average score of π. And *don't* get me started on his d4, d8, d12, d20, and dTeapot. The contents of Derek's dice bag should probably be a state secret, but every mathematician we've sent to study them has required months of therapy afterwards, so now we leave them in the custody of their creator.

The purpose of rolling dice is to generate a random number—one as close to truly random as you can get. True randomness is apparently rather difficult to approach using computational—which is to say, magical—techniques. Derek's irrational dice don't merely generate truly random numbers; rolling them is like throwing chaff in the face of an oracle's radar vision. Forecasting Ops hate them. They blur the future. And that's why I brought them, and their carrier, along on this mission. They're backup for my imposter syndrome.

"Derek?" I repeat his name to get his attention.

"What?" He shakes himself.

"Comstock, phone, snap to it."

Janice looks unhappy. "Wait, you're just going to walk into a—"

Jim cracks his knuckles. "Papers?" he asks me.

"They'll be here by ten." The special passports with diplomatic visas will arrive by courier later this morning. Jim is an officially accredited representative of H.M. Government. I'm an actual legislator. It's not bulletproof and it won't keep the Nazgûl from messing with us, but this is DC and the ordinary cops are used to dealing with foreign VIPs. Or *not* dealing with them, because they can't legally arrest someone with diplomatic immunity, and the mountain of paperwork (not to mention negative press attention) that results from shooting a foreign diplomat is memorably traumatic. "Let's do breakfast, then get ready."

Derek phones Mr. Tancredy's voicemail and leaves a message, reading from my tablet, as Jim cooks up breakfast—scrambled eggs, a metric ton of toast, orange juice, and some nameless fried meat that claims to be bacon but isn't. Since he's distracting himself in the kitchen, I have a quiet word with Janice, who goes to the grid in the living room and reconfigures it for its original purpose. While Jim and I are off meeting the President, she'll see if she can scrounge up enough extra components to make a portable isolation grid for Jim, but it doesn't look promising. If we had some way of backtracking to the source of a V syndrome contagion . . . but no. And I'm wasting too much time overthinking this shit.

After breakfast Jim and I dress as if we're about to spend a day in front of a parliamentary committee. I wear my anti-sunlight body stocking under my business suit, and Janice helps me with the latex face paint so I look less artificial than usual—more TV news presenter, less alien android. I stash an emergency makeup kit in the backpack full of gear Janice and Derek laid in for us yesterday when we called to say we'd lost our luggage, along with a basic first-aid pack. Then we sit around and wait.

At nine thirty the doorbell rings. Derek answers it, and signs for a slim envelope. I open it and quickly flip through my passport before handing Jim his own. *Her Britannic Majesty's Secretary of State requests and requires in the Name of Her Majesty all those whom it may concern* . . . with an added bound-in insert that says in flowery diplo-speak *Yeah, we're* serious *this time*. Oh my, it's official: I'm now a representative of the government. Being me, I tuck a short but extremely sharp ceramic knife blade between the pages. Because you never know when you'll get thirsty.

Jim scrutinizes his new passport with a faint frown. He doesn't fool me: I hear his pulse accelerate unevenly. "It's really happening," he says.

"Yes, it is."

Janice is not the world's most sensitive person, but she picks up on what's going on. She grabs Derek by the sleeve of his cardigan and leads him in the direction of the grid in the living room, asking him something about timesheets. I meet Jim's gaze. "Feel anything unusual?" I ask, too casually.

He shrugs. "Should I?" The frown deepens. "Nothing like yesterday's attack on the train, if that's what you're asking."

"Well, okay—" My phone vibrates for attention and I glance at it. "That's the Colorado Springs team. They're about to come through. That's our ten-minute warning." I swallow and look back at him.

"How long will they take to get here?" he asks.

"I have no idea." Could be thirty seconds, or thirty minutes. Anything more than three hours would be bad, very bad. The ghost roads distort distance and time. They also need to be nailed down at both ends lest the travelers end up lost forever. I raise my voice: "Janice? I just got the yellow alert from Jon. We need to bring the grid up in anchor mode." Jim just nods at me silently, and for a moment I wish I hated him. It'd make this so much easier.

I raise my voice again: "Janice? When you're done there, I'd like you to spend some time with Jim, with Alex's visualizer. See if you can make it clear to him."

To infect someone with PHANG, it's not enough just to look at an eyeball-melting, higher-dimensional projection. You need to *understand* it, not just admire it. I'm not a programmer or a mathematician, although I've picked up some stuff over the years. (You can't work in the Laundry or run a team of software devs and not do that.) It took Alex several hours of one-to-one tuition to get it into my head (before we realized that it wasn't such a good idea, of course).

Jim is a cop. Admittedly he's a very senior one with a postgraduate degree. He can write spreadsheet macros and run regression analyses of crime hotspot statistics, but whatever paranormal abilities he's got are strictly superhero track, not ritual or computational. It's no surprise that Jim couldn't figure it out on his own. And Janice didn't work her way through a PhD at Oxford as a part-time teaching assistant the way Alex did: her teaching skills are non-existent. So this is a long shot—it's just better than doing nothing.

But before Janice can take Jim aside, Derek rushes in. "I got a reply!" he says excitedly. "I got a reply! The President wants to meet you at eleven!" He waves a sheet of paper covered in scrawled instructions. "Here!"

Jim and I stand as I take the paper and glance at it. "Okay," I tell Derek, "we're on our way. If we're not back and you don't hear from us by one o'clock, assume we're blown and execute Plan C."

"But try and hang on for the Colorado team before you evacuate," Jim adds thoughtfully. Then, to me, with a sardonic wink: "The game's afoot."

"What the fucking fuck is *that*?" Brains demands, momentarily losing his cool as Jon waves the *that* under his nose.

"It's a blood wand!" Jon tells him excitedly. "I made it overnight?! Say hello to blood wand!"

The blood wand resembles an extremely regrettable cross between a toilet brush and a tampon, although Brains isn't entirely sure about the latter (neither he nor his husband have much use for such things). The blood wand is of elephantine proportions, a handle bearing a cylindrical mass of compressed bloody cotton wool. As Brains recoils he realizes that the bloodstains seem to form some sort of grotesque design. Feeling slightly faint, he fans his face and hides behind the spirit of scientific enquiry: "What's it for?" he asks.

Pete grimaces and hides his face, shoulders shaking. (Brains assumes that, being of the heterosexual persuasion, Pete is more familiar with such objects.) "Presumably the period fairy uses it to banish the cramp demon?" he suggests, which Brains refuses to even attempt to understand. "Or maybe it's a divining tool?"

"Yes-good!" Jon nods vigorously. "Blood is a potent store of *mana,* the blood of magi in particular. Draw the portal diagram and I will open the way and lead you to She Who Is To Be Obeyed."

Brains frowns, racking his brains for movie references. "Ursula Andress?" he offers, before realizing that, of course, being a goddamn alien, Jon is a complete cinematic illiterate, so—"Wait, you mean Baroness Karnstein?"

"Yes-yes!" Jon bounces up and down on the balls of her feet.

"How much coffee did we have this morning?" Pete asks, suspicion dawning.

"All of it!"

Brains absorbs this fact slowly. The room he and Pete shared didn't come with a filter machine, but there was an industrial-sized one in the motel lobby. *If Jon drank the entire jug—*

"How many times did you refill it?" asks Pete.

"Only three times! It kept running out!"

Brains glances at the vicar. "Are we going to need a tranquilizer dart?" he murmurs.

Pete shakes his head. "That's really nice, Jon," he says calmly. "Now, why don't you sit down on the sofa while Brains and I take care of the portal setup? We'll call you when we're ready for you to energize it." Then, in what Brains can only characterize as a stroke of genius, he adds, "Have you ever played Candy Crush Saga? No? Here, it's on my phone, let me show you how . . ."

It takes five minutes to get the vibrating *alfär* mage settled on the sofa bed with Pete's smartphone, but pretty soon she's hunched over the palmtop, mumbling angrily to herself as the game's theme tune spills from the tinny speaker at a manic tempo.

Pete makes eye contact with Brains. "Let's get this show on the road," he says, and Brains can only agree.

Brains's morning takes a turn for the better after that. He's worked on grid layouts so many times that it's almost automatic these days, but he keeps the schematic for this one to hand on his tablet and refers to it frequently, double-checking his work— if he gets any part of it wrong they could become horribly lost. There's a checklist, too, and Pete talks him through it as calmly as he'd lead a Sunday service. In fact, he's almost as soothing as Jon is disturbing. Between them they get the intricately nested circles and pentacles of the conductive diagram laid out in under an hour, during which time Jon blows right through Pete's all-time high score in the game. Finally, Brains gets a text from DC to say that the receiver is ready for them.

And then it's time to go.

It's an annoyingly bright day outside, but there's enough overcast to keep it from frying me, and it's cold enough that wearing opaque tights and gloves isn't too unusual. Jim's carrying a huge backpack. He'll need it later if our contact is good to go with either Plan A or Plan B.

We wait just inside the doorway for an Uber to the next-but-one nearest subway stop, then catch a train into town. The DC subway is an annoyingly sparse network compared to London or New York, but there are a couple of interchanges. We split up at L'Enfant Plaza and ride separate trains for a while, then meet up again at King Street and head for the rendezvous near Rosslyn. There are a bunch of buses and an airport interchange at the station so it's both busy and has enough fan-in/fan-out to smudge our movement footprint. Jim confirms he's not being followed before I meet him. I don't spot anyone on my tail, either. (I wish PHANGs came with the traditional—alas, entirely fictional— vampire's invisibility to cameras and mirrors, but all I've got is an inability to see my own reflection, which is just a nuisance.)

The exit from the Metro station is overshadowed by bland concrete offices with underground parking. The middle of the street is a ramp leading down to an underpass. Jim and I proceed arm in arm towards the rendezvous near a garage entrance. We're a few minutes late so I'm tense, a little nervous, when one of the ubiquitous Escalades with blacked-out rear windows pulls up beside us and the rear passenger window winds down. "Hello?" someone calls from the front seat. "Hello?"

I turn, putting myself on the far side of the pavement from the car, with Jim between us. "Hey," says Jim, then pauses. "You must be looking for—"

"The Kennedy Memorial." That's the passphrase.

"It's in the cemetery. You can't miss it," Jim gives the counter-phrase.

"Want a ride?" The passenger-row door pops open.

Jim clambers in first and slides sideways across the bench seat. I follow him into the walnut and leather interior, then shut the door. The green-tinted windows pleasantly dim the outside light. Our driver moves off without waiting for us to strap ourselves in, but he keeps his speed down. I don't look round and don't make any sudden moves, but carefully pull the seatbelt around me. Bodyguards with guns generally like it if the person in the row in front of them is strapped down.

"Your papers, please," says the man behind me.

"I'm going to open my handbag," I tell him, wait a few seconds, then withdraw my passport. Jim has his own in hand. He takes mine and passes them back.

"James Grey, Mhari Murphy." There is a pause. "Diplomatic cover—Baroness Karnstein? 'Carmilla'? Really?"

"House of Lords Special Forces," Jim says drily.

"I'm a member of the government," I add. *At least, until the PM decides otherwise.* "Jim is here as my plus-one and PPO." Personal Protection Officer.

A momentary hitch, then: "Detective Chief Superintendent Grey, Special Branch—that's the, uh, anti-terrorist police, isn't it?"

"I cover the metahuman beat."

"Meta—oh. I get it. What do you do to rate a Special as a bodyguard, Baroness?" Our passports reappear over the back of the seat and Jim accepts them.

"You can look me up in *Burke's Peerage*. Or Hansard." *Hah bloody hah.* "The Prime Minister personally sent me with a message for the President. Ears only."

"You can deliver it now," says the man with the gun.

"Not until I see the President. I really *must* insist."

"Oh all right then," says a different voice, laden with sardonic humor, and I can't help myself: I look round and do a wide-eyed double-take, because sitting in the jump seat next to the man with the gun is another man, with a very famous face that keeps slipping out of focus whenever I try to look directly at him. "You can tell me anyway."

"That's quite some glamour," Jim says appreciatively while I'm still boggling. "Where'd you get it?"

"Our friends in the Comstock Office have a few tricks up their sleeves. What can I say?" The President shrugs and flashes me a million-dollar smile. "We'll take whatever help we can get. Now, what does Mr. Everyman have to say to me?"

"What—" I lick my lips, temporarily flummoxed. Part of me can't help freezing up in an agony of disbelief: *I'm riding around Washington DC in a limo, casually chatting with the President? Me? This is some kind of joke*—I grab my imposter syndrome by the scruff of its neck and throw it out the window, because I've got a job to do and it's getting in the way. *Get a grip, Mhari*— "Sorry. The short version is: we know about your problem. His Majesty doesn't want the Operational Phenomenology Agency to take over the US government—that's unvarnished national self-interest speaking, by the way. They scare the crap out of us. So we've set up an operation that will crack open their glamour and give you an opportunity to take back control. But it requires your active participation to work." I smile, careful not to show him too much tooth. "You have questions. Yes?"

Arthur frowns. "*His* Majesty?"

"Let's not mince words. Our Queen is just the ceremonial head of state, and she's pushing ninety. She's good for ribbon-cutting and after-dinner speeches, but not so much with the ass-kicking these days." (She's very good at playing the role of the Nation's Favorite Grandmother, but the couple of times I've met her she struck me as being deeply unimpressed by the current century.) "The PM, in contrast, is around for the long haul, and upon Her Majesty's death or abdication there may be some constitutional changes to recognize His peculiar suitability for leading the nation through this time of crisis."

The President's frown deepens towards a scowl. "Mr. Everyman isn't strictly human, Baroness. Nor, as I understand things, are you. What do you have to say about that?"

I flap my jaw for a few seconds, processing, then Jim catches my eye. "With respect, Mr. President," he interrupts smoothly, "the Baroness *started out* human, and if a cure for her unfortunate condition becomes available I'm certain she'll take it in a second." I nod vehemently. "On the other hand, the Prime Minister role-plays humanity as his chosen character class. And the OPA threw away their humanity and never looked back."

I swallow. "Most of them were never human to begin with. Or they're thing-enablers. Whatever. The fact remains, it's up to you to decide who you're willing to make common cause with, or how broad a definition of human you're willing to apply. I'd just like to observe that desperate times make for strange bedfellows."

After a few seconds Arthur nods. "What's in it for you guys?"

"We get to dodge the end of our world. That's what the OPA are working towards—with the executive oversight tier out of the way, they're free to pursue projects that will doom us all." I hesitate. "The truth is . . . our PM needs worshippers. He's an ancient horror, but He's also a narcissist that's adopted our species as His pet project. Sure, He enjoys tormenting us, some of us, some of the time—but if we go extinct, He won't be able to do that any more. So He's taken over the UK for His personal captive audience. In contrast, the thing the OPA want to summon doesn't need anyone or any *thing*. Raising it might destroy our universe, but the people running the OPA don't care because their religious framework tells them that this would be a good thing." *Who's your homie going to be, Hitler or Stalin?*

Of course I can't tell him that, or describe the New Management's longer-term plans: the gleaming chrome-and-glass Tzompantli rising over the sacrifice terminals on Oxford Street, the blood foaming in the gutters beneath the obsidian sky. I can't warn him about the vampire priests of the Morningstar Empire ascendant once more in Ultima Britannia, of the beginning of the end of human history. I can't speak of an endless future of barrel-bodied, bat-winged dragons with dangling tentacles coasting silently above the heads of terrified serfs. Of cloning tanks and charnel factories and legions of the damned swarming east beneath the blood-encrusted banner of the Union Jack, cannibalizing Europe.

Nor can I tell him—lest the SA's command override cause my arterial blood vessels to burst and my eyeballs to catch fire—about Long-Term Continuity Operations and the Resistance. (A pity: that would probably sway him emphatically in our direction. But if I told him, word might leak out and get back to Downing Street, and then the PM might well decide, *après moi le déluge*.)

It's too bad that I have to keep the future to myself, because some nightmares cry out to be shared.

"Tell me about this plan to break the OPA's amnesia spell," says the President, "and tell me what it'll cost us. Then I'll make up my mind."

So I tell him, in detail, which takes about half an hour as his security team drive us aimlessly around the conquered capital city.

And then, God help us, he says "Yes."

Pete steps inside the diagram Brains has drawn on the floor of the motel room, and watches as Jon bounces around outside it, twitching and making lip-smacking noises of approval as she shakes her bog brush. She seems to be checking it for correctness, but he isn't entirely sure, which is more disturbing than he's willing to admit. Brains sidles slightly closer. "Do you think this is entirely safe?" he asks.

"Wait—" Jon has stopped pacing the perimeter. Now she steps inside the circle with them. A sudden flash of red and Pete recoils. "What! Hey, did you need to—"

Jon squeezes her right fist over the head of the brush as blood trickles down her forearm from the razor-slash she just incised in her wrist. She grins toothily at Pete. "Hey-hey, we're on our way!" she shouts, stabbing the blood wand at the cardinal points of the grid. With a sizzling flash of electric blue light, the world around them fades out.

They stand on an infinite indigo plain, barely brighter than the not-sky overhead. A thin haze like clouds of diamond dust sparkles and glimmers across the night, curling and fading fractally across the pitch-black darkness beyond. Pete shivers. Something tells him that this is not a place where he can survive for long.

"Come on-on!" Jon tells them, then skips away, waving her bloody tool from side to side.

Brains freezes for a couple of seconds, then mutters something about elves under his breath. He charges after her. Pete glances over his shoulder briefly. The landscape behind is barren and trackless, and Jon and Brains are already dwindling, as with each step they recede a good fraction of a kilometer. A momentary terror of being lost sweeps over him and he hurries to catch up.

There's no obvious path, but Jon seems to know where she's going. This must seem like a walk in the park compared to the ghost road the Host marched along when it came to its earthly exile, Pete realizes. His separation anxiety subsides as he catches up with the other two, but now a deeper, more enervating horror grips him. This is a realm without people, without gods, without life—but not inherently hostile, not like the vacuum of space. It's a realm of potential, waiting to be filled by new creation. Or perhaps an infinity of creations. He's heard of such interstitial places of course, but to find himself walking through one is skin-crawlingly disturbing. Even though Pete is too sophisticated for Biblical literalism, he has a sense of standing outside of creation. *I can't get out of here soon enough,* he thinks, and glances at his smartwatch—a birthday present from his wife—only to see that it has crashed and frozen on reboot, mocking him with an image of the apple from the tree of knowledge, one bite down.

"Numbers mean what I want them to mean in this place!" Jon announces gaily. "Come along, hippety-hop!"

"How much further?" Brains demands.

"Not far! Hippety-hop, hurry or the clowns will eat our toes!"

"Clowns?"

Pete notices that neither he nor Brains cast any kind of shadow, but a warped penumbra surrounds Jon's feet. It moves, but only loosely matches time with her steps.

"Clowns!"

Jon points across the plain towards a distant flicker of electric blue. Another portal, Pete realizes. "Is that where we're going?" he asks.

"Yes-yes! Must outrun the clowns!" Jon trills, skipping along.

"Clowns?" Brains sounds worried.

"What clowns?" Pete asks.

"Those clowns!"

Jon points towards the distant flickering light. Which is flickering, Pete finally sees, because something is passing in front of it. Something humanoid a long way away that casts a terrible shadow.

What kind of clowns live in an interstitial space? he wonders, then looks to Jon and realizes that perhaps her command of spoken English vocabulary is imperfect.

"What *are* they?" Brains demands.

"Clowns! Like me, only not-not because they belong to the Nazgûl!" She sounds happy. "We fight, yes-yes?"

Oh dear Christ, Pete thinks dismally. *They got between us and the anchor*. As the oncoming magi in silver bodysuits race towards him, he realizes: *We're going to die.*

The President has graciously agreed to the PM's modest proposal. His man with a gun—a senior Secret Service officer called Mattingley—puts his pistol away, and our driver is running Jim and me across town towards a different Metro station, when a curious sense that we're not alone steals over me.

"We've picked up a shadow," says Jim.

"Can't be—" Mattingley stops. "Cho?"

The driver grunts assent. "Yeah, I see him. And the silver Prius that just turned in ahead of us. Two-car box tail, maybe more."

Rapid-fire jargon heavily infested with numbers and codenames is exchanged across us. I'm not the only one at a loss, judging from Arthur's plaintive, "What's happening?"

"We've been made, sir. Sir and ma'am," Mattingley adds to Jim and myself as an afterthought.

"Well, our guests had better stay with us until it's dealt with," says the President. His voice is warm and reassuring. "I apologize for the inconvenience," he adds, as if being mousetrapped by hostiles with guns is a routine irritation.

"What's your plan?" asks Jim. "Assume we're along for the ride."

"Aim for the highway and get the hell out of town," says Mattingley. "We're in a KZ here. Cho? Hit it."

"Yes, *sir*." The officer riding shotgun places an electronic gadget on the dash as the driver floors the accelerator. Ahead of us, stoplights suddenly turn green as we shoot forward and swerve around the silver Prius. The Prius may be part of a tail, but if so they're prudent enough to get out of the way of the monster truck we're riding in. Seconds later we're out of the junction and taking a hard right onto a six-lane highway, but there's a distant chittering rumble at the back of my head and it's clear that in breaking the box we've turned ourselves into a conspicuously visible target.

I get my head down and wait for my new phone to boot up—if we've been made there's no longer any point in religiously staying dark. "Jim. You ready to go at short notice?"

"What? You mean—" He shakes his head. "Neither of us are dressed for it, and I can't go that far anyway. We need the survival suits, helmets, and harness."

Dammit, he's right. I grab the overhead handle as we screech sideways into a gap between two semitrailers, then accelerate forward again. Flashing blue lights reflect in the windshield, but then I realize they're from inside the car—I guess there are some perks to having a Secret Service ride, even if it's not the presidential armored limo. My phone comes up and I enter my PIN, then check my inbox.

"Your ride will be ready to take off in about ninety minutes," I tell them. "Then it'll take another two hours and ten minutes to come overhead." Technically, 302 Heavy *could* take off, light its afterburners, and be over DC in an hour and a quarter—just as long as the pilots pay no attention to the Patriot missile batteries around DC or the F-22 squadron at Langley AFB, and are willing to leave a trail of broken windows down the entire Eastern Seaboard. Oh, and as long as they don't care about making the pickup. In practice, the plan calls for 302 Heavy to stay subsonic and broadcast a civilian airliner call sign, staying well outside the capital city's defensive perimeter. "You need to be ready to fly by two thirty to two fifty. Go to a safe location not less than ten miles north of I-495 and not less than ten miles west of Baltimore, then have Mr. Tancredy contact Derek with the details, no later than three o'clock. Jim will pick you—" I glance over my shoulder at the rear window behind the President. "—duck!"

With a loud crack, the rear window turns opaque. A nearly invisible sheet of something transparent vibrates, just inside it, absorbing the force of the bullet.

"*Fuck.*" The President winds up in the legwell of the back seat with Officer Mattingley sprawled atop him, putting his body between his charge and the shooter.

"A tire shot that went wide, I think," Jim remarks coolly as Mattingley yelps angrily into his headset. I point my camera at the starred-over window and fire up OFCUT, which requires another PIN *and* a fingerprint—I swear if they made phones with blood samplers it'd take a drop to unlock—then scan. I can't quite hear anything, but—

"Playmates," I announce. "Two PHANGs in a Dodge Charger, one shooter. You want to deal with them, Jim? I might smudge my makeup."

"Happy to oblige," he says, opening the passenger door and stepping out into the traffic at sixty miles per hour. Then, while I'm grabbing for the door to close it, he goes full Officer Friendly on them. Well, about 80 percent Officer Friendly. He doesn't have the suit of armor with the custody helmet and flashing blue light on top, so all he brings to the fight is a solidly built silverback-executive-looking guy in a business suit who can fly and punch through walls. Not Superman, but his Hollywood stunt double. The shooter leaning out of the Dodge gets off a couple of shots but they go wide, then Jim gets his hands under the driver-side door sill and flips the car on its side. I wince because it's trailing sparks like a Roman candle went off under it. That's one hostile down, with the highway behind us conveniently blocked as one of the semitrailers we overtook earlier jackknifes.

But then our driver slams on the brakes and I nearly go flying through the front windscreen, saved only by my seatbelt. My mouth dries up like magic and my teeth ache as I feel a silvery shimmery sense: we've got company and they've blocked the road ahead of us.

"Wait here," I tell Mattingley.

"You can't—" he says, then shuts up as I bare my fangs at him. I unbutton my collar and pull the hood of my bodysuit over my face, then bail out and go *fast*.

As I accelerate, the voices in the back of my head rise from a distant hiss of static to a deafening locust-swarm roar, hungry for blood. Gravity weakens, the air flows thick and surprisingly hot, daylight reddens, and everything around me seems to slow.

I hit the ground and roll to my feet, taking in the situation. The Escalade is swerving onto the shoulder, preparing to drive around the roadblock. Behind it, I glimpse Jim peeling the roof off the Dodge in slow motion. Someone inside the car is waving a gun around and I hear a dull, hollow boom as they pull the trigger, but Jim is behind them and I'm not too worried.

In front of us, the Prius stops and pops all four doors. Faceless mannequins in skintight silver Lycra climb out, not yet going to speed. Two of them have assault rifles and they're raising them to hose me down as I pull my phone up. "Say cheese," I say.

Bang. Looks like their bodysuits are just metallized spandex, which gives zero protection against basilisk weapons. Unfortunately my suit's no better, and while one of them is now a toppling pillar of flaming charcoal with white bones poking out, the other shooter is aiming at me. Something is wrong with this picture and it takes me a split second and a diving roll to realize what it is: they may be PHANGs but they don't have the superspeed thing down. If they did, I'd be bleeding out already.

Thud. (Pause.) *Thud.* (Pause.) *Thud.* I roll frantically, then kick off the ground and dash round the back of a large pickup truck as the shooter with the M16 goes full auto and tries to track me. Too late I register the propane cylinder on the truck's load bed. Is the silver shooter stupid enough to light up a tanker less than twenty meters away? *Yes he fucking is,* and his mates are rushing around the cab to meet me, and I'm willing to bet that they've got handguns or super-strength or something. *Yippee.* I haven't had this much fun since I was in the Transhuman Police, mixing it up with superpowered neo-Nazis, and by *fun* I mean *fuck me I demand a pay rise and a nice quiet office job—*

It comes to me as I close with the jokers that I can't get enough air. Super-speed has a huge drawback: I could leave Usain Bolt in the dust over a hundred meter sprint (if metahumans weren't banned from sporting events under IOC rules), but getting air in and out of my lungs is murder and I'll collapse from heatstroke in less than a minute if I keep it up. I've got to end this *fast*—

The two hostiles are spreading out around the direction I'm running in and one of them is raising a pistol in a two-handed stance that means trouble, so I sprint at him and punch as hard as I can. Blinding agony engulfs my fist and a spike of sound rams my ears as he pulls the trigger, but his gun goes spinning up and away. I shoulder-barge him with my remaining momentum and it's like hitting a brick wall. Numb and staggering, I topple over his body as his sidekick turns. There's still no sign they can go fast—I actually took them by surprise—but now I'm flat on the ground and my right hand is a solid ball of fire that won't un-fold properly. If I can't get up in the next second he'll be on me, and I can't *breathe*—

Something black and vaguely rectangular sails overhead like the Detroit iron angel of automotive death. It's the hood of the Dodge Charger, and it cuts Goon the Second off at the waist in a spray of gore. Everything goes red for a moment and I can't see, and I can tell I'm slowing down because the automatic gun-fire is speeding up. The idiot shooter is spraying bullets with ran-dom enthusiasm. I gasp for air, desperate to breathe. It feels like I'm burning up. There's an incredibly strong smell, something like rotten eggs, chokingly intense, as liquid squirts out of holes in the propane tank and runs boiling across the surface of the highway. "Mhari—" Arms like a car crusher lock tight around me and I scream as my damaged hand bounces off the ground. "I've got you," says Fuckboy. "Punching out now."

"But OSCAR—"

"He'll meet us at the rendezvous. Come *on*." Then I'm look-ing down at the concrete roadbed and lane-divider stripes from above as they recede. He's holding me against his chest like a stray kitten he's picked up with a hand around its ribs, and the white stripes begin to unroll at speed. Gale-force wind tugs at my clothes. I fight to take a deep breath, and that's when the propane vapor evaporating from the puddle beneath the leaking tank ignites and hell's doors slam open behind us.

10: FLIGHT PLAN

Jon is fraying at the seams: Jonquil is tattered shreds of memory, but Yarisol is happily in her element here in the ghost roads. It's not exactly a *safe* space (there are things that live here, unseen, for to see is to be seen and to be seen is to be *understood* and to be understood is to come to the end of mortal existence), but she's come this way many a time before, sneaking behind the backs and minds of her cruel and vindictive trainers. Finding a stakeout at the exit node is nothing new to her. Furthermore, it's a not-newness she knows how to deal with. Violently.

The playground bullies (Jonquil's metaphor, not Yarisol's) cluster around the glowing portal, looking in. It's a stakeout in *Washington DC,* the capital of the enemy's empire in this universe. Yarisol peers past them, employing the inner eye visualization trick that lets her see the informational density of the world around her. The landscape of this place is a fictional construct mapped to the *mana* flow of the space beneath it. In the near distance, a few miles away in the real world, a gigantic labyrinth of power glows around a dreadful star-bright kernel that defies scrutiny. Other lines and arcs of power form a graph of energy flowing around the boulevards and avenues of the ceremonial capital. Jonquil's memories of a documentary about DC's construction return to prompt her: there is strong ritual magic here, a binding at the center of empire. The *urük* may lack the sophistication of *alfär* magic but they are not completely ignorant. The British must have known this, for they burned the White House—and the Library of Congress—in 1814, before the binding came to full power. But the sacrificial repository at Arlington, its proximity to the Pentagon, and its distance from the Library . . . it all makes sense to Yarisol.

Patrolling the ghost roads around their labyrinthine hub, the Nazgûl's minions have stumbled upon the anchor that the team in DC have established for Jon to home in on. Now they're waiting to see who uses it. *Too bad for them,* she thinks, nursing the glow of righteous retribution. Seen by her inner eye, the four playground bullies are shadowy humanoid figures, greenish jellyfish with tendrils limning central nervous systems surrounded by the dull red glow of freshly fed peripheral tissues. They're magi, but curiously weak and uniform in appearance. They crouch around the glowing beacon, looking inwards as if they think it's an entry point rather than an endpoint.

Jon examines her two companions, hunkered down just ahead of her. They're the pinkish-orange of healthy humans, although Brains shows a faint stippling of dry rot around his head—an early sign of K-parasites attracted by the rich flavor of his thoughts. Neither of them are fighters, so this is all on her. "Stay," she hisses at them, then darts forward, summoning her full power and turning it on the enemy.

Good: the nearest Nazgûl mage sparkles and bursts into flames as abruptly as if she'd dropped a high-tension power line in his puddle. His neighbor to the left is thrown off his feet and tumbles backwards. Less good: the one on the right staggers but keeps his balance and turns towards her, snapping a directional shield into position with a flick of his fingers. *Worst*: the fourth mage doesn't waste time with a shield but shouts a word of unbinding at her. It's a weapon specific to these implied spaces, fuzzing and dismantling any structure it encounters. It's also highly directional. Jon anticipated resistance, and her dive and roll takes her out of the entropic effect, though she feels the backwash: her hair crackling and feathering, her clothing taking on the form of a leathery integument.

"Fuck!" One of her companions shouts behind her. She ignores them, goes *fast,* frantically mouthing words of control and binding and despair. The enemy shield bearer has concentrated single-mindedly on blocking simple attacks. He succumbs instead to creeping dread and curls in on himself, shuddering and wailing in terror. The chittering of her helpers rises to a crackling roar as she throws up a shield of her own. Playground bully number two won't stay down: he's sitting up, firing a handgun at the *urük. This will not do!* Jon throws a second jet of heat at him, and his hair catches fire and smokes most satisfactorily. She scrambles aside and circles the remaining active threat, which is bully number four.

Closing to within twenty meters—*oh for a handgun,* Jonquil's ghost laments—Yarisol comes to the fore and blocks. The enemy is slow, so slow, and doesn't seem able to go fast. His blood is weak. Their loss, Jon's gain. A bolt of unmaking draws a frozen line through the not-air where she was standing moments earlier but she's no longer there, somersaulting in an arc above the plane of intersecting realities.

A deep, long-drawn-out shout rises from a human throat behind her as bully number four's shield lights up. Good, one of the *urük* has a basilisk on their phone. It's little more than a distraction in this place, but bully number four is indeed distracted and turns to deal with the new threat. Their aim isn't great and the bolt of unmaking they fire goes astray. The distraction is exactly what Jon needs, and as she comes down off her arc she strikes at the enemy with words of love and contagion and gravity. The last one works: regardless of their resistance to changes of emotional or epidemiological state, enemy magi splatter very satisfactorily when you squish them.

"Yes-yes! We win! Wiktory!" Jon chants as the terror-stricken enemy's back arches and they go into clonic seizures. She capers and waves her fist triumphantly at the dead sky. Then an apprehension that all is not right steals over her. "What-what?" she demands, dropping back into real time and looking round.

Brains is kneeling by a supine form. "Over here!" he calls. He's kneeling over Pete, compressing his left arm. Blood wells up between Brains's fingers.

Shoving her blood thirst to the back of her head with practiced brutality, Jon strides towards him, breaking stride to duck under the two frozen gashes the enemy sorcerer ripped in their local reality. "What happening?"

"It's Pete! He's been shot." In the grip of Yarisol's ascendency she's terrible at reading *urük* faces, but Brains seems distressed. Yarisol focuses, sharpening down into Jon, and recognizes that Pete has been hit by a blood strike. "What's happening to—"

"Where is his ward?" Jon snaps.

"Burned out? By the lakeshore, remember? We were using our phones as backup. The OFCUT toolkit includes a protection app, but—"

"—That's no good here." Jon peers at Pete. He's not fitting and he hasn't caught fire or bled out, but there's something wrong with him. Something familiar as well. Blood calls to blood, and evidently the enemy *urük* magi have worked out a few tricks—enough to be dangerous to unprotected mortals, anyway. "Oh," she says. She snorts, amused, and a fragment of Jonquil makes her say, "Rats deserting the sinking ship?"

"What does *that* mean?" Brains demands angrily. "Can you save him?"

"Sure," Jon says carelessly. "He's not in any danger? But we must enter the gateway first." The blue-glowing circle on the ground pulses soothingly. "The others can staunch the bleeding?" She thinks for a moment. "You should avoid getting his blood on yourself, you know? And stay away from his mouth, at least until he's been castrated: he'll be very thirsty when he wakes up."

"What—"

"He's been blood-shot," Jon explains patiently. "Hit by a bullet with an inscribed grid carrying some of the shooter mage's V-symbionts. It creates a feeding link—take the feeder to the blood, rather than vice versa." She pauses in thought for a moment. "Very elegant, any wound is rapidly fatal and the victim's *mana* is transferred to the shooter. But then the shooter died, leaving the symbionts in need of a new host, yah? Pete will be fine once he learns to feed?!" She flashes Brains a brief grin, then does a double take at his expression of dismay. "Is something wrong?"

Tell me if you've heard this one: a vampire and a superhero walk into an ambush—

I must have lost consciousness for a bit, because when I wake up Jim is holding me in a bridal carry, my right hand burns like it's been dipped in molten lead, and the world is far too bright and is zooming in and out of focus. But at least we're not flying any more. Jim peers at me anxiously. "Can you hear me, love?"

"Put me down. I feel sick."

It comes to me that the reason my hand feels like the Spanish Inquisition have been testing new pilliwinks on it is that it's clenched in a fist around something solid. Jim gingerly lowers me to my feet and I force my fingers to unclench, agonizingly slowly. Pain crosses my palm with lines of molten silver as my hand opens and something that might once have been a smartphone falls out. It tinkles as it hits the pavement. *"Shit. Ow."* Memo to self: do not punch vampires while holding a phone. I'm insanely lucky the battery didn't catch—

—fire—

"Whoa!" Jim swiftly pulls me two steps back from the pyre.

My hand is still burning. I raise it and look, then shove it in my pocket hurriedly, even though it hurts so badly I want to cry. The palm of my bodysuit is ripped, exposing skin that is starting to blister and smolder in the daylight. "Need gloves," I explain. "Feel sick." Both Jims look at me with evident concern before I get my eyeballs pointing in the same direction. "Sym-sym-*things* will fix the concussion and broken hand," I explain, "*if* sunlight doesn't finish me." I take a tentative step back, nearly trip and go over, but manage to regain my balance. I take a deep breath. "Sitrep."

"We're about five blocks away. I walked the last two carrying you and the gear bag. Nobody followed us that I could see. There were two cars. I think it was a simple tail that went wrong when we spotted it. They weren't ready and now they're dead."

"So they had a tail on the President." That's bad, really bad. After a fuzzy moment—my eyelids keep trying to tell me I'm tired and they want to close—I realize something else. "My phone's toast. You need to call Derek and let him know. Team should move."

"Do you have Derek's number?" he asks mildly.

"It was on my—" I feel like kicking myself. "Shit."

I force my eyes to stay open and focused on Jim, even though it's too hot and bright and everything around me is burning. "Nothing for it, we'll have to run on auto. Derek should have your number on his list—"

As if on cue, Jim's breast pocket begins to play the theme from *Z Cars*.

"Jim speaking." He looks at me. "Yes, she's here." He holds the phone out to me: "It's for you."

"Hello? Mhari? Listen, Pete and Brains just got here with someone who looks like Jonquil only Pete's been turned and they were jumped by PHANGs on the way in and it looks like our site's compromised so we're about to—"

"Derek." I squeeze my eyes shut. *Prioritize. What's most important to the mission?* "Tell me. West or east?"

"What?"

"Dice, man! Tell me. Go west or go east?"

"Is that your big question?" I can almost hear his eyes rolling from here.

"Yes." I grit my teeth and wait. There is a long pause. I listen for a telltale rattle but his phone's microphone is too clever to pick up background noise.

"Dice say . . . east? Yes, east: Go east, whatever that means?"

"Thank you." I take a deep breath, then open my eyes again. "Derek, thank you. My phone's broken, so once you get the rendezvous details from the Comstock guy text them to Jim, then get everyone home safely. You should mobilize *immediately*. Remember the Moscow rules apply, as they say. Jim and I will meet you on the other side."

"Other side of *what*?" His voice rises in alarm.

"Other side of the Atlantic, silly," I lie through my teeth. *I am such a shit,* I think guiltily. Then it sours into resentment at the PM for putting me in this position. I pull my cheek back from Jim's hand and nod at him and he hangs up.

"What's that about?" he asks.

"I got Derek to roll the dice. Doing it this far ahead means there's some risk of enemy oracles getting a fix on our future direction once the initial uncertainty dies down, but if we get separated—" I swallow. "—you're to carry on with the plan and go west, *not* east. Can you do that?"

"Yes, I—" his voice catches. "What else did he say?"

"Too fucking much. It's our worst-case scenario for the pawns on the board, I'm afraid." I peer at him glumly. We haven't been half as smart as I thought we were: I just hope we can salvage something from this. Like, oh—"Jim. Tell me how you feel?"

"How do I . . . ?" He chuckles disbelievingly. "*All things considered* I'm doing *great*." He peers at me. "Is that concussion speaking?"

"No, it's just my suspicious paranoid nature wondering why the hell you're not dead yet." I lean against him and he wraps a strong arm around my shoulders, supporting me. "Let's walk. Uh, slower?" We move at an arthritic shuffle at first. How he's managing that, propping me up while carrying his overstuffed backpack, is beyond me. The world is still slowly spinning, and it's too bright and fuzzy at the edges and my hand is a dull throbbing lump, but I'm not about to throw up. "Anyway. Here's what I've got. Derek said Team West were ambushed and Pete's been turned. And of course Pete will have heard me ask Derek for a roll and Derek called it for east, so that's good."

"I could call him back—"

"No, don't. Derek will text us when he receives the rendez-vous details, but apart from that, the less chatter the better. What he was telling us was, Pete's been infected with enemy PHANG symbionts. But for a moment I wondered if he meant 'turned' in the other tradecraft sense, and then I began to ask myself, what's the difference?"

"Eh?" Jim shakes his head. "You're not a—"

"The opposition PHANGs are all *wrong*. No super-speed, not a lot of thaumic power. In New York they felt like they were all one creature, some sort of hive-mind." Deep breath time. "Jim, if an officer is injured in the line of duty, what do you do?"

"You evacuate them to receive medical care. It's a no-brainer. You're saying . . . they were trying to tag us? Not kill? So that, what, we'd evacuate our injured? Pete? Me?"

I take another deep breath, feeling shaky. "Next question. Do you know the origin of the term Fifth Column?"

I feel his arm go tense. "Mhari Murphy, you are *not* telling me I'm—"

"No, let me retry. Did you ever see that *Futurama* episode with the Brain Slugs?"

"Wait, what—"

There's only one explanation that fits, really. "Somehow they turned Pete. They'd probably have caught and turned Brains, too, if we hadn't sent Yarisol along for the ride. They got their PHANGs into you, and it's only a matter of time before they drain you or turn you. Probably they planned to grab and turn our entire team as we bail out." There's a Starbucks on the other side of the street, on the next block. "They had the President in a sandbox the whole time, until we accidentally blew the doors off it. The V-parasites they're using aren't free-range symbionts: they've been bred, or enslaved, to do a very specific job. But aside from that one thing, they're not very good. Fancy a fancy coffee?"

Jim sighs. "You're planning something, aren't you?" he complains.

"Yes." I thump him lightly on the shoulder. "I don't feel like waiting for the walk light and jaywalking's illegal in this state: pick me up and fly me over."

Jim does his square-jawed superhero thing and scoops me up in a carry, then levitates across the street, narrowly missing an overhead electrical cable before settling onto the pavement. He walks through the door of the semi-deserted cafe, then approaches the counter, startling the hell out of a barista before he remembers to put me down. Clearing his throat: "I'll have a venti latte with two extra shots. To sit in, thanks."

"And I'll have a double espresso, please." I smile, then remember to yank my hood back off my face. "We'll be in the back booth," I add, then wobble slightly.

"What," Jim mutters as he sits down opposite me and dumps his bag, "are you thinking?"

I glance round. It's dark in the back—no windows—which is good. And the cafe is just about dead right now. We've somehow missed the lunchtime rush. Also good. "Give me your phone. Unlocked, please."

"Why?" He complies all the same. I tap into OFCUT, go into secure messaging, and fire off a FLASH message, eyes-only, to the Senior Auditor, cc'd to Persephone in case the SA is out of action, and Mrs. MacDougal in Human Resources, who is a level-headed sort and will know what needs to be done. (Dear God—and by God, I do *not* mean the Black Pharaoh—the mountain of paperwork this is going to create for me when I get home will be brutal.)

While I'm finger-typing with my off hand, the barista comes by with our order. (Tipping large in an empty cafe is good for that kind of personal service.) Jim sips his latte and keeps an eye on the entrance and the door to the back room, while I follow up with another message, this time describing what I'm about to do next, only carefully framed in the past tense, because it's better to beg forgiveness than ask permission.

Then I back out into OFCUT, sign in again using an extra ID and password that is approved for Jim's account but he doesn't know about because I'm not stupid enough to tell him every-thing, and load up Alex's visualizer. *Right, here goes nothing.* "Pass me the first-aid kit, Jim?" I say, looking straight at him as I flip his phone around so that the animation is running on the table in front of him.

"Mhari?" He rummages in his bag, then puts the first-aid gear on the table and looks back at me.

"Whatever you do, don't move," I tell him. I go fast, lean across the table, yank the ward out from under his collar, and wrap my arms around his upper arms, pinning him in place. Then I bite through my lower lip and kiss him bloody.

A blue flash of light in a darkened living room surrounded by blackout curtains: three figures appear in the middle of a cat's cradle of network cables and compute nodes laid out on the car-pet. Predictably, one of the three takes a step forward and trips over a wire. As this is Brains, and Pete is leaning heavily on his shoulder, they both go down. This prompts some very inappro-priate swearing from the member of the clergy. Derek is a be-mused witness as Brains cries, "This is a clear health and safety violation!"

It's been a tense, stressful morning. Janice is in a grumpy mood, bristling at everyone even though it's Mhari she's pissed off at, because of her unrealistic expectations of Janice's ability to magically conjure up an isolation grid using pocket lint. Or per-haps simply because Mhari is quietly frantic over Jim's PHANG infection and is spreading her stress around. Either way, Derek doesn't have anything more to do until Mhari calls him to roll the dice, which only makes Janice worse, because anxiety loves company almost as much as misery. Even after Mhari and Jim's departure, the atmosphere in the safe house remains tense. So, having packed their kit, Derek and Janice take it in turns to watch the grid. And it just so happens that Derek is on duty when the gate to the dream road opens and the team from Colorado tumbles out.

The next few minutes are loud, confusing, and alarming. Pete is bleeding from a gunshot wound to his left arm—bloody but not life-threatening, *except* Brains, who is usually almost psychotically laconic, is completely losing his shit over it. He's also utterly paranoid about the bleeding, and yells at Derek, "Don't touch it! Don't get blood on you! It's deadly!"

Pete, eyes screwed shut, grunts. "Get. Janice."

Jon adds: "Bring tampons!"

So Derek scuttles into the hallway. "Janice?" he calls. "Janice? We've got visitors! They want tampons? Do you have any?"

A snarl of vampire rage answers him from the third bedroom. Derek decides prudence is the better part of valor and dives back into the living room. "She's coming," he reports breathlessly. "I think!"

Ten minutes later everything is under precarious control. Janice loudly explains that Derek interrupted her in the process of patching a serious security hole that had just come to light, affecting all their compute nodes. "This is easier," she adds as she slides a tampon into the hole in Pete's arm. "The army figured it out in Iraq: they had large numbers of women in combat positions for the first time and it turns out sterile, expanding, blood-absorbent cylinders have more than one use. Who knew? Now if you'll excuse me, I have a bunch of *very sick* computers to nurse and I'm thirsty"—she looks at Pete in perplexity—"why don't I want to bite you?"

Pete's jaw clenches. Then, after a moment, he relaxes. "Go," he whispers.

Jon has wandered through into the kitchen and is staring wide-eyed at the oversized appliances. "Where's the kettle?" she asks Derek.

"There." He points at the tin kettle sitting on the stovetop.

"No, I mean the real kettle, the one that plugs in?"

"This is America: electric kettles are a Communist plot, and tea is a Chinese conspiracy. Would you like some coffee instead? They haven't figured out it comes from Arabia yet."

The blonde woman who isn't *quite* Jonquil nods vigorously. "Yes, I think I would certainly like some coffee-coffee!" For a moment Derek sees a flicker of *alfär* magic, a curtain brushing aside to show him the strange magus from the prisoner-of-war camp, but then it flips back into place again. She jitters around the kitchen as if she's too wired to sit down. Abruptly she turns to face Derek, although her gaze slides past his eyes: "You are human, yes?"

Derek freezes, a coffee capsule poised above the Keurig machine. "What if I am?"

"Brains is still human," Jon observes. "So are you." She leans close: "But Pete-Pete isn't," she confides. Derek recoils as she grins, carefully keeping her lips sealed, and rolls her eyes. "Outnumnumnumbered!"

Derek pushes the button on the capsule machine. "Would you please get to the point? Threatening to drink the blood of your co-workers is harassment," he adds pointedly. This hybrid of Yarisol and Jonquil probably knows that, but it never hurts to remind. A moment of doubt: "What happened to Pete?"

"The enemy has magi!" Jon waves her hands. "They shot him with a blood bullet! But then," she confides, "I killed them. So he's infected, too."

"Jim was bitten, do you think—"

"I'm getting thirsty," Jon adds, "but I can cope for now." For a moment her sense of identity veers alarmingly into Jonquil territory: "Sweetie, Pete and I—and Janice, too, I think—we need to nip out for a bite if we're still here this evening, paint the town red. Otherwise you humans won't be safe around us, *capisce?*" A hand flashes out and pinches Derek's cheek. "Mm, plump and juicy!" Her pupils are dilated and the backs of her eyes flash emerald at him. Paralyzed, he can't look away. Then the coffee machine beeps and she looks at it, and he hastily gets out of her

way. "Mm, espresso!" she says, and cradles her cup appreciatively, humanity reasserting itself. Derek doesn't have the nerve
to tell her he used decaf. Instead, hands shaking slightly, he brews
up enough coffee for everyone—decaf for PHANGs, regular
with an extra shot for himself and Brains. He has a feeling they're
going to need it.

Back in the living room, Pete is topless. Brains, wearing blue
latex gloves and a paper breathing mask, is rolling a long bandage around Pete's chest and shoulder. He's treating Pete with the
degree of care due a statue carved from time-expired explosives.
"What—" Derek asks, then nearly swallows his tongue as he sees
the silver lines of an elder sign peeping out from under a corner
of the bandage. He tries again: "Does it hurt?"

"Not now, thanks to Janice." Pete's eyes track towards the far
side of the room, where Janice is building a stack of unplugged
compute nodes and laying out the cables side by side, grouped
by color and length. "There's a macro the *alfär* magi taught our
people. For battlefield minor wound management." A macro being a command that triggers a whole bunch of computational
invocations in one go.

"What do they do with major wounds?" asks Derek.

"They reclassify the victim as ammunition and feed them to
the magi."

"Don't you throw up on me now!" Brains tells Pete. "Hold
this." He presses Pete's hand against one end of the bandage
while he reaches for the micropore tape. Soon, he's finished.
"Okay, that should hold for a while."

"Where did you learn first aid?" Derek asks. "Was it on the
training course for active ops?"

"No, I did it back in Cub Scouts." Brains peels off the gloves
and drops them in a bin bag, then drenches himself in alcohol
hand rub. He looks at the PHANGs: "I think we're safe for now.
If you could take the trash out? Please? It's not like this waste is
a serious health hazard to you people."

"I'll do it!" Jon capers around, grabbing Pete's discarded shirt and jacket and the bag of rubbish and anything else that might conceivably be contaminated and isn't nailed down. "Taking out the trash! Right now!"

"What's our status?" Pete asks.

Derek shakes his head. "Baroness Karnstein and Mr. Grey left about an hour and a half ago. She said they'd be back in not less than two hours if all went to plan." He pulls out a small notepad. "Flights . . . everyone on the team is checked in, as of an hour ago. I have your e-ticket numbers if you want to obtain boarding passes. No need to be at the airport until five o'clock." He takes a deep breath. "I'm just waiting for a saving throw and then we're all done."

"Right." Brains glances at Pete thoughtfully. "So . . . airport at five. That's still daylight, isn't it? What time is sunset?"

"Sunset? Full dark isn't until six fifteen." Derek blinks owlishly behind his thick glasses. "Why? Oh."

Janice comes out of her sulking corner and advances on Pete. She drops into a crouch before him. "Let me see him."

She touches his face and Pete flinches, then grimaces. "That feels weird," he says. "Like spiders. Lots of baby spiders."

"You'll get used to it," she tells him unsympathetically. "Clothing, gloves, a hat. I think I've got enough Liquid Skin for your face, but it's going to look a bit weird. Might squick the airport security people, get you some extra attention."

"He could wear it to the luggage drop-off, then peel it off in the bathroom," Derek thinks aloud. "Go through security with bare skin, the departure area is windowless except at the gates, isn't it? So he should be okay if he sticks indoors until after sunset. When we arrive . . ."

"We can arrange for someone to pick him up at UK immigration." Brains nods. "Does he need to feed before we get him home?"

Pete screws his eyes shut. "I'm not thirsty," he insists.

Eyes meet over his head. Nobody believes him, but nobody's willing to call him out.

"We may need to move out sooner," Derek says in the silence.

"What? But we only just got here!" Brains looks disgusted.

"You were attacked," Derek points out. "Tell me where it happened."

"Four hostiles were waiting—" Brains's eyes widen. "Oh shit."

"I killed them! Me are deadly!" Jon is as proud of her accomplishment as a farm cat with a nest of dead mice.

"*Oh shit* is, I think, the correct response." Pete slowly pushes himself upright. "We've got however long it'll be before someone notices their goons haven't checked in and comes looking. I'm going to need help getting dressed," he adds, swaying slowly.

Derek is already pulling out his phone. "How do I send her a mess—oh, yes, here."

"What are you—"

"Letting the Baroness know we're bailing on her." He twitches at Pete: "We need to ditch everything but hand luggage and evacuate to Fallback Bravo." To Janice: "Can you book two Ubers to collect us in fifteen minutes?"

"Going where?" she demands, hands on hips.

"Here, let me show you." He flips through his notepad, then hands it to her. "We're going to have to risk a direct ride in daylight. You and J-Jon should be all right, but someone's going to have to stay with Pete, keep him covered and ensure"—he nibbles his lower lip—"no upsets."

Reader, I've never tried to turn someone before. Directly or indirectly, it makes me an accessory to future murders. But there's a first time for everything; also, I'm not a politician, even though I play-act one when the boss tells me to—I'm allowed to change my mind when my understanding of the facts changes. *Click, click, click* and the puzzle pieces slide into a different shape.

As of now, the mission is a wash if I *don't* infect Jim with PHANG syndrome—and if the mission fails, sooner or later a whole lot more people will die.

Let me explain my reasoning. I am one of a group who were

infected with PHANG syndrome as an experiment by an ancient sorcerer embedded within the Laundry. We—me, Janice, Alex, the other survivors—have as much free will as anyone else, just as long as we get the occasional blood meal to keep our parasites fed. It's like, oh, having a potentially fatal but treatable medical condition that nonetheless keeps you locked into a job that gives you medical insurance that covers it. You *might* survive outside in the cold . . . but you might not. Are you feeling lucky, vamp?

But we now know of other PHANG strains. K syndrome parasites may be a related life-form, or not. The V-symbionts that infest *alfär* magi are *definitely* related—so much so that I for one thought they were the same as my own infection. Silly me! *Alfär* magi are almost all male: the only female one we know of—Yarisol, or Jon as she currently self-identifies—is distinctly non-neurotypical, even for a psychopathic elf. And the *alfär* also castrate their mages. (Well, except for Yarisol.) Why do they do that? Cassie told us it's to keep them under control, but she's not an expert. I'm going to go out on a limb here and guess that amplifying their hosts' natural aggression may be a survival trait for V-symbionts in the wild, but is slightly less desirable if you're trying to enslave them as living weapons.

Which brings me to the zentai mannequins. Who all taste of the same thought leader, and don't do super-speed. The OPA runs on enslaved extradimensional horrors, and the US prison-industrial system can be counted on to provide a supply chain of blood and bodies for a cadre of PHANGs. But free will is the last thing the Nazgûl would want in their tools. To their way of thinking, PHANGs are self-replicating muscle, a zombie horde that can infect its targets, infiltrating their organizations. So I can totally see them selectively breeding a strain of V-symbionts for unquestioning obedience—the perfect mass-produced vampire minion.

Pete's been infected by the Nazgûl strain of PHANG. It's probably too late to do anything for him, other than provide secure and humane containment. He's still himself, I think—but the disturbing way the mannequins all act as extensions of a common will don't give me grounds for optimism.

Jim, however . . .

Jim has been parasitized but not turned. He's in that cell in the execution shed, waiting on death row alongside Mr. Kadir. He could die at any moment. That *alone* is a mission kill for us— we can't stake the President's life on his survival, or continue the primary mission if the enemy realize they have a (metaphorical) bomb wired to his brain. But there are worse prospects: they might decide that Jim is a more valuable asset than whoever's got their fangs in his neck, and shoot the host. At which point, all those V-symbionts will pile into Jim, and Jim, too, will become part of the Nazgûl Vampire Borg, if you'll pardon the mixed metaphor.

But I've *got* this. I'm here, embracing Jim in the shady booth in the back of the cafe, bleeding inside his mouth as I kiss him. If I shovel my own V-symbionts into him and point his eyeballs at the visualizer and do my fucking best to walk him through the conversion process, I *might* be able to outcompete the hostile parasites and infect him with my own. He's *mine,* dammit, and I intend to save him . . . assuming my symbionts take the hint and don't eat him by mistake. Assuming he doesn't have some kind of massive anaphylactic reaction to being cross-infected by two strains of competing parasites simultaneously, on top of his existing low-level K-parasite load. Assuming the enemy doesn't try to kill him *right now*.

Which is why I kiss him like this is our last goodbye, our last chance ever, and the end of the road. Because, God help me, I might be killing him.

"Well this is bad," says Derek. "Mhari's still with Jim. She says to remind everyone we're on Moscow rules, and evacuate ASAP." He puts the phone down.

"What are Moscow rules?" asks Janice, looking annoyed and puzzled.

Derek twitches. He thought *everyone* who's filled out the basic Intro to Fieldwork workbook or role-played a game of *Espionage!* knew that. "Look them up on Wikipedia," he suggests. Then he relents. "They're tradecraft rules for working in hostile territory. Assume we're being followed, trust your gut, take nothing for granted."

"We need to go, now," he adds. "Where are those Ubers?"

Two cars are waiting outside the safe house. Derek bundles Janice into the first one, with carefully framed instructions to look after Pete, who is riding with her with a paper shopping bag scribed with a no-see-'em ward pulled down over his head. He seems largely uninterested in anything, sits hunched around his abdomen as if an ulcer is burning away at his stomach, responds to questions only in monosyllables. Derek is quite—English understatement—*worried* about him. Concerned, even. Being shot is unquestionably justification for feeling under the weather, as is the whole infected-with-vampirism thing, but Pete's changed behavior is so uncharacteristic that it's almost as if he's had a total change of personality. But there's no time to waste. The next car arrives and he climbs into it with Brains and Jon, who sits in the front passenger seat, gawking in all directions as if the experience is wholly new to her.

They travel in silence to the fallback house, unload their bags, and go inside. The curtains are drawn. Janice is pacing the living room like a caged animal, while Pete flops bonelessly on the sofa. "Airport baggage drop opens in three hours," Janice whinges. "Why are we even here?"

Derek puffs his chest up. "I'm waiting for a call, then I have to relay some information to Jim's phone. Then I'm done here. If you want to head to the airport early you can do that, but loitering at airports is one of the things security organizations watch for."

"Jim's phone." Brains looks at him. "What happened to Mhari?"

"She broke hers again." Derek huffs. "I think. I spoke to her—"

"—I hear you," says Pete, turning his head in Derek's direction. Derek knows he should find Pete's resumption of dialog encouraging, but the lack of human warmth in his words undermines any spark of fellow feeling. "Janice, have you got the makeup kit?" She nods. "Can you do Pete's face? Then—" He thinks for a moment. "—the two of you head out. Find a restaurant in town, take your time over lunch, do some shopping, do whatever it is couples do when they've checked out of a hotel on their last day and are waiting for their flight home—" He deliberately ignores her expression of studied incredulity. "You can hit the airport before check-in time if you want, just keep moving."

"You. Want. Us. To act like a couple."

Brains chips in: "It's called role-play, not foreplay. Anyway, nobody in this town knows who you are."

"And thank fuck for *that*." She gives Derek a final token glare but subsides grumpily.

"Brains, Jon, you stick with me for now." To be honest, he should send Brains packing, but there's Jon to consider, and Derek's afraid to be on his own with the weirdly bouncy blonde. Jon seems to oscillate between effervescent social butterfly and obsessive-compulsive blood-mage. That isn't so bad, but it's not obvious what triggers the shift. "I've got to wait where there's cell service, until—"

Derek's phone rings, just as Janice starts chivvying Pete to get off the sofa. "Come *on*," she urges him, "you need to get your slap on and then we can go and hunt down some lunch."

Derek answers his phone. "Yes?"

"Derek?"

"Gilbert—" He pauses. "—let me get a pen." He reaches for his notepad and scribbles, one-handed, phone wedged between shoulder and ear. "Got that. Okay, let me repeat that." He reads back a set of GPS coordinates. "Correct? Good. Okay, I'll pass it on. If you don't hear back from me, we're good."

He hangs up, then photographs the page of his notepad, and is entirely focused on attaching the image to a secure message when Pete grimaces apologetically, says "I'm really sorry," and lunges for his throat.

Derek's brain freezes. "What—" His fingertip hovering over the "send" button, he holds the phone away from the interruption before he quite registers that Pete has yanked him against his chest, one-handed, and is gnawing on his jugular. He drops notepad and phone as he pushes against Pete's arm.

"Hey!" Brains shouts, rising. Janice, who was rummaging in her bag, looks up with a hiss, eyes flaring with emerald light. A burning pressure clenches around Derek's neck, stopping the breath in his throat. His view of the room begins to narrow. "Stop that!"

Derek goes limp, hot dampness pumping across his chin. Pete is making a glutinous snuffling sound, as if he's trying to breathe while chugging a yard of ale. Someone punches Pete in the head, inhumanly hard and fast—one of the other PHANGs, perhaps, but Derek can't quite figure out what's happening. Everything is confusing and fuzzy-edged. There's another sharp jerk, then a crackling sound as Jon twists Pete's head sharply away from Derek's throat, and keeps twisting until it's pointing backwards.

Derek lies on the carpet, feeling surprisingly comfortable apart from the searingly numb void in the side of his throat. He knows there's something he should do, but he can't quite remember what it is. *Ah. I should be dying,* he thinks. This realization brings him no great sense of satisfaction. Upset people are babbling across him, something about the laws of sympathy and contagion and Pete's infection and, and—

Janice crouches on the bloodstained carpet beside him and peers into his eyes. "Derek?" she says. "Blink if you can hear me?"

Derek wheezes a sad bubbling eruction through the hole in his throat. Speech seems to be impossible for the time being. He blinks at her repeatedly. His hands and feet feel very far away, and he's profoundly tired. Thirsty, too, but mostly tired. There's something he should have done, but he's not sure what, and that realization bugs him.

Janice's face disappears for a moment. "He's conscious," he hears her tell the others. Her voice is muffled by the odd buzzing, crackling sound in his ears, like a swarm of billions of locusts converging on him from a thousand miles away.

"What about Pete—"

"Don't ask. What the *fuck* happened?"

Where's my phone? Derek wonders. *I need to hit "send" . . .* He tries to raise his right hand, manages to lift it a couple of inches off the floor. Everything weighs too much.

"He should be dead. I mean, look at the blood, it went everywhere—"

"Pete went for him. Why the fuck would he even *do* that? It's not like him! He wouldn't hurt a—"

"Pete-Pete are not being himself since he is blood-shot," chirps Yarisol, her Jonquil overlay shredded by stress. "Pete has the bad blood magic, Nazgûl blood magic. Hear through his ears, see through his eyes. They make, made him, attack Derek."

"Why now?" Brains asks tensely. "Why not hours ago? Why the *fuck*—"

"Derek just took a phone call," Janice says, dull-voiced. "He was waiting for a call. He hung up, then Pete went for him."

"Fuck—"

Legs squish across the carpet before Derek's face. An alien thirst grinds away at his guts, and there's an enticing smell-sense-*something* wafting his way. The rich smell of life uneaten. Unnoticed by the others, his eyes glow green. *There's something I need to do,* he thinks, as the locust swarm at the back of his head encourages him, *Yes, do it.* Across the impossible range of carpet, he glimpses debris: an upside-down notepad, a pen, a smartphone. *I just need to see the message again . . .* his arm quivers, and then he moves his hand towards his throat.

"Hey, he's moving!" It's Janice, suddenly vulnerable and human, all her spiky defenses dissolved by chaos. "Derek?" She touches his shoulder, then leans closer. "I swear the fucking hole in his throat is closing—"

"Shit, cable ties, *now!*" snaps Brains.

"What for?" Janice asks.

"Pete."

"In my backpack, I always carry some." Brains bolts across the room. *That makes sense,* Derek thinks foggily. The numbness in his throat is already receding. PHANGs can take a lot of damage and if Pete bounces back from acute spinal trauma—*Friendly now,* sing the locusts of imagination—they'll need to immobilize him. To prevent future neck-biting. *No need for that,* the locusts point out, *now you're one of* us.

Derek finally manages to touch his throat. It's sticky and feels wrong but it doesn't hurt. He pushes his palm against the bite. Dental tracheotomy. Whatever. Breathing becomes incrementally easier, although lots of thick phlegm, or some other liquid, bubbles up. He can swallow, now. *Need the phone.*

"Derek?" asks Janice. "Are you trying to talk?"

He blinks rapidly.

"Is it the phone call? You were meant to call Jim?"

He blinks rapidly again.

"Huh." Janice picks up his phone. "Hey, you were writing a message. Want me to—"

"*No!*" shouts Brains.

Derek hisses and levers himself laboriously up from the carpet. Janice's eyes go wide. Brows lowering, she stares suspiciously, then looks at Brains. "What?"

"—Nazgûl PHANG they rooted Pete and used Pete to root Derek trying to intercept the message *don't let him see those coordinates*—"

"Gotcha." Derek lurches to his knees as Janice dances back a step. His vision grays: all he can hear are the locusts of infinity, telling him to rise and feed. "Huh, well, okay, Jim, was it?" Derek tries to obey and stand up, but everything's too heavy. "Sending it now," Janice tells him casually, then bends his phone into a pretzel between fingers and thumb. She drops it in the puddle of blood: a moment later it begins to smoke and fizzle. Hope has not completely fled: his eyes turn to the notepad. It's lying face-down in the splatter from his throat, but if it hasn't soaked up any blood it might be—

"I don't *think* so!" Yarisol singsongs as she pushes him face-down in the carpet and picks up the notepad. "Not yours, bad boy!" She drops it on the burning smartphone. The flames spread.

Demoralized and exhausted, the locusts allow Derek to succumb to unconsciousness.

There's a side-street just off Maryland Route 32, after it crosses Interstate 70, near West Friendship, an affluent exurban development outside DC. An anonymous white crew-cab rumbles along the narrow blacktop between rows of trees and low brick walls. Memorials sprout like mushrooms in the shade among the shrubs: the memorial gardens around Crestlawn Cemetery.

Officer Mattingley's fingertips are white with tension on the steering wheel. His tired eyes scan restlessly as he searches the arcs and loops and tiny traffic circles of the cemetery grounds. There are plenty of discreet signs to steer the bereaved to the resting places of their dearly departed, but they're not positioned to be read from inside a moving vehicle other than a golf cart or a motor mower. Officer Cho rides shotgun beside him, gun tucked discreetly below window level. Periodically his head tilts back or sideways, and he shakes it vigorously, fighting off the impulse to micro-sleep. They've been on the go for too long, and the slow attrition of the protection team isn't helping: if the Brits don't show up, pretty soon there'll come a point when everyone falls asleep simultaneously.

OSCAR rides in the back seat. Two other cars are parked on the street outside the cemetery, guarding the approaches. They're all that's left of the improvised Presidential Protection Detail, and even their rides are stolen from a Ford dealership's lot. (OSCAR hastily scribbled an Executive Order, committing to pay for the trucks from the White House budget, before they hot-wired the vehicles.)

"Looks like a nice day for a walk in the park," OSCAR announces. He raises a fist to cover his mouth, concealing a yawn. "How far to go?"

Officer Cho glances at the GPS. "About two hundred yards, sir. We're three minutes early."

Mattingley: "I really wouldn't recommend—"

"Overruled. If the bad guys have gotten a snatch team past Murph and Sylvia, then the game's up, isn't it?" Mattingley shakes his head in denial, but his heart's not in it. The President continues: "They're not going to shoot me, that's not what this is about. Anyway, I've got the suit." He's wearing a zippered-up nylon flying jacket and baggy combat pants over close-fitting body armor, ceramic plates embedded in Kevlar. It makes him look bearish, layered up against the risk of a winter storm on a fair-weather afternoon. "Stop the car, I want to get out and walk. One last time."

"Sir—" Mattingley begins.

"Just do it, Nick," Cho says tiredly. Mattingley casts his subordinate a look of explosive disbelief—*Mutiny!*—then reconsiders and gently squeezes the brake pedal.

"I can't recommend this, sir."

"Tough." OSCAR gives him a thin-lipped smirk as he pops the door open.

Cho is out of the car a heartbeat before the President. He scans the vicinity, his short-barreled assault rifle at the ready. Mattingley's shoes hit the ground a second later, his hand traveling to the butt of his service pistol. They're alone in the cemetery grounds, apart from the birdsong and the distant rumble of traffic on the interstate. "Clear?"

"Clear."

The President starts walking. It's a fair day: the temperature is well above freezing. The two officers follow as he approaches a five-way intersection of footpaths. "Which way?"

Mattingley consults the GPS again. "Second left, sir." Cho darts ahead; the senior officer takes up the rear as OSCAR makes his way towards a copse of well-manicured trees, their mostly bare branches overshadowing a platoon of perfectly aligned headstones.

The President is about ten meters away from the nearest tree when a compact shadow flits across the lawn towards him. "Incoming!" Cho brings his rifle up and Mattingley draws his pistol as a tall man, clad from head to foot in motorcycle leathers and a helmet with a full-face visor, lands lightly before them, hands raised. "Show your face."

"If I do that, I'll go up in flames," the visitor says calmly. "Senior Officer Mattingley, we meet again. I'm Jim Grey. Baroness Karnstein and I ran into a spot of bother after we left you in traffic, coming up on three hours ago."

Cho sidesteps and keeps his rifle leveled at Jim, but reverts to scanning for threats from all quarters. "What happened?" asks the President.

"Vampires don't exist," Jim says, with ironic emphasis. "Tell everyone, all right? The plan is still on and the clock is ticking. We've got eight minutes to get you kitted out and airborne, no second chances. Are you good to go, sir?"

The President swallows, just as the compact airband scanner in Jim's front pocket emits a burst of static. "Let's do this," he says.

Mattingley closes his eyes with deliberate gravitas. "As officer in charge of your personal protection team I've really got to say that this is the stupidest, worst, no-good idea *ever*—"

"Hey." The President grins, although it's false bravado: "If it worked for the CIA in Tibet in the fifties, it's good enough for me." He looks at Jim. "What do you need me to do?"

"Can I move?" Jim asks Cho, then lowers his hands without waiting, and shrugs out of his backpack, opens it, and pulls out a bundle of mountaineering rope, a five-point suspension harness, and a compact parachute: "Let's get you wrapped up, sir . . ."

Jim straps the President into the harness and parachute, then pulls another harness on over his own leathers. Then he hooks them together using the climbing rope, connected by a coupling that'll open the President's parachute if the rope breaks. (Nobody wants to risk splattering the President all over Maryland if the pickup goes wrong.) "Check us?" he asks Mattingley.

"This looks secure," Mattingley admits grudgingly.

Jim rummages in his backpack for the last component: another helmet. This one isn't a biker's lid. It's olive-drab, with a mirror-finished visor designed to close over a fighter pilot's oxygen mask. "Found this in an army surplus store," he comments as OSCAR tightens the chin strap. "It gets quite cold up where we're going. Uh. Three minutes. Are you ready?"

"I'm ready," says the President.

He turns and gives Mattingley the thumbs up, just as Mattingley's walkie-talkie crackles. "Contact! Contact on three!"

Mattingley's eyes widen. "Go! Go!" He waves at Jim. "We've got company!"

Cho is already stalking back towards the parked pickup truck as Officer Friendly takes hold of the President's ropes and ascends into the Maryland sky.

So here's the thing: it turns out that infecting people with PHANG symbionts isn't the hard part. The hard part is living with yourself afterwards, when you sit alone in the booth at the back of a cafe staring at the lip-smear on the rim of your espresso cup as it cools, wondering how many executions they'll have to schedule, how much fear they'll have to stir up to rubber-stamp the vote to extend the death penalty, to keep him fed.

I can live with feelings of inadequacy and paranoia about my elevation to the peerage. That's just imposter syndrome, and it's so common we have a name for it. I can deal with the superhero stuff and the juvenile James Bond shit when I have to. I refuse to regret dallying with Jim: he's my Fuckboy, and you'll have to fucking live with it.

But by turning him, I indirectly signed a bunch of execution warrants. Or helped with a number of assisted suicides if we get off lightly, but I have to assume the worst. If we survive this mission, you can add two or three deaths a year to his side of the balance sheet. That's the price of simply staying alive. If he has to use them to fuel his paranormal powers it'll cost even more lives. Jim is forty-eight. Give him another forty years—a normal male life expectancy these days—and do the math.

Like most cops, Jim has some inflexible moral boundaries. He may think he's thought things through and that he's prioritizing the mission, putting the national interest first, or some similar bullshit notion, but I don't believe him. I don't think he's enough of a monster in his soul to survive the realization that he's become a monster in the flesh. So I've got to work very hard to ignore the horror. If I notice the charnel house there's a chance that he'll see me noticing it, and once he finds himself unable to ignore it he'll break, and then he'll burn and I'll lose him anyway.

I sit in the booth and stare at the dregs of my coffee while the stain on the edge of the cup darkens to the color of rust. Remember the way he flinched in surprise when I bit my lip, then froze as I caught his gaze. Thrusting my tongue into his mouth past the wasp-sear of pain in my lip, watching his pupils dilate as he sucked, the sinuous warmth of his tongue as he kissed me back. His eyes gradually glazing as I picked up his phone and held it next to my cheek, screen held where he had no choice but to see it. The astonishing sense of thrusting *into* him, pumping something I can't quite grasp that is nevertheless desperate to fill up a host with a new and different life. The huge and deadly and weirdly perverse turn-on—I get an intense shiver, an erotic chill, from remembering it—as I fuck his brain with V-symbionts.

"Are you okay, ma'am?"

It's the barista, leaning over my table. He smiles and he's taller than I am so of course I smile back up at him warily, social training kicking in. "I'm . . . fine." I'm not fine, actually: I'm a monster who has just fought a running battle, regenerated a mild concussion and a broken hand, and used her V-symbionts to turn her human boyfriend into an executioner. It comes to me that I'm unbelievably thirsty.

"Did that guy just dump you?" the barista asks in a tone of voice I don't care for. I realize we're alone in the cafe: we've been alone for some time.

"No, he didn't dump me," I say very evenly as I push my coffee cup away.

"Your mouth—is that blood?" He reaches out and touches my lip. I pull back and he grabs my chin. "I think he *did* dump you."

He sounds excited, which is *a really bad mistake* because it stirs up the dull roaring in the back of my head. We're alone and my job isn't done yet, and *you should go now,* the human part of me thinks at him. "Come back here with me," he says, "I've got something for that." He grabs my wrist firmly and pulls me towards the storeroom door, which is ajar. *Oh you silly boy,* I think, but I'm too tired to resist and he smells heavenly, and also: hitting on a woman alone in a cafe, *really*?

I let him lead me into the storeroom and turn me around. He pushes me back against the inward-opening door. There are no other exits. *Huh, fancy that.* He stares at my face hungrily. "I've got what you need, bitch," he tells me, pressing down on my shoulders.

Well, that *makes things easy,* I think, unzipping the dime-store rapist's fly. He's already sprouting wood, his cock hardening, the vein on top of it pulsing and full of blood. I lick my lips. "Suck me dry," he demands, tightening his fingers in my hair, so I take his cock and give him exactly what he asked for, if not exactly what he expected.

Afterwards, I leave him curled on his side among the cleaning supplies, as if he simply took a nap during a quiet period and never woke up. *Who's the monster now?* I think vindictively as I step over him. Everything feels warm and happy. Even the day-star glaring down outside the front window can't hurt me, for I have my sunblock on. I take a minute in the restroom to tidy my hair, reapply my lipstick, and make sure my passport is close to hand, then I walk past the impatient customers waiting at the counter and step outside to face the music.

Back during the Second World War, helicopters barely existed. They certainly weren't an off-the-shelf solution to the problem of plucking a spy or a crashed pilot into the sky and bringing them home. Which is why British and American special forces began experimenting with skyhooks.

At first, the hapless evacuee would be tied to a cable suspended between the tops of two tall poles. A cargo plane would make a low pass overhead, trailing a grappling hook on the end of a rope: if it made contact, the human cargo would be yanked from the ground and winched aboard. Later, they got rid of the poles and raised the tether using a helium balloon. The Fulton Surface-to-Air Recovery System, STARS, got a workout during the Cold War, but mostly in the movies: it works, but it's a stunt—under almost all circumstances, it's easier to send a helicopter.

But these are not normal circumstances; these are desperate times.

So desperate that they call for a superhero and a Concorde.

(Best of British, right? I mean, if he existed I'd have sent for James Bond, and bugger the cocktail and baccarat bill. But alas, he's a fictional character. So we had to make do with what we've got, and I improvised.)

Now, boarding a Concorde in flight is, shall we say, just slightly harder than a regular STARS pickup.

For starters, STARS usually used a prop-powered transport aircraft, flying low and about as slow as it could go without falling out of the sky. A Concorde turns into a lawn dart if it slows below two hundred old-money miles per hour, so it has to make a much faster pickup.

Secondly, a Concorde in flight is dagger-sharp. You can't just open the doors and snag a passing passenger. Anything that gets too close to its belly is liable to get sucked into one of the four Rolls-Royce Olympus engines clustered near the tail—the same engines (and same number of them) that power the Royal Navy's shiny new aircraft carriers. The term "flying Cuisinart" springs to mind.

Luckily, where there's a will there's a way. It turns out someone was thinking ahead when they drafted the requirements for 666 Squadron's aircraft, and jumping out, or dropping *things* out, was on the list, along with the blood bag–warming oven and the summoning grid. The passenger retrieval mechanism was the only major modification necessary.

The other special ingredient is Officer Friendly. Who, despite rumor, is *not* actually stronger than a locomotive or able to leap tall buildings at a single bound, let alone squeeze coal into diamond in his grip. However, Jim *is* able to fly while wearing body armor and dangling a President on the end of a climbing rope.

So here's the plan, as drafted by the 666 Squadron mission planners:

302 Heavy staged out to Goose Bay a week ahead of our schedule, then prepped for flight. With a range of 4500 nautical miles, a Concorde B can just about do Newfoundland to Washington DC, then fly another 3000 nautical miles. More with the aid of a pre-positioned tanker aircraft or two.

Of course the airspace around Washington DC is heavily guarded with surface-to-air missile batteries, a pair of F-16s on combat air patrol, and more F-15s ready to scramble at short notice. Which is why 302 Heavy takes off under a carefully contrived flight plan consisting of vicious lies and innuendo.

Some six hours before 302 Heavy approached DC, UK Air Traffic Control announces the departure of a cargo 747 from Heathrow, heading northwest across the Atlantic. It doesn't exist. However, the details of the nonexistent flight get handed off to Shanwick Oceanic—the air traffic control sector over the northeast Atlantic—and are updated as if it's flying towards North America, out of range of radar. Meanwhile, a Dutch air force KC-10 tanker that has been waiting in Reykjavik as part of a NATO exercise takes off and heads for the northwest corner of Shanwick's airspace.

In due course 302 Heavy takes off from Goose Bay and heads out into the Gander oceanic sector, over the West Atlantic, staying slow and low—that is, at a mere Mach 0.85 at 30,000 feet. Once out of range of coastal radar, 302 Heavy transitions to Shanwick Oceanic, saying goodbye to North American air traffic control, and makes rendezvous with the tanker.

With fuel tanks filled to the brim, 302 Heavy turns southwest and joins the North Atlantic tracks, adopting the call sign of the fictional 747 bound for Nassau. Flying subsonic at thirty thousand feet, a sharp-eyed plane spotter *might* notice something hinky as it passes overhead . . . but it is following a flight path a couple of hundred miles offshore.

As it comes due east of DC, 302 Heavy flips its transponder beacon to code 7600. A minute later, it squawks 7700, turns sharply west towards Baltimore, and begins to descend. Code 7600 means loss of communications, or radio failure; Code 7700 means there's an emergency. DC traffic control are alerted, but as far as they know what they're seeing is a cargo 747 in unspecified trouble, slowing and descending through ten thousand feet towards Runway 28 at BWI.

302 Heavy misses its approach to Baltimore airport. In doing so it turns northwest, away from DC, and slows to two hundred knots at six thousand feet. The missed landing approach puts it two miles north of Crestlawn Cemetery—with its belly hatch open, trailing a 200-meter-long cable and a giant high-tech butterfly net.

Crestlawn Cemetery is located a few miles outside the northern edge of the Washington DC Air Defense Identification Zone. It's at extreme range for the NASAMS long-range air defense missiles around the Capitol. A freighter squawking an emergency code, skirting the ADIZ at only two hundred knots, is cause for concern but not an immediate shoot-down. As it happens, a pair of F-16s flying out of Bolling AFB are airborne and on assignment to the capital's air defenses under Operation Noble Eagle today. But curiously—and absolutely *not* by accident—three light planes are buzzing around the southeast periphery of the ADIZ, generating piles of paperwork and keeping the fighter jocks busy. It's astonishing what you can get an idiot with a private pilot's license to do if you offer them enough bitcoins or threaten to send their stash of kiddie porn to the FBI. And it's astonishing how many weekend flyers there are in the US. Go figure.

666 Squadron are able to do this because from the 1950s to the 1980s the RAF's mission planners regularly gamed how to sneak a four-engined bomber into attack range of the Capitol as a training exercise. Rumor has it that during one Red Flag run in the early '70s a Vulcan actually dropped a paint can on the White House lawn. They tried to warn their USAF counterparts about the risk of a sneak attack, but got the usual bureaucratic not-invented-here runaround—nobody likes a smart-arse. Besides, the received wisdom was that bombers were obsolete in the direct nuclear strike role. Then the Cold War ended. But the RAF kept the plans on file, because you should never say never . . .

In an Airbnb in DC, arguing in a blood-drenched living room:

"They're compromised. The OPA has rooted their nervous systems. Also, they're both too badly injured to fly out. What do we do now?"

"Fuck. Derek and Pete need a hospital set up for PHANG support, plus a terminal donor or three each. There's no way—"

"If we had some donors, we could fix them up. You'd be astonished how fast a PHANG can heal when you pump them full of Type O negative."

"Yeah, and if we went on a dementia-killing spree in the neighborhood and somehow got them patched up and in clean clothes, what then? They're OPA assets now. Everything they know belongs to the OPA. You know what the, the Prime Minister would expect us to do."

"All-Highest is also All-Ruthless! Yes?"

"I know but I can't—" (pause) "—friends. *Fuck*. I know his wife. He's got a four-year-old daughter."

"So you could maybe kill Derek because he's got no life, but the Vicar is off-limits because he spawned—"

"No, fuck you, that's not it at all! It's just not right!"

"The Baroness wouldn't blink twice, she'd ice them for the good of the state. She's cold."

(Reader, that's not true.)

"*I* could kill them for you! Just a little bit?"

"Shut up, Jon, you're not helping."

"Thinking here." (A pause.) "There's no way to turn them back, I take it?"

"I don't think so. Pete was a problem from the moment he was shot. Then I broke his neck when he took a bite out of Derek, but that made enough of his symbionts jump ship to cross-infect, not just feed. So now we have two problems."

"If you hadn't broken his neck—"

"Derek would be dead, not compromised." (A pause.) "This wasn't a situation we could have come out on top of. Hell, we're lucky to be alive. If Pete told them where—"

"Oh you did *not* just say that."

(Sirens, in the distance.)

"Memorize these words, Jon: all you need to do is repeatedly say *I assert diplomatic immunity*, and show them your passport. You've got it, yes, the one with the extra pages? Good. Repeat after me: *I assert diplomatic immunity*—"

"—Bet you it doesn't work any better than saying *I believe in Tinker Bell*—"

"—Shut up. Let's practice saying it together: *I assert diplomatic immunity*—"

(Sirens, getting closer.)

(Fade to gray.)

11: A DEAD GOD DID IT AND RAN AWAY

They have the block surrounded when I emerge, blinking behind my Ray-Bans in the early afternoon sunlight.

American cops are so heavily militarized these days that the only way I can tell the difference between them and the army is the color of their body armor—that, and the army is less trigger-happy. They've got the street cordoned off at both ends of the block, with armored cars and SWAT teams hanging back behind the barriers. I can't see them, but I hear the thudding beat of helicopter rotors overhead, reverberating between the ten-story office blocks. When I glance up at the roofline opposite, I see a row of shiny silver statues looking down on me.

Reader, I am not suicidal. Nor am I Keanu Fucking Reeves, and this is not *The Matrix*: I hold my arms up, my passport clenched in my right hand, and I wait.

After a minute or so, one of the giant armored trucks that has been blocking a gap in the barriers roars into life and reverses out of the way. A huge black Cadillac limousine creeps past. It rolls slowly down the street and parks just beyond the Starbucks. The front passenger door opens and a zentai-suited minion climbs out. It opens the door of the passenger compartment, then freezes in place, watching me.

I look up at the skyline beyond the limo. *There*: behind and below the motionless row of spam-PHANGs I see a brief glint of light reflected from a sniper's scope. I lower my gaze, and slowly—*slowly*—walk towards the open door of the car.

"You can lower your arms and put your diplomatic passport

away, Baroness, we know who you are." The woman in the back of the limousine sounds amused. "Ride with me, please."

As I stoop to enter the darkened interior of the limo I tense involuntarily: the buzz and chitter of the Nazgûl symbionts rises to the grating screech of a cicada swarm. But as I slide across the slick leather of the bench seat and the uniformed minion closes the door, it stops abruptly. There's a heavy *thunk* that I feel in my inner ears. The car is airtight as well as armored and thaumproof. The light dims noticeably; the windows are heavily tinted, and as thick as my fist. The armor's so heavy that the interior of the limo is surprisingly cramped. The woman sitting opposite me smiles in the twilight, giving me a brief flash of needle-sharp teeth. "Welcome to the Beast," she says. "Not many people ever get to ride in one of these."

"The Beast?"

"The White House has no current occupant, so I borrowed it. Nice wheels." I size up my host as I fiddle with my seat belt. She's got straight blonde hair and ice-blue eyes, but beneath the carefully applied makeup she looks as if she's undergone plastic surgery to give her the face of an idealized female senior executive. Her trappings are conservative-leaning boardroom—black suit, nice blouse, heels—accessorized with pearl stud earrings, and a discreet silver necklace strung with the rune-inscribed finger bones of infants. An aura of ominous power swirls around her like a funnel cloud. "Allow me to introduce myself, baroness: I am the Deputy Director."

"The Deputy . . . ?"

"You can call me DeeDee for short." Her face flickers momentarily between ingratiating charm and concentration-camp nightmare, as if her humanity is a mask. "I used to have a name of my own, but names give your enemies power over you. Anonymity is so much more convenient, don't you think?"

I swallow a burp of stale blood-and-coffee breath, the contents of my stomach threatening to repeat on me. I'm so scared I could throw up: *She's one of us! Only with a link to one of* them! *Fuck!* For the past couple of days I've been thinking *going to die now* too often for comfort, but this time I know it's true. If an ancient horror invites you into its limousine at gunpoint—

"I'm taking you to see My Lord. He would hear your message, Baroness—or is that Ambassador?"

Panic flaps my lips inadvisably: "What if I say no?"

"I wasn't asking." DeeDee smiles, not entirely unfriendly, and for a moment I see a reflection of my future time-flensed skull in her eyes. "One does not say 'No' to the Mouthpiece of the Lord of Sleep."

Why aren't I carrying a suicide pill? Part of me gibbers. Even my V-symbionts are terrified. Because who the hell can the Lord of Sleep be other than He Who Is Not Dead But Lies Dreaming in the Deep?

DeeDee leans forward and touches my knee: "Interfering in our affairs wasn't very clever of you. Especially disrupting our tail on the Uncrowned King."

"The President, you mean?" She winces when I say the title.

"We'll get him back," she says, self-assurance personified. "You'd better *hope* we get him back. If we can't, the Lord of Sleep has expressed a preference for you as his replacement."

"Me?" I can't help myself.

"You. It's quite an honor, you know." I don't know exactly what she's talking about, but it sounds horrid. Succumbing to my cowardly side, I change the subject.

"Is it true, then? Has your Lord awakened?"

"Not yet." But her body language proclaims her proud anticipation. "For the time being, He makes His wishes known through His Mouthpiece."

I make a huge effort not to hyperventilate and rub my sweat-moistened palms on my skirt. *I am totally* not *ready for this*. This is what His Majesty really sent me for, I realize. Forget the thing with the President; the reason He sent *me,* the reason He insisted I lead my team in person, was because He intended me to convey a message to this . . . Mouthpiece . . .

Within the shielded darkness of the President's limousine a geas unlocks in my head, and I can finally remember the message the PM wants me to convey to his counterpart.

OSCAR stops yelling as they climb through two thousand feet of air. Jim can't tell if he was screaming from fear or yodeling in exhilaration. Given the President's pre-politics bad-boy reputation, it could be either: he did his own movie stunts, after all. But the screaming was a distraction, and Jim can't afford to be distracted right now. He's got a plane to catch—and he can't see it yet.

Here is an A-level physics problem . . .

A Concorde with a full fuel load stalls at approximately 310 kilometers per hour at standard temperature and pressure (sea level, 20 Celsius). A human body reaches terminal velocity in air at the velocity where the force acting on it due to gravitational attraction is equal to the aerodynamic drag it experiences: approximately 200 kilometers per hour if spread-eagled and at sea-level pressure, but considerably higher if streamlined, and/or at higher altitude (hence lower pressure). How much force does Jim have to exert to reach a velocity of 310 kilometers per hour at 2400 meters altitude, if Jim has a mass of 95 kilograms and his passenger has a mass of 88 kilograms? (See provided table of constants for drag coefficients in different configurations.) Extra credit: What is the minimum breaking strain of the rope OSCAR is hanging on?

Jim isn't in free fall, but he's pushing through dense air at a speed greater than his terminal velocity while towing a passenger. He's pushing his power to the max in the ascent, trying to get nearly two and a half kilometers up in time to transition to horizontal flight and get up to speed before the white dot in the distance runs him down and smashes him like a rabbit under an express train—or misses him altogether. He's burning *mana* at a prodigious rate, and he hasn't been fed his first blood meal yet. What is it like in Jim's head?

Jim is *thirsty*. It's a wreck-survivor-crawling-through-the-desert kind of thirst, a lovesick thirst, combined with a monstrous chittering at the back of his cranium and a cage of starved rats gnawing on his stomach. He has successfully absorbed a cohort of V-symbionts, and the risk of K syndrome is receding, but he's burning his own thaumic passengers in this race for altitude and speed, and the V-symbionts are *hungry*.

To make matters worse, he is trailing a glorious banquet on the end of a nylon rope. OSCAR doesn't realize it, but he is no mere human. His countrymen may have forgotten him, but for years he's been the focus for a nation's dreams and sense of common cause. Jim's symbionts yearn for the President's rich accumulation of *mana*. There is a reason the nation houses its Uncrowned King in a heavily warded palace within a city laid out on a grid of symbolic power. To the inhuman feeders, he's a golden glowing beacon of hope and liberty and comfort, dripping with delicious nutrient juices like a well-cooked Thanksgiving turkey: even the half-neutered Nazgûl PHANGs were able to sense him and stalk him.

Jim is a sworn officer of the law, an immensely self-disciplined and intelligent supercop . . . and yet he is as tempted as an alcoholic carrying a crate of vintage single-malt Scotch whisky.

Passing through seven thousand feet (according to the GPS strapped to his left wrist), Jim switches on the compact radio beacon in his combat pants' left pocket, orients in the direction of the coast, leans backwards until he's recumbent, and pushes as hard as he can against the immovable Earth beneath. The wind is a sullen roar around his helmet, and the cable vibrates like a bowstring. OSCAR is a dead weight, a pendulum tugged backwards by the slipstream as Jim sees his speed readout inch upwards. Two hundred and twenty kilometers per hour. (Too slow.) Two hundred and thirty. (Pile on the throttle—*so hungry now*—and stare at the sky.) Two hundred and forty. *Not going to make it,* he thinks, almost despairing. *Need to eat.* He can *feel* OSCAR, knows that if he could tap the President's mojo he could make the rendezvous, no problemo—

His airband scanner crackles again, but between the slipstream gale and his helmet he can't hear what it's saying. Hopefully it's the first officer of 302 Heavy announcing they've got him on the under-nose camera. More likely it's ATC or the US Air Force, F-16s closing, possessed pilots with green worms spiraling dimly in their eyes at the controls as they search the skies for intruders. No matter. Jim lets the hunger goad him ever faster. *There's blood aboard the pickup,* he tells himself, hoping the deafening chorus within his skull is paying attention. Sharp canines cut aching grooves through his desiccating gums.

There—

A white dot bisected by a horizontal line against the blue sky, a painfully bright flare of sunlight reflecting off a mirror-polished cockpit window. It's distant and dawdling, just hanging in the air, slowly creeping closer. But perspective foreshortening is deceptive. Those inches are measured in kilometers and it's covering ground faster than a Formula 1 race car. Seconds pass. Jim points his feet at the tip of the onrushing spear and throws everything he's got into a last, desperate sprint. With a rumble like an express train blowing past, a giant needle-sharp shadow rushes past a hundred meters above his face. Jim gets a brief glimpse of the belly of the beast, an open hatch before the engines roar overhead and rattle his brains in his skull. Then a giant net clamps tight around him with a jolt like a parachute opening.

The next two minutes pass in a blur of controlled chaos. The capture net tugs harder and vibrates as a hidden motor somewhere behind Jim's head winches it in. The roaring and buffeting rise to a monstrous crescendo as he's dragged underneath the long stinger of the aircraft's tail, below and between the boxy engine pods and then in front of the hoarse, bellowing air inlet ramps. Finally the net squeezes down into a rope as it hauls him up and over the lip of a shield-shaped hatch, into a low-ceilinged compartment beneath the floor of the cabin. Hands grab him and drag him forward, heave another squirming netted figure through the closing hatch. Then the screeching hunger in his head expands to fill the universe, and Jim knows nothing more for a while.

The next time Jim becomes aware of his surroundings, he's strapped down in a cramped, backward-facing blue leather chair in a tunnel-like room with curved walls. A bloke in a green flight suit is closing a trapdoor in the floor. A woman leans over him. "Thirty seconds," she tells him, her tone bossy as a primary school teacher. "It's in the microwave, just wait, all right?"

Jim tries to nod but what comes out is a snarl. The Air Force technician recoils. Because the room is tilting and the guy with the trapdoor is off balance, he goes over on his arse and scrambles backwards until he hits a wall. This is unaccountably funny— *the prey can't get away*—and Jim laughs uproariously. Meanwhile, the hall monitor who is perpetually sober and on station in the back of his mind is quietly horrified. *What am I turning into?*

"Drink." Hands extend a beaker of crimson liquid towards his face. Without thinking, moving faster than he realized was possible, Jim grabs it and tips it down his throat. Hot ecstasy spreads through his stomach and flashes out into all his limbs, lighting them up silvery-bright, like a strangely dry orgasm. *It's the symbionts' way of rewarding you, reinforcing the behavior they desire,* he remembers his girl Mhari explaining: *It's addictive, you've got to stay in control.* He shudders, revolted by the discovery that he actually quite *likes* this, wonders if feeding with Mhari would be like sex, or something better—

Another mug appears, only for the contents to vanish into the sucking black hole in his stomach. After an agonizing delay for warming, there's a third. They all smell wonderful and taste subtly distinctive.

"Are you functional now?" asks the schoolmistressy one. Subtext: *Have you got your shit together?* (Clearly, the Air Force don't put their back-seaters through British Airways' cabin-crew school.)

"I'm"—Jim forces the words out—"I'm good, I've had enough." He closes his eyes and holds the empties out. He hasn't had enough: he's not sure there's enough blood in the entire universe to fill his hunger. But he's back in control. The donors, he *knows* this instinctively, were healthy adults in the prime of life. No hospice-care terminal-release forms were involved. These bags of blood came courtesy of execution warrants. Complicity: it's a bitch. He shudders. "Back in control now."

Jim tiredly slips his gloves off, then begins to unfasten his helmet. "Glad you're with us, sir," says the airman with the hatch. Teacher has disappeared, back towards the front of the cabin which is behind him.

The floor is still tilting down as he looks towards the tail, but now he's not burning up Jim notices the tiny, deep-set windows. He twists round and sees two more rows of rear-facing seats, then a corridor leading to a row of engineering stations and a cramped galley. The windrush outside the fuselage is loud, and the sky is darkening by the second: they're climbing far faster than any normal airliner, faster than an early jet fighter. *Fuck me, I'm on a Concorde!* he thinks, then remembers to ask, "How's the passenger?"

"He's up front. Sir, I'm supposed to ask you for a direction—"

"Plan West," says Jim. He closes his eyes. "Chase the sunset."

"Great. Be right back."

The airman rushes past him in the direction of the forward cabin, and Jim leans back against his headrest. A terrible postcoital lassitude creeps over him, but the side of his face feels hot and prickly where it's exposed to the daylight filtering through the nearest window. He rubs his cheek and suddenly realizes it's excruciatingly sore, like really bad sunburn. *Two minutes of indirect sunlight filtered through three layers of glass,* he realizes.

No more beach holidays. Wondering how the President is doing, he unclips his lap belt and shrugs out of the shoulder restraints. Then he stands and heads towards the cockpit.

Air forces love bragging rights: Who's got the most planes, the most firepower, the highest, the fastest? Bragging rights get you budget approval for more and shinier (higher, faster) toys. Which is why, back in the 1980s and 1990s, the US Air Force *really* resented the fact that both British Airways *and* Air France beat them like a broken piñata when it came to total hours of supersonic flight.

Everyone knows that supersonic warplanes are, well, supersonic. What most people don't realize is that it's more accurate to call them supersonic-*capable*. They're rarely called upon to break the sound barrier. Doing so puts enormous wear and tear on engines and airframe, guzzles fuel at a ridiculous rate, and annoys the hell out of everyone on the ground within earshot. Only a few modern fourth-generation jets, notably the F-22 and Eurofighter Typhoon II, are capable of supercruise, extended supersonic flight without afterburner assist. Even then, they can only supercruise at a relatively sedate Mach 1.5. Going flat-out still takes fuel-hungry afterburners, and these fighters can only sustain their top speed of Mach 2.2 to Mach 2.4 for about ten minutes. (Mach 1.5 is a little over 900 miles per hour. Mach 2.2 is 1300 miles per hour.) So most military pilots seldom, or never, fly supersonic.

Concorde is *all* about the supersonic—it set the record for the longest supersonic range of any aircraft, and nothing has ever beaten it. Cruising at Mach 2.2, serving cocktails to VIP passengers at flight levels normally occupied by SR-71 spy planes, the six British Airways Concordes shuttling between London and New York used to rack up more supersonic hours annually than the entire US Air Force.

As Jim and OSCAR were being winched in through the belly

hatch of 302 Heavy, airborne intercept controllers were direct-ing the pair of F-16s on patrol over Washington DC to check out a pair of Beechcraft wobbling dangerously close to the air defense zone. The unidentified blob making two hundred knots a few thousand feet up, thirty to forty miles north and squawking 7700, is next on their to-do list. But once the belly hatch closes and seals, 302 Heavy's captain turns northwest, pushes the throttles all the way forward past the reheat stops, and pulls the nose up in a full power climb.

Three minutes later the F-16s get a flash alert to go to full afterburner. But they're too late.

302 Heavy, climbing through thirty thousand feet and accelerating towards supersonic transition, is over a hundred miles ahead of the DC air patrol fighters. Three minutes later, 302 Heavy passes through fifty thousand feet, accelerating towards a thousand miles per hour. A stern chase is a long chase, and the pair of F-16s are sprinting to catch up with a marathon runner with a mile-long head start. Eighteen minutes after receiving their first advisory about 302 Heavy, the F-16 pilots report bingo fuel and turn away to rendezvous with a tanker, never having closed to within a hundred miles of the target. Meanwhile, 302 Heavy isn't even up to cruising speed yet.

There are two seats in the compartment behind the cockpit, positioned left and right of the aisle. They both face bays of radio equipment and defensive avionics. Right now, both seats are occupied. OSCAR, sitting in the port seat, is looking around wide-eyed. He sat in a space shuttle's cockpit once, but not in flight; this is the highest and fastest he's ever been, the sky fading to indigo and the curvature of the Earth's surface becoming visible. On the other side of the aisle an RAF Squadron Leader—the equivalent of a major—is punching buttons, configuring the VHF radio to relay the output of a hastily retrofitted ENDEC module in one of the racks that line the long tunnel of electronics behind the cockpit.

"What do I do?" asks the President. "I mean, how does this even work?"

"It works the same way as the kit on Air Force One, sir," Bradshaw says diffidently. He's clearly trying not to boggle at the identity of the man in the seat next to him, and finding it difficult. "Once you're ready to talk, I set you up by broadcasting a Presidential Emergency Action Notification. You then push to talk—that switch there, sir—and everything you say gets encoded on the carrier signal and relayed by the FEMA Emergency Alert System. The nearest Primary Entry Point—a suitably equipped radio station—picks it up and rebroadcasts it to all the neighboring PEPs. It cuts into all FM and AM radio broadcasts and a whole bunch more channels as well: cable television, Sirius XM, digital radio, even cellphones. The EAS isn't very secure—it's meant to be easy for the President to interrupt ongoing broadcasts, and it's been hacked in the past—but just to make sure, we've got a hacked repeater in the Midwest that'll keep rebroadcasting you until someone takes an axe to it."

"Right. Right." OSCAR nods vigorously. "All I have to do is work out what to tell the nation—" He waves his pen at the blank sheet of paper on the fold-down table before him.

Unnoticed by OSCAR but very visible in the cockpit windscreen, the Earth is tilting gradually to the right as 302 Heavy banks left, turning west. In just twenty minutes they've flown halfway to New York, trailing a double whip crack of noise up the eastern seaboard. A pair of F-15s have just scrambled from Bolling AFB, but the F-16s already in the air have given up the pursuit.

"Not to worry, sir," Bradshaw reassures him. "The F-15s with orders to shoot us down that took off three minutes ago don't have enough fuel to get within missile range before their tanks run dry. You've got at least half an hour before we come within extreme range of the next airfield that can generate an intercept: *plenty* of time."

OSCAR shakes his head, the corners of his eyes wrinkling with fatigue. Then he starts writing.

Washington traffic is notorious, but we're south of the Potomac to begin with. As soon as the limousine inches past the parked MRAP we're enveloped by a cortege of motorcycle outriders and blacked-out SUVs so ostentatious that Her Majesty would die of embarrassment if they tried it on her back home. We're so visible I have to fight the urge to crouch down in my seat—but then I realize here in DC your importance is telegraphed by the size of the gridlock in your wake. This is just DeeDee's equivalent of prancing around Westminster in an ermine-lined stole. Anyway, the traffic is getting out of our way and the lights are changing in our favor. As we proceed north towards Pentagon City under the guns of a Marine Corps helicopter, I stiffen my back and try to look unimpressed.

"Why are you doing this?" I ask myself, staring out the window.

I don't mean to speak aloud but the words slip out, and DeeDee assumes they're directed at her. "What, trying to save the world?"

"World-saving is not exactly how I would describe raising the Lord of Sleep."

"Oh, but it is." Her voice drips studied irony. "I might equally well ask what the hell your people thought they were doing, surrendering to the Black Pharaoh?"

Ouch. That's a low blow. "At least we get to keep our free will," I shoot back at her. *Up to a point.* "It seemed like the least-worst option to secure national survival, at least in the short term." Or so it looked when Mahogany Row had their backs to the wall because the idiots in the Cabinet had utterly and irreversibly fucked up, under the influence of an occult Non-State Actor. Now we're just playing it by ear.

"Whereas we are looking for a better outcome," she replies

after a momentary pause. "To save the United States from the Lovecraftian Singularity."

I hold my tongue. I want to say that I think she's going about it the wrong way, but I don't have all the facts, and besides, people in glass houses shouldn't throw stones. However—"Isn't the Lord of Sleep just about the most mind-mangling and sanity-destroying example of a level-six Anthropic Threat, though? I mean, really, Cthulhu herself? How do you justify *that*?"

She snorts softly. After a second or two it turns into a low chuckle: "Oh, you crack me up. You're not thinking big enough. I guess that's what comes of living on a small island surrounded by the ruins of a dead empire: it narrows your horizons. Did you really think there was *only one planet* at stake in this game? Or that the Lord of Sleep was the worst thing we could throw in with? There are things out there in the night where light cannot exist that make Cthulhu look like a Care Bear. Things beyond life, things beyond intellect, beyond mathematically defined reality. Ask yourself what the Black Pharaoh, the Lord of Sleep, and their ilk are fleeing. Ask what gives the Elder Gods their nightmares. Ask yourself what your Prime Minister isn't telling you. Ask yourself what is worse than your entire species dying and being erased from the history of the cosmos, what could be worse than the worst hell human imagination can conceive of . . ."

She trails off reflectively. I suppress a shudder as the car jolts across a sleeping policeman and slows, nosing down into a subterranean parking garage. I look at DeeDee, and see that in the darkened belly of the Beast her eyes glow with an inner luminescence: a pale green light that I recognize after a moment. Like every other PHANG I'm blind to my own reflection, but I know what other powerful blood-mages look like, wrapped in the power and the glory.

"How did you, personally, get here?" I ask, filling the silence.

"The usual way." She shrugs. "Up through the ranks, same as you. They sentenced me to thirty years of boredom, for—"

"—Trying to change the system from within," I join her, nodding along, and she flashes me a delighted smile of recognition. For a dizzy moment I feel my perspective pivot. There's no cunning glamour at work here, just an utterly unexpected instant of bonding over Leonard Cohen. We've arrived in the same place from opposite directions, and for a second I find myself wishing we weren't enemies because I know where she's coming from, and it's so rare to find somebody who actually understands me. I glance away just as the car bottoms out and drives through an impressively thick steel blast door. *Damn it, I hope I don't have to kill her,* I tell myself, knowing that she's probably thinking the same about me. The worst curse you can inflict on a monster is an excess of empathy.

We park. "I'll have to take your phone," DeeDee says apologetically as we climb out; "it won't work down here anyway."

"I left it in the cafe's trash. It didn't survive the traffic stop earlier in the day." A thought strikes me. "Do you have the time?"

DeeDee wears an old-fashioned wind-up watch. "Three forty," she tells me. "Follow the blood guard."

The blood guard in question is our zentai-suited shotgun rider from the front compartment. Something about the hierarchical setup feels familiar: "Yours?" I ask her, surprised.

"Mine," she confirms, then cackles delightedly, "they're all mine, from the top down! I used to be the head vampire wrangler," she explains. "Our kind make excellent muscle when they're properly bound."

"A hierarchical geas?" I ask.

"Yes. Of course, not everyone in the org chart was down with that, but after we cleaned house the survivors came around."

We pick up five more cut-price PHANGs. They form a phalanx around me and steer me towards a side door. We pass the first of several checkpoints on our way into the huge office complex. The SUVs are parking behind DeeDee's armored limo, and a couple of flunkies in suits who might as well have "administrative assistant" tattooed on their foreheads fall in alongside her, speaking quietly. Evidently they're bringing her up to speed on the classified gossip that came in during our ride. I don't need to see her face to guess that she's not smiling any more. West, not east. For my part, I'm thinking furiously. This setup reminds me of the *alfär*: it's a classic authoritarian dominance hierarchy enforced by magic compulsion, which is pretty much what you'd expect from an inhuman ancient nightmare that hasn't bothered to develop a theory of mind for humans. It means they have a single point of failure, as my geekier co-workers would describe it. Unfortunately that single point of failure seems to be buried under the Pentagon, and unlike the *alfär*, the Nazgûl are a bureaucracy, with all that implies—

We proceed inward and downward through naked basement corridors with pipes and suspended cable runs hanging from the ceiling, past shiny security gates set in concrete. Eventually we come to a short stairwell, then more doors, and a much narrower corridor, the walls of which are covered with fat cable bundles. "Keep going," says one of my gimp-suited guards, startling me badly—I hadn't realized they could speak at all. His voice is deep but hoarse from lack of use.

This is not good. I managed to shrug off the existential dread for a bit when DeeDee and I were talking, but (catacombs, vampires, the temple of an Elder God in the Pentagon subbasement) I'd be lying if I said I was in a happy place. And that's before I address the cause of my nagging sense of dread. What if Fuckboy's failed, what if 302 Heavy didn't make the pickup on time, what if DeeDee's minions succeeded in getting to the rendezvous? What if . . .

When you get down to it, there's not a lot of difference between a dank, dripping stone-walled dungeon with chains dangling from the walls and a dark, stuffy underground server room with cable runs snaking everywhere, especially if they're both occupied by a giant over-elaborate ward surrounded by motionless vampires who guard a corpse animated by a dead god's emissary. It's a good thing I refreshed myself before I came here, because there's something joyless and deadening in the air, as if what this room really holds is the decaying miscarried fetus of the human future. Anyone who lingers here will sicken and die, just as if they were stranded in the pyramid on a dead world where once the photo-reconnaissance Concordes flew.

I follow the clacking of DeeDee's heels all the way to the start of the labyrinth because I'd rather not be frog-marched. The labyrinth seems to be some sort of soul trap, I realize, designed to confuse the occupant and stop them emerging prematurely, or—no, it's to contain their energy. Ley lines converge on this room, burning with power. They follow the paths established by the US Defense Department's communication network, going all the way back to the 1930s. Bureaucracies run on telephone lines, and network cables channel occult energy. Every bitcoin proof-of-work mined is an incremental addition to a vast distributed summoning ritual powering the demon-soul at the heart of the maze, the computational equivalent of a Buddhist prayer wheel spinning in a Himalayan breeze. The power flowing into this room today is implied—the network links and server farms of today's government agencies are vaster by far than anything that came through this hub when it was built—but it still sets my skin tingling, like the static charge near the base of an energized supergrid pylon.

DeeDee stalks towards the maze, then pauses on the threshold. "Follow in my footsteps," she murmurs. "Do not deviate from the path or bad things will happen. To you, I mean." She starts walking again.

At the heart of the labyrinth we come before a strange throne. Clamped atop it sits a corpse as pitifully maltreated as any of the Residual Human Resources the Laundry harvests from those who die in the line of duty. As with a zombie, the body is technically dead but animated by a controlling daemon. But the feeders that control RHRs are trivial wisps of mind-eating menace. The thing atop the throne below the Pentagon is anything but trivial.

As I approach the throne, the body moves slightly, straightening upwards, then slumping around its bloated belly. It buzzes and hums like a swarm of wild bees. Its face is a mass of bruises, expressionless but rippling slightly as something hidden behind its cheekbones curls and moves. A shiny segmented foot peeps from one sleeve of the orange jumpsuit, black with barbed yellow bristles circling it like a lace cuff.

"*Approach,*" hums the corpse. My feet bear me forward despite my reluctance. There's a geas associated with the labyrinth, a huge and powerful compulsion I'm as helpless to disobey as a soap bubble circling a drain.

DeeDee takes up a position before the throne. Her eyes glow brightly in the darkness. She bows deeply to her Lord's representative on Earth. "*I obey,*" she says in strongly accented Old Enochian. I curse myself for not having studied the language more intensively. It's like being presented to the pope and discovering he intends to interview you in Church Latin.

The corpse's head tilts towards me. The eyes are milky and flat with the onset of desiccation. The thing behind the fleshy mask clicks and crackles. "*Ambassador,*" it says to me. "*Thou art—*" I think the next word is *recognized.* "*So. Speak.*"

"*I—*" I clear my throat and extemporize. "*I don't speak this tongue—*" then words I don't understand begin to well up inside my throat. Mhari Murphy takes a back seat inside the head of Baroness Karnstein, Emissary of the Court of the Black Pharaoh. I speak eloquently if painfully (Old Enochian was not designed for human vocal cords), uttering words the Prime Minister embedded in my mind during our last meeting, and as the words come, so does a loose and very approximate translation of their meaning. Something like this:

"*Greetings from the Throne of N'yar Lat-Hotep to the Mouthpiece of the Lord of Sleep and Master of Nightmares, Dread Cthulhu. We take note of thy most excellent amusements and diversions, of the pall of forgetfulness spread by thy followers across this continent, thy plans for the sundering of worlds and the immanent return of thy true personage, the construction*

*of the Dam of Dreams and the War against the Cold Ones. There
is much that is debatable here, and some that is admirable. However, we feel that our purposes are best served by slowing thy
headlong rush into war until such time as we have held joint
counsel with all of our peers who are awakening in this epoch.*
So consider your chain duly yanked, motherfucker."

Without conscious volition, I punch the Mouthpiece in what
is left of his face.

Let me note that at this point I'm a passenger in my own body.
It's a really strange sensation, like watching myself on TV: only
this is real life and my arms and legs have taken on an eerie life of
their own. They move through preprogrammed motions scripted
by His Darkness. I'm not much of a puncher to be honest, although
I did a self-defense course once and passed basic police auxiliary
training. V syndrome gives me added speed and strength, but
against a real opponent I'd be toast. Luckily for me, the Mouthpiece is expecting diplomacy—and its human host is chained down
and rotting from the inside out.

I hit its nose and its face splatters like an overripe plum. Red-
tinged liquor squirts out, along with a stomach-curdling stench
of decay. An eerie keening sound rises from around us, and it
begins to split vertically. I glimpse a chitinous gleam inside. My fists
pull back in time to block as an arm swipes at me, flesh sloughing
off to expose a barbed claw.

The Mouthpiece lunges and jolts to a stop as the chains come
taut. Flesh compresses and bubbles around its steel collar. It
chirrs at me, a grating crackle that has nothing to do with mam-
malian mouthparts. I expectorate, spitting a gobbet of bloody
saliva as the Mandate's Will allows me a moment to take stock.
I can hear Him giggling, audible all the way from London. DeeDee
stares at me in outrage: "What," she demands, "do you think
you're doing?"

Oh fuck, I think. I swallow, regaining control of larynx and
limbs now that His B'stardness is done with me. "I assert diplomatic immunity!" I yell. "I'm a valuable bargaining chip and kill-

ing me won't buy you anything! I had nothing to do with this, it was all the Black Pharaoh's fault!" *A mad god made me do it, then ran away.* My fists rise again, without me willing it to happen. "Help!"

DeeDee's fingers curve into clawlike mudras, violet light rippling across her skin. "I think you're beyond help," she snarls over the moist squishing sounds as the Mouthpiece's human remains fall apart. A blanket of raw power folds itself around my skin and twists suffocatingly tight. "You stole the Uncrowned King so you're next in line to host the Mouthpiece." *Oh, was that what you wanted the President for?* Outside the grid, the blood guards are closing in on the entrance to the labyrinth.

The exposed Mouthpiece buzzes deafeningly as it hurls itself repeatedly against its chains. The ovipositor extending from its segmented and sickly yellow abdomen twitches and pulses. Glistening wings, freed from their envelope of human meat, ripple and spread behind its thorax as it turns a cluster of seven compound eyes towards me. It's not a true wasp—insect book-lungs just don't scale up: also, the chitinous exoskeleton is articulated like a suit of armor, plates sliding over each other as if supported by some inner structure—and behind the clashing mandibles lurk nematocysts tipped with barbed stingers. With my body no longer my own to control, a weird calm descends on me. If this is indeed a specialized instar of Cthulhu's kind, tailored for existence within our biosphere, the original body plan must be like nothing that ever evolved on Earth.

DeeDee splays her fingers and the world flashes pink. The next thing I know, my ears are ringing. Whatever she zapped me with should have killed me, but instead I find a matching darkness rippling around my hands. The Black Pharaoh's Will flows through me, searing and chill. "Just die already!" DeeDee snaps, triggering another death macro that sizzles uselessly against the Will that animates my marionette body. While she is busy trying to murder me she's distracted. Her dolls stumble dizzily in the maze around us, at a loss without her guidance. By rights I should be toast, but the PM is protecting me—at least until she realizes she can draw on the power of the Mouthpiece.

As I watch, she steps sideways to place herself before the throne, facing me across the dais. *She's going to do it,* I realize sickly. I nearly black out at a sudden spike of agony as the damaged fingers of my left hand twist, joints crackling, and sketch a symbol in the air that forms a blind spot in my vision. "Now look what you've made me do!" she snaps at me. Then she steps backward into the embrace of the Lord of Sleep's avatar, arms spread wide to welcome in her god.

The Mouthpiece's wings abruptly still as it embraces DeeDee from behind with four black barbed arms. Its abdomen pulses, sucking back, then thrusts sharply against her hips, rippling and squirting. She gasps and her eyes widen, lips forming a perfect "O" of shock and pain as she welcomes the new Mouthpiece into her—*of course* Cthulhu's brood reproduce through traumatic insemination—and then her eyes roll back in their sockets and her arms and legs twitch, a crimson glow rippling outwards as the Lord of Sleep's will burns through her peripheral nervous system.

I thought I was doomed before, but I've been wrong every time. This time? It's the real deal.

The toilets on the Concorde are famously cramped, and Jim is too big to fit inside, bundled up in multiple layers as he is. So he peels off his harness and boots, then his flight jacket and body armor. When he's down to just the sunlight-resistant body stocking he pulls the pants and boots on again, and finally gets the bathroom break he's been gagging for ever since he forgot to go before leaving Starbucks.

The interior of a Concorde is divided into compartments by claustrophobic tunnels, like a chain of linked sausages. Jim makes his way forward from the seats in the rear compartment, past a toilet and galley, then into the next compartment. He does

a double-take as he sees the bare floor with the permanent invocation grid—a glorified pentacle—that fills the middle of the compartment, in front of the stations for the flight sorcerers and the
other ritual equipment. But the grid is powered down, the sacrificial altar folded against the wall, and the manacles unoccupied: it's safe to cross.

There's a large LED display on the front wall to the left of
the tunnel leading to the cockpit. It's currently reading 1280 mph.
As Jim watches it rises to 1290. 302 Heavy is in cruise-climb
flight, rising gradually as it burns a quarter of a ton of fuel per
minute.

"Mr. Grey?" It's the primary school teacher. She's seated at an
equipment console: "Can I help you?" she asks.

"I'm beyond help, I'm afraid. I was just curious," he says, sizing her up reflexively for a moment. This time he recognizes the
Flight Lieutenant's shoulder-stripes. "I should go back—"

"No, you'd better take a seat right here." She points at an unoccupied position in front of a console on the opposite side of
the plane. "Strap in, if we hit clear air turbulence at speed I don't
want you bouncing off the ceiling. I need to notify the flight deck
so they can shut down the rear cabin aircon pack." She turns
back to her console and speaks into her headset as Jim fastens
his three-point safety harness.

"Why is the air conditioning important?" he asks.

"At this speed the Concorde's skin is at oven temperature due
to friction. At cruising speed the passenger birds wasted a fifth
of their engine power on cooling the cabin. Now that you're
up"—she unstraps and goes aft to slide a partition across the
tunnel to the rear of the plane—"we can go faster or higher.
Whichever the skipper needs."

"How fast is fast?"

"Depends. During flight testing in the seventies, one of the
prototypes hit 1500 miles per hour and held it for half an hour,
but that's not recommended: it's a good way to weaken the wing
spars. If the skipper does it we'll be grounded for a C check

afterwards—that's at least two months in the hangar, being pulled apart and put back together again. Could be a complete hull loss." She winks at him. "On the other hand—"

Lights begin blinking for attention on her console, which features an ancient-looking CRT tube display covered in cryptic green and red glyphs. Suddenly her attention is entirely focussed on the panel in front of her. A few seconds later she updates the flight deck, then Jim. "Air route traffic control center ZDC just ordered a complete ground stop. MARSA in effect, GIANT KILLER calling our path. Uh, got a ground stop at ZHU Center, now ZDV Center joining in as well—looks like they're grounding everything. Quit-36, flight of two F-15s on active air defense scramble out of Truax Field, heading on an intercept for our ground track." A pause. "No sir, unless they've got tanker support already positioned they can't touch us—"

A couple of minutes crawl by. Jim focuses on the pulse in the Defensive Systems Operator's jugular and tries to remain calm. A clattering, and footsteps from the tunnel behind him, finally get his attention. It's OSCAR and another officer coming aft. The President nods tensely as he passes Jim's chair. He clutches some sheets of paper in one hand, as tightly as if they're the launch codes for the nuclear arsenal. "Constable."

Jim salutes with deliberate irony: the President can't be expected to be familiar with foreign police ranks, but it's the fastest and steepest demotion Jim's ever had. "Sir."

"This way," prompts the airman. There's a fold-down jump seat next to the containment grid in the floor, opposite the altar, and the RO sets it up and swings it out over the grid then motions the President into it. "Headset." He plugs the President into an overhead panel. "I just need to set up, then give you the signal to record your speech, sir." Moving over to Jim's seat, the airman leans past him and flips three switches. A row of pilot LEDs embedded in the floor all the way around the grid light up red. "Okay, you're ready to go online, sir," he tells the President.

Then he flips a fourth switch, the invocation grid turns green, and the President begins to read his script.

My fellow Americans, you are receiving this broadcast because our nation is under insidious attack by an enemy within our own borders.

I am your President, the elected Commander-in-Chief of this nation. I have sworn to defend the Constitution, and I have served as chief executive of this great nation of ours for more than six years. Then, three months ago, you were made to forget me.

Today, I am obliged to tell you that magic is real—every bit as real as the superheroes of New York and the dragons of the Rocky Mountains. Unfortunately, the government organization tasked with defending our nation against black magic and demonic attacks has gone rogue. I do not yet know why this happened; but for whatever reason, this classified agency decided to make everyone *forget* that your President exists.

This was an illegal action on their part, done without an executive order, a law passed by Congress, or the scrutiny of the Supreme Court. They conducted a magical ritual that compels you—everyone in America—to forget my existence every time you fall asleep. In doing so they vastly exceeded their authority, going far outside the boundaries of law, and violating the Constitution by altering your memories without due process.

This is an outrage. I am appalled, as I am sure you are too. But I am awake, and as you hear my voice, you should be awakened. Hear my voice. I am your President. You must remember that, at all costs. Fight back! Before you go to sleep, write yourself a note. If your friends or family members sleep, remind them when they awaken. If you work in a shop, or office, tell everyone you see, every day: I exist, I am the President, this is an attempted coup, and we must awaken the fighting spirit of our great nation if we are to survive.

We are awakening. We shall not sleep. We shall search, cease-lessly, until the enemies who tried to make us forget our eternal truths and liberties are rooted out, and their foul schemes are brought to justice.

Please spread the word. Thank you, and God bless America.

So, about the Prime Minister's plan.

When His Darkness set me up with this *Mission: Impossible* caper, there was only ever one goal: to buy us time. The Nazgûl are not our friends. Forget the so-called Special Relationship; it's been a dead letter for decades, more an aspirational touchstone for fossils on the 1922 Committee to fret over than anything meaningful. The truth is, the New Management harbors some degree of concern for human survival, however minimal. The Nazgûl don't. They're terrifically powerful, and their objective is to bring about the Lovecraftian Singularity and awaken the Lord of Sleep by dismantling half the solar system. This would be an extinction event for humanity. We can't let it happen. It is also a who-poisoned-my-beehives event for the Black Pharaoh, which is why He's trying to prevent it. (We bring Him honey: He keeps us around.)

The New Management has got something that the OPA lacks: legitimacy. The Prime Minister may be an alien nightmare, but He took control through constitutionally sound means. Granted, these means may have legal historians weeping and clutching their heads for centuries to come, but in the final analysis it was entirely aboveboard and we have only got ourselves to blame for this mess.

The Nazgûl, in stark contrast, did not win any elections, were not handed any magic swords by watery tarts, and aren't even members of the House of Lords. They simply seized control by making everyone forget their superiors existed.

However, the Nazgûl were sloppy and their amnesia plot has a weakness: the President. He's one of the few ordinary US citizens who the forgetfulness glamour can't get its claws into. People exposed to him *remember*. If they'd arrested him immediately, they'd have risked him waking up his captors. Worse: the OPA are not the only US government occult agency. They did a number on their rivals such as the Occult Texts Division of the Postal Inspectorate (the Comstock Office), but when you start peeling the bureaucratic onion there's always another layer. Leaving the President in a sandbox with a pared-back bodyguard probably seemed like a good idea at the time, a magnet to draw institutional enemies of the Nazgûl out of hiding. But some of their opponents are foreign agencies, and by focussing solely on domestic threats they fucked up.

Now, His Darkness has a certain reputation for deviousness. He always zigs when they expect Him to zag, and this caper is no exception. Thus Plan East, and Plan West.

Derek's oracle-defeating dice roll suggested Plan East.

Plan East called for Concorde to turn northeast and hit the afterburners once OSCAR was aboard, not slowing down until it reached the Bristol Channel and final approach for Heathrow. The President, now an asylum seeker, would make obeisance before the throne of His Dark Majesty. In return for sanctuary, the PM would relieve him of all the *mana* accumulated from centuries of secular worship by hundreds of millions of Americans.[11] In other words, it's a straightforward magic heist, facilitated by a team of expendables and the only flying supersonic airliner in the world: the sort of scheme a totalitarian brute squad staffed by Cthulhu-worshipping bureaucrats would buy into uncritically . . .

But then there's Plan West.

---

[11] Non-destructively, I hope. We discussed the proposed mechanism at some length in a COBRA meeting. The phrase, "you *cannot* sacrifice the President" was uttered. Eventually the PM conceded that it would set a bad precedent for future international negotiations. But I've a nagging sense that he'd love nothing more than a VIP decoration for the top of his Tzompantli.

Plan West calls for the presidential executive transport to turn west and fly like a bat out of hell from coast to coast, broadcasting via the Emergency Alert System as it steers a wide course around Air Force bases capable of mounting an intercept attempt.

Shooting down a Concorde in flight is almost impossible. During the Cold War, NATO air defenses in Europe regularly used Concorde charter flights for intercept practice, because it was the nearest match for the fastest Soviet bomber, the Tu-160 Blackjack. It turns out that unless they knew *exactly* when and where it would show up on radar, they could never get a missile lock.

Of course, the plan assumes they'll try to shoot it down—we're counting on it, to distract them from trying to shut down the EAS for at least the first hour. Eventually they'll figure out that it's simpler to lock us out of the radio network. But we've got a fallback: the modified ROM Brains slipped into the entry-point hardware at WOCZ-FM, hacked to prevent them switching it off remotely. This should buy us another hour, or even two, during which OSCAR's voice can reach upwards of a hundred million Americans.

Finally, running low on fuel, 302 Heavy is to hurtle west across Oregon, out across the Pacific, then turn northeast and make an emergency landing in Seattle. The plane will probably never fly again, but the shitstorm produced by the sudden reappearance of a missing president is bound to liven up a dying news cycle.

These weren't the only plans we brainstormed. But we—Mahogany Row, I mean—managed to talk His Darkness down from Plans North and South. We are living through the early days of a darker aeon, and the world is not yet ready to see the PM's giant glass-and-chrome skull rack capped with the screaming undead head of the President. Nor is it considered appropriate to break the glamour by brute force, sacrificing OSCAR sixty thousand feet over the American heartland in order to rain regal blood on the cornfields of Iowa.

(I mean, it *could* work, if we had access to Air Force One and could convince an American agency to do the job . . . but as foreigners? The optics are terrible. Nope, not going there.)

Anyway, if you've been paying attention, you will have noticed there are a couple of explanations missing from this account. One is the minor detail that when Derek said "east," Jim told the pilots to fly west.

And the second is an accounting of who lived and who died.[12]

Matrix-time recap:

If Jim has done his part, he and the President of the United States are flying cross-country at upwards of Mach 2, broadcasting a wake-up call loud enough to raise the dead. He's sitting in a defensive grid in case the Nazgûl try to fry his brain remotely, and 302 Heavy is listening in on the military chatter and taking evasive action before the fighters can get close—there are *some* advantages to pulling this stunt in the airspace of a NATO ally, and one of them is being able to listen to their encrypted military communications because we use the same kit.

OSCAR might be able to wake up his people, but it won't be enough if the power behind the glamour is still on the loose. The PM can't leave his home territory, so he sent me as his proxy, a weapon disguised as a diplomat. Politicians aren't supposed to get their hands dirty with wet work, but I've known all along I'm not qualified for this—it's not really imposter syndrome if you really *are* a fake. Nor are my targets—DeeDee and the

[12] There is a third missing piece of the puzzle: and that is what the SA told me under conditions of ultimate secrecy. (But you will not learn about the plans for Extended Continuity Operations from me: my tongue is locked—that pesky low-level geas—and if I tell you any more I'll die.)

Mouthpiece—afforded the benefits of sovereign immunity. Not without actually admitting that they've held a coup, anyway. So the gloves are off and someone isn't going to get out of here alive.

(Probably me.)

Back to the Pentagon basement:

DeeDee jitters and twitches atop the throne of the Mouthpiece as if she's sitting in an electric chair. A bruised-looking purple aura surrounds her head: glowing red runes ripple across her skin. I spare a glance over my shoulder. The blood guards in the labyrinth have collapsed, collateral damage from the seizure gripping their controller. The grid around the dais is lit up yellow and lethal. If I approach her, it'll fry me. If I try to leave, I'm in the middle of the Pentagon basement and the PHANGs will be bound to recover before I can escape. If I wait, DeeDee will recover. And as the new Mouthpiece, she's a lot closer to her Lord's focus of power than I am.

I realize I'm running out of time as I look around the dais and take in the various ritual objects laid out around us, the bone scepter and the skull chalice—

Oh.

I stumble forward and grab for the chalice with my right hand. It has a history: taken and used as an ashtray by Stalin, lost to Jimmy Carter in a game of poker by a very drunk Leonid Brezhnev in 1977. As ritual objects go Hitler's plated skull is totally tacky, but totally appropriate for what I have in mind. I kneel down and drag it close. *The boss will need . . . oh, yes.* I pull out my passport, shake it, and grab the ceramic knife. Then I grit my teeth as without conscious volition my right hand shoves my left sleeve up and slashes lengthwise down the inside of my forearm, opening it from elbow to wrist.

The pain in my left hand was bad enough already: this is shocking and total. My V-symbionts deafen me with their shrieking protest. I gasp for breath and try not to double up as venous blood drips—*not squirting, thank fuck, I missed the artery*—and trickles rapidly down my arm. I hold my damaged hand over the upturned cup and squeeze my arm with my other hand, trying to open the vein further. The dripping turns to a steady flow. I nearly black out again but some external force keeps me conscious through the agony. If this keeps up for too long I won't just fill the chalice, I'll bleed out. On the other hand, if I *don't* go through with it I'm dead anyway. My Lord and I are of one mind right now: the only way out is in. My symbionts are outraged. They aren't party to my pact with the Black Pharaoh, the pact enforced by my oath of office.

The chalice is less than a quarter full when I stumble to my feet. Black spots pulse in my vision. I feel nauseous, and there's a steel band pressing behind my eyes. My arm is on fire and my fingers are tight skins of agony, but they form hooks inside Hitler's eye sockets and scoop up the goblet nevertheless.

Behind me, the zentai puppets begin to stir. The thing in DeeDee's flesh stops twitching, and her eyelids flicker open. She makes a low, moaning sound. Blood bubbles from the side of her mouth as she tries to sit up. Behind her, the old Mouthpiece is a quiescent husk, like a ghastly leather seat cushion that supports her impaled body atop the iron throne.

"Hello, sister," the Prime Minister speaks through me, and as DeeDee looks at me and opens her mouth to speak I throw the chalice at her. The blood goes everywhere—including into her open eyes and mouth.

For a moment I wonder if it's failed. But then I feel the Mandate's Will fill me, pouring thickly through my skin and infusing the blood dripping down my arm. The V-symbionts still wail, but now they're listening as well, and I feel their sense of anticipation. I feel something else, too, the sound of the parasites bound to the will of the thing on the throne. The hunger fades as my symbionts feed on their weaker kin, supplanting their control over the puppets. I open a pair of eyes I didn't have a moment ago and find myself staring at the back of my own head. Then another pair of eyes, and another, as one by one all of DeeDee's minions come on line and make obeisance to the thing I've invited into my head.

Did I mention the OPA-bred symbionts were bred for a very specific trait—obedience to an overriding will? Did I observe that they're a whole lot weaker than my own feral infection, acquired by way of a certain London banking institution's research group? Did I inject symbionts into Jim, already parasitized by Nazgûl PHANGs, and steal him back for my own lineage?

This is the same, only on a larger scale.

I throw my puppets at the iron throne one by one. They sizzle and burn on the powered-up grid. This keeps the thing colonizing DeeDee distracted for a precious minute while two of my clumsy half-dominated bodies fumble with a power-distribution board, in the end yanking a three-phase cable out of the wall by brute force. The grid goes down abruptly, with a loud bang from the circuit-breaker box. The smell of roasting meat and burning hair fills the room, and I throw more bodies at DeeDee, dogpiling her with stolen vampire minions.

There's a pink flash and sizzling zap of lightning: bodies go flying. But DeeDee isn't fully integrated yet, not functional as the Mouthpiece of the Lord of Sleep. Her body is still mostly human, and damaged at that, impaled on her predecessor's stinger-like ovipositor. Quality counts, but quantity has a quality all of its own: the puppets bite and claw at her and she screams incoherently. *Flash*. Bite. *Zap*. I pick up the scepter in my right hand and step onto the dais. "*Maximize thy entropy*," DeeDee chants, mangling her Old Enochian abominably, but the scepter catches the worst of the curse. The bone handle blackens and chars and the jeweled cap flares violet, hurting my eyes and burning my exposed skin. More pain comes in waves now, and my vision keeps fading to gray. I position two of the puppets to prop me up under each armpit and push me towards the thing on the throne.

"Do something," I mumble, hoping like hell that the PM is still in the loop, that He's still riding my nervous system like a horrible parasite, because *anything* is better than what the Mouthpiece will do to me if I fail here: "*Do* something? Anything—"

"*Like this?*" I seem to hear His voice mocking me as my right arm rises and the scepter stabs towards DeeDee. Clawed legs lash out from behind the cover of her torso, and I know that if any of them touch me something horrible will happen. But my wrist twists painfully, and the head of the scepter thumps against one of the legs, and there's a pink flash that eats my vision and a noise so loud I hear only ringing silence afterwards.

An indeterminate time later, I come to. I'm lying on the floor and my left arm is a throbbing ache from elbow to fingertips. Also, my head hurts, my ears ache, and there are greenish-yellow blotches in front of my eyes. I roll over painfully, push myself up with my right arm, and take stock.

The puppet-PHANGs on the dais resemble man-shaped charcoal briquettes, with skeletal grins and exposed ribs poking through their carbonized husks. I'm alive because they caught the worst of the blast: the scepter, or maybe His Darkness, shielded me from the backwash. The throne where DeeDee was sitting was at ground zero—

Nope, not looking, definitely don't need any more nightmare fuel.

A handful of puppets are still ambulatory, and a whispery memory of His Majesty's Will prompts me to shove them forward to clear the charred remains from the containment grid. They're so easy to push around it's like having a dozen extra pairs of hands and eyes. They still have minds, but they're so weak they tear like tissue if I push them too hard. I shudder. Alex and Janice and the other PHANGs I know—never mind Yarisol—they'd swear and punch me if I tried to work them like this. Maybe I'm stronger than I realized. Or His Dreadfulness has done something to me, given me an unasked-for power-up. Either way, I'm thankful for the help, because right now I'm weak from blood loss and shock and too drained to fight off a feisty kitten.

With the bodies cleared out of the way the damage doesn't look too bad. I stand in front of the dais and contemplate the complex circle inscribed on the floor around it. It's a summoning grid, obviously, with containment on top—currently powered down and unoccupied, thank you, DeeDee. If I knew how to make one of these things work, or had my phone, maybe I could do something useful—exactly what, I don't know. It's becoming apparent to me that while I was boned previously, I am still boned, only in a different manner. Instead of facing a DeeDee hell-bent on sacrificing me to a giant parasitoid wasp-thing from another dimension, I'm trapped in a labyrinth in the basement of the Pentagon with no way out. *Hmm.* At least I've still got my passport and diplomatic visa, I realize, even though it's bent and bloodstained. "I assert diplomatic immunity," I mutter under my breath. "As if."

"Boss?" Someone calls from the far side of the room. I turn round so fast I nearly black out.

A new puppet has arrived. He's standing in the entrance to the bunker and there's something weirdly familiar about him. I blink through his eyes and realize he's not in control of his own body, any more than I was in the driving seat when the PM took over during my little contretemps with the Mouthpiece. Someone else is with him—

"Who's there?"

"It's us!"

I hear the words twice, and that's when I realize it's Brains, and the puppet I'm riding is—*fuck, it's Pete.* I stare. Yes, it's Pete the Vicar—a loose string from DeeDee's harp—with Brains, who appears to be himself, Jon, or Yarisol, or whatever she's calling herself today, and Janice. Those three I can feel but not control. Another four blood guards cluster around them, forlorn as abandoned dolls. Prisoners: DeeDee had them rounded up and was bringing them here for some undisclosed purpose—sacrifice, probably.

"Derek?"

"We had to leave him." Brains looks haggard. "Pete's been——"

"Shit. I know." I slide my will into Pete's limbs. He's there and protests vaporously, but it's like thrusting a hand inside an empty glove. I walk him towards me. "Pete is about to join me in the labyrinth. Follow in his exact footsteps. We need to get out of here."

Pete's been compromised, but the boss stole DeeDee's geas on the OPA's PHANGs. If I wasn't half dead right now I could try and bring him the whole way over to the dark side the way I did Jim, but it'll have to wait. There is no overriding urgency here: the mission is over. Anyway, there may be no point in salvaging him. Pete understands all too well what PHANGs are about, and I've got a feeling he'll only stick around long enough to say goodbye to his family before he walks into the sunrise.

"What have you *done,* Mhari?" asks Brains.

"Long story, no time right now. Janice, can you do something with this grid? Get us home?"

Janice cocks her head on one side and squints at the control panel. "You're in luck, kind of," she says. "Unfortunately I don't have my gear bag or I could say for sure, but this looks like it's set up for entangled translocation, being in two places simultaneously. If we had an anchor——"

"An anchor?" echoes Jon.

"Coordinates for another grid that *just happened* to be ready and waiting for us to lock onto——"

The ghostly tittering of an eldritch prankster echoes between my ears, and I wince. "I can give you an anchor," I say. Or rather, His Darkness can give her an anchor. He left *very precise* instructions in my head, wrapped up with a ribbon, or maybe a whoopee cushion. "Just set it up to bilocate and get us all inside. Your parameters are——" My tongue begins to flap without any input on my part.

Janice looks at me strangely, but nods and gets to work.

"That's not you-you, is it?" asks Jon, peering at me, wide-eyed.

"I have no idea what you're talking about." I show her my best poker face. Who am I, anyway? I have the most disturbing sense of alienation, as if the Republic of Me is recovering from a state of emergency and martial law.

"Where's Jim?" she pushes.

"Elsewhere." I shrug, uncomfortable with her line of questioning. "Alive, I hope." I think I'd know if one I made had died, not that I've got much experience in that area.

"Come on," calls Brains, "all aboard the nowhere express! By the way, can you say where we're going?"

"Yes, Brains." Sick dread settles in the pit of my stomach. Of course, if the PM was serious about everyone on this mission being disposable, now would be the ideal time for a little mopping up. Even though He relayed very explicit instructions through me—but you can't live your life as if you're perpetually expecting to be betrayed by your leader. "We're going home," I say, picking up the chalice as Janice throws the knife switch.

By three o'clock on the west coast, 302 Heavy has flown a little over 4000 miles. They're running close to their minimum reserve level of fuel. All that's left now is the matter of deciding where to land and face the music.

"Do you think it worked?" asks the President.

Jim shrugs, uncomfortable at being put on the spot. "I couldn't say, sir. But"—he glances at the DSO and raises an eyebrow—"how long since the last intercept attempt?"

"Oh, they stopped nearly an hour ago." She grins broadly. "The chatter got *interesting*."

On the front bulkhead, the display shows their speed dropping below a thousand miles per hour and altitude descending through fifty thousand feet. 302 Heavy has completed its run across the Midwest and up the Pacific coast, staying as far away as possible from Nellis AFB in Nevada, home of the only fighters in the continental United States that have a good chance of shooting down a Concorde. The advanced F-22s there are able to fly higher and cruise faster than F-15s, but they're mostly deployed in overseas hotspots, not on domestic air interception duty. If they were, Plan West would have been unacceptably dangerous. As it is, after the encounter with the pair of F-16s patrolling near DC, three different pairs of F-15s tried to intercept the Concorde. The first two attempts failed. The third . . .

"I think you really confused that major, sir," offers the DSO.

The President nods, wearily. "I'm going to have to follow that up. I mean, I hope I'm in a position to—you know what I mean. Because he's going to be in a world of grief when he lands."

"Yes, he will be." She nods. "On the other hand, we were squawking a genuine IFF code on a standard NATO frequency and had the right encryption keys for his voice channel, and if he got close enough to see us—well, I wouldn't want to make that judgment call—"

Her headset chatters for a few seconds, diverting her attention. "Yes, sir, I'll tell him." She makes eye contact. "That's the skipper. We're on approach for Sea-Tac. Tower are definitely woke but keeping a lid on it. We have a pair of Air National Guard F-16s inbound as escorts, they're woke too but the skipper says please can you to talk to them *personally,* just in case. I can hook you up right now . . ."

Over the next ten minutes, Jim listens in as the President shoots the shit with a pair of fighter pilots who are putting their best professional face on not freaking out, as they converge on the supersonic airliner that's squawking its ID as Executive One. He's tired, his eyes burning from the diffuse sunlight filtered through the tiny windows, and he's *thirsty*. He can't help glancing between the President and the Defensive Systems Operator, focusing on the pink flush of their skin, the pulse in the DSO's wrist, the rumble of blood in her veins. This is all new to him, and it's going to take some getting used to—to not thinking about the origin stories of each little plum-dark bag of life-juice, to not seeing the people around him as a walking buffet, to never lying on a beach in the noonday sun, to all the things he's going to have to give up—

"Sir?" He blinks. It's the airman who hauled him aboard. The loadmaster. "Sir, would you mind taking a seat in the rear cabin for landing?"

"Of course." Jim stands up and they head up the aisle towards the back of the cabin. He finds himself licking his lips. "Is there a spare bag of go-juice in the galley?" he asks.

"Uh, I'll just check, if you could strap yourself in—"

Jim takes his seat. A numinous sense of guilt washes over him. He's no saint. He's not a criminal, but all law-abiding citizens are guilty of doing shitty things from time to time. This, however, feels like he's stepped across a line. He's about to raise his voice to say he changed his mind when the airman returns, holding a cup full of warm blood. "This is the last one, sir." He holds it out for Jim to take, and Jim notices he's wearing latex gloves.

Jim sighs. "I changed my—" He takes the cup and swallows his words along with his qualms. *They wouldn't have loaded the blood bags if they didn't want me—or other PHANGs—alive,* he reasons. *As tools of the state.* It feels like a dirty and self-serving argument for state-sanctioned killing, and the liquid ecstasy leaves an unclean aftertaste.

"We've got a three-ring circus waiting for us when we land, sir," says the loadmaster, strapping himself into a seat on the other side of the cabin. "The governor, local heads of the FBI and Secret Service offices, camera crews from the major news agencies, and a whole bunch of police. Also, the resident from the British government office. The consul from San Francisco is en route, along with legal counsel. You'll be needed for a press conference when you've been debriefed, but until then we're supposed to keep quiet. We broke an unbelievable number of rules and regulations and committed several felonies that carry serious prison time, mostly aviation-related offenses. Your man up front is the ultimate get-out-of-jail card, but let's not push our luck."

"Let's not," Jim agrees. The crackling whispers in his skull have fallen into a satiated sleep. He glances out the window at the F-16s holding formation some distance away. Sunlight reflects painfully bright from their cockpit canopies. It's an honor guard, not an intercept. *We made it,* he realizes. *I wonder if Mhari succeeded.*

EPILOGUE: DEBRIEF

Three days later:

Evening in London. I follow Iris into the Prime Minister's study at 10 Downing Street. "He'll be along in a few minutes," she says, giving me an unreadable look. "Make yourself at home."

I nod, then take a seat at the coffee table with my back to the bay window and drawn curtains. There are refreshments served on fine bone china: tea, scones with clotted cream, strawberry jam the color of fresh blood. I carefully position my gift-wrapped parcel on the table as Iris sits opposite me and busies herself with the teapot. I ignore the food: I'm not hungry right now. There are butterflies in my chest. Finally she sits back and looks at me. "I know what you did," she says. "Thank you."

I feel nauseous. "Did you tell Him?" *How did you find out?*

"*I* didn't tell Him." Her smile is worthy of Catherine de' Medici. No wonder she's survived six months as His chief courtier. "Your substitute was good, but not good enough to fool a mother, let alone the PM. You should probably avoid Jonquil for a while—she's sore about missing out." Her smile turns cold. "But thank you for keeping her safe."

Brr. Now the version of Catherine de' Medici she's channeling is about to call for her poisoner. I nod, unable to frame an appropriate reply. *I'm sorry I kidnapped your daughter and hid her in a POW camp* seems somehow inadequate. Also, sorry (not sorry).

I'm still trying to work out whether my tea is safe to drink when the door behind us opens and I feel the Prime Minister's presence. We rise as one, turn, and bow deeply. It's not normal protocol but it feels like the right thing to do in the presence of the People's Mandate.

"Baroness, fancy meeting you again! What a pleasant surprise!" He sits down and we follow suit.

I show Him the fakiest smile I dare, and flash a little fang. "So pleased to be here," I say, hoping desperately that they're not my famous last words. I still don't know why He waited until now to summon me. I slide the gift-wrapped package towards him. "I brought you a present."

After the bloodbath in DC, I spent a few very disagreeable hours stumbling and screaming along a ghost road with the other survivors. When we reached the end of the road it turned out to be a summoning circuit the PM had drawn on the middle of the State Dining Room, ruining a priceless nineteenth-century Persian carpet, and coincidentally spoiling the day for the Parliamentary and Diplomatic Protection Group cops on the front door (who were rather upset by the sudden appearance of a group of blood-stained intruders in the Prime Minister's residence).

We got it sorted out eventually. Nobody got machine-gunned or staked, or even arrested: it turns out He'd simply forgotten to tell them He was expecting visitors. My diplomatic passport helped cool things down then Iris arrived, led us through the not terribly secret tunnel to the Foreign Office basement, and arranged transport to a secure medical facility. I was then given no less than three transfusions from separate donors, along with a wholly unnecessary tetanus shot. I don't want to think too hard about the logistics of those transfusions, by the way. Janice and Jar—no, Jon—needed blood, too, and so will the others, if they don't end themselves. Or if they're ever released, in Jim's case.

If.

I look at the PM. "This is where you give me a well-deserved chewing out," I say briskly, putting my head on the block because there's no point in delaying the inevitable reckoning. "Needless to say, you'll have my resignation letter if you want it."

The PM's smile is like a dead star rising above the horizon of an airless moon. "Baroness, I have *always* had your resignation letter. It's not something you write yourself." He crosses His legs and laces His fingertips around His knee. He doesn't seem to be angry or upset; if anything, He's . . . *pleased*? "But before we discuss that, I'd like to hear you explain what you think you did wrong."

"What . . ." Words fail me. "Wrong?" My voice rises. "I lost the DM!" (A unique, highly specialized, impossible-to-replace operative.) "Two other members of my team—only seven bodies to begin with—were infected with hostile V-parasites along the way! I had to turn one of them or the mission would have been a total washout! All but one of us were captured by the opposition, and, and . . ." I swallow. "They were waiting for us. It was a trap."

"These things happen." The PM shrugs. He raises his teacup—eighteenth-century Wedgewood—and blows gently across it. "What about the big picture?"

"I did—I didn't—" I flap, then take a deep breath: "We got the President aboard the transport and we rooted the entry-point system and I suppose *that* side of the mission worked perfectly, although I couldn't bring him home for you." I've seen the intel estimates. Right after his flight, almost a hundred and sixty million Americans were awake and aware that they'd lost their President for three months. It was tantalizingly close to a majority of the population. But then the numbers stalled, and ever since then they've been falling. It seems people don't *want* to be awake these days. Apocalypses are easier slept through than experienced.

"And the Mouthpiece?" I can't focus on His face but I can imagine Him raising an eyebrow.

"Well and truly punched." But it doesn't matter, because there's a new Mouthpiece, and she's probably pissed off at me for getting blood on her Armani. "For what it's worth . . ."

"Yes, well, we can't have everything we want." He puts his cup down. "I am mildly disappointed that you didn't bring me the President, but even *I* can see that he is more useful leading the resistance than as a Christmas tree decoration." I shudder. There are reports of burning cities on the Eastern Seaboard, where night and sleep had already fallen by the time 302 Heavy completed its mission. "And besides, you brought me such a lovely present!"

Iris takes this as her cue to pick up my parcel and slice a thumbnail through the tape. She unfolds the paper and presents the contents to the Prime Minister for his appraisal. He glances at the chalice briefly, as if to confirm something, then looks at me.

"Such an excellent gift! It will fit in perfectly with the other decorations at Marble Arch. You have excellent taste, Baroness, and whatever you may believe, I am not displeased by the outcome of your operation. On the contrary: your offer to resign is *denied*."

"My—my—"

His savage grin reduces me to silence. "Your problem, Baroness, is that you pay too much attention to the brushstrokes and too little to the frame. I ignore your lesser flaws because you are a never-ending source of amusement, but your belief in your own helplessness grates after a while. Just remember who you work for and you'll be fine." His amusement vanishes as abruptly as a summer mist beneath the light of a supernova. "But do *please* keep in mind what happens to those who bite the feeding hand." He rises, cradling Hitler's skull in his left hand. "I shall have another little job for you to organize next Monday, but you might as well take the rest of the week off: you've earned it."

The best thing about being a workaholic with a train-wreck for a personal life is never having to worry about finding something to do in your spare time.

The worst thing about being a workaholic with a train-wreck for a personal life is what happens to you when you have *too much* spare time.

I go home, shower, change into pajamas, eat, then sit on the futon and stare blankly at the wall for about an hour. I don't dare turn on the TV: I might accidentally stumble across a news channel, and then I'd have to buy another TV after I finished punching it. The internet on my laptop is just as bad, all clickbait headlines—*Ten Improvements Cthulhu's Awakening Will Bring to American Politics (and you won't believe number six!)*—but the alternative is Facebook, and Dad forwarding Crazy Uncle conspiracy theories about the PM by way of his Pastor, or Jenny talking about her boring fiancée. If not that, she'll be moaning on her wall in an attempt to guilt-trip me into being a bridesmaid, trying to rope me into her wedding plans, because that's what big sisters are for, and she won't take "I can't show skin in daylight" for an answer. (She's only doing it to annoy, with a side order of "my maid of honor is a baroness" thrown in, because who could resist?)

Eventually the wall-staring gets to be too much for me, so I reach behind the futon and flail around in the Waitrose box. The first four wine bottles I touch are empty, but I hit paydirt with number five, another Minervois. I pull it out and swig straight from the neck like an utter heathen. I hesitate briefly between my first mouthful and my second. Maybe if I hadn't left my phone in a trash can in DC I could call some friends and go out for a night on the tiles instead of drinking alone, but when you're forced back to the late 1990s laptop experience everything is unbearably cumbersome, so why bother? I take that second gulp, and then a third, and I'm halfway down the bottle before I hear a tapping at the window casement.

I slide the glass door open, letting the cold in. His breath steams. He smells of stale blood and beer, maddeningly sexy and stale all at once. "Hey."

"Hey," he replies. "I tried to call but you're not answering. Do you have to invite me in, or is that another dumb myth?"

I mash my lips against his mouth and hang on for dear life as he picks me up and carries me across the threshold. We surface for air in a heap on the futon. I accidentally kicked the wine bottle over on the carpet but that's okay: it was already half-empty. The French window is still open and the wind blows the night and magic inside. My arms are full of Fuckboy and all is well with the world. "They let you go!" I squeak as I catch my breath.

"They let *everyone* go, although the plane will probably never fly again." He sends one hand on an expedition inside my pajama top and I wriggle happily. "They shipped us to Vancouver the day before yesterday and we flew home the long way, via Tokyo and Dubai."

"But the daylight—"

"Special arrangements were made. *Never* joke about flying cattle-class ever again."

"You must be exhausted?"

"I am." But he came here all the same.

"What about Sally?" His sixteen-year-old daughter.

"She's fine." I feel his shrug. "She can drive Liz mad for another week." Liz is Jim's ex. "I haven't figured out what to tell them yet. I was hoping you could help with that."

"Tell them about—" My brain freezes. "—about PHANG?" That's still classified.

"No, about us." That's even *worse,* I think, but then he pulls me tight and kisses me again. There's nothing tentative about it: I can feel his erection through chinos and pajamas. I start to undress him while he continues, "I thought I'd lost you."

Me, too. "But you haven't."

"I didn't know"—my God, his hands are everywhere, it's *wonderful*—"you'd made it until after we landed." I move to straddle him as he continues: "I was so fucking *scared,* Mhari, you and Sally are why I'm still alive"—I kiss him but he won't shut up—"please will you marry me?"

"What?" The question blindsides me, although I should have seen it coming. I sit up, and he takes the opportunity to pull my top up and over my head, trapping my arms. It takes a huge effort of will not to moan and rub myself against him because I'm so turned on I'm flashing ivory.

He holds out his hand and offers me a familiar-looking diamond-and-emerald engagement ring. I handed it back to the jeweler a couple of days ago, thinking that was the last time I'd see it. "Please will you—"

"—Yes, yes, I heard you the first time." My future life flashes before my eyes. Jenny being *incredibly* pissed off at me because she *will* see it as big sister trying to upstage her big day. Cow-eyed resentment from Sally for usurping her mum's place in her father's affections, even though that ship sailed years ago. The PM smiling horribly over tea and cake as He reminds me that all our tomorrows belong to Him and, oh, by the way, Jim and I are hostages against each other's loyalty to the regime. My gut-gnawing terror of losing him on a mission. *His* gut-gnawing terror of losing *me* on a mission. Jim, a serial shagger, and me, commitment-phobic, expecting each other to change our spots. Lying awake hugging our survival guilt tight, talking shop at dead of night as we try to justify our continued right to exist and, by existing, to kill relentlessly. *Two* workaholics with train wrecks for personal lives, entangled forever? "I'd have to be mad."

His face falls. "You don't want to—"

"Sanity can fuck right off," I say, shrugging out of my pajama top. Then, before he can ask me whether that was a *yes* or a *no*, I add, "I'll do it, on one condition."

"What's that?"

"*You* can break the news to my sister . . ."

ACKNOWLEDGMENTS

I'd like to thank my agent, Caitlin Blasdell; all my editors who have worked on this series at various times (Marty Halpern, Andrew J. Wilson, Ginjer Buchanan, Rebecca Brewer, Jenni Hill, Patrick Nielsen Hayden, and Theresa Nielsen Hayden); and various test readers and informants: K. B. Spangler, Seth Dickinson, Erik Olson, Genevieve Cogman, Sean Fagan, Stewart Wilson, Dan Ritter, Lynn Ann Morse, and many others.

extras

orbit

www.orbitbooks.net

about the author

Charles Stross is a full-time science fiction writer and resident of Edinburgh, Scotland. The author of seven Hugo-nominated novels and winner of the 2005, 2010 and 2014 Hugo Awards for best novella ('The Concrete Jungle', 'Palimpsest' and 'Equoid'), Stross's works have been translated into over twelve languages.

Like many writers, Stross has had a variety of careers, occupations and job-shaped catastrophes in the past, from pharmacist (he quit after the second police stake-out) to first code monkey on the team of a successful dot-com start-up (with brilliant timing he tried to change employer just as the bubble burst). Along the way he collected degrees in Pharmacy and Computer Science, making him the world's first officially qualified cyberpunk writer (just as cyberpunk died).

In 2013, he was Creative in Residence at the UK-wide Centre for Creativity, Regulation, Enterprise and Technology, researching the business models and regulation of industries such as music, film, TV, computer games and publishing.

Find out more about Charles Stross and other Orbit authors by registering for the free monthly newsletter at www.orbitbooks.net.

if you enjoyed

THE LABYRINTH INDEX

look out for

THE GIRL WHO COULD MOVE
SH*T WITH HER MIND

by

Jackson Ford

FOR TEAGAN FROST, SH*T JUST GOT REAL.

*Teagan Frost is having a hard time keeping it together. Sure,
she's got telekinetic powers — a skill that the government is all too
happy to make use of, sending her on secret break-in missions that no
ordinary human could carry out. But all she really wants to do is
kick back, have a beer, and pretend she's normal for once.*

*But then a body turns up at the site of her last job — murdered in a
way that only someone like Teagan could have pulled off. She's got
twenty-four hours to clear her name — and it's not just her life at stake.
If she can't unravel the conspiracy in time, her hometown of
Los Angeles will be in the crosshairs of an underground
battle that's on the brink of exploding . . .*

ONE

Teagan

On second thoughts, throwing myself out the window of a sky-scraper may not have been the best idea.

Not because I'm going to die or anything. I've totally got that under control.

It wasn't smart because I had to bring Annie Cruz with me. And Annie, it turns out, is a screamer. Her fists hammer on my back, her voice piecing my eardrums, even over the rushing air.

I don't know what she's worried about. Pro tip: if you're going to take a high dive off the 82nd floor, make sure you do it with a psychokinetic holding your hand. Being able to move objects with your mind is useful in all sorts of situations.

I'll admit, this one is a little tricky. Plummeting at close to terminal velocity, surrounded by a hurricane of glass from the window we smashed through, the lights of Los Angeles whirling around us and Annie screaming and the rushing air blowing the stupid clip-on tie from my security guard disguise into my face: not ideal. Doesn't matter though – I've got this.

I can't actually apply any force to either Annie's body or mine. Organic matter like human tissue doesn't respond to me, which is something I don't really have time to get into right now. But I can manipulate anything inorganic. Bricks, glass, metal, the fridge door, a sixpack, the TV remote, the zipper on your pants.

And belt buckles.

I've had some practice at this whole moving-shit-with-your-mind thing. I've already reached out, grabbed hold of the big metal buckles on our belts. We're probably going to have some bruises tomorrow, but it's a hell of a lot better than getting gunned down in a penthouse or splatting all over Figueroa Street.

I solidify my mental grip around the two buckles, then force them upwards, using my energy to counteract our downward motion. We start to slow, my belt tightening, hips starting to ache as the buckles take the weight –

– and immediately snap.

OK, yeah. Definitely not the best idea.

TWO

Teagan

Rewind. Twenty minutes ago.

We're in the sub-basement of the giant Edmonds Building, our footsteps muffled by thick carpet. The lighting in the corridor is surprisingly low down here, almost cosy, which doesn't matter much because Annie is seriously fucking with my groove.

I like to listen to music on our ops, OK? It calms me down, helps me focus. A little late-90s rap – some Blackstar, some Jurassic 5, some Outkast. Nothing too aggressive or even all that loud. I'm just reaching the good part of "So Fresh, So Clean" when Annie taps me on the shoulder. "Yo, take that shit out. We working."

Ugh. I was sure I'd hidden my earbud, threading the cord up underneath the starchy blue rent-a-cop shirt and tucking it under my hair.

I hunt for the volume switch on my phone, still not looking at Annie. She responds by reaching back and jerking the earbud out.

"Hey!"

"I said, fucking quit it."

"What, not an OutKast fan? Or do you only like their early stuff?" I hold up an earbud. "I don't mind sharing. You want the left or the right?"

"Cute. Put it away."

We turn the corner, heading for a big set of double doors at the far end. My collar's too tight. I pull at it, wincing, but it barely moves. Annie and I are dressed identically: blue shirts, black clip-on ties, black pants and puffer jackets in a very cheap shade of navy. Huge belts, leather, with thick metal buckles.

Paul picked up the uniforms for us. I tried to tell him that while Annie might be able to pass as a security guard, nobody was going to believe that the Edmonds Building would employ a short, not-very-fit woman with spiky black hair and a face that *still* gets her ID'd at the liquor store. Even though I've been able to buy my own drinks like a big girl for a whole year now.

I couldn't be more different to Annie. You know how some club bouncers have huge muscles and a shit-ton of tattoos and piercings? You know how people still fuck with them, starting fights and smashing bottles? Annie is like that one bouncer with zero tattoos, standing in the corner with her arms folded and a scowl that could sour milk. The bouncer no one fucks with because the last person who did ended up scattered over a six-mile radius. We might not see eye to eye on music – or on anything, because she's taller than me – but I'm still very glad she's on my side.

My earpiece chirps – my *other* one, the black number in my right ear. "Annie, Teagan," says Paul. "Come in. Over."

"We're almost at the server room," Annie says. She sends another disgusted look at my dangling earbud.

Silence. No response.

"You there?" Annie says.

"Sorry, was waiting for you to say *over*. Thought you hadn't finished. Over."

"Seriously?" I say. "We're still using your radio slang?"

"It's not slang. It's protocol. Just wanted to give you a heads-up – Reggie's activated the alarm on the second floor. Basement should be clear of personnel." A pause. "Over."

"Yeah, copy." Annie says. She's a lot more patient with Paul than I am, which I genuinely don't understand.

The double doors are like the fire doors you see in apartment buildings. The one on the right has a big sign on it, white lettering on a black background: AUTHORISED PERSONNEL ONLY. And on the wall next to it, a biometric lock.

Annie looks over at me. "You're up."

My tax form says that I work for a company called China Shop Movers. That's the name on the paperwork, anyway. What we actually do is work for the government – specifically, for a high-level spook named Tanner.

For some jobs, you need a black-ops team and a fleet of Apache choppers with heat-seeking missiles. For others, you need a psychokinetic with a music-hating support team who can make a lot less noise and get things done in a fraction of the time. You need a completely deniable group of civilians who can do stuff that even a special forces soldier would struggle with. That's us. We are fast, quiet, effective and deadly.

Go ahead: make the fart joke. Tanner didn't laugh when I made it either.

The people we take down are threats to national security. Drug lords, terrorist cells, human traffickers. We don't bust in with guns blazing. We don't need to – not with my ability. I've planted a tracking device on a limo at LAX, waving hello to the thick-necked goon standing alongside the car while I zipped the tiny black box up behind his back and onto the chassis. I've kept the bad guys' safeties on at a hostage exchange – good thing too, because they tried to start shooting the second they had the money and got one hell of a surprise when their guns didn't work. And I've been on plenty of break-ins. Windows? Cars? Big old metal safes? Not a problem. When you can move things with your mind, there's not a lot the world can do to keep you out.

Take the lock on AUTHORISED PERSONNEL ONLY, for instance.

You're supposed to put your finger on the little reader, let it scan your fingerprint, and you're in. If you're breaking in, you either need to hack off a finger (messy), take someone hostage (messy, annoying), hack it locally (time-consuming and boring), or blow it off (fun, but kind of noisy).

My psychokinesia – PK – means I can feel every object around me: its texture, its weight, its relation to other objects. It's a constant flood of stimuli. When I was little, Mom and Dad made me run through exercises, getting me to really focus in on a single object at a time – a glass, a toy car, a pencil. They made me move them around, describe them in excruciating detail. It took a long time, but I managed to deal with it. Now I can sense the objects around me in the same way you sense the clothes you're wearing. You know they're there, you're aware of them, but you don't *think* about them.

If I focus on an object, like the lock – the wires, the latch assembly, the emergency battery, the individual screws on the latch and strike panels – it's as if I send out a part of myself to wrap around it, like you'd wrap your hand around a glass. And then, if I'm locked on, I can move it. I don't have to jerk my head or hold out my hand or screw up my face like in the movies, either. I tried it once, for fun, and felt like an idiot.

It takes me about three seconds to find the latch and slide it back. The mechanism won't move unless it receives the correct signal from the fingerprint reader – or unless someone reaches inside and moves it with her mind. It's actually a pretty solid security system. I've definitely seen worse. But whoever built it obviously didn't take into account the existence of a psychokinetic, so I guess he's totally fired now.

"And we're good." I hop to my feet, using my PK to pull the handle down. I haven't even touched the door.

"Hm." Annie tilts her head. "Nice work."

"Was that a compliment? Annie, are you dying? Has the cancer spread to your brain?"

"Let's just get this over with."

We're on this operation because of a clothing tycoon named Steven Chase. He runs a chain of high-end sportswear stores called Ultra, which just means they're Foot Locker stores without the referee jerseys. If that was all he was doing, he'd never have appeared on China Shop's radar, but it appears Mr Chase has been a very naughty boy.

Tanner got a tip that he was embezzling money from his company. Again, not something we'd normally give a shit about, but he's not exactly using it to buy a third Ferrari. He's funnelling it to some very shady people in the Ukraine and Saudi

Arabia, which is when government types like Tanner start to get mighty twitchy.

Now, the US government *could* get a wiretap to confirm the tip. But even if you go through a secret court, there'll be some kind of paper trail. Better a discreet call gets made to the offices of a certain moving company in Los Angeles, who can look into the matter without anything being written down.

And before you start telling me I'm on the wrong side, that I'm doing the work of the government, who are the real bad guys here, and violating a dozen laws and generally being a pawn of the state, just know that I've seen evidence of what people like Chase do. I have no problem messing with their shit.

We're not actually going anywhere near Steven Chase's office. Reggie could hack his computer directly, but it would require a brute-force attack or getting him to click on a link in an email. People don't do that any more, unless you promise fulfilment of their *very* specific sexual fantasies. The research on that is more trouble than it's worth, and you'll have nightmares for months.

Chase is in town tonight. He flew in for a dinner or an awards show or whatever rich people do for fun, and it's his habit to come back to the office afterwards. He should be there now, up on the 30th floor. He'll work until two or three, catch a couple hours of sleep, then grab a red-eye back to New York. Which works just fine for us.

If you can access the fibre network itself – which you can do in the server room, obviously – you can clamp a special coupler right on to the cable and just siphon off the data as it passes by. Of course, actually doing this is messy and complicated and requires a lot of elements to line up just right … unless you have me.

The cables from every floor in the building run down to this room. The plan is to identify Chase's cable, attach a coupler to it, then read all the traffic while sipping mai tais on our back porch. Or in my case scarfing Thai food and drinking many, many beers in my tiny apartment, but whatever.

Chase might encrypt his email, of course, but encryption targets the body of the email, not the sender or subject line. If he emails anyone in the Ukraine or Saudi, we'll know about it. It'll be enough for Tanner to send in the big guns.

The server room is even more dimly lit than the corridor. The server banks stand like monoliths in an old tomb, giving off a subsonic hum that rumbles under the frigid air conditioning. Annie tilts her chin up even further, as if sniffing the air. She points to one side of the door. "Wait there."

"Yes, sir, O mighty boss lady."

She ignores me, eyes scanning the server stacks. I don't really know how she's going to find the correct one – that was the part of the planning session where they lost me. All I know is that when she does, she's going to trace it back to where it vanishes into the floor or wall. We'll open up a panel, and I'll use my PK to float the coupler inside, attaching it to the cable. It can siphon data, away from the eyes of the building's technicians, who would almost certainly recognise it on sight.

As Annie steps behind one of the servers, I slip my earbud back in. May as well listen to some music while—

"Shit," Annie says.

It's a quiet curse, but I catch it just fine. I make my way over to find her staring at a clusterfuck of tangled cables spilling out of one of the servers. The floor is a scattered mess of tools and loose connections. A half-eaten sandwich, dribbling a slice of tomato, sits propped on a closed laptop.

"Is it supposed to look like that?" I ask.

Annie ignores me. 'Paul, we've got a problem. Over."

"What is it? Over."

"Techs have been in. It wasn't like this this morning; Jerian would have told me."

Jerian – one of Annie's Army. Her anonymous network of janitors, cleaners, cashiers, security guards, drug dealers, nail artists, Uber drivers, cooks, receptionists and IT guys. Annie Cruz may not appreciate good hip-hop, but she has a very deep network of connects stretching all the way across LA.

"Copy, Annie. Can you still attach the coupler? Over."

Annie frowns at the mess of cables. "Yeah. But it'll take a while. Over."

Joy.

"Understood," Paul says. "But we can only run interference for so long on our end. You'd better move. Over."

Annie scowls, crouching down to look at the cables. She takes one between thumb and forefinger, like it's something nasty she has to dispose of. Then she stands up, marching back towards the server-room doors.

"Um. Hi? Annie?" I jog after her, earbud bouncing against my shoulder. "Cables are back there."

"Change of plan." She keys her earpiece. "Paul? Tell Reggie to switch over the cameras on the 30th floor. Over"

"Say again? Over."

"We're going up."

I don't catch Paul's response. Instead, I sprint to catch up with Annie, getting to her just she pushes through the doors. "Are you gonna tell me why we've suddenly abandoned the plan, or—"

"We can't hide the coupler if they got people poking around the cables." She reaches the elevator, thumbing the up button. "We need to go to the source."

"I thought the whole point was *not* to go near this guy. Aren't we supposed to be super-secret and stealthy and shit?"

"We're not going to his office, genius. We're going to the fibre hub on his floor."

"The what now?"

"The fibre hub. Every floor has one. It's where the cables from each office go. We'll be able to find the right one a lot faster from there."

The interior of the elevator is clean and new, with a touchscreen interface to select your floor. A taped sign next to it says that floors 50–80 are currently off limits while refurbishment and additional construction is completed, thank you for your patience, management. I remember seeing that when we rolled up: a big chunk of the building covered in scaffolding, with temporary elevators attached to the outside, and a giant crane in a vacant lot across the street.

When the elevator opens on the 30th floor, there's someone standing in front of it. There's a horrible moment where I think it's Steven Chase himself. But I've seen pictures of Chase, who looks like an actor in an ad for haemorrhoid cream – running on the beach, tanned and glowing, stoked that his rectum is finally itch-free. This guy is ... not that. He has lawyer written all over him: two-tone shirt, two-tone hair, one-tone orange skin. Tie knot as big as my fist. Probably a few haemorrhoid issues of his own.

He eyes us. "Going down?"

"We're stepping off here, sir," Annie says, doing just that.

He moves into the elevator, mouth twisted in a disapproving frown as his eyes pass over me. Probably not used to seeing someone my age working security in a building like this. I have to resist the urge to wink at him.

I haven't seen inside any of the offices yet, but whoever built this place obviously didn't have any budget leftover for the hallways. There's a foot-high strip of what looks like marble-textured plastic running along at chest height. There are buzzing fluorescent lights in the ceiling, and the floor is covered with that weird, flat, fuzzy carpet which always has little lint balls dotted over it.

"Jesus, who picked out the paint?" The wall above the plastic marble is a shade of purple that's probably called something like Executive Mojo.

"Who cares?" Annie says. "Damn building shouldn't even be here."

I sigh. This again.

She taps the fake marble. "You know they displaced a bunch of historical buildings for this? They just moved in and forced a purchase."

I sigh. Annie's always had a real hard-on for the city's history. "Yeah, I know. You told me before."

"And you saw that notice in the elevator. They just built this place. They already having to fix it up again. And the spots they bought out – mom-and-pop places. Historical buildings. City didn't give a fuck."

"Mm-hmm."

"I'm just saying. It's messed up, man."

"Can we get this done before the heat death of the universe? Please?"

It doesn't take us long to find the right office. Paul helps, using the blueprints he's pulled up to guide us along, occasionally telling Annie that this isn't a good idea and that she needs to hurry. I pop the lock, just like before – it's even easier this time – and we step inside.

There's no Executive Mojo here. It's a basic space, with a desk and terminal for a technician and a big, clearly marked access panel on the wall. By the desk, someone has left a toolbox full of computer paraphernalia, overflowing with wires and connectors. Maybe the same dickhead who left the half-eaten sandwich in the server room. I should leave a note telling him to clean up his shit.

The access panel is off to one side, slightly raised from the surface of the wall. Annie pops it, revealing a nest of thin cables. She attaches the coupler, which looks like a bulldog clip from the future, then checks her phone, reading the data that comes off it. With a grunt, she moves the coupler to the second cable. We have to get the correct one, and the only way to do that is to identify Chase from his traffic.

There are floor-to-ceiling windows on my left, and the view over the glittering city takes my breath away. We're only on the 30th floor, not even close to the top of the building, but I can still see a hell of long way. A police helicopter hovers in the distance, too far for us to hear, its blinking tail lights just visible. The view looks north, out towards Burbank and Glendale, and on the horizon, there's the telltale orange glow of wildfires.

The sight pulls up some bad memories. Of all the cities Tanner had to put me, it had to be the one where things burn.

It's bad this year. Usually, it's some kid with fireworks or a tourist dropping a cigarette that starts it up, but this time the grass was so dry that it caught on its own. Every TV in the last couple of days has had big breaking news alerts flashing on them. The ones tuned to Fox News – you get a few, even in California – have given it a nickname. HELLSTORM. Because of course they have.

This year's fire has been creeping towards Burbank and Glendale, chewing through Wildwood Canyon and the Verdugo Hills. The flames have made LA even smoggier than usual. A fire chief on one of the TVs – a guy who managed to look both calm and mightily pissed off at the same time – said that they didn't think the fires would reach the city.

"Teagan."

"Huh?"

"You got your voodoo, right?" She nods to the coupler. "Float it up into the wall."

"Oh. Yeah. Good idea."

The panel is wide enough for me to lean in, craning my head back. The space is dusty, a small shower of fine grit nearly making me sneeze. Annie shines a torch, but I don't need it. She's got the correct cable pinched between thumb and forefinger. It's the work of a few seconds for me to find it with my *voodoo* and pull it slightly outwards from its buddies, float the coupler across and clamp it on. Annie flicks the torch off, and the coupler is swallowed by the shadows.

What can I say? I'm handy.

"Aight," Annie says, snapping the panel shut. "Paul? We're good. Over."

"Copy that. We're getting traffic already. Skedaddle on out of there. Over."

Skedaddle? I mouth the word at Annie, who ignores me. She replaces the panel, slotting it back into place, then turns to go.

As we step out of the tech's office, a voice reaches us from the other end of the hallway: "Hey."

Two security guards. No, three. Real ones. Walking in close formation, heading right for us. The one in the centre is a big white guy with a huge chest-length beard, peak pulled down over his eyes. He's scary, but it's the other two I'm worried about. They're young, with wide eyes and hands already on their holsters, fingers twitching.

Ah, shit.

Enter the monthly
Orbit sweepstakes at
www.orbitloot.com

With a different prize every month,
from advance copies of books by
your favourite authors to exclusive
merchandise packs,
**we think you'll find something
you love.**